ARIA DAZE

Glory

Happy Harlots Book One

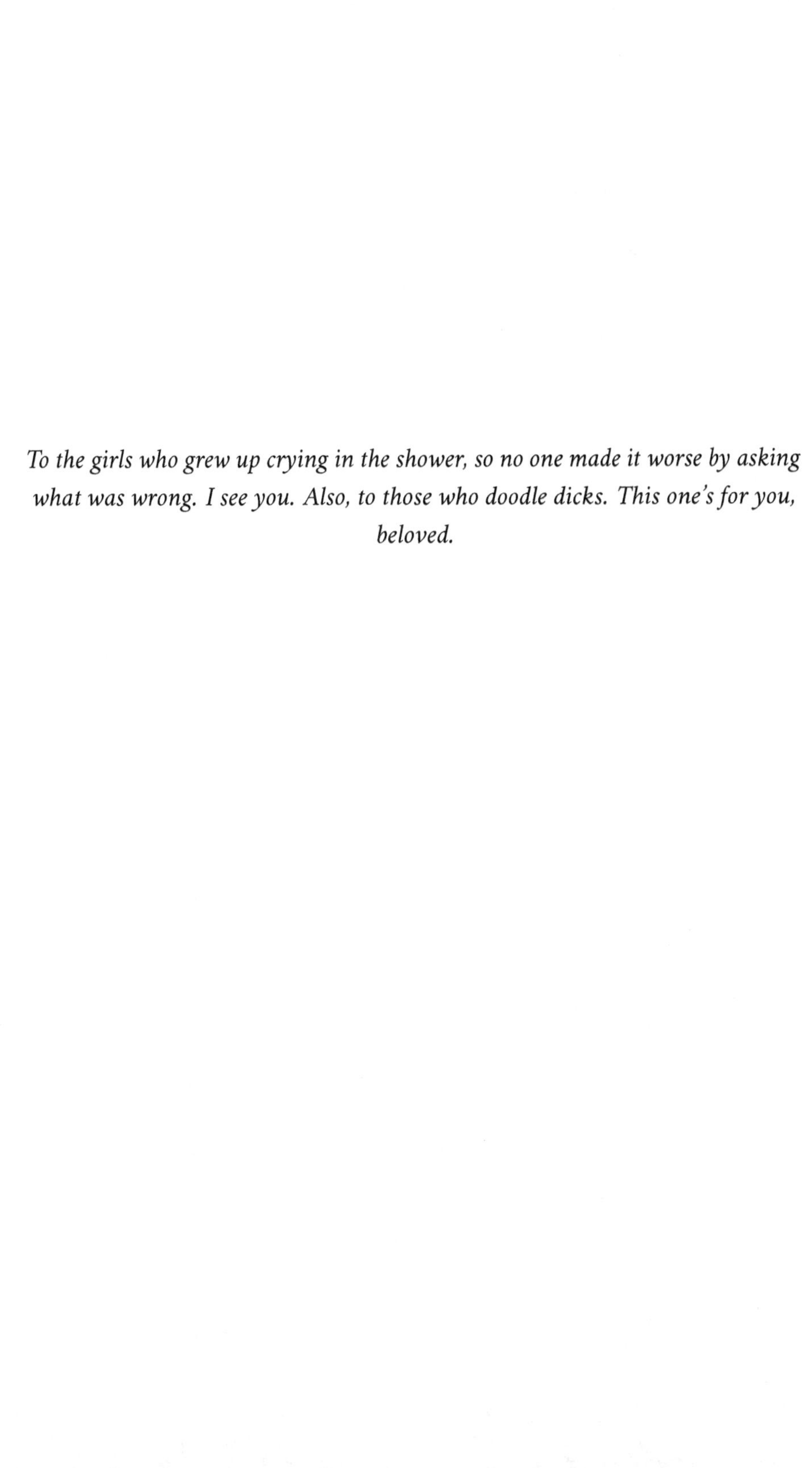

To the girls who grew up crying in the shower, so no one made it worse by asking what was wrong. I see you. Also, to those who doodle dicks. This one's for you, beloved.

Contents

Preface

So how did we get here, writing books about glory holes? Well, your author is adventurous and came across one in real life. Since I have virtually no shame surrounding sex I said, "Oh, that'd be cool to put in a book." and now here we are. But glory holes aside, this book is an ode to the oldest daughters. The girls who should've been able to put ten+ years of experience on their resume at age eighteen. The strong ones. Birth order has been proven to affect so much of life and relationships, especially for the eldest. So this book is a reminder that you do not have to do it all, nor should you be expected to. The best people will know that, and they will put in *effort* to take care of your heart.

Happy reading!

Trigger Warnings

This book contains themes that may be distressing to some readers. Please review the following information before diving in. Your mental health matters!

- Talk of Statutory Rape (Not committed.)
- Religious Trauma
- Parental Neglect
- Homophobia (Slurs and hateful verbiage surrounding sexual prefer- ence.)
- Death Of A Loved One
- Mentions Of COVID-19
- Manipulation
- Depression
- Narcissism
- Suicidal Ideation
- Alcoholism
- Medical Bias
- Cheating

One

Genesis

My name is Gloria, and I think I'm a succubus. I know they're not *technically* real, but if they were, I'd be their leader. I love everything associated with orgasms, especially men's. I like feeling their hot cum sticking to my used holes, I like hearing their ragged breath whimper my praises, and I especially like when they get overwhelmed and bow their backs, eager to release their frustrations. It soothes my depraved, hungry mind for a few days so I can continue to dominate at work and support my community. It gives me back the power taken from me by these ridiculous patriarchal expectations, and it's also damn fun. So that's why I think I'm a succubus. Because I, Gloria Esther King, pull my strength from the sins of men. Instead of the glory of God.

Before you assume this is because someone touched me, I use drugs, or because my parents let me run wild, never setting a boundary or saying no, let me clarify some things. The House Of King is a good Christian house where I had a stern, but loving, upbringing. My father comes from a long line of pastors and my mother from an equally long line of schoolteachers. Their union yielded four children, with my siblings being standard-issue and mild-mannered. So the problem is definitely me.

My mother first noticed it when I was about seven. I would doodle little obscenities in the margins of my notebooks, mostly breast. Ink-drawn tits were basically my signature for a while, but my mother wasn't worried. She must have shrugged it off as simple self-curiosity until it evolved into something worse in my pre-teens. Big, veiny, hairy dicks. She had the same concerns as most. She was worried that someone had exposed me to something or themselves, and that's where my perversions stemmed from, but the truth was much worse. So she and my father spent nearly two weeks trying to coax a statement out of me that didn't exist. I was simply a pervert, and while I was happy to leave it, I knew I had to be honest when they started questioning my brother.

Marcus still stands as one of the two only people I've ever loved outside my parents. He was a good big brother when we were kids. Picking on me when necessary, strengthening me for the real world, and protecting me always. I'm still his pride and joy to this day, and that's why I'd never let his character be called into judgment. I remember my stomach tightening with anxiety and fear before my cracked lips parted to tell the truth.

"No one touched me! I was watching the men's locker room!" I shouted.

There was a hole barely big enough for a rat to squeeze through in our church's upstairs study room. It was so small that the only evidence of its existence was the light that peered through when you moved the chair over in the dark. I noticed it one day after kissing a little boy from my youth group. He hurried away when the pastor called, and I stayed behind to practice more doodles. I doodled often on Sundays. My father was strict, but even he could understand a young mind's tendency to wander. So he left me upstairs after the third sermon to draw. I followed the same routine as usual that day. Kiss a boy, wait for him to panic, then draw. But when I moved the chair to get comfortable, I found something else worthy of my time. *Dicks.* There was a shower room downstairs for our homeless members and clergymen. It braved heavy traffic on Sundays, especially in the summer, so I spent three months of my time memorizing the privates of its frequent fliers. Especially brother Myer-Smythe. His dick was my favorite. Veiny, thick, long, and drooping over his balls like a partially deflated balloon animal. My mother nearly fainted while I fought to keep the smile off my face, while my father curled his fist into a tight ball. So yeah, I'm the problem.

My daddy had the hole repaired, and my access to privacy was of course revoked. But that didn't stop my fascination with penises. I often tried to bribe Marcus' friends to show me theirs with the little bit of allowance I got, and while I was lucky half the time, Franklin Myer-Smythe eventually snubbed my luck by snitching on me. At just four years my senior, he felt he was suited to tell me how I ought to behave. And while his concerns did have some merit, he was mostly full of shit. He was just mad about his boyfriend. So after he blew up my spot, I was confined to solitude while my parents searched for a solution through God. But after many, many, failed attempts at correcting my behavior through prayer, they turned to science.

Turns out Zoloft worked faster than the Lord above us could, and I spent my teen years dedicated to a strict routine to curb my urges. It's been fourteen years since I started meds, and while I was upset at first, I can admit they helped me. I graduated as a high school salutatorian, a college valedictorian, and a law school prodigy. Highly desired by both of my chosen specialties. I was offered the best jobs, got the greatest benefits, ad made the most money. So I had a pretty good life, and I owed it all to a little orange pill that dried my pussy up like a dream deferred.

But I'm grown now, and at the ripe age of 27, I decided that I wasn't going to be ashamed of my hypersexuality. Especially after hearing dozens of stories of other women having issues with the opposite. I decided to embrace my insatiable lust and go with it. I am who I am, and I am a whore. So I skip my meds Thursday and Friday nights, put on my tightest dress and highest heels, and head into town to have some damn good fun. I've had a thing for glory holes lately, and it might just be the namesake, but I can't help myself. Using some faceless schlub as a dildo is the perfect way to end a hectic week, especially if I lose a case. I usually find a seedy club or swingers bar to scratch my itch, but I've taken on a different challenge recently. *Gay bars.* Gay bars have the best glory holes. Triple-lined with duct tape, clean, with condoms provided. And I also like that gay men keep their dicks clean. Clean dicks taste better, especially when they cum down my throat. It was finally Friday, and tonight was no exception. So I put on a skintight leather dress, a pair of heels that could make a seasoned dominatrix keel, and lined my lips with sinfully red lipstick. I caught a glimpse of myself in the mirror and grinned. Yeah, tonight was gonna be good.

I arrived at Adam And Steve's a quarter after nine and it was already packed. Luckily, I knew Adam personally, so I got to skip right past the thick security guard who wouldn't give me his number and head inside. I didn't jump straight into it though. I nursed a margarita while watching the crowd. A sea of moisturized, glittering bodies were busy rippling against each other, basking in neon club lights, entrancing me. Especially the fems. If I wasn't violently craving dick I probably would have gone after the cute brown skin fem with the purple hair. She kept glancing at me, and she looked fun and soft, but I needed something hard for tonight.

I finished my drinks around 10:30 and decided to make my way to the men's room. Hopefully, no one paid me too much mind, and if they did, hopefully they assumed I was trans. That thought made my mind wander to the last trans girlie I met. Her dick was tattooed and she had a fat ass. *"Focus Gloria!"* I told myself. This wasn't about Sonni, it was about tonight. Me, a sketchy hole, and an equally sketchy penis. Bad decisions all around, not cute girls who wanted a cat, a girlfriend, and matching Christmas pajamas. No, no, no.

I try not to get into relationships if I can help it. Sometimes situationships get close, but I usually nip it in the bud before anyone can get hurt. Contrary to popular belief, I do have a heart, and the last thing I want is to open up to someone and have them spit on it because I'm sexually non-monogamous. So I just decided to bypass all of that and cuddle my best friend on occasion, let my family absorb my free time, and suck dicks and eat coochies until my jaw hurts. That way every human need is taken care of, and I never let things get out of hand with my lil friends.

Anyway, back to tonight. I got comfortable in the big stall while I waited. A few people ran in and out, but I still didn't have a contender after an hour. I was almost ready to pack it up and try the direct approach, but then I heard my calling card. A zipper and no urine stream proceeding it. Finally, it was showtime. Most frequent fliers knew about the glory hole, including Adam. So naturally, there was a laminated instruction card taped inside both stalls. I knocked on the divider once and the person knocked back twice, indicating that they wanted to play. So I kicked a condom under the thin space between our stalls and eagerly waited for a response.

My Dick Donor must've also been eager because they ripped that pack and knocked back in record time. I knocked twice, indicating I was ready, but I don't think I could ever be ready for what I saw. A big head pushed through the hole before the rest fell over to my side, and it was perfect. It was deep brown, heavy in my hand, with veins on the surface straining against the condom, plus it was uncut. It was rare to see an uncut dick nowadays, but they were my absolute favorite. It jumped at me, demanding my attention, and I narrowed my eyes at it. I knew I never had it, but it looked oddly familiar. It also looked like a challenge. I normally stuck to a head-only rule for lil holes in the walls, but I think I would pass away if I didn't at least try to back down that one.

What can I say? I'm an opportunist. So I braced myself on the wall in front of me and eased down Goliath's dick. I was soaking wet, but I didn't have any other choice except to go slow. Cause when the head entered me, I had to throw my hand over my mouth to contain my yelp. Big was somehow an understatement. I'm not real religious anymore, but I had to call on The Father, The Spirit, and The Holy Ghost to make it down their length. I was perfectly full and stretched to the max, which was honestly rare for me. I liked dicks of all sizes, but I was accustomed to medium ones. Not backbreakers.

I finally reached the base and Captain Dingle groaned and cussed, saying something about how tight I was. I loved dirty talk, but my voice was way too recognizable. It was high-pitched and shrill, just like my school teacher mama. So unless I wanted to deny my truth and have folks thinking my mama was running around utilizing local glory holes, I kept my mouth shut. That didn't stop me from humming with relief though. My shit was throbbing every time I thrusted against that big-ass dick. Plus it didn't hurt that my donor was meeting my pace by stroking back. I could imagine them being an absolute menace without a barrier between us, so it was a good thing that wasn't an option.

The first rule of hypersexuality was to never expect too much from your partners. Most people were normal, and they got their serotonin from shit like hobbies and hugs, so they never wanted it as much as you. They never needed it. Never craved it. But my donor had blown my expectations outta the sky. It had been ten minutes and we were still going. I know because I heard three different songs come over the speakers and at least six different folks shuffle in and out, some cheering on our debauchery. I think they wanted it too, and fuck, that shit was hot.

Six songs had played since we started and we were still at it, but I needed it to stop because I was about to pass out. They were making me cum. I think they might've even been doing it on purpose because they used whatever sliver of room they had to change angles repeatedly. It was rare that I came during penetration without toys, and it was even rarer that a stranger had my wetness rushing down my shaky legs. They switched angles again, making the hinges on the stall groan as they did, and I was fighting a losing battle against containing my moans. So I let out a little pant with my next cresting wave of pleasure before it crashed down and ruined me.

That was a mistake though, because my donor showed their ass as soon as I did. They rammed into me so hard that I almost lost my balance, and I had to grip the toilet paper holder to remain upright. Then I made another mistake by trying to catch their rhythm because it was far too superior to anything I was used to. So there my dumb dickmatized ass was, struggling not to moan while a horse-dicked stranger knocked the Mario coins out my shit. Then as if things wasn't bad enough, their shit got harder, the strokes got faster, and my pussy clenched tighter. *Oh no.* I thought. The pressure overwhelmed me before I realized what was happening. My stomach tightened while warm liquid sprayed out of me, soaking the floor, my donor, and myself. I squirted in a fucking public bathroom. The insatiable whore in me didn't know rather to be impressed or ashamed, but who could tell since she had been temporarily relieved of duty.

My donor's orgasm succeeded mine, making me cum one last time before they withdrew their sticky twitching dick, and a bitch was spent. There was nothing poetic about what happened. I was a sweaty, shaking, crumpled mess. My body hurt and I was out of breath, plus I was also completely sexually satisfied. Usually, I was the one doing the fucking, but that night I had been fucked. It was a perfect night of rare encounters, and I owed it all to Adam's nasty ass, a roll of duct tape, and a perfect stranger.

I caught my breath and fixed myself in the little door mirror while I waited for my donor to leave. Good dick aside, I needed them to stay a stranger. The kind of sex we had was dangerous and had the tendency to complicate things, and I was in no mood for complicated. I heard the lock on their door snick before light from their exit flooded the pleasure chute that was still dripping with my cum. Yeah, I needed to tell Adam about that. Bleach was needed.

One song later, the water stopped running, the door swung open, and my donor left with a loud, but satisfied sigh. For some reason that made me blush, and I had to shake off the weirdly warm feeling before opening my door. No, thank you to whatever that was. That exchange was supposed to be purely physical, and that warmth felt real emotional. I decided I was gonna numb that with a shot or two before heading home. I was taking a self-care day the next day anyway, so it'd be easy to nurse my hangover. But that plan was ruined as soon as I exited my stall and looked up. Shit had gotten complicated.

Two

Chapter Two

Franklin

I had a rough week. I usually had hard weeks because I hated my job, but that disdain was particularly apparent on Monday morning. A nervous secretary wheeled a literal cart of files to my desk before passing me a note from my uncle.

"Happy Monday, Frank And Beans. I approved your PTO, but you know you gotta work hard to play hard. This is due before you leave next week."

Only Curtis was capable of such villainy. I had to take PTO to attend my aunt's funeral. His fucking sister! But he insisted that I wasn't gonna get special treatment just because I was his nephew, and the nigga was not lying.

Not to toot my own dysfunctional horn, but I was smart. I burned through books like chain smokers burned through cartons, I was a chemistry and math prodigy, and I had a couple of patents under my belt. My life probably could've been comfortable and peaceful at this point, but unfortunately, I had fallen into the most unbeneficial pit of nepotism I've ever seen.

See, my uncle Curtis was a habitual fuck up. I remember my mama side eyeing him plenty while he talked about his latest get-rich-quick scheme over strained family dinners. I was seven when I started to see right through the bullshit, and do you know how crazy that is? I ain't even know how to wash my dick properly but I knew my uncle was full of it. Unfortunately, my dad refused to face the music, and he funded much of Curtis's bullshit despite my mother's vocal displeasure.

The damage it caused their marriage was catastrophic, and it leaked over into my childhood. I dried way too many of my mama's tears, so I promised myself I would never disregard and disrespect my partner if I was ever lucky enough to get someone. That was highly improbable considering my not-so-sunny disposition and fucked up work schedule, but still, a nigga could dream.

Anyway, back to how I got stuck sitting in a cubicle I couldn't even fully extend my legs at. Remember what I said about my dad funding my uncle's bullshit? Yeah, he had done it big back in 2010. I had just graduated from the top of both my majors at the ever-prestigious Stanford and my parents put on their best bandaids to celebrate me. I could tell shit was iffy, but they were smiling, laughing, and making the best of it. So I was happy to pretend we were a normal family and not one that was so verbally abusive that I had an anxiety attack every time I heard any kind of elevated tone. I was drinking age though, so that was water under the bridge at that point.

My mama was busy covering me in an alarmingly bright red lipstick while my uncle and dad strolled around chatting. I should've been more concerned but I honestly didn't care what they were doing as long as they didn't piss my mama off. She had it hard enough dealing with everything at home and with the church. I just wanted her to enjoy one day, be proud, and be happy. But Gregory Myer-Smythe was once again on a mission to fuck up a good time. He left my uncle's side and rushed back to me with a moronic grin. A grin that made me hate my own smile. Mostly because it was way too toothy, partially because I wondered if that's all my mama saw when she looked at me.

"Good news, Son!" he called. "I found you a job, and the best part is, it's close to home," he said.

My entire face scrunched up. I wasn't sure what part of that news was good. It certainly wasn't the prospect of a job involving Curtis, and it definitely wasn't the location. The only good things about Dallas were my mama, my best friend Marcus, and a certain 4c-haired, wild child with an affinity for good leather and greasy fries. She was probably the best thing, and she wasn't even talking to me at the moment. Fuck, her lil ass could hold a grudge.

"Say something," he urged.

I probably should have just walked away, but I think everything was finally coming up, and it splashed against my throat and chest like stomach acid courtesy of Taco Bell induced heartburn.

"I ain't ask you to do that," I spat.

My mama tried to hold my hand to comfort me, but it was too late.

"I ain't ask you to find me no fucking job, I ain't ask you to dig in my personal business, and I really ain't even want you here after you told me what you told me. So why…"

My mama tugged my hand and her eyes briefly flitted to the gathering crowd. I was about to show my entire ass on the manicured lawn of a PWI, minutes after they handed me a shiny new degree. So I tucked all twenty-two years of rotten, festering rage back into the pit of my stomach before putting on my best Barbie smile.

"Tell me about the job," I said calmly.

To make a long story short, without my mother's knowledge or consent, my father had given my uncle twenty-thousand dollars. Damn near their whole retirement fund. Apparently, Curtis was starting a drop shipping company and he needed a bookkeeper. Is that what I wanted to do with a one hundred-twenty-thousand dollar degree? Absolutely not. I wanted to work a few high-paying nine-to-fives before eventually breaking away from corporate life and then I wanted to spend the rest of my days making candles. I wanted to move away, experience living in a new area, and finally heal from the wounds that nobody besides Glory ever saw. I wanted peace, and this shit with Curtis sounded like the exact opposite of peace. But when I looked at my mama, I saw nothing but regret, anger, and mostly fear. She had trusted this bible-thumping idiot in an effort to be a good, god-fearing woman, and now her peace was on the line.

My mama gave me so much when her cup was only a quarter full, and she deserved a break. So I did what any loving son would. I took the job for my mama. I drew up a solid contract with help from an equally grumpy friend detailing the length of time and the circumstances of my employment. If my uncle wanted me to manage his shit, he had to give my parents back their money, **all of it,** and he couldn't ask Regina Myer-Smythe for shit until then. Not even a bottle of water, and I was standing on that.

Of course, he took it as distrust, which it absolutely was, and he used his position of power to make my professional life hell. So here I was, nearly a decade later, still working off my father's mistakes. Then the icing on the cake was the "misplaced" receipts being delivered to my already crowded desk at seven P.M on a hectic Friday evening. I immediately imagined dousing the entire office in Shell gasoline and throwing a match behind me as I left when I looked down at the nonsensical reports and mismatched receipts. Yeah, I needed a break. And not just a funeral with an open bar. I needed to be distracted with something or someone.

So I found myself at Adam and Steve's a little after ten. Adam knew how to run a club, cause the music was thumping, the drinks were strong, and I heard there was a glory hole in the men's. (not that I ever tried it.) Plus it was one of the only black-owned gay clubs in Dallas. That made flirting a whole lot easier for me, even though I was still pretty bad at it. Case and point, the cute boy I accidentally scared away.

"So are you a transplant, or did you grow up here?" he asked.

"I grew up here. I wanted to leave ten years ago, but my uncle trapped me into working for him because he essentially swindled my parents out of their retirement. So now I'm just kinda stuck, aha."

He grimaced and I instantly knew I overshared.

"Oh, damn. That's crazy," he replied.

That's crazy? Yeah, this mission was DED. I wasn't fucking shit tonight.

"Yeah," I huffed awkwardly.

"Have a goodnight, beautiful," he called, skirting back into the crowd.

As painful as that was, I'm actually real glad that he didn't beat a dead horse. Especially since Suze was watching.

"Didn't work out?" she asked.

"You know it didn't, Suze," I hissed.

She laughed before patting my hand patronizingly.

"You could always take me for a spin," she joked.

Suze had made that joke before, and part of me knew she was serious, but I'm what I like to call a reluctant bisexual. I prefer to date men, because men are easier and often emotionally unavailable, so it works out for my tendency to create distance. Women, however, are soft, round, intuitive, and emotionally perceptive. Those qualities are not great for me. I also get possessive and protective with women quick because of what happened to my mama and Glory. That's probably something to unpack in therapy, but I can't afford that. So for now I just try to avoid women. Because they can easily take me for all I'm worth, which already ain't shit.

"Hard pass, Suze. I'm a looker, not a toucher," I replied.

Suze shrugged it off before fixing me another pineapple jalapeno martini. That was another reason I couldn't fuck Suze. She was the only bartender in Fort Worth I trusted to make my drinks. So I definitely needed to keep my dick to myself unless I wanted my weekly cocktails made with 90% juice and 10% spit.

She slid me the festive drink with an unhinged grin, and I was concerned she was going to ask again.

"You could always try out the pleasure chute in the men's room," she suggested.

My initial concern was misplaced and replaced by pure dread.

"First off, Suze, please don't ever say pleasure chute again. Second off, I cannot stick my dick in a glory hole!" I whisper-yelled.

"You could," she shrugged. "It's not like it's unconsenting sex. There's instructions, condoms, and anonymity. Clearly you're not having any luck the other way."

Damn it. I hated that she was right, but the cute boy I scared away was my third failed attempt of the night. Still, using a glory hole to scratch my itch felt wrong.

"Ion know, Suze. I don't like the moral implications of using a stranger's body for my own selfish needs."

Suze huffed, clearly fed up with my nonsense, and backed away from the bar with raised hands.

"I'm not holding a gun to your head, Fab. I'm just giving you options beside your left hand."

I had to laugh even though she was being an asshole about it. But minutes passed as my drinks depleted, and I wasn't any closer to my original goal. I hated small talk, I hated social politics, and I didn't wanna try. I tried every single day, all the time. The only thing trying had ever gotten me was a shitty cubicle, a probably condemned studio apartment, and a decade-long silent treatment. I wanted something easy, I needed it. So I finished my drinks, took an extra shot, and made my way to the men's room.

It was surprisingly clean for a glory hole. I don't know what I expected, but the ones I saw in porn were nightmare fuel. Then again, this was Adam. A nigga so meticulous that he did deep cleans twice a day. The whole club smelled like bleach if you came in before seven, so I'm sure it was clean.

Fuck it.

I was gonna stick my dick in a glory hole. I unzipped my pants to get to it, but I was startled by a knock. *Is that how it remains anonymous?* I thought. Suze did say there were instructions. I quickly found them on a laminated printout hanging behind the mirror.

"Knock twice if you want to play."

Shit, that was easy. I knocked back and a Skyns was slid to my feet a few seconds later. I practically flew to open it and put it on. Luckily I had tequila dick and my shit was already semi-hard. So it didn't take long for me to let them know I was ready.

A singular knock of consent from the receiver let me know it was show time. I knocked back before slowly easing my dick through the duct tape transporter. Then I felt soft hands run down the length of my shaft. God, I hoped it wasn't a fem on the other side, but I guess that's why the anonymity was good. Hopefully, their shit was wet enough to keep me from becoming a Batman villain, they would get theirs, and we would part ways amicably an… Oh my fucking God. They interrupted my internal monologue by sliding down my shit, and while I'm basically a hermit crab, I know what good pussy feels like.

"Fuck, you so damn tight," I mumbled.

Tight was an understatement. Their shit was like Pentagon security. Then it was wetter than water. My dick was basically in a personal hot tub with massage jets. Yeah, Suze knew what the fuck she was talking about. I needed this.

I think I needed it a little too much though, because my foot was on the toilet seat, my stall was shaking, and I was hitting my receiver's shit from any and all possible angles. I thought that they were tight before, but when they came? Fuck, my life flashed before my eyes. I looked good in a tux. I could see myself being a soccer dad and baking cupcakes on the weekend. We could vacation in the mountains during the summers, the girls would have their own rooms, and my bean-head-ass son would have his own basketball hoop in the backyard. That probably should have been the point that I stopped and came back to earth, but then my receiver gasped. It was so sharp, light, and pretty. And it went straight to my dick.

I think I blacked out momentarily. Cause I broke the toilet paper dispenser somewhere between hearing their gasp and feeling them cum on me then the floor. I ain't mean to, but my hands needed something to grab. Probably because if I had it my way I would've been gripping the fuck outta that ass. I was glad their orgasm was so strong though, because it meant I couldn't delay my own much longer, and that was good because I was three strokes away from tearing down Adam's stall to satisfy my need to touch.

Fuck.

Relief washed over me in a wave I couldn't swim against. I had bucked so hard that a few of my pubes caught a peeling piece of the tape. So I got the best nut of my life and a free wax. We finally came to a halt and my entire body collapsed against the vinyl wall of a public bathroom. All that was left to do was to pull out and get rid of the evidence.

You can do it.

I had to hype myself up to exit them because even though I was definitely spent, they still felt so fucking good. It wasn't even sexual despite the fact that I was inside of them. It was just… comforting. I hadn't known comfort in years, but all good things must come to an end. So I withdrew, and they came again. Yes, that also went straight to my brain. Especially when I saw my dick looking like a microwaved honey bun back on my side of things. Fuck anonymity, I needed to know who did that shit to me, because that felt realer than any of the dates I forced myself to go on this past decade. I ain't even hate myself afterwards.

I think I found my distraction.

Of course, my fem was shy. Or maybe just cautious. Which I couldn't blame them for, because here I was, waiting on them to show their face like a fucking weirdo. I stood still for five minutes hoping they'd leave first, but it wasn't happening for me. So I decided to get creepily creative. I opened my door, washed my hands, fixed myself, and then sighed while I pretended to exit the bathroom. I even walked in place so that they would hear my footsteps trailing off.

I then realized I was too smart for my own good. I also realized I was crazy. What the fuck was I doing? Trying to trap some person into what? Dating me? A frequent flier situation? Was the pussy really that good?

All my concerns were valid, but I ain't have time to address them because my fem was coming out of the stall before I could actually leave. And I was wholly unprepared to face my new reality.

"Frankie," she gasped.

Gloria Esther King. She stood before me in all her, well, Glory. Her doll eyes were wider than usual, her kinky curls were wildly askew, and that round mouth of hers that had no problem displaying her usual bratty pout was hanging wide open. I realized why when she absentmindedly tugged the riding hem of her dress.

I had just blew her back out.

"Gloria," I started, voice shaking. "Please tell me that wasn't you on the other side of that stall."

Glory took two steps back, creating distance between us that pissed me off more.

"What, no! I was just…"

"Glory," I growled. "Don't lie to my fucking face."

"Franklin," she whispered, confirming my fears.

I couldn't help myself. All my shit was falling out at my feet. She hadn't talked to me in over ten fucking years but there she was smelling like my sex. So I locked the door and confronted her. Like the possessive lunatic I was becoming.

"Gloria, what the fuck are you doing? You just going around fucking strangers through walls? I thought you were on meds?"

I didn't realize I rushed her until she cowered. Glory was tall for a woman, but I still towered over her and she was understandably scared.

So I backed off. I backed off and pinched the bridge of my nose, hoping that it was just some fucked up continuation of my recurring nightmares, but it wasn't. Glory was still standing in front of me in the middle of a public bathroom. My Glory. The one person I tried my very hardest not to fuck. Then I went and ruined all my hard work in one night with a couple of drinks and an impulsive decision. Fuck the relief and comfort, I was pissed.

"ANSWER ME, GLORIA!" I screamed.

Tears cut through her iridescent-blue highlighter as she clutched her chest with trembling hands. She already had anxiety and I was scaring her. This was bad.

"Franklin, I'm sorry. But I'm a grownup, and you don't get to tell me what I should be doing to satisfy myself in my free time," she choked.

"Heh. You're satisfied, Glory? Are you proud of yourself?" I laughed.

"Yes," she answered bluntly.

It wasn't Glory's fault, but I was just so overwhelmed. This wasn't what I was expecting or what I wanted. I wanted something easy, and Glory was anything but.

"Gloria, I don't even know what to say to that," I chuckled. "You want me to be happy that you're satisfied fucking random ass people in public?"

"I don't want you to be anything, Frankie. I want you to be you, and I want to leave. This was supposed to be anonymous," she replied.

"Anonymous?" I said, moving closer. "You shouldn't be doing this shit, period!" I roared.

Glory slid her hand down her face, undoubtedly attempting to erase some of the stress off her expression. She had always been careful about frown lines.

"Frankie! What is this about? Cause you were doing the exact same thing, and I've known you to be an asshole, but not a hypocrite! Is this because I didn't go to your graduation? Cause if so, I'm sorry! I'm sorry I wasn't there for you, but I was still mad! You stabbed me in the back and basically got my freedom stripped because you were jealous!" she shouted.

No.

That's not what happened. I didn't stab her in the back. I was looking out for her. I was always looking for her. Except for right now. Right now I was shutting down and trying to look out for myself.

Self-awareness was wasted on me.

"No!" I shouted. "This isn't about some shit that happened ten years ago! It's about the fact that you tricked me into fucking you!"

Glory lowered her gaze, and it was successful in making me feel small and stupid.

"I did not trick you, Franklin. You non-verbally consented, stuck your dick through a wall, and you got what you got," she hissed.

I should've stopped there, but I didn't.

"I withdraw my consent! I would've never done that shit if I knew I was sticking my dick in you! You tricked me! You basically raped me!" I screamed.

It was true. I would have left if I knew she was on the other side of that hole, but I knew I hurt her feelings. I knew I did. Glory never cried in front of people, and she had a killer poker face, but the slight quiver of her upper lip told me everything I needed to know.

"Don't say that, Frankie. We both know it's not true. You were a willing participant," she stated.

"I was willing for a stranger. Not you, Gloria. I wanted anyone else but you."

She looked away for a second and her fist curled, imprinting the point of her coffin nails on her palm.

"What's so wrong with me?" she asked, watching the floor.

All these years and she still didn't know. She didn't know how much her avoidance hurt me. She didn't know how much I missed her. She didn't know how much I cared.

"You're you, Glory, and I'm me. And I would have never willingly fucked you," I huffed. "You know that. So you raped me, and I'm pressing charges."

I didn't mean it.

I know I didn't mean it, but I was so hurt, and I was so tired, and Glory was just in the right place at the wrong time. She rushed past me, pushing me into the trash bin so she could unlock the door.

"Fine, Frankie. Press charges. I'll see you in court," she called.

She left and forcibly slammed the door behind herself, piquing my anxiety and PTSD, which she never did on purpose. Yeah, I fucked up. I fucked up bad.

Chapter Three

G lory

I didn't bother changing. I just pulled a sweatshirt over my dress and started driving. It was nearly midnight. So my parents were definitely in bed, my best friend, Caris, was leaving for a work trip in the morning, and Halle… Well, who knows what Halle had going on, but I knew I couldn't go to her. There was only one person I could cry to at midnight, and I found myself standing outside his house with a peace offering to Alayssa, who answered the door.

"I'm really sorry," I sobbed. "I promise I won't do this all the time."

By this, I mean pop by. It wasn't really a thing I did, but I still didn't want to make it a habit. Especially since Alayssa was four months pregnant with my niece.

"Glory, girl boo. You pop by once every two years and feel bad about it every time. You acting like you Michael or something. He be bringing grocery totes with him," she said, taking the cookies and waving dismissively.

She made me laugh though. Visits from Michael were problematic and that's why he was banned from my crib. I was not a Walmart, and my shit was not rollback prices.

"I'll get Marcus. He's upstairs sketching," she called.

Alayssa disappeared up the steps and I was left with a cup of chamomile and a plush knitted blanket. I got comfortable and flicked through their cable before finding something decent on HBO, then I heard the old man creak down the steps. I feel like he planned to scold me at first, but I'm sure he changed his mind after seeing my water-logged mascara and snotty nose.

"Glory, what happened? You need me to get a clean gun?" he asked.

I had to remind him that I was a lawyer and Daddy was a pastor.

"Shit, I'm just asking," he said, holding his hands up. "So what happened?"

"How much do you wanna know?" I asked.

"Whatever you feel like you need to tell me," he shrugged.

Marcus. My first friend. He never judged, belittled, or snitched. He was really my Ace.

"Let's start with the first thing," I mumbled. "I talked to Franklin."

I woke up to a throbbing head and a hot rag.

"You look like shit," Marcus chuckled, holding out the scratchy washcloth to me.

"Gee thanks," I shot back. "You're not looking too hot yourself, touch of gray."

Marcus rolled his eyes before hollering back into the kitchen, making me wince. I knew he did it to be ornery.

"She hungover, babe! Can you just fix her some rice and bacon!"

Man, my brother knew me well. A little too well. But it was cool. I was gonna wipe my face, eat his food, and harass him while I could.

"Some husband you are. Got that woman barefoot and pregnant, chained to the kitchen," I mumbled.

I thought he'd say something back, but I got a throw pillow to the forehead instead. Luckily I didn't get hit with another cause his wife had spider-senses.

"Don't be fucking up my couches, Marcus!" Alayssa called.

I laughed at his somber expression of defeat before he softened his tone and called back,

"Sorry, Bae!"

Ha! He got in trouble. I know that was a childish thought for a late twenty-something, but a win is a win.

Alayssa was a woman of many hats. She was a retired nurse, a blogger, a fashionista, and a caterer. I was trying to get better about listening to my fullness queues but she made that exceptionally hard for me. Especially with her fried breakfast potatoes. Them shits were so fucking fluffy on the inside I could cry.

She was also incredibly clever.

I had no intention of doing a retelling of last night's events, but she waited until I was full, lethargic, and unable to flee to ask about it.

"What happened last night, Glory?" she started.

Dammit. I knew I should've been wary of those potatoes.

"Nothing. It was just a regular-degular night," I replied.

"A regular night that made you cry and drive forty minutes to your big brother's house?" she asked.

She was also relentless.

"Alayssa, it's coo. I'm good. It was no big deal," I shrugged.

"It kinda was," Marcus mumbled.

I narrowed my eyes at him before shifting my gaze to the fruit bowl. I was gonna get my lick back in blood if he didn't shut the fuck up.

"Just saying," he tutted.

I tried to plan my exit but Alayssa was looking back at me with her good mom eyes. Damn, she was gonna be good at this. I felt bad for my niece already.

"Fine! I had sex with someone, they were mad, and they threatened to press charges against me for rape," I explained.

"Whoa, whoa, whoa!" Marcus shouted. "Franklin tryna say you raped him?"

Oh yeah. I was embarrassed, so I kinda left that out of my recap last night. For good reason too.

"Fuck that. I'm calling him," Marcus announced.

"NO!" Me and Alayssa said at the same time.

Everything was still too fresh and part of me suspected that Franklin didn't even mean it. It was probably a bluff because he was pissed. It was a shitty, potentially career-ruining bluff, but a bluff nonetheless. Besides, Marcus had the tendency to overreact.

"So what, Glory? You just wanna see how it shakes out in court? That's a bad plan," Marcus spat.

"That's not the plan, Marc. This won't make it to court."

"You don't know that," he replied.

"I do."

"Based off what? Some friendship y'all had when we were kids? People change, Glory."

I knew that. I knew that because I barely recognized Franklin's voice last night. Marcus was my first friend, and Franklin was my second. His parents went to our father's church, and he would come over after service sometimes to play with Marcus. That was ironic though because he eventually started coming over just to spend time with me. My parents were fine with it though. Frankie was smart, and we had a lot in common. Then, as I got older, I guess they hoped he would be a good influence, and he was. Except there was one problem. Franklin was queer. I knew Franklin was queer before I knew exactly what queer was. We used to dress up for tea parties, try on makeup, and braid each other's hair. Then when I was about eight, he told me that I looked better in bright neon pink instead of pastel because it made my skin "pop" more. He was gayer than rainbows shooting out of spinner pasties. I wasn't bothered though. It was cute, and he was just Frankie, queerness and all.

That was until he had his first crush on a boy. He started acting all weird around him, started acting weird around me, and then he started avoiding me.

It hurt.

It hurt me bad, but that wasn't what killed our relationship. It happened when I was thirteen, and I was on Christian house arrest. No church, no friends, no TV, no drawing. I was allowed only a bible and my meager weekly allowance of $5. I was bored, and I was going through puberty, so I was horny. Unfortunately, masturbation had lost its charm two weeks into my solitude, and I couldn't even draw myself new inspiration. So what did I do instead? I hired sex workers. Okay, not really, but I did get a few of my brother's friends to show me their dicks for my stashed allowance, and one even let me touch it. I was elated, and I went back to masturbating. I didn't think anyone besides the three boys knew about it so I continued on with life. That was until I found myself sitting across the table from Franklin and my parents.

"Gloria," my father boomed. "We need to have a conversation."

Boy, did we. Franklin had snitched on me. I guess he was upset that I saw his boyfriend's dick, but I really wasn't even trying to. He offered to show it to me and I couldn't say no fast enough before he pulled down his pants. It wasn't my fault, and Frankie would've known that if he just asked. I never wanted to lose the only other person I truly loved. But I did.

So now here I was, fourteen years later, still dealing with the consequences of someone else's actions. Still missing the little boy who used to let me put barrettes in his hair. Still angry about losing his friendship. All while he was making it perfectly clear that he was disgusted by me. I thought some things were forever, but that wasn't true. Because Franklin Jameson Myer-Smythe didn't want me anymore.

"Glory," Marcus whispered, snapping me out of my thoughts. "You good?"

I nodded before gathering the strength to speak. I wasn't good yet, but I was gonna be.

"I'm chilling, Marc," I replied, rising from the table. "Don't worry about this thing with Franklin. I got it figured out."

"Mm," he grumbled. "Text one of us when you make it home."

I smiled at him before kissing Alayssa on the top of her lil head.

"Gotcha. Thanks for breakfast, and for letting me crash on y'alls bougie-ass couch!" I called.

I climbed in my car, threw my heels in the back, then checked my phone, and sure enough there was a text waiting on me.

"Don't worry about the couch. We'll send a cleaning invoice to your office next week, drool face."

He was being an ass, but I had to laugh. Only Marcus.

I went home and cried under a too-hot shower while scrubbing the club glitter off. Once I stripped my skin the only thing left to do was eat then find some ass or something. Luckily I had a few numbers in mind, but if they weren't down I guess I could try to pimp that handsome ass Afro-Colombian lawyer from S&D outta some dick. I didn't really do coworkers like that but he still flirted with me despite the fact that I had been icing him out for months, and rumor had it, he was also asking about me. What was his name again? Oh yeah, it was…

Four

Chapter Four

Cash

Ah, Mondays. The best day of the week. Now I know most people hate Mondays, but I find them beneficial. Why? Because most of my opposing counsel spend their weekends out and about, and if they're young, they usually come into court tired, cranky, and hungover. I, on the other hand, come in moisturized, nourished, and magnificent. I don't party, I don't drink, and I keep a tight routine. So when Monday comes around I'm ready to win, and I usually do, except against *her.*

I like poetry, but not by white men. Their muses don't compete with mine. White men write of blue eyes, raven hair, and skin of cream. My muse had raven skin, eyes of tourmaline, and a smile of ivory.

Gloria.

Her name is Gloria. For a while, I was convinced she didn't know I existed, and that was a blow to my ego. Most people not only noticed me, they wanted me. Then there was Gloria. A woman who would break me down so badly in the courtroom that it gave me imposter syndrome. Then she'd walk her fine ass right past me in the hall with a tepid but polite smile and a gentle wave. Eventually, I got bold and flirted with her, but she never gave me the time of day. Hell, she never gave anyone the time of day. That made me curious, so I started asking around. I knew nothing about her besides her first and last name, so I'm sure that crept most of the other legals out. But Mr. Gemison humored me. Man, I loved nosey old black men.

"Gloria King. She's one of a kind. Smart and real sweet. Mama's a schoolteacher, Daddy's a pastor. She volunteers down at the women's shelter all the time. Hell of a cook too. She'd make somebody young real happy. Too bad she doesn't do relationships," he laughed.

"Like, at all?" I stuttered.

He looked at me like I hadn't been the first idiot to think I could be the exception, and hell, I probably wasn't. I knew I wasn't. Gloria turned heads no matter what she was doing. From DAs and officers to judges and inmates alike. Everybody wanted to behold Glory.

"At all," he said gravely. "Besides, she'd eat you alive."

"Don't I know it." I thought.

I had come to terms with that fact months ago. Gloria was strutting through the halls with a Robert, not a bob, and she had on some badass red bottoms with a cream and oxblood suit. She looked like an angel. Probably an angel of death, but an angel nonetheless. She walked past me, smelling all good, looking all fine, and all I could do was imagine her heels crushing my windpipe. So yeah, Gloria was gonna eat me alive. Whenever she finally noticed me. God, I hoped she noticed me. Maybe she would today though because it was Monday. It was larceny Monday to be exact and guess who my opposing counsel was? Gloria King.

She was in a fire-ass flare-legged black suit with a gray lace bodysuit, her bob was robbing, and her stilettos were sharper than my good knives. She looked good like always, but something was off. She hardly ever spoke to me outside of the courtroom so it couldn't have been her conversation. She wasn't one to fake smile either, so it definitely wasn't that. I wanted to ask if something was on her mind, but we had five minutes until our docket. So my curiosity would have to wait. Maybe she'd be in the mood to gloat when she inevitably won.

"Ms. King, do you have anything else you'd like to add?" Justice Davidson drolled.

I was in utter fucking shock because Gloria was losing. She never lost, and especially not to me. I had four constants. My mom always called me on Bingo Wednesdays for our weekly chat. My wax lady always missed that one spot at the top of my ass crack. My neighbor always tried to set me up with her gay son. Then on Mondays, I always lost my first case of the day to Gloria King.

Something was definitely wrong.

Gloria sighed while running her palm down her face to smooth the stress-induced creases,

"Not at this time, your honor."

Davidson scoffed as if he expected that reply before slamming his gavel against the podium.

"Then we'll take a brief recess until this Thursday. I hope you can build a stronger argument than this, King," he sneered.

One of the many things I admired about Gloria was her stellar poker face. Her eyes, lips, and brows were relaxed no matter what. She was usually a mountain. Except for this time. Davidson filed out with the rest of the room and her upper lip quivered just slightly when he passed her. It just barely happened, and you didn't have to blink to miss it. I should've missed it, but I didn't, and I was glad I didn't.

Because Gloria was pissed.

Then I was busy trying to figure out why when I should've been celebrating finally getting ahead of her.

Mr. Gemison was right. She was gonna eat me alive. She was gonna eat me alive and I was gone die happy about it. God, I was hopeless.

I noticed her hips swaying before I noticed anything else. Those endless legs of hers were moving a mile a minute like she was rushing to be somewhere. If you didn't know Gloria, you wouldn't know that she didn't rush. She strolled and occasionally sauntered, but the differences were just barely noticeable. So to everyone else on the third floor, she was behaving perfectly normal, and I was being a fucking weirdo, rushing after her like she was a secret agent in an action movie, who seduced me to steal my passport.

"Gloria, wait!" I called.

I wasn't expecting her to stop, but she did.

Her body stopped moving before her hair did, and it flicked over her shoulder when she turned to face me.

"Cassius, to what do I owe the pleasure?" she replied.

Damn. My name sounded so good coming out of her mouth. Too good.

"Focus, nigga!" My mind snapped.

Right, she asked why I was bothering her. I could handle that. All I had to do was be normal and answer in a complete sentence.

"I err, ruh, shit," I muttered, gawking at her.

Damn, her eyes were gorgeous. Even with her cold stare. Her gaze made me question why and how I was allowed to become a lawyer. I'm sure this was why I kept losing to her.

"Um, Gloria, hi. Good morning," I corrected.

Gloria pulled her wrist forward to check if it was still morning. Then she looked disappointed with said fact.

"Good Morning, Cassius," she sighed.

I haven't blushed in years, but the way this fine-ass woman said my name had my face hot.

"Focus..."

Right, focus. Focus on asking Gloria what was wrong.

Shit.

Why was this so hard? I had asked plenty of people what was bothering them. It was a conversation standard.

"Cause you never really cared how anyone else felt." My monologue

answered.

That was a level of truth I was uncomfortable with. I really didn't care how anyone else felt, and while it had recently changed, it was evident when I was younger. See, people had been telling me I was pretty since I could talk.

"Cash is gone be a lil heartbreaker. Cash is so handsome. You better watch Cash around ya lil girls!"

To be fair they needed to watch me around their sons too. A nigga would swing whichever way I felt like swinging in the moment. I was a greedy pansexual playboy with a big bank account. So I ripped through bodies like strippers ripped through fishnets. I partied and perused, but I never took anyone or anything too seriously.

Then my mama got sick.

My mama is quite literally my hero. Always has been, and always will be. See, Dalia Anna was serious about that mom life. She supported me and my sister Cookie through everything. I'm talking bake sales, soccer practice, and dance recitals. She also suffered through two years of me attempting to learn the clarinet. Emphasis on *attempting*. Then, when I was eight, I told her and my daddy I might like boys. I was scared shitless because I had heard plenty of people say I had a lil sugar in my tank and my daddy would be pissed every time. He would cuss and yell, and he even put my grandma out for it once. Then there was my mama. I told her and nothing changed. Nothing at all. She just smiled and said,

"Duh, Mijo. I know my kids. Go lay down, baby."

We moved out of that house the very next day. My mama divorced my daddy the year after, and she'd been doing it all by herself ever since. She gave up a ten-year marriage because my daddy didn't support me. So I gave her everything when she got diagnosed with ovarian cancer three years ago. I stopped partying, I dropped my habits, I dropped my distractions. I let her have my free time for whatever she needed. Whether it was to cry, yell, or just watch Grey's Anatomy. Sometimes it was all three. Sometimes it was nothing at all. But we got through it, it made us stronger, and it changed me for the better.

Which led me to right now. Where I was standing in front of a woman who kinda reminded me of my mama, trying my best to put fifteen years of playboy know-how to work and not be awkward.

"Look. You seem off like you're having a bad day, or a long day, or just a day. So I wanted to check on you, and offer you a drink when you're done with everything," I rambled.

So much for not being awkward. At least I got it out. Gloria hadn't scoffed at me yet which was usually a given when a man was audacious enough to speak to her. I noticed she was nicer to the ladies.

Her eyes finally expressed something other than indifference. Maybe surprise. Maybe annoyance. I was dying to find out either way.

She parted her cherry-painted lips to speak, drawing me into the trap of her little pink tongue and gleaming ivory smile.

"I don't really go out with coworkers," she said, piercing my heart.

I probably should've given up, but there was a glint in her eye that told me I just might have a chance if I pushed back just a bit. Nothing too crazy though. She probably just wanted to see if I had a spine.

I did, and I'd blow hers out if I ever got the chance.

"What about with friends then?" I asked. "I know this place with really great fries and I'm a good listener."

And I was. Especially when it was her.

She cocked her head onto her shoulder just slightly, exposing her neck and rounded chin. I think she was trying to figure out the best way to break something on me, and I was truthfully ready. But then she surprised me.

"Ok. I'll think about it and let you know. Have a good rest of your day, Cassius," she sang.

I think she stunned me because I didn't realize she had boarded the elevator until it closed.

Holy shit. Gloria King didn't outright turn me down.

I loved Mondays.

It had been a decent day. Nothing had gone terribly wrong, but there wasn't any noticeable excitement either. I was just kinda done. Fatigued from boredom, and bored of fatigue. So I started packing up my shit around four. I usually didn't leave until six, but I knew I wasn't gonna get anything else done. Besides, there was nothing more for me to do. Until my phone chimed.

"Hey, Cassius. This is Glory. I hope you don't mind, I got your number from your assistant."

Fuck! Gloria texted me. She was amazing. This was amazing. I just didn't know what to say.

"Is that drink offer still on the table?"

Never mind, I was golden. Even I knew how to spell yes.

I met Gloria two hours later at a little happy hour spot. I wasn't expecting to see her in regular clothes, but I was really glad I did. It was late July and she was dressed in a pretty burgundy knit dress with a high split, a pair of flat strappy sandals, and big earrings. I think I liked her in regular shoes more than I did heels. I'm not sure why, she just looked comfortable. I liked her comfortable.

"Hi, Gloria," I said, taking the adjacent stool. "How was the rest of your day?"

She sat down whatever fruity-ass drink she was nursing before turning to me, and her eyes were full of something unfamiliar. I think it was laughter.

"Ok, first things first. If we're friends, you gotta stop calling me Gloria," she said.

"Done. I'll call you whatever you want," I bumbled.

Jesus fuck. There was coming on strong, then there was that. I was coming on like commercial paint thinner.

"Glory is fine," she laughed.

Commercial paint thinner aside, I hadn't fucked up too bad yet.

"Deal, and please call me Cash. My mama's the only person who calls me Cassius, and I let her slide since she picked the name."

Glory laughed again, but it wasn't as reserved as the first time. It wasn't reserved at all. It was a loud melodic symphony of shrill peaks and gentle, breathy valleys, and it was better than anything I ever heard come out of a woman's mouth. I needed to find an estate planner because this was not gone work out for me. That nosey-ass black man was right. She was about to pray-mantis my shit.

"What happened this morning?" I asked. "We kinda got this routine where you embarrass me, win your case, and then pretend I don't exist," I joked.

"I don't pretend you don't exist!" she gasped.

"You kinda do, shawty. But I ain't mad. I'm a masochist anyway," I shrugged. "So what happened?"

Glory stirred her drink aimlessly before her stoic mask faltered. Then I heard one of the most heartbreaking sighs ever.

"My personal life kinda imploded, and I'm off my shit. So I guess I was just emotional with everything I got going on. The defendant is one of the residents at Second Path, the women's shelter. She's had a hard life," she murmured.

That nosey old black man was right again. Glory was a sweetheart. I rubbed her back gently to ease some of her tension and that calmed her quivering lip.

"I get it," I confessed. "We're humans first. Even if some people forget that somewhere along the way. But I'm proud of you for really fighting for your defendant. You just gotta tighten up against Davidson's coon ass."

Glory's big eyes got even bigger when she realized I knew.

"Oh my God. I thought I was the only one who noticed!" she gasped. "That nigga is insufferable!"

"Nah, it's not just you. Trust me. I thought he was one of them shits from Get Out at first. He looks dead in the eyes," I laughed.

She once again graced me with the most beautiful laugh I've ever heard and my brain went off the deep end.

"She's the one," my subconscious mumbled.

"Ok, I've had three drinks and you've had an impressive amount of fries and two virgin daiquiris. What's going on, Cash?" Glory asked.

Shit, she noticed. We had been hanging out and talking for an hour but I didn't want to end it by telling her that I didn't drink. I'm not sure why my elective sobriety made me nervous when it came to Gloria, but I think I was scared she'd get bored. Jaguars are finicky that way.

"Um, I kinda don't drink. I mean, I did, once upon a time, but not anymore. Unless it's the holidays or a special occasion. But I know it's kind of the thing for lawyers to do when they're stressed and I couldn't take you to the art museum."

I was expecting the worst but she laughed again.

"You definitely could've taken me to the art museum to destress. I wanna go see the new Amna Rei exhibit."

"You know her!?" I asked with far too much excitement.

Glory nodded before flashing me that bright kilowatt smile.

"I love her. Her work makes me remember why I love painting."

"You paint?"

"Yeah," Glory shrugged, nibbling her bottom lip. "I mostly sketch, but sometimes I paint when I need the colors to blend a certain way or if I'm shading something complicated. Do you draw or…"

"Oh no, I'm mostly an admirer and occasionally a collector. Sometimes I write poetry, but, um. It's just for fun," I said nervously.

"I think that's the only reason we should have hobbies," Glory whispered. "For fun. Regular life is unfun enough."

She said the last part so hushed it hurt. For some reason that made me want to hold her hand and kiss her temples while I told her everything was gonna be alright. God, I was simple. All it took was a pretty smile and pensive eyes to turn me on my ass.

Oh well.

"Can you show me some of your work?" I asked gently.

Gloria looked at me with something new. Fondness. Or maybe I was tripping. I convinced myself I was until she opened her phone to show me her art.

It was stunning.

It was black people in their full glory. Kinky curls, and oiled skin, and teeth with big gaps. I scrolled through the entire album in awe until I came to a huge oil painting. It was different from the others, yet so familiar. It looked like love, effort, and history. All the little details married together beautifully to create an absolute masterpiece. Plus that nigga was fine as fuck.

"This is amazing. Is this yo boyfriend?" I asked, attempting to tie back the fear in my voice.

I guess Glory saw right through me cause she snorted before rubbing my now-tense arm.

"Nah. Frankie's a childhood friend. Besides, I'm sure Mr. Gemison told you I don't date," she yawned.

Damn, this is why she always beat me. She was way smarter than I.

"He did mention that. He also told me that you volunteer a lot and that you can make a mean pot of greens. So I'm at least tryna stay in the running until Thanksgiving. I got a G wagon so I'm sure it'd be very beneficial for your annual coat drive."

Damn, that was good. I'm not sure what happened, but Suave Cash was back, and Glory liked Suave Cash from the looks of it. Her eyes dropped to my lips while she leaned toward me, demanding every single kilowatt of brainpower I had to spare. Leaving me with only enough to keep me breathing.

"Cassius," she whispered, closing the space between us. "I'd eat you alive."

"I know," I gulped. "I'm counting on it. Just not tonight, because you are very drunk."

Curse my mama for raising me right and giving me a conscience! I ain't mean that, but still. Glory looked at me like I shot her puppy before focusing back on her drink. I had finally fucked up, but it was the right thing to do, and I wanted Glory to want me in the right state of mind. Cause I wanted her always.

"Come on, pretty lady," I cooed. "Let's get you home."

I had not fucked up, but I was about to. Gloria had her nails wrapped around my throat like I was her favorite bitch, and fuck I wanted to be. Especially with how she was kissing me. Her warm minty tongue wrapped around mine with precision while her teeth rested in my bottom lip, and the hand that wasn't choking me was busy surveying the rest of my real estate. She was almost to my hardwood deck and the patio doors were sliding open. We needed to pump the brakes.

"Glory, we're in public," I moaned, struggling to pull away.

"Then come upstairs," she purred seductively. Dangerously.

"I can't do that."

"Why not, Cassius?"

"Because you're drunk," I said firmly.

Glory kissed her teeth like I was the one in the wrong here. I was trying my best not to be a rapey weirdo while she was trying her best to get folded like an ironing board.

"I won't be in thirty minutes, Cash! So just come upstairs, let me sit on your face, and then I'll be sober enough for you to stick your dick in me."

I thought the bar exam was hard, but this was hell. I could oblige this beautiful woman who was unfortunately inebriated and have the time of my life. Or I could go home, put a frozen pizza in the oven, and beat off.

Fuck.

I hoped I had a plain cheese.

"Look, Glory. I'd really like nothing more than to have you ride my face like I'm a merry-go-round, but you are drunk, and you cannot give consent. Unhand me, get some rest, then ask me when you're sober. And if you good for me right now, I might even eat your ass later."

Who was I kidding? I was definitely gone eat her ass, but Glory didn't need to know that.

Those round lips pulled into a bratty pout that was testing the limits of my integrity and my drawls, but I guess I was firm enough for her to listen. She pulled away in defeat, but not before giving me one more gentle kiss.

"Thanks, Cash. I had fun tonight," she whispered.

I cupped her cute round chin in my palm before doing something I had wanted to do all day. I kissed her temple and squeezed her hand.

"Anytime, Glory," I replied. "Have a good night."

She let out a tired little sigh while I opened her door. Which was so adorable it made my heart hurt.

"You too, Cassius. Text me when you make it home."

I had to stop myself from texting her immediately, because the delusional ass nigga in me was telling me she was gone be my new home.

Yeah. I was cooked.

Five

Chapter Five

Glory

Ugh. Men ruin everything. It would've been so easy for Cash to come upstairs and let me have my way with him, but he just had to have morals and shit. That was sweet but inconvenient. Annoying even. Because it was now Thursday and I was feeling belligerent despite my best efforts to tamp down my urges. Maybe I wasn't trying hard enough though. I kept letting my mind wander back to bow-shaped lips, hazel-colored almond eyes, and moisturized chestnut skin. Skin I wanted to sink my teeth into.

There was only one problem. I worked with Cassius, and he was a good man, Savannah. He was the type of man that kissed you too long before he left for the day. He was the type of man to give you his jacket after you left yours being hard-headed, he was the type of man to rub your feet after a date, and he was the type of man I needed to avoid. I fucked up by getting that drink though. Because heaven forbid I fucked him with the way I was feeling. I liked talking to him, I enjoyed his company, and we had shit in common. Shit like art, music, and nerve-wracking ass mamas

39

that we adored. Then he saw me. Most men didn't even see me as human, yet Cassius noticed that I was off. AND HE LISTENED! He ain't try to fix, he just listened! He was the second man I ever met in all my twenty-seven years who knew how to listen without fixing.

I liked him. Fuck, I liked him. I didn't even have to fuck him first either. He thought I was ignoring him, but I was avoiding his ass. Because I knew I'd like him from the moment he parted those kissable ass lips, and I did. That would make it so much harder when I inevitably broke his heart.

Now I know what you're thinking.

"Just don't break his heart, Glory. Duh."

Trust me, that sounds great in theory, but it's only going to take once for my urges to become too much for him. One day I'd be everything he ever wanted, then the next day I'd be a disgusting, selfish, whore with no self-control. I know I will. I've read the story too many times to wish for something different.

So Cassius Monroe had to be off limits because I didn't want him bad enough to break his heart. Which I definitely would.

"What the hell?" I mumbled.

I went to work early hoping to distract myself from my increasingly complicated love life, only to find my office filled with peonies. There was only one fucker sweet enough to remember that I liked peonies over roses, and he was busy bringing sexual assault charges against me.

"Aren't they beautiful?" Tilly, my assistant, clapped. "They were delivered an hour ago."

"From who?" I questioned.

Tilly brought her hand to her chest just slightly before flicking a note card in my direction.

"Mr. Cash Monroe," she purred, annunciating every syllable of his last name.

"Don't say his name like that," I barked.

Tilly raised her hands in surrender before giving me the look. Cash had a reputation that rivaled mine. Love em and leave em. Except there was no love. He never seriously entertained anyone in our circuit or outside of it from what I heard. Which was odd, cause the man was fine as fuck, as Tilly mentioned twenty times previous.

"I'm just saying, boss. The fine ass man is shooting his shot."

She jumped on her toes while flicking her wrist, then she made an air basket. "KOBE!" she exclaimed.

"Go sit down somewhere before I fire yo country ass," I tutted.

Tilly shrugged and reluctantly left my office to man her desk, leaving me time to focus on the task at hand.

Ripping Cash a new one.

"Good morning, Glory," Cash cooed into the phone. His voice was all velvety and soft when he said it. Like he was wrapping my brain in a cashmere throw. But I didn't want him wrapping me in anything. Especially not those thick and veiny muscular arms or his plump lips. *Especially.*

"Don't you try to Rico Suave my shit!" I shouted. "What's your deal? What's with the flowers?"

Cash's butter-smooth laugh filled the line, soothing my irritation.

"I like you, Glory. So I bought you flowers," he answered honestly. "I figured you liked peonies because you seem to paint them a lot."

Fuck. The nigga was perceptive and thoughtful.

Shit.

Damn.

"Cassius, I meant it when I said I'd eat you alive. You'll leave me alone if you know what's good for you," I warned.

"You promise, Glory? Cause I like it rough," he chuckled.

A handsome man with deep pockets, good conversation, and no sense of self-preservation? Fuck, the universe was tempting me.

"Goodbye, Cassius. Stop sending me flowers," I gritted.

The very next day he sent me twice as many instead. This went on for an entire week until I arrived early Monday to reject the deliveries. So the following Tuesday he switched to sending me lunch. And it was from my favorite taqueria that I briefly, emphasis on *briefly,* mentioned. I loved the food because the meat was tender and the tortillas were irregular from the use of an old hand press. They were located in a grocery store on the east side of town, and they didn't deliver.

Fucking Cassius Monroe.

I should have just said no to drinks. I had every opportunity to go home and wallow. I had every intention to do that after losing my shit with Davidson. Then Cash popped up, all happy to be here and shit.

I really should have just gone back to how it was before. Interactions and conversations limited to the scope of our profession. That would be easy. That would be best. So why was I standing outside of Cash's office, fist raised, ready to knock?

"Come in, Glory," he boomed.

Well, I'll be damned. Maybe he was a little too perceptive.

I entered, shutting the door firmly behind myself before striding to that ridiculously oversized desk of his.

"Cassius."

He propped his head on his hands before looking up at me with a challenging smile.

"Glory."

"Stop what you're doing. You're not slick, and you're not the first one to think you can bypass my rules," I warned.

I expected him to get nervous or for his expression to mirror defeat, but this cocky nigga was checking his nails. I noticed they were freshly manicured too.

"Cassius!" I screeched.

"I love it when you say my full name," he grinned.

"Are you really this delusional?" I asked.

"Yes."

"Why?" I groaned.

"Because I like you. I know you got your lil rules, and I know many have tried and failed, but I feel like I've gotten closer than most, and I really am tryna make it until Thanksgiving."

I'm not sure why that got me, but it did. Risk vs reward was losing to desire.

"Stand up," I demanded.

Cash, completely entranced, jumped at my command. I had to bite my lip, because temptation was an understatement. Cassius Monroe was an outright trap.

A trap that I was falling into heart first.

"Kiss me," I barked.

Cash immediately rounded the desk and came over to me. His eyes flickered with pure adoration while we stood chest to chest, then he leaned forward stopping just short of my lips.

He was a brat.

I liked those.

"Kiss. Me. Now," I hissed, no room for softness in my tone.

Cash smiled against my lips before parting his to meet my demand, and, God, it felt so fucking right. We were the same height so it was easy for me to grip his throat and run my fingers over his downy waves. It was so easy for me to tilt my chin and press close to deepen our kiss, and it was easy for me to unbuckle his pants.

I thought he might stop me since he had morals, but he didn't. He just paused long enough to lock the door and tell his nervous assistant, Marisa, to hold all his calls. Then he picked my big ass up and put me on his desk.

I'm not a light lady. For one, I'm five-foot-eight. For two, I'm 50% tit, and for three, even without the tit, I'm still firmly plus-sized. I've never been anything smaller than a size eighteen in adulthood. It's not like I cared, but I was impressed when someone could lift me. Especially since

Cash wasn't much bigger than me. Clearly, that wasn't a deterrent for him though, because he kneeled before me after propping me on the desk and practically ripping my pants off.

"Can I taste you?" he asked so sweetly.

I rubbed the swirl on the crown of his head before spreading my legs, and the look on Cash's face was golden. See, my situation is always pretty situated. I got a wax schedule tighter than most folks' booty holes, I keep honeypot wipes in every handbag I own, and I got coochie deodorant to keep shit fresh while I'm at work. What threw him off was likely the butterfly jewelry dangling over my bigger-than-average clit. He was so cute when he was nervous. So my answer was an unequivocal,

"Yes."

Cash wasted no time putting his lips on mine. First, it was just sweet, playful kisses. Then he gently swept my folds with the tip of his tongue before taking my clit into his mouth and sucking it.

Fuck.

He was a good little whore.

I almost wanted to keep him if not for the looming threat of my breaking his heart.

"Get it together, Glory!"

I've had good eaters before, and I never thought about keeping them. I was just frustrated and Cash was just doing a lil zig zaggy thing with his tongue that made me want to strip butterball ass naked. Shit, this was a bad idea.

I take that back. It was not a bad idea. I mean it was, but it wasn't. See, I never get tired of cumming. I love it, I wish I could do it all day every day. I usually keep a serious rotation of contenders, toys, and play spaces, and I've only been worn out once, which was that incident with Frankie.

Until now.

I expected Cash to get lockjaw twenty minutes ago, but he'd been happily munching my box for the last thirty-five minutes as if we didn't have jobs.

If I was in court today, I'd be screwed. I really should've really stopped him before we got to this point, but he was just so fucking good.

Too good.

"Cash, wait. Wait, wait, wait," I panted, trying to hold it in.

If the pressure building in my pussy was any indication, we were about to have a Steamboat Geyser situation. But Cash didn't listen. He kept licking like he was trying to get to the center of a tootsie roll pop, and he was certainly working to get a mouthful.

"CASSIUS! I said, wa…. Fuuccckkkk…" I groaned.

My vision split in two while I struggled to regain my fleeting breath. I came so hard that my ears were ringing and I temporarily forgot where I was. Eventually, my vision re-merged and focused on Cash who was sitting in between my legs, licking my squirt off his bottom lip with a smile like it was spilled juice that he wanted to savor.

"Did I do a good job, Glory?" he asked.

What kind of question was that? I never squirted from head, especially not in the middle of a work day, and here he was asking if it was good?

That shit was amazing.

Immaculate.

Then I remembered how Cash liked to kiss. Baby Boy was a sub if I ever saw one, and he just wanted praise.

"You did so good, sweetness. So good."

I stretched out my hand to rub his soft curls and Cassius nuzzled my palm like a happy Labrador.

"You're such a good boy," I said innocently.

I wish I hadn't said that because it made my cheeks warm. It reminded me that I actually liked him. It reminded me that Cash was a good man. It reminded me that I was me.

"Fuck," I cussed.

Cash stood ready to help. Ready to fix whatever was bothering me. Ready to do whatever I asked. That made me sad, and I started fucking crying.

Shit.

I hadn't cried in years before that shit with Frankie last week, and now I was crying all the time. I was boo-fucking-hooing in this nice ass office after I got my pussy ate like a parfait because I was scared of hurting him. I never gave a fuck about hurting a cis-gendered man before. I missed being dead inside. This emotion shit was for the fucking birds.

"Glory, tell me what's wrong," Cash cooed gently.

He wiped my tears, cradled my head, and patted my back while I cried off a $60 tube of "waterproof" mascara. Fuck he was good.

It also didn't help that Cash was warm and comforting. He was a little bit of a plush pal so his chest was firm yet soft, and he smelled divine. Like lavender, cedar, and teakwood. I wanted to bottle that shit up and huff it.

"I like you," I blurted out.

I didn't mean to say that, but he was just so damn comforting. I don't think I've ever described a man that I fucked as comforting. Except for Frankie, but Frankie was being an ass.

"I like you too," Cash said matter-factly. "So what's the problem?"

Why I was inclined to tell him the truth, I'm not sure. But I did. It was better to rip the band-aid off early anyway. Cause this was feeling way too right.

"I'm gonna break your heart," I whispered, still clutched against his chest.

"Why do you think that?" he laughed.

"Because I'm me," I answered. "It's kind of my thing."

Cassius swept a strand of hair behind my ear before pecking my forehead a few times. He seemed marginally unconcerned with my confession.

"Well, I happen to think that you're pretty great. You funny, and sweet, and so very smart. So I'm having a hard time believing you just gone break my heart for the hell of it. So tell me, Glory," he said, tilting my chin to meet his hopeful gaze. "Why are you being so hard on yourself?"

I told him. I told him everything about my hypersexuality, my pretty much constant state of want, and how I had the tendency to fuck things up when

I needed more, and he just said,

"Ok."

"Ok?" I stammered.

"Yeah, Ok," Cash reiterated. "So you're sexually non-monogamous. That's not really a deal breaker for me. My biggest deal breakers are rapists, racists, and Scorpios," he shrugged.

"I'm a Pisces," I laughed.

Cash sucked air through a grimace before rising from the seat across from me.

"Ion know about them either, but for you, I'll make it work."

"Cash," I sighed, falling into his embrace.

"Look, Glory. I'm pan, so I know good and well that sexuality and relationships fall on a spectrum. If you need to get your rocks off and I'm not available, I'm not tripping. We'll just get tested after every new partner and be honest with each other. Ok?"

I released the breath I had been holding in. He wasn't disgusted by me, and he wasn't trying to change me. He liked me for me, even the horny bits. Cassius Monroe was a breath of fresh air.

"Ok, but I gotta be honest about something now," I whispered.

"What's up, shawty?" Cash asked.

"I'm still really fucking horny. So I'd like you to pull down your pants if you wouldn't mind."

Cash's smooth-ass laugh filled the room before he kissed my forehead.

"I got you," he said, reaching in his desk for a condom.

That threw me off. I was usually the one with condoms stored in every conceivable space.

"Cash, are you a whore?" I asked.

Cash bit his lip before flashing me that cute-ass smile of his.

"Yes. Well, a retired one now, but I'd like to be your favorite if you let me," he purred.

Oh, we were way past that.

"Hurry up and pull your pants down," I said with far too much excitement.

Cash's dick was perfect by my standard. It was medium length, girthy, and curved. He was also waxed, putting his adorable crescent moon-shaped birthmark on display.

He wasted no time rolling the condom down, but his enthusiasm slowed when I spread my legs.

Shit.

I hoped he wasn't having regrets.

"Cassius," I cooed, lifting his chin. "What's wrong?"

Cash nuzzled my hand again while his fingers found their way to my clit.

"You make me nervous," he whispered.

This fine-ass man was nervous about me. God, I didn't know men could be so adorable.

"Don't be nervous, Cash. It's just me," I replied while covering him in kisses.

I pulled him close while spreading my legs enough for our pelvises to meet. Then I rolled my hips forward, forcing Cash inside me.

"Fuck," we groaned.

Cash felt so good. He was nervous for nothing because I was instantly addicted. Especially with how well I stretched around his hook. He was a perfect fit, and I did not mean that figuratively. His entire dick could rest inside me comfortably. It was a type of satisfaction that I never knew I needed. Especially when I tightened around all of him. Especially during his tender, languid strokes. It was almost better than the head.

I never liked slow sex before, and I think that's because I try to keep sex as unemotional as possible. But Cash was a lover boy through and through, and his excited kisses, slow twines, and gentle touches were welcomed. I think they were even wanted because I was clinging to him, making eye contact, and kissing back.

Yeah.

He was my favorite.

Especially when he made me cum. My legs would shake and his eyes would roll back. It felt like my pleasure was his pleasure. He was such a good boy. Especially when he let me choke him. My hand gripped around his exposed throat, soliciting a little moan. A moan that was smooth, deep, and laced with appreciation.

"Good job, Cassius. Keep moaning for me, baby," I panted.

Cash's sharp canines pierced his supple bottom lip when he met my gaze. He was in ecstasy, and the feeling was mutual.

"Glory…" he whimpered. "Why do you feel so fucking good?"

His eyes were watering and something about his truly overwhelmed state was punching my ticket. Maybe I liked that he was vulnerable. Maybe I liked the praise. Maybe my good Christian parents actually did birth a succubus, and maybe that's why I was obsessed with making Cash cum.

Who knows?

I grabbed him by the throat and pressed the two fingers I'd been rubbing my clit with against his tongue.

"Speed up," I demanded.

Cash shook his head, refusing my request. So I tightened my grip against his Adam's apple.

"Speed up, Cassius," I barked.

Cash softened his eyes and held my hip in search of amnesty.

"Glory, I'll cum," he whimpered.

Poor, nervous, Cash. He really just wanted to do a good job. I eased my grip on him just enough to pull my fingers out of his mouth and kiss him. His tension relaxed a little with the tender lip lock, and I softened my tone.

"That's the point, Cash, sweetheart. I really want you to cum. So speed up for me, baby. Speed up so I can feel you cum for me."

Cash sped up. He sped up so much that the desk was shaking, the awards on the walls were rattling, and I was cumming again. Maybe it was from his pelvis rubbing against my clit. Maybe it was because I liked being fucked rough and careless despite my newfound appreciation for soft sex. Maybe it's because I liked Cash. Or maybe it was all three. I was grateful, whatever the reason. Because while Cassius Monroe was busy pounding me into a well-maintained desktop calendar, I was being pulled through a serious simultaneous orgasm that left me sated. And I got to ride that wave while looking into the prettiest hazel eyes God ever took the time to make.

Chapter Six

Frankie

I wonder what Glory was doing. I had been wondering what Glory was doing for the past ten years, but I was experiencing an uptick in curiosity since last Friday. After I accidentally fucked her.

Shit.

I freaked out on her for no reason. I mean, there was a reason, but it was my reason. The way I felt wasn't her responsibility, and that was partly why I kept my distance. See, Glory wasn't bothered to know that she fucked me. She still looked satisfied up until I went and hurt her feelings. And that was very bad. Because that meant she found me sexually attractive. Which meant she might be interested in doing it again, and I couldn't handle having sex with Glory again.

Because I was in love with her.

I didn't mean to be, but I think I always was. It started out innocent when she was just a drooly, menacing toddler who gave me a nickname.

"Frankie and beans!" she cheered.

They had introduced me to her as Franklin, but that had been my nickname from that day forth until she dropped the beans. Then it was just Frankie. My parents set up play dates with the Kings hoping I'd make friends with their son, but eventually, I became friends with their first daughter. I really wasn't sure how it happened, it just kinda did. She was four years younger than me and that's leagues apart when you're kids. But she was clever, funny, and incredibly sweet.

I had a moment in church one day when Pastor King raised his voice to deliver a scripture. It sounded too much like yelling, and it sent me into a full panic attack. I lied and said I had to pee and instead left to find somewhere quiet. Which led me upstairs where I accidentally stumbled upon Glory who was drawing in an unoccupied office. Mrs. King did her hair twice a week and she still managed to have poofy, half-braided tresses every Sunday. When everyone asked about it, they simply said that she was a rough four-year-old. She was four. Glory was four, and a preacher's daughter, and she was drawing a skull with concerningly accurate detail. But she was still four, so I wondered if she'd ask me a thousand questions, or tell someone I was there, or laugh at me, but she just walked over and rested her head on my shoulder.

"Sometimes he gets loud," she said softly.

She then handed me a coloring pencil after dividing a fresh piece of paper in half.

"Draw with me," she demanded.

So there I was, eight years old, with a hot face full of salty tears, and I was being soothed by a little girl with wild hair who was quite literally half my age.

"Ok," I mumbled.

My love for her only grew with age. Every passing year made Glory brighter, funnier, and sweeter. When she learned that some people didn't have homes, she wanted to spend her weekends volunteering. When she learned that Marcus had his first crush, she proofread his love note. When she learned that I hated Fran Drescher's voice, she perfected her impression of her and dressed up as The Nanny for Spirit Week. Everything she learned she mastered, and that included me.

"You like him," she whispered while corn-rolling my hair.

We were in her room watching the other boys play football out of her window, and I would move and fuck up her parts every time he ran back toward the house. I knew exactly what she was talking about, but I was still heavily in denial of my sexuality.

"What? He's a boy!" I replied.

"So?" she shrugged. *"I like girls all the time. They're good kissers."*

"I don't like him," I mumbled. *"I'm not gay."*

"Yes you are," she said plainly. *"I know you are, and that's ok. I won't tell anyone."*

"Essie, you're twelve. You don't know what gay is."

She laughed in my face as soon as I said that. I knew better. We both knew better. Hell, the Pope probably knew better at this point.

"You can like boys and girls, Frankie. It's ok to have a crush on Elias. There are gay penguins and gay lions."

She leaned forward to kiss me on the nose, and I think that's the exact moment I fell in love with her. Before that I just adored her, but after that I was hers.

"Just don't forget about me when you get a boyfriend. Ok?"

"Ok," I mumbled.

I was hopelessly in love with her. Even still, I knew my affection for Glory was inappropriate. She was too young for a boyfriend and far too young for a sixteen-year-old boyfriend at that. I was halfway through high school, and she had just started sixth grade. Intelligence and emotional maturity aside, Glory was a baby, and I wanted her to grow at her own pace, not mine. Or anyone else's for that matter.

"You seen Glory?" Elias asked.

Glory was on house arrest for spying on the men's locker room. I wasn't allowed to visit her even though Mrs.King thought'd it be good for her to have some benign company. I didn't think I was benign, and I think she knew I loved Glory, but she also knew I'd never do anything to hurt her or put her at risk.

"*Nah, she's in trouble. So we can't hang out,*" I answered.

"*Damn, what she do?*" he asked.

I shrugged. I didn't make it a habit of telling Glory's business. I knew she had been drawing dicks for months before she got caught. Honestly, she was good at it. I wasn't gonna stop her shine.

"*Shit. You should ask her to hang out with us when she gets off punishment,*" Elias suggested.

I leaned back onto my palms to watch the sunset over the horizon. I honestly didn't like sharing Glory's time, but I hoped she could help me conquer my anxiety about hanging out with Elias in public. She helped me conquer it any other time.

"*Yeah, I think she gets off in two weeks. I can ask her. Whatchu wanna do?*"

"*Fuck,*" he answered plainly.

My stomach turned inside out when he said that. Elias was a year older than me and five older than Glory. My Glory. My sweet baby who volunteered all the time and did shitty sitcom impressions.

"*Excuse me?*" I barked.

His face twisted and I realized how fucking ugly he was. Especially since he was trying to take advantage of Glory.

"*What? I thought you liked Glory? She got some big ass titties and...*"

"*She's twelve,*" I growled.

"*Yeah, twelve going on eighteen. She fast as fuck. She was just paying us to see our dicks. Baby girl ain't as innocent as she likes to play. She could probably show us s...*"

I honestly can't tell you what he said after that. I didn't come down from my dark cloud until Mr. King pulled me off of him. I spent twenty minutes beating Elias Oscar's ass on the Pastor's manicured lawn during group Bible study.

"*Franklin! What has gotten into you?*" my mama shrieked.

Everyone saw me tryna choke Elias out. His parents also went to the King's church, so did his grandparents, and they were pissed that I had fucked up their precious pedophile.

"Lazarus, we're calling the police," Mrs. Oscar said.

Mr. King held his hand out with one pointer finger before turning back to me.

"Give the boy a chance to tell us what happened," he instructed.

I didn't even realize I was crying until the tears slid into my scratches. If I told him right there everyone was gonna know Glory's business. I would not only blow up her spot, but I'd embarrass her, and she'd be condemned to church gossip for something she truly couldn't control. I didn't want that for her.

"I'd like to talk alone, Sir," I mumbled.

Mr. King sighed, but he obliged me. We went to his office to talk, and I reluctantly told him everything. I told him about Glory paying to see dicks. I told him about Elias' plot to spit roast her. Then I think I accidentally told on myself because he leaned back in his chair and looked at me differently.

"You did the right thing, Franklin. Thank you for telling me and using discretion," he said.

Then he inhaled. It was so sharp it could've stabbed me straight on through.

"But, you and Gloria will be spending less time together from here on out."

I know why he said it. Anyone with eyes could see I loved her, but it didn't hurt any less. It didn't make me want to fight any less.

"Sir, I would never do anything to Glory. I would never disre..."

He silenced me with a single raised palm. Then he left his desk, walked to the bar cart, and poured two single malt whiskeys, one shorter than the other.

He slid me the glass in silence and urged me to drink. I was nervous but he insisted I'd need it. So when I finally did, he continued.

"Franklin. I know you're a good kid, and eventually, you'll be a good man. I

don't doubt that you'd do everything in your power to keep Glory safe. I can see that from today," he waved.

"But you are in love with Gloria. As much as that disturbs me, I know it is what it is. God describes love as one of the most powerful forces ever created, and it is. You'll give Gloria whatever she wants to make her smile. You do it now. But her urges are too strong, so if she were to ask you for your body, which I'm sure she would eventually, you'd probably give it to her."

I'd give Glory the shoes off my feet, the food off my plate, the air out my lungs, I'd give her anything. I couldn't really argue because it was true. So I drank. Whiskey burned, but it burned for less time than hot tears did.

"I can't let you do that, Franklin. I can't allow you to love my daughter in that way. I'm sorry. I know you need her, but you love her too much. Y'all are too young, and Glory has to learn self-control," Mr. King sighed.

So we sat down a few days later. Glory sat across from me. Her curious nutmeg eyes were roving over my expression for some sort of hint as to what was happening. Then Mr. King said,

"We need to have a conversation."

Then we did, and it was me and Glory's last.

Turns out Mr. King didn't have to separate us because she cut me off herself. She didn't have all the details because she was twelve, but she knew enough to know I told on her, and I guess that was all she needed to know. She stopped talking to me, stopped hugging me, stopped looking at me, and gave me back everything I'd ever given her, including her favorite sketchbook. But I think she ended up keeping a part of me without either of us knowing, because I'd only been half full ever since.

Which leads me to now. Where I'm at this funeral for my aunt who I honestly loved but can't feel anything for. I haven't felt anything in years. Scratch that, I haven't felt anything since last Friday, and before that, I hadn't felt anything in years. I don't even enjoy cooking anymore. That's probably why my diet is largely single-malt whiskey, bananas, rice, and clearance meat. At least liquor makes me feel something. I get kinda warm and fuzzy, and that reminds me of her.

"Frank, did you hear your uncle?" my dad asked.

I broke my trance and looked down at my empty cup. It was only twelve and I had been drinking before the sun rose. Can you abuse an open bar? Probably. I probably crossed that line four drinks ago. What was I doing? Oh yeah, trying to feel something. Or maybe trying to kill what I was now feeling.

"Uh, not really? Sorry, my mind is just elsewhere," I answered.

"Oh, is it Glory?" my mama asked.

It was pretty much always Glory. If it wasn't Glory, it was shit necessary to survive. Food, water, clothes, shelter, Glory's smile.

"Is that his girlfriend?" Auntie Sheryl asked.

"Sh..."

I cut my mom off. I was a grown-ass man and I didn't want anyone else explaining Glory.

"Glory isn't my girlfriend. She's a lady that I've been in love with since I was sixteen years old. She's been mad at me this past decade though. So we're not talking right now and I've been falling apart because she was one of the best things I ever got to experience in my brief, terrifying, miserable existence."

Everyone was looking at me like I was off my shit, and I kinda was, so I decided to make a decision I probably should have made five years ago.

"Excuse me, I have somewhere else to be," I mumbled.

I caught the first flight home three hours later on an airline that was actually a health violation. But it was cheap, it was fast, and I needed to be back in Dallas. Glory lived in downtown Dallas, but I was heading to Fort Worth. It was Friday night and I already knew where she likely was.

"Ah, Mr. I revoke consent," Adam taunted. He waved a well-manicured hand to the ridiculously buff bodyguard Glory liked to flirt with, allowing me in.

"Come on, let's have a lil chit-chat," Adam called.

I sat down across from Adam and a new copy of the "pleasure chute" rules. There was a new line added right underneath how to consent, detailing a lifetime banishment for anyone who tried to falsely cry sexual assault after willingly using the second from the left stall.

"Adam…" I groaned. "It's more complicated than this," I said, motioning to the laminated rule sheet.

"Fab, I know. I know it's more complicated than twelve rules on a sheet of paper, but we are not kids anymore, and Glory has a job!" he shouted.

"I have a job too," I mumbled.

Adam brought his hands to his chest and rang them out with his laughter.

"Yes, Fab. We wouldn't want you to get disbarred from your job as an MLM's bookkeeper," he snickered. "Be fucking forreal, nigga. You can't press charges against Glory because you're upset that you're still in love with her! Take a number or grow a spine, Fab! It's 2019, she's not twelve anymore. She's been out in this world and she's thriving in it. She can handle the truth."

Adam was right, but I honestly didn't know if I could handle telling her. Cause she could hear me out and still decide I wasn't worth the headache. Then what? What was I supposed to do?

"Glory is not gonna piss on your heart, Fab," Adam sighed.

"You don't know that. I heard she eating these niggas alive out here," I shrugged.

"Stop listening to my daddy's nosey ass. That man is a gossip fodder. Shit, it's where I get it from," he chuckled. "But look man, this cannot keep going on. Y'all are hurting each other more by pretending there's nothing between y'all than just addressing it and taking what comes."

He said that like the pain was mutual. Like Glory was going days without sleeping because of somebody she was friends with years ago.

"Glory is not tripping off me," I chuckled hopelessly.

Adam reached over and patted my hand with a somber expression.

"Caris told me about the bathroom cause she called them crying, saying you didn't want her. So keep telling yourself that, Fab," he sighed.

Seven

Chapter Seven

Frankie

Glory didn't go out on Friday, or Saturday, and she was still avoiding church after an incident involving Halle's husband. Apparently she saw him kissing another woman then literally busted his balls.

God, I loved her strong-willed ass.

So here it was Monday, and I was at her office, unannounced, uninvited, and ready to take Adam's advice.

"Tilly," I said calmly.

Maybelline Tillman, or Tilly, went to school with us. She was two grades above Glory and two under me so she was the perfect buffer between us for a while. She had been there for everything, including Elias. So she knew what actually happened, and she knew that I was in love with Gloria. Plus she owed me a favor.

"No, no, no! Franklin, no! You cannot use your favor right now!" she exclaimed, waving me off.

I chuckled. I never came to Glory's office, so she must've known something was up. Tilly was as loyal as they came. She was always one hundred. Although I needed her to dial that back like ten right then.

"You ain't even hear me out," I laughed. "I know I'm asking for a lot, so I got something to sweeten the pot."

"You ain't got shit I want, Fab. Not that damn bad, she gone fire me, and…"

I held out my offering. A literal golden ticket that granted it's user access to an exclusive influencer event. A scene Tilly was tryna make it in. My uncle was big on YouTube and he was invited every year with the option to bring three guest, but it was never my kind of thing.

Tilly snatched it up like it was a map to the fountain of youth. I knew she would.

"Fine. Whatchu want, Fab?"

I held out my bag. It was truffle fries and burgers from a little spot near my side of town. I got my driver's license right when I turned sixteen, and Mr. King used to let me drive Glory to grab lunch there on Saturdays.

"Fab, she's seeing somebody," Tilly mumbled.

That should have made me keel over and throw up on that nice ass carpet, but it made me curious instead. Because Gloria King didn't date.

"Right now?" I asked, tilting my head to look in her office.

"No, not right this second! She's out getting lunch with another lawyer," she explained.

Another Lawyer? Oh, yeah. Homie was about to get flambeed. That didn't concern me though. What did concern me was an overdue conversation I was about to have and the apology that needed to come with it. It almost made me want to drink, but I needed to have a clear mind when I talked to her. What happened at Adam's was a shit show, and it was partially because I was too fucked up to manage my emotions. I could now though, and I was feeling determined.

"I don't give a fuck about whatever stiff ass suit she at lunch with. That's not my business. I wanna talk to her and tell her the truth, so are you gonna help me or do I need to take my ticket back?" I asked.

"Fine!" she hissed, unlocking the door. "Put in a good word for me with

Adam when she fires my dumb ass!"

I got comfortable at Glory's desk while I waited. Tilly suggested that I utilize the couch, but that seemed too impersonal for me. I liked getting on Glory's last nerve. That was kind of my brand when it came to her. I got to be annoying, goofy, and chaotic. I wanted to enjoy that part of me one last time in case this confession shit went south, because I know that's the part that stayed behind with her.

It didn't take long for me to notice something among the pictures on her desk though. It stood out like a sore thumb despite the abundance of family pictures, awards, vacation shots, and headshots. It was a picture of a lanky, pimple-faced, teenage boy hugging a wild-haired, baby-faced, brat who stuck her tongue out for the photo. My baby-faced brat.

"Frankie," she gasped.

I slowly lowered the photo to reveal my grown-up brat. She looked at mc the same way she looked at me the Friday before last. With surprise.

"What are you doing here?" she asked, shirking her blazer and purse.

Glory had been dressing since she was born. I remember her picking out her own outfits at three years old and then picking out Marcus's and Halle's to coordinate with her. That hadn't changed in the last 14 years. She was still killing it with a pair of tailored mocha-colored slacks, a printed silk blouse, and...

"What the fuck you do to your hair?" I asked.

Glory flicked the short, asymmetrical bob over her shoulder with a grimace.

"It's a wig, Frankie. Ain't nobody got time to be fighting with my hair every morning. What are you doing here?" she asked again.

I motioned to the spread I set up on her desk.

"I came to bring you and Bobert Bobton some lunch," I laughed.

Glory sucked her teeth when she looked at the fries. She probably didn't expect me to bust out the nostalgia.

"I'm not hungry," she tutted.

Her stomach growled loudly immediately after she declared that. I thought Tilly said she was out to lunch.

"So the nigga you using your lunch hour to fuck on couldn't even feed you?" I asked, munching on a fry.

Glory paused her motion, fingers touching her palms, lip twitching violently.

"I'm gone kill you, kill Tilly, bring her back to life, fire her, then kill her again," she muttered.

I could tell she was serious by the way her lip was twitching. It quivered when she was sad or mildly upset, but it twitched when she was pissed.

I stood from my claimed spot at her desk and guided her into her chair before pushing some fries toward her.

"You should really take advantage of the fries. You're not you when you're hungry," I laughed.

"Franklin!" she hissed, partially interrupted by her growling belly.

Her hands were shaking which told me she had probably been living off coffee, dick, and a dream all day. She needed to food, and I needed her to be ok.

"Look, you can yell at me in twenty minutes once the fries run out, but please, Glory. Eat, baby," I whispered, pushing her meal forward.

Her hard-headed ass listened. She ate her lunch, feet swinging as she did, rolling her shoulders with a modified happy dance she had been doing since she was two. I could've watched her all day to make up for all the variations of that dance I missed over the years, but she was fed up with my waiting game as soon as she dusted the seasoning off her fingers.

"Hey! I was eating that!" I exclaimed while she binned the fry cartons and burger wrappers.

"The seasoning, Frankie? Curtis doing you that bad?" she grimaced.

Honestly, he was. A nigga hadn't seen a raise since Obama was in office.

"Why are you here, Frankie? Or do you go by Fab now? Is this about your case? Cause I haven't seen the charges come through yet," she sneered. "Who comes and visits their alleged rapist? I thought I di..."

"GLORY, STOP!" I boomed.

She was hurt and probably confused, and I'm sure none of anything that was happening made sense to her. It barely made sense to me.

"I'm not pressing charges, an..."

"Oh, really?" she said sarcastically.

She wasn't gonna make it easy for me. She never did. I guess that's what I loved about her. She was the only difficult thing that ever worked out for me.

"Glory," I whined. "Please, just let me get through this."

I was shaking, sweating, and shit. Maybe because I was nervous. Probably because I ain't had a drink in twenty-four hours since I thought of this plan.

Shit.

That was the moment I realized I might've been an alcoholic.

That was something for another time, though. Right then I was apologizing.

"Gloria, I'm sorry. I'm sorry about Adam's, and I'm sorry about snitching, and I'm sorry for making you cry both times. I hate seeing you cry, it eats at my heart. I freaked out because we have not said two words to each other in over ten years, and then suddenly I was inside you. It fucked with my head because I wanted you, not just your pussy," I sobbed.

"I did not want to stick my dick in you..."

"Gee thanks, Frankie. I get it," she sneered.

"Hush dammit, and let me finish! I did not want to stick my dick in you under those circumstances. Glory, I..." I had to stop because the nerves were getting to me. I was feeling lightheaded because this was it. I was gonna do it, I was gonna... Pass out? The room spun violently before my shaking body crashed to the floor. Oh, fuck. Maybe the alcohol thing should've been addressed sooner.

"EVERYBODY BACK THE FUCK UP!' Glory shouted.

I woke up from the sound of her voice, in a white room with an itchy gown and way too many people. I was still dizzy though so I couldn't focus on anyone in particular. Except Glory. My sweet angel. Wait, was she wearing white?

"Shit, did I die?" I moaned, throat burning and voice prickly.

"No, fuck face!" Glory hissed. "You did not fucking die, you passed out in my office with the shakes."

She pointed to her father and mine, who were standing off in a corner, chatting.

"I thought you two liars said he was taking care of himself!?"

Shit, was she asking about me all these years?

"Gloria, that's not nice," Mrs. King scolded.

"Mama, I love you dearly, but you and I both know I don't give a damn about being nice to grown men," she retorted.

That much was true, Glory was good for checking the drawls off a nigga.

"So what? You've been drinking your life away, Frankie? Huh?"

Damn, I guess that included me.

"I don't think that question is appropriate all things considered, Gloria," Greg said.

"You don't think it's appropriate, considering what?" she asked. "Considering that your son could've died, or considering that he's so fucking depressed from fixing your shit that he turns to a bottle to cope?"

"Glory!" Mr. King chided.

"Ain't no, Glory nothing!" she raged. "Matter a fact, since everybody wanna sit up here and act stupid, act like my questions ain't got no merit, get out!"

Glory was bold, but she never spoke to Mr.King with such recklessness. She was either mad, scared, or both.

"You can't make us leave," Gregory tutted.

Glory snatched her head back, urging him to place a wager against her abilities to move mountains.

"Frankie, tell the nurse you want everyone except me to leave," she said softly.

"What?" my dad asked. "He's not gone do that."

Mr. King's expression dropped because he knew I was liable to do whatever she told me to. All those years apart hadn't changed a single thing. Except for the fact that I had fucked her. Yeah, she wanted me to make everybody leave and I was gone do that.

"I'd like everyone except Gloria to leave," I said, sounding like an entranced parrot.

My mama turned back to me in utter disbelief. She knew me better than most, and even she didn't understand the pull Gloria had on me.

"Franklin, you can't..."

"Please, leave y'all," I said again, adding bass.

Grumbles, head shakes, and grimaces were exchanged while four people filed out of an alarmingly small hospital room. Then it was just me and her.

"Frankie," she said, softening her normally authoritative tone. "Why are you d..."

"I love you, Gloria," I rushed.

My timing could've been better, but I did almost take myself out this morning, and Glory deserved the truth.

"Wha..."

"No, let me talk. I love you, and I have for a while. Since I was sixteen, maybe longer, but I know for sure that I fell in love with you at sixteen. But you were too young for me, and you had me wrapped around your finger, and your daddy knew you did. I w..."

"He did this to us?" she asked.

"No, Glory. Listen, he didn't want some boy growing you up before you were ready. I get it, trust me I do," I explained.

"You wouldn't have done anything to me, Frankie. You kn..."

"No, you're right, I wouldn't have, because I love you. But if you would've asked me, really asked me, I would've done it. I know that's so fucking wrong and weird cause you were a baby, but it's the truth. You would've wanted to eventually, and you would've asked, and I would've done it, because I'd do anything to make you happy."

Gloria sat still for a while, processing a confession I probably should've made a few years earlier in a different setting. Then she looked at me, took a deep breath, then slapped the shit out of me.

"YOU LEFT ME OVER A FUCKING HYPOTHETICAL?" she screamed.

I really ain't know how to reply. I was confused, and after that slap, turned on. But I guess she was right, the whole situation was technically hypothetical.

Still.

"You wouldn't even talk to me, Glory! What was I supposed to do?" I hollered.

Glory tried to smooth the creases out of her expression but they had decided to vacation there for a while. I was once again line dancing on her nerves. Some things truly never change. Not even with fourteen years.

"You were supposed to fight, Frankie! You fought me on everything else, all of the time! Why couldn't you fight me on the one thing that mattered? I waited for you, I waited for you for years, and you just… GAVE UP! AND THEN TRIED TO KILL YOURSELF!"

Don't say it. Don't say it. Don't say it.

"You're being dramatic. I ain't try to jump, I just drink a lil," I mumbled.

I knew I fucked up as soon as the words popped in my head, but I couldn't help myself. I needed some humor to cope with everything.

Glory's lip twitched upward into an unhinged smile before she started laughing. It wasn't her normal, carefree laugh. It was the maniacal laugh of her coffee-bogged alter-ego. Then one that usually chilled back until she was bleeding.

"I'm being dramatic?" she asked.

If there was ever a time to be quiet it was now, but that's not what I did.

"Yes, Glory," I sighed. "You ar…"

She started beating me with my own shitty hospital pillow. That shit hurt too, she had a swing rivaling Cool Papa Bell.

"Glory!" I shouted. "Glory, shit! I was just joking!"

I gripped around her waist to slow her rampage and my touch instantly soothed her. Just like it used to do when we were kids.

"I missed you so fucking much," she cried. "You stupid, irritating, asshole. You could've just fucking told me. You could've told me years ago," she cried.

The little troll at the club was right. We had been hurting for no reason other than pride. Glory had been missing me as much as I missed her. Based on the way she was holding me, she might have missed me even more.

Eight

Chapter Eight

G lory

I took the entire week off work. Mostly because Franklin had been admitted for alcoholism, and partly because I was emotionally spent. This idiot had been busy loving me for fourteen years. It was stupid, reckless, and selfish cause he honestly had no business loving me.

But he did.

Then the worst part? I know I loved him too. It had probably been going on for just as long and I'm not entirely sure my Daddy was wrong to put a stop to it. Sure, it sucked to have my heart ripped away and shipped off to California, but Lazarus King was right. I would've taken Franklin for all he was worth. I would've asked him to have sex with me way before I was emotionally ready, and although reluctantly, he would've done it. I was too young for him then, but there's too much shit between us now. Shit like his very necessary recovery, the sex we had that I still dream about, and my thing with Cash.

I like Cash. I like Cash a lot. He's sweet, funny, and down to earth. I can talk to him about all my work and art shit, and he's so fucking considerate. I gave him the cliff-note about the whole situation and he sent groceries to my house. Good groceries at that! Everything was organic, the bananas were green, and he even included my favorite wine. Wine that paired with pasta that I now had the ingredients for. Then, as if that wasn't enough, he came over Tuesday night, cooked me steak and potatoes, then let me ride his face. I wish every Tuesday was like that.

Then there was Frankie. An anxious, impulsive, asshole who did his very best to get under my skin at any given time. But he could also be sweet. So damn sweet. Like the time he sent me a stress relief candle during my junior undergrad finals week after my mama mentioned I was having a hard time. Or the time he bribed Halle to slip me a book he'd thought I'd like. Or when he beat Elias Oscar's ass for trying to have sex with me at twelve, while I was five years his junior. Tilly told me about that a week ago since I was sour after bumping into him at Adam's. All this time I believed he was upset about a boy when that couldn't have been further from the truth. He was protecting me just like he promised he would. He was protecting me even from myself.

So I liked Cash cause of our potential future, and I loved Frankie because of our history. I liked having sex with both of them, and they both liked having sex with me. Frankie admitted to that on Monday after I got done crying. Apparently, he was thinking about kids when he was in my shit, like the absolute menace he was.

"Gloria King! You cannot have two boyfriends! That's greedy!"

"Technically I could."

"No! Pick one! You aren't Solomon! You can't have a harem!"

Do two men qualify as a harem? I feel like you'd need to have at least three. Not that I was interested in adding a third man to the mix. Two had me drowning, and not in a good way. I'd been doing very little fucking and a whole lot of feeling. Something had to give and soon.

Speaking of giving. Life is definitely a gift, because I'm truly unsure how Frankie has managed to remain alive. What do I mean by that, you ask? He had gotten released from the hospital and set up with outpatient rehab, but he wasn't ready to deal with his parents after dipping from Mary's funeral and passing out, so he asked me to come get him. I really didn't mind anyway. I missed him terribly, especially after going cold turkey for fourteen years. But I was wholly unprepared for the experience that was his apartment.

"Frankie, what the absolute fuck?" I mumbled.

There were bottles **everywhere.** In fairness, they weren't just thrown around. Frankie's OCD meant they were organized. He had bottle pyramids, bottle sculptures, and bottle sand art. Bottles occupied the corners, the counters, and the bathroom. There were at least a hundred in the living room alone, and then his pantry?

Empty.

Wait, I take that back. He had half of a five pound bag of brown rice in there. So it wasn't *technically* empty.

"Yeah, seeing this with fresh eyes is kinda alarming," Frankie whispered.

"Kind of!? You've been single-highhandedly financing Haystack Whiskey for what, five years, and you think it's kinda alarming?" I shouted.

"First off, Miss ma'am, this is a ten year collection. I saved my first one and I just never really stopped. Second off, rude. I don't need you judging me. This isn't very support person of you."

He was right. I wasn't being very supportive, but this was way outside of what I was expecting. Especially the pity rice.

"I'm sorry, Frankie. It's just... scary. You passing out was scary, the hospital was scary, this is scary."

Franklin absentmindedly reached for my hand while scanning the perimeter of his living room.

"Yeah, you're right. It's scary for me too," he whispered.

I gave his hand a gentle squeeze before pulling him along to the bathroom.

"Take everything you don't want me to throw away," I commanded.

"What?" Frankie asked. "Why?"

Bottle Tropica aside, Franklin's apartment was hazardous. The door didn't lock all the way because of the rotting wood frame, the kitchen sink had red mold growing underneath it, and there was a concerning amount of roaches scurrying by for an apartment devoid of food. The whole building needed to be condemned, but they were taking advantage of people like Frankie. People with low coinage and no other options. So I was gonna have somebody look into this for everybody else, but he needed to leave.

"You're moving out," I answered plainly.

"Glory, no," he stammered. "I can't move back in with my parents. You think this was a slow death, I really will jump. Especially with the screaming."

Franklin had PTSD from loud sounds because his mama had a habit of screaming whenever she didn't get her way. I guess her son was just collateral damage to her and that's why I never liked Regina. I could never really figure out why, she was just... weird. Like toxic positivity, Jesus is my drug, weird. I for sure never liked Greg. He was a fucking idiot. An idiot with a big dick, but an idiot nonetheless.

Holy shit.

Franklin was hung like a horse. I'm not sure why this was the time that I remembered that, but it was, and it made me blush. Most people inherit their father's eyes or some shit, but Franklin inherited his dad's big ole dick. That's why it looked so familiar. Ew. That memory now made me wildly uncomfortable.

"You're not moving in with Regrory. I got an apartment downtown," I explained.

Franklin was quick to throw a disgusted glance in my direction.

"Glory, no. I'm not bumming off my girlfriend," he said firmly.

Was Franklin my boyfriend? I mean we kissed the other day and we did *other stuff* previously, but that didn't mean he was my boyfriend. Cash was my boyfriend. I couldn't have two boyfriends.

"Relax, it's a spare I rent out so my ho…"

I realized what I was about to say. I rented out an entire apartment so my hoes didn't know where I actually lived. That sounded like some nigga shit. Then the way I treated my last hookup? I was basically a dude with tits and some fire ass box at this point.

"So my homies can crash," I laughed.

Franklin didn't buy that shit for one second.

"No thanks," he replied.

"It's not optional, Frankie. You're leaving, tuh-day. You can take your clothes, work shit, and body products. Everything else will be replaced."

"Glory," Franklin gritted.

I guess he was trying be all big and bad. Too bad that didn't work on me. He was leaving, and that was final.

"Frankie, I'm tired of talking about this. You're leaving this roach infested shoe box. There's no food here, it's unreasonably damp, and I'm pretty sure you have raccoons in the wall!"

I kept hearing chittering and I thought I was tripping until I heard claws scratch against the drywall.

"Doug is cool," Frankie shrugged. "He likes hot dogs."

My God. It just kept getting worse. He was feeding it and it was eating better than him. Frankie was living off rice and cheap whiskey while a wall-dwelling trash bandit was eating hot dogs.

"Hmmmkay," I grumbled, trying not to implode. "Please pack yo clothes. Do you need boxes?"

Frankie opened his closet and gathered his laundry basket. There were exactly ten articles of clothing in there, and half of that was undies. That made me so incredibly sad because he needed so much more than what he had.

"Nah, this is it. I guess I'll buy another shirt and a pair of pants when I get paid since they cut me outta my shit."

Fuck. I forgot to tell him about his job.

"Actually, Fran…"

There was a knock at the door. Actually there was a knock and then the door creaked open. I guess the wood finally gave out.

"Aye, Fab. How you feeling?" Curtis called.

Curtis Myer-Smythe. Franklin's only uncle, and the very first con artist I ever met. He had a penchant for insensitive jokes, fucking up other people's money, married women, and screwing Frankie over.

I leaned around the bathroom wall and he jumped when he spotted me. "Shit, Glory, I uh…"

He paled like he'd seen a ghost, and the way I was feeling, I just might've been his worst nightmare.

"Curtis," I said plainly.

"I was just," he stammered. "I was just stopping by to see when Frank And Beans was coming back to work."

He glanced at Franklin with an expression mirroring fear-coated humor.

"Yo PTO almost out. Wouldn't want you to get written up," he laughed.

My head snatched back while my bottom lip spread to convey my surprise. There was bold, then there was Curtis.

Poor Frankie was gone answer him too.

"I'm kinda in the middle of recovering from almost dying," Frankie grumbled.

"I get that, Neph, and I know that's hard," he started.

He knew almost losing your life at thirty to be just hard? This nigga was insufferable, but I wanted to see how far Frankie was gone allow him to go.

"But business doesn't stop just because you do. You can't just drop the ball on your re…"

That was enough. I didn't want to hear anything else from him or his stupid ass brother. I reached in my purse and slammed the confirmation into his chest.

"Frankie has been employed by you for well over a year, and you have more than one hundred employees. That means he's entitled to twelve weeks of unpaid leave under FMLA which he will be taking. Your HR department received all completed paperwork from his doctor this morning. Here's the confirmation receipt and your signature."

The room got a whole lot smaller while Curtis looked between the two of us, then he tried for Franklin one last time.

"You taking the whole twelve weeks, Fab?" he asked.

"Yes, he's taking the whole twelve weeks," I answered.

He looked at me as if I were conspiring against the current government. Little men always did have big opinions on women they couldn't control.

"She speaking for you now, Fab?" Curtis sneered.

Frankie tucked his lip for safe keeping and nodded painfully before shooting me a look, begging me to be amicable about the rest of the conversation.

"Damn, I ain't know Gloria had you like that," he laughed.

Amicable was about to be placed on a shelf, high out of reach.

"What am I supposed to do about my book keeping?" he asked, directing the question at me.

"Hire a temp," I offered plainly. "Frankie shouldn't be the only one in the accounting department anyway. Especially not with how much you pay him."

"I'm hearing you, Glory, I am. Frank And Beans is just the best," he sighed.

"Yep. Frankie's good at a lot of things. But right now he's focused on healing. So if that's all you needed, we got somewhere else to be."

For all the things Curtis was, there was still one thing he wasn't. He wasn't stupid by any stretch of the word. So he stepped aside and let me drag Frankie out of this fucked up cycle he helped him create.

Chapter Nine

"Sit your basket down, Frankie. No one's gonna pop out the closet on you," I sighed.

We were in the spare. I'm glad I had it fully furnished to make it convincing, because the clothes were the only things salvageable. Even his toothbrush had to go. Twenty years ago I thought Franklin would do great things. He was eleven trying to make his way through Homer's Iliad because there was a quote he wanted to understand better. Then he got accepted into Stanford and I was sure he was gonna do great things. Things like teaching under-served youth, mentoring little boys who were just as jumpy as him, and eventually retiring and doing something he actually enjoyed. Like making stress relief candles that didn't make my nose itch, or opening a private library. Instead, he had been guilt tripped into basically working for free to get his parent's retirement back. Two grown ass adults who made their bed and truthfully should've slept in it, but they had always taken advantage of Frankie. I just wished I woulda been there to stop it that time.

"Glory," he called. "What's wrong?"

I sighed, causing Frankie to pad over and rest his chin on top of my head. He had been doing that for as long as I could remember, and it had been effective for as long as I could remember. Frankie had always been taller than me. I thought I might catch up for a little while when I started puberty, but he went and had a growth spurt at fifteen that shot him up to his final height of six foot two. I was quick to take advantage of his height. The lil lanky string bean did all my out of reach bidding, including getting down my good cereal that I hid from Marcus and Michael. My daddy was right. I had Frankie wrapped around my finger.

"Just thinking," I yawned. "It's been a long week."

"I'm sorry, baby. I ain't mean to blow your life up," he murmured.

"Stop apologizing," I chided. "You said sorry for what you were responsible for saying sorry for. I don't need an apology for every little inconvenience or road bump."

Franklin sucked his teeth before rolling his eyes, proving that very little had changed between us despite our hiatus.

"Don't you roll your eyes at me, you overgrown giraffe!" I shrieked.

"I'm not listening to you," Frankie called. "I'm bout to soak in this nice ass tub you got. Yo hoes get treated good!"

I snorted in disbelief of his audacity. A man who had six pairs of drawls to his name had an attitude with me, and I was letting it slide.

Love is so stupid.

"This a nice robe, Essie. This that nigga's?" Frankie asked.

We were sitting on the couch watching Halloween movies, and he was back to calling me Essie. A nickname only he had access to. Then I was back to letting him. If this was my karma for being a sexual degenerate, then it was well done. Cause this was torture.

"No, it's not," I answered plainly, urging him to drop it.

"This a nice apartment. How much is rent?" he asked.

Nope. Not happening. Even if I was expecting it, which I wasn't, this apartment was about two thirds of Franklin's thin salary.

"You don't have a job, Frankie."

"I'm on leave from my job," he corrected.

"No. I think you should quit," I whispered.

There were so many reasons why I wanted Frankie to quit working for Curtis. The pay, their relationship, the work conditions, and the truth. The actual truth of why he didn't want any one else working in accounting.

"How long have you been scrubbing his money?" I asked.

Franklin's eyes cut away from mine to stare at a sculpture. He'd probably always been doing it. That's probably the whole reason for his involvement. Curtis needed someone he could trust and or blackmail.

"It's bad enough I'm bumming off my girlfriend, Essie. I'm not finna be an unemployed bum too."

There that title was again. I was a lot of things to Frankie, but I could not be his girlfriend.

"I ain't your girlfriend, Frankie," I sighed. "We can't go together."

I expected him to accept defeat with a sigh, but that part of him seemed exclusive to his relationships with other people. I always got a fight.

"Yes we can go together. You not twelve no more," he shrugged.

Fair argument, but still a no.

"I can't be your girlfriend," I reiterated.

"Yes you can," he tutted.

"No I cannot,"

"But you wanna be," he said matter of factly.

Did I wanna be Franklin Myer-Smythe's girlfriend? Who's to say? Is a lunar cycle 28 days? Does precipitation mean rain? Do annuals die in the winter and come back in the spring?

Yes, the answer was yes. But I could not have two boyfriends. Even I knew that was greedy.

"That doesn't matter, Frankie. I'm seeing someone," I admitted.

"You seeing someone? You don't date, Essie," he said while brushing his thumb over my chin.

Yes, I generally didn't date. But Cash wasn't a general circumstance.

"I made an exception, Frankie," I groaned.

I was once again thrown off by my own expectations.

"Make another one then," he demanded.

I wasn't expecting Frankie to say that. I wasn't expecting him to say anything. I was expecting him to get jealous, shut down, and stew about it.

"What, Frankie? No, I'm not breaking up with him! I like him! I lo... like you too, but..."

He interrupted me with raised hands, "You ain't gotta break up with ole dude. Just make another exception."

I couldn't tell if he was serious or not and that bothered me. The fact that I was even entertaining his madness also bothered me. Plus I was horny, and Frankie was being Frankie. Which meant he was being unfairly handsome. Franklin hated the sensation of clippers so his hair had been growing since he was old enough to escape from the barber's chair. It was always kept in two long cornrows that fell at his hips. He was tall and lean with muscular arms and strong calves developed from years of evening walks and heaving around boxes. He had acne as a kid but now his skin was smoother than whipped meringue, and it reminded me of the red clay roads my daddy drove down when we visited Mississippi for Christmas. But his eyes were my favorite thing about him. They were down turned with irises the color of Bermuda Black Rum, and lined with a thick row of long fluffy lashes that met his equally fluffy brows when he blinked. Then his soup coolers drew me in with an anxious nibble. Showing off the two gold slugs on his bottom canines that accentuated his plump heart shaped lips and natural mauve and cocoa coloring.

"I can't have two boyfriends, Frankie," I said in a disappointed, hushed whisper.

I don't know who I was tryna convince more. Me or him. But he didn't care. Not really. Franklin searched my eyes for the approval he so desperately wanted, and when he found it staring back at him, he leaned in to kiss me. I couldn't help it. I kissed him back. I knew I shouldn't have, but I had been wanting to since I was nine and he was thirteen, and it felt so fucking good. It felt like cool rain, burning sunshine, and a crisp autumn breeze all wrapped up in one. It felt like every single season I had endured without him, and it felt like something I never wanted to be without again.

I think he knew that though.

He pulled away just enough to cup my chin and tilt my gaze to meet his. Franklin Jameson Myer-Smythe was pulling me into an orbit I didn't have the willpower to escape from. Then he said everything he had promised me with that kiss out loud.

"You can have whatever you want, Glory. I'll give you whatever you want," he whispered. "It's your world and I'm just living in it."

I wanted him. I think I always wanted him. The desire had formed before I could conceive what want was or how deep it could root. I'm sure that's why my daddy put space between us. Because want would've consumed me before I had a chance to grow into myself.

It was consuming me right now because I had a thousand urgent thoughts in my mind before he pressed his lips to mine, and now the only thing swirling around in my brain was a pair of lambent, brown, down turned eyes, a heart-shaped mouth, and the feel of his thick coily hair wrapping around my fingers while I kissed his Adam's apple.

"Tell me what you want, Essie," Franklin groaned.

"I want you, Frankie," I whispered, holding his jaw. "I've always wanted you."

Those were famous final words according to his smile.

"Breathe." I kept reminding myself air was necessary even when I was purposely getting choked. Especially since I was losing a lot with all that moaning I was doing.

"Frankie," I whimpered.

"No," he growled, twisting his wrist from my grip.

Franklin often described himself as a reluctant bisexual, with reluctance falling onto his attraction to women. I'm not sure why he feels that way since he refused to tell me, so I had done my best not to make assumptions about the reason. Still I have to admit it shaped my expectations of what he'd be like with a woman.

I thought he'd be gentle.

I thought he'd be a pushover.

I thought he'd let me have my way in bed like he let me have my way everywhere else.

I was wrong.

I was wrong, and unprepared, and now I was laying in his arms practically comatose because not only was Frankie dominant, but he was obsessed with watching me cum.

"Good job, Essie. Look at that pretty pussy jump," he chuckled.

A dressing mirror usually occupied the right corner of the bedroom, but he had pulled at the foot of the bed so I could watch myself fall apart.

Over and over.

And over again.

His thumb carefully rolled over the ridges of my anus, making me shiver from his feather light touch.

"You got such a pretty booty hole, Glory. It's all tight and shit. Ain't had it dug out in a while?" he asked.

Weirdly enough, no. I limited usage of my holes to my mouth, coochie, and sometimes belly button. Sometimes I used butt plugs, but that was kind of a solo mission.

"I don't do butt stuff. I never really trusted anybody to be gentle."

Caris told me about someone accidentally splitting their ass from being too rough and that killed it for me. I wasn't about to be whoopie cushioning out here.

"You trust me?" Frankie asked.

"Yes," I said without hesitation. "I trust you."

Frankie flashed me an enduring smile full of pretty sharp teeth.

"I know, Essie. It's gone stay that way too."

I thought that meant he was done exploring that avenue but I heard a bottle squirt before his thumb pressed downward, easing it's way inside of me. It wasn't too bad. It felt like the butt plugs I was used to.

"Is this ok?" Frankie asked, rubbing my clit to relax me.

"Yes, Frankie. I like it," I moaned.

He removed his thumb and added two fingers instead.

"What about this?" he inquired.

It was stretching me more than I was used to, but it still felt good. The pressure was traveling straight to my pussy, making me cum.

"Oh fuck," I cried, trying to brace the wave.

"Good girl, Essie. You're cumming so loud and strong," he cooed. "Let's do one more, okay?"

"Ok-ayyy…" I whimpered breathlessly.

Franklin flipped me onto my stomach before pressing one more finger inside of me, then he rolled a condom on and arched my back so my hips met his.

"Frankie," I gasped, settling into the sensation.

I don't think I'd ever get used to his unethically large dick stretching me out. It hurt in a good way but it was also overwhelming being filled in two out of three holes.

So I squirted.

It rushed down my belly and Franklin's before pooling on the dark sheets.

"Aw, Essie. You made a mess, love," Franklin moaned.

He leaned over for a vibrator before laying his wet stomach against my back.

"Keep doing that shit," he purred, pressing the toy against me.

Every time I let my body relax, I came again. I had been cumming for at least an hour, and my back was so well beaten that I had been resigned to prone by the collective vote of my core muscles.

Then Franklin flipped me onto my back to lick between my legs. Surprise,

surprise, he was a good eater. His wide, hot tongue felt good on my sore box. Especially when he licked in an all-encompassing circle. Eventually, his focus was exclusive to my clit, and he sucked me with an urgency that made my vision whiten.

"Frankie, why?" I cried.

He waited until I stopped cumming to flash me a devilish smile.

"I wanted to see you cum close up. Unless…"

He spread his long legs, forming a triangle with his feet and hips before thrusting back inside me.

"Unless you asking about this. In which case, I missed looking at your face," he hummed.

Who knew a man could be so sweet while fucking me balls deep on his tip toes?

He was always sweet though. Even when he was getting on my last nerve. Even when we were apart. I think our sex was penance for my distance though, because he was fucking me worse than the first time.

Maybe it's because he needed it more. Maybe I did too.

Franklin's diction synced with the cadence of his thrust, clipping his sentences as his lungs fought to suck in enough air.

"I. Missed. You. So. Much. Essie," he panted.

I was crying again. I think my eyes started watering from an orgasm and they couldn't stop.

I missed him too.

Unfortunately Frankie was gonna put me into a coma if I let him continue. So I tried to slow his rhythm, but my hands were thrown over my head and pinned there.

"No," he barked. "Take it. Take all of me."

"Frankie," I gasped.

"Take me, Essie," he whimpered. "Take me for everything. Take me as yours."

I should have refused, but Franklin asked me, so I did. Just like he knew I would.

Ten

Chapter Ten

"SHIT!"

It was dark out. I had fallen asleep in Franklin's arms and it was dark out. I scrambled through the covers looking for a phone, any phone, and I was lucky to find mine.

"Oh thank God, I'm not late yet," I sighed, scrambling out of bed.

"Essie," Frankie whined, clinging to my waist. "Just tell him you'll see him tomorrow or something."

He thought I was worried about another man. Jealousy was cute on him.

"Frankie, hush. I'm going to go meet Caris," I explained.

"Oh, aight. Can you bring me back a plate if they cooked?" he asked.

"What? Frankie, no! I'm not coming back here."

"Why not?" he asked, all pouty in the eyes.

His puppy eyes weren't about to trap me in this comfortable, warm-ass bed. So I stood, only to immediately fall flat on my ass.

"Shit, Glory!" Frankie shouted, rushing to scoop me up.

I had to let him because my legs were so sore that I could hardly stand. It was like I walked up three flights of steps after trying a Dora Milaje leg day. Franklin had fucked me so much that I literally couldn't walk straight.

"What did you do to me?" I simpered, struggling to catch my breath.

Franklin laughed like the shit was funny.

"We had sex, Essie. Isn't that what you wanted?" he said, leaning toward my lips.

There he was again, offering himself to the beast. Normally I'd jump at the chance, but I had thirty minutes to make it forty minutes away and I was still naked and wigless. Plus I wasn't in the mood.

What?

I wasn't in the mood, and I was pretty much always in the mood. I was usually in a new mood before I could even finish relieving a mood. The only thing that kept me from fucking all day was my love of making money to spend it. Now, I was just… spent.

Between Frankie and Cash, I was spent.

I wasn't sure if this was the best thing to ever happen or the worst.

"Oh, you're trouble," I admitted, leaving Frankie's lap.

"I need time away from you."

I found a box braid wig and a wrap dress while Frankie scowled at me.

"Wayment, Stella. I thought we was getting our groove back?" he asked.

Clever.

"Franklin. I love you, I really do, but I think Lazarus was right to keep us apart, because you turn my brain into goo. I had fifty things to do and the only thing I achieved today was an orgasm!"

"Several," he corrected.

Funny.

"Good night, Franklin," I scoffed.

"Hey, Glory?" he called.

"Yes, Frankie?"

"You love me?"

Shit. Damn. Fuck. Consarn it! I wasn't cut out for this emotion shit!

"I gotta go, Franklin," I huffed, slamming the door.

I ran to the garage, started my car, and let OnStar read my latest texts.

"*I love you too, Essie.*"

Did I say fuck already? Cause fuuuuuccckkk.

"So, let me get this straight, you fucked Cash on Tuesday?"

"Correct."

"You fucked Frankie… recently, from the smell of it."

I crossed my ankles before putting my hands over my lap, slightly ashamed that I didn't have time for a bird bath.

"Also yes," I sighed.

"Now you're unhorny?"

I mean, I would've used a different word, but I guess.

"Mmhm,"

"And you don't know who to pick?"

"Nope," I shrugged.

Caris clapped their hands together in brilliance over the world's simplest solution.

"Why not both?" they exclaimed.

I could give them forty reasons why having two men was a bad idea, but I was willing to settle for the top three.

"I cannot have two boyfriends. For one, Lazarus would have my neck. For two, they could get jealous and then make me choose anyway. Then three, two men is greedy! Then it's two good men! It's women unfortunate enough to share the same bum ass BD with three other chicks! I can't just take two!" I argued.

Caris broke it down real simple for me.

"Fuck yo daddy, you grown. You high-key need two boyfriends cause you've been a fucking menace this past year, and ain't they both bi? They might hit it off. Y'all could be a triad," they shrugged.

"Caris, I can't set my boyfriends up with each other! That's fucking crazy!" I shouted. "What do I say? *Hi, I think y'all would hit it off. You both like books, anime, and fucking the shit out of me.*"

"Oh, excuse me! Says the lady who has a monthly face sitter's club subscription!"

"Actually, I need to cancel that," I murmured.

"So you are keeping them both?" they asked.

"Caris, no!"

"Fine! We'll do a comparison chart since you're so fucking unfun!" they shouted.

"Who has better head?"

"They both have good head," I answered.

"I said better, Glory."

"Ugh, fine. Cash has better head."

"Ok, point for Cash… and, who's a better cook?"

Cash's steak and potatoes was good, but even still I knew he couldn't hold a candle to Frankie. Frankie used to read cookbooks for the hell of it and now he can make a mean ass Shepard's pie.

"Frankie," I nodded.

"You ain't never lied!" Caris clapped. "I'm still dreaming about them short ribs."

"Me too. That was the best meat I ever had," I sighed.

"Oh, speaking of meat, who has better dick?" Caris asked with raised brows.

This was truly unfair. They were so different, it was like apples and oranges.

"I don't know, Car. Can we skip and come back?"

"No, Glory. This is the last question, and you done skipped it thrice," they chided.

"Fine, ok! Um, Cash takes me on down to Stroke Springs. He's soft, slow, and submissive, and you know I love a good brat," I sighed.

"And Fab?" they asked.

"Frankie, is just… unexpected. He always puts his all into it. He fucked me like he ain't get enough hugs as a child. I can feel the angst. That nigga is the definition of pound town, but he's still… I don't know? Gentle?"

The word finally came to me and I snapped to change my answer.

"No, attentive! He made me watch myself cum in a mirror. And he be sticking and licking."

"And point for Fabbbb," Caris cheered.

"What are we looking like?" I asked, cracking one eye open.

"Let's see. Cash is a better cuddler, Fab makes you laugh more. Cash has deep pockets, Fab is hung like a buffalo…"

"Caris! Focus!" I hissed.

"It's a tie, babe. Both of them have 24 points. They both seem great for you on paper. They both adore you. What do you want me to say that hasn't been said?"

I didn't know what I wanted them to say. I didn't even know what I wanted. I wanted everything all the time. Boys, girls, fae, theys, and thems. I wanted to eat braised short ribs and redskin mashed potatoes while sipping an elaborate drink that contained no alcohol. I wanted to enshrined in an a candle too pretty to burn and memorialized in affectionate poetry detailing my midnight skin. I wanted to hold Cash and be held by Frankie. I wanted them both.

Both.

"I can't pick, I'm just gonna break up with them both," I cried.

"Whoa what the fuck? Are you crying? Gloria!" Caris exclaimed.

I didn't cry around people. I hardly ever cried in general. The last good cry I had was at my Grandpa's homegoing. Then all of this happened. This had been the most complicated, tumultuous, wonderful month of my young life, and I never wanted to feel this again.

Cash

Glory's been acting weird. She's always a lil distant, but lately she's been straight out avoiding me. I tried to ask Tilly if something was going on, but she just stared straight ahead as if she'd seen a ghost or something. I couldn't catch her in court. I couldn't catch her at home. She'd been avoiding my calls, and hardly responding to my texts. If I didn't know any better, I'd think she was trying to break up with me.

Fuck.

I just had to be an exception. Rules are in place to keep people safe. People that wouldn't survive without them. People like me.

"Glory, are we breaking up? Cause you haven't wanted to sit on my face in days, and I'm trying not to be a clingy weirdo but I thought things were going good and now you're just avoiding me."

She had me sending postcards and shit. I was trying my best not to write a letter too, but something just felt off. I didn't think that this was a case of unreciprocated feelings or bad chemistry cause it wasn't. She still checked in with Marisa to make sure I was ok. She still sent me cool places she saw that she thought were worth a visit. Her hands still twitched every time I got near her in court. Like she wanted to squeeze me. Like she needed help doing it. If she wasn't gonna reach out first, then I was gonna meet her where she was. On whatever corner of emotionally constipated and self-sabotage she was standing at.

Frankie

Glory's been playing that little distance game she likes to play. Why? I'm not sure. I tried to bribe Caris with food but they refused to get involved.

All they said was, *"I tried, Fab. I was rooting for y'all."*

Y'all.

I wondered what they meant by that. Was that y'all as in me and Glory, or y'all is in me and Glory's other nigga? Cause one of those y'alls meant shit was about to get dicey for a whole lot of folks. If Glory was breaking up with both of us, that meant she couldn't choose. Either she couldn't or didn't want to. Or she was doing something I liked to call emotional implosion. Sometimes she starts feeling too much good and she gets scared that she doesn't deserve it. I'm guessing Lazarus had something to do with that. He always believed that sexual liberty was the worst kind of sin, and he shamed her for it at every turn. Told her that her life was gonna be shit until she came back to God. Mrs. King was willing to let Glory be Glory, but her father was her first and biggest hater.

He didn't want her to go to law school because he wanted her to get married before everyone found out about who she was. I guess it was inconvenient for an abstinence pusher to have a daughter who was quite literally obsessed with sex. He didn't want her to wear her hair out because it was too unruly and unprofessional. I guess it reflected too much of her unruly personality, and the rest? The nigga was just antiblack. I used to look up to Mr. King like he was a prophet or something, but age and distance had me realizing that he was just as flawed as the rest of us. Then my grown-up heart didn't like that Glory suffered for his short comings.

Anyway, back to Glory and her little plot to dump both of us. I ain't know the other dude, but I knew he had to be feeling it to if she'd been doing him like she was doing me. So I guess I was gonna help him in an effort to help myself. There would be no imploding, self-sabotaging, or emotional avoidance this time around. Glory was gone have to face the music.

Chapter Eleven

Cash

The music was jumping. Adam and Steve's lived up to the hype. Shit, I wished I knew about it in my hoe phase because my head would've been on a swivel. I'm sure that's why Glory loved this place so much. Apparently, Mr.Gemison's son, Adam, was the owner. Adam grew up with Glory, so she always got discounted drinks, guaranteed entry, and whatever else she wanted.

At least I wasn't the only one under her spell.

"What? What do you mean you can't serve me? I just wanted a club soda!"

I overheard a conversation between a patron and the bartender. A slender man leaned over the counter pointing to the nozzle for club soda while the bartender shook her head vigorously.

"She'd have my fucking skin if she knew I was even talking to you. Take your bottled water and go. Your money is no good to any of us."

Damn, I wonder who he pissed off. Niggas do be on bullshit. Especially fine ones. Damn, he was hella fine. Damn! His hair was all the way down to his ass.

I think he caught me staring, and he blushed like he was embarrassed.

"Uh, hi," he waved.

"Hey," I said cooly.

"Can I get you anything, hun?" the bartender from earlier asked.

Oh yeah. This was a bar. People typically drank at bars.

"Just a Shirley Temple please. I actually don't drink," I explained.

"Oh, shit! Fab!" she called. "There you go, a sober friend," she sneered, motioning us together.

The last nigga named Fab that I knew was a cold-blooded killer. I represented him after he dug a muhfuckas larynx out with a spoon. He even looked like the current Fab. Or maybe the current Fab just looked familiar? This fine-ass man had too many red flags.

"How'd you get the name Fab?" I asked.

Tall Lloyd shrugged before flashing me a goofy smile. An adorable goofy smile.

"It's an abbreviation for my childhood nickname. Frankie And Beans."

I think that was the cutest shit I ever heard. Refusal to serve aside, he might not be so bad.

"How'd you get banned from the bar?" I asked.

I'm honestly not sure why I was so curious. It was just something about him. He had smooth reddish brown skin and a bright smile. Then his laugh? I thought Glory had a cute laugh, but his shit was beautiful. Melodic and hypnotic.

"Snare of my own creation. I'm a recovering alcoholic, and I have a very influential friend. So I guess she's making things easy for me. It's kinda hard to relapse if no one will look your way."

He tested that theory by leaning to the left slightly, locking eyes with another bartender. The bartender in question stopped flirting with their money maker and immediately fled to the other end of the counter. His friend was very influential indeed.

His eyes then widened in surprise.

"My bad. I got issues with oversharing," he grimaced.

"Nah, don't sweat it," I shrugged. "I get it. I stopped drinking five years ago. I wasn't quite in alcoholism yet, but I was still overdoing it."

"Here's your Shirley Temple, hun," the bartender cooed.

"Thanks, Suze," Fab called.

"Stop talking to me, Fab!" she retorted.

We locked eyes before breaking out into laughter. Whoever his friend was meant business. I've never seen so many people fall in line so easily.

Except with Glory.

I missed her.

"What brought you out tonight?" Fab asked, swirling his bottle of water to make temporary bubbles.

"I was hoping to bump into a friend, but I think it's too early. I'm not mad though, the music fire."

I knew it was too early. Glory was a night owl made functional by the miracle of coffee. I just wanted to catch her before she could catch me.

"Same, I know I'm early, but I hoped my friends would keep me company!" he said, raising his tone slightly.

Suze flipped him the bird then went back to cleaning glasses and pouring shots, making us both chuckle. She was serious about not talking to Fab.

"Although the current company isn't too bad," he said with a nervous smirk.

"Nah, not at all," I laughed back. "I'm Cash."

"So, wayment. You walked in on your roommate doing…"

"Paraphilic Infantilism, yes. Pretending to be a baby for… I really can't tell you. I be trying not to kink shame, but nuhuh."

"Aye, I get it. I broke up with this girl I was seeing because she told me to shit on her chest. I was like, *"Oh no, not the scat pack."*"

"Dookie!? Who the fuck gets turned on by dookie?" Fab asked.

I just shook my head. I remember thinking giving head and eating ass was nasty. Then I grew up.

"Ion know, man. Being grown is not what I expected. I thought I was gone stay up until two A.M, hunch, and eat garbage all the time. Now hot chips give me heartburn, and I can barely make it through an episode of Jojo's Bizzare Adventure," I sighed.

"Shit, I get it. I thought I'd be doing something way different than pulling my hair out over uncategorized business expenses and looking for good socks," he said.

"These new socks do be ass," I shrugged.

"Super ass," he laughed.

Talking to Fab was an unexpected highlight. I came to the club nervous as hell and ready to get my heartbroken, but I met a cool ass dude instead. Fab liked to read, he made candles, and he liked manga and anime. He was funny, he was smart, and he was exceptionally kind to everyone there even though they barely wanted to look at him. He even bought a woman a loaded fry to sober her up after noticing another nigga being creepy and trying to get her drunk. This fine ass man was actually a catch. Hopefully we'd run back into each after Glory was done smashing my heart into a thousand tiny pieces. Because before I knew it, we had been talking for two hours. It didn't even feel like two hours. It felt like I had known him my whole life. It felt oddly right. I guess that's just because we had so much in common.

"It's way different being in here sober," Fab mumbled.

There was a weird sense of loss hanging over that statement. Like he was grieving that part of him. I get it though. Sometimes you get comfortable in experiences that no longer serve you, and you don't realize it until you're on the outside looking in.

"Yeah?" I asked.

"Yeah," he sighed. "It's too much going on for me and I tried to hit on some of these ugly ass dudes. Beer goggles is real."

Oh shit. Was Fab gay? I was partially kidding about running back into him earlier. He seemed like an exclusive lady's man from our conversations. Maybe my gaydar had been busted from Glory sitting on my face so much.

"Wait, are you," I turned down my wrist to make the motion.

"Oh, yeah. Big time," he chuckled.

I guess that made sense. He was a frequent flier at a gay club, and he was friends with someone there who had enough power there to get him blacklisted from the bar.

"Are you…?" he asked cautiously.

"Oh, absolutely. I'm a greedy pansexual," I joked.

"See, I liked to describe myself as a reluctant bisexual. Reluctant with my attraction to women. I let them get away with murder cause I wanna give them the world," he laughed.

Me and Fab had way too much in common. Art, books, music, manga. If I wasn't actively in the middle of something with Glory I'd shoot my shot. Too bad. I'm greedy, but not that greedy. At least I don't think I am.

"I'm kinda in the same boat. Not with all women, but this one lady in particular… She got my stupid ass wide open."

"Same, my lady ghosting me right now though. I think it's getting a little too emotional for her since I told her I loved her," Fab sighed.

"Damn, it's that bad?" I asked.

"It's complicated," he shrugged. "We were friends before we were anything else. She has trouble with love and other aforementioned things because of how she was raised. She doesn't fit into the boxes her family wanted her to fit in so that made her feel like love was out of reach for her."

That sounded so familiar. Too familiar.

"That sounds like Glory," I sighed

"Glory?" Fab exclaimed.

"HEY, GLORY!" someone shouted.

Glory

"Caris!" I hissed, ducking down. "What the fuck!?"

I came to Adam's hoping to get out of my head and into someone else's pants only to run into the exact set of problems I've been trying to avoid.

"Glory! Stand up, bitch! This has gone on long enough!" Caris shouted.

"I still don't know what to do!" I hissed back.

At first I was dead set on axing them both and calling this an educational moment. What not to do when you're trying to avoid relationships 101. But then Frankie dropped dinner off after a bad case. It was roasted lamb and apple chutney, which was so damn good it almost broke the tie. Then Cash's determined ass popped up with a bouquet of peonies and vibrators! Points for creativity and consideration, because I had burned out the motor in my wand days earlier.

So yeah, I was back at square one. I was emotionally overwhelmed, unbelievably horny, still indecisive, and now I was about to get caught up because they were both looking in my general direction.

"Gloria Esther King, if you don't straighten your fucking back and go talk to them!" Caris chided.

That sounded so simple coming out of their mouth. Like I could just waltz right over and say,

"Hi, I've been fucking you both and also mistreating you both because I'm bad with handling pleasant emotions."

Yeah, no. I was super good on that.

"I'm scared!" I shouted.

Caris narrowed their eyes at me before shrugging dismissively in my direction.

"Well get unscared, because they're both headed this way."

I wished I could snap out of existence in that exact moment. Where is Thanos when you need him?

Frankie

The night was taking an unexpected turn. I had every intention of leaving Adam And Steve's with a Glory-induced migraine, instead I was sitting across from her, something.

"How you know Glory?" I asked.

"We work together, I'm her boyfriend," Cash explained.

"Wait, you're the suit? You're her another nigga?"

Cash's meticulous brow scrunched before he ejected his bottom lip.

"I'm the other nigga?" he asked.

I guess realization was seeping in on all sides cause Cash shuffled in his seat, startled by a memory.

"Wayment, wayment. Frankie And Beans. You're Frankie! You're the nigga in her paintings!"

I know there were more important things to focus on. Things such as Glory's avoidant behavior, the fact that I was flirting with her boyfriend, and the fact that she was definitely in this club somewhere. But I couldn't help myself.

"Wait, she paints me?" I asked.

Cash grimaced before hanging his head.

"Yes! She's fucking in love with you. It makes so much sense! What am I? A rebound?" he asked.

"Nah, can't be. Because I kinda asked her to break up with you and she told me to fuck off."

"What?" Cash asked, voice brightening.

"Yeah, apparently she really likes you. She said you're sweet and shit. I honestly don't give a damn as long as you treat her right, but she said can't have two boyfriends."

"I mean… she could," Cash shrugged. "I wouldn't mind sharing with you."

What was happening? Was I seriously ok with sharing Glory? I mean Cash was cool as shit. Successful, funny, cute. He had a fire ass smile and his eyes were top tier. They were hazel brown and they pinched high when he laughed. I understood why Glory had a hard time choosing if this was my competition.

"Wait…" I stammered.

The math was mathing. Glory couldn't pick between us. So she was avoiding us both hoping to make one of us pick for her. That or she was gonna dump both of us.

"What?" Cash asked nervously.

"She's tryna drop our asses. She must've gotten emotionally overwhelmed trying to pick," I explained.

"So we both about to get dumped?" he asked.

Glory was always the one in charge. No matter what or who. That was clear from how different me and Cash were. He was a junior partner at a prestigious law firm and I was an anxious accountant. She was in charge with him, she was in charge with me, and she was still in charge right now. But not anymore. I was done appeasing an emotionally stunted tyrant.

"Not if I can help it. Here's what we about to do."

Chapter Twelve

We walked over to Glory who was hiding behind Caris. Luckily they refused to open the office door.

"Car," I waved.

"Frankie," they nodded.

"How'd you like the ribs?" I asked.

"You sold me out for a plate!?" Glory hissed.

Ope, there it was. She had fucked up.

"How'd they sell you out? Was I not supposed to know you were here?" I asked.

Silence.

"Mmhm. Anyway, have you met Cash?" I asked.

Cash stepped forward, offering Glory his hand, but she just stared right through him.

"Sorry, let me introduce myself," he chuckled. "Hi, I'm Cassius Monroe. I work as a prosecuting lawyer for Spencer And Diehl, I'm 29 years old, and I'm Glory's boyfriend."

I snatched my head back dramatically, putting on a show since she thought we were clown ass niggas.

"Oh, what a coincidence!" I exclaimed. "I'm also Glory's boyfriend! Only she hasn't been talking to me recently. I think she's avoiding me," I pouted.

Cash snatched his head back in equally dramatic fashion before clutching his pearls.

"She hasn't been talking to me either! I thought I was tripping at first, but her other boyfriend got me up to speed!" he exclaimed.

We both turned to face her. She was already staring right back, trying to burn a hole through us with her tight gaze. Too bad it wasn't working for her this time.

"Gloria, we need to talk," we said simultaneously. "All three of us," I finished.

So now we were in Cash's nice ass uptown townhouse, sipping on lemonade that was unfairly good.

"What's in this one?" I asked, coating my mouth with another spicy, sweet sip.

"Candied jalapeno and mango lemonade," Cash answered proudly.

He had told me he got into experimenting with soft drinks after giving up drinking and that was the wrong word. He was perfecting these shits. This was the third lemonade I had, and it was bussing just like the cranberry and the guava one.

"I need like two gallons of this if it's cool with you," I sighed, sipping again.

"Deal," he said, poking my knee. "But only if you make me a stress relief candle."

"Excuse me!" Glory shrieked. "Are y'all just gonna keep pretending like I'm not sitting right here?

Cash looked at her with a pulled lip.

"You see this, Fab? Now she wanna talk to us," he chuckled.

"I think it's because we were flirting a lil bit," I admitted.

"You call that a little bit?" he asked.

"Yeah," I said, angling my thumb and pointer finger. "Poquito."

"ACCHMM," Glory scoffed, trying to reclaim our focus.

She was irritated that she couldn't divide and conquer. Must suck to finally be outdone after twenty-seven years.

"Yes, Essie sweetheart. You got something to add?" I asked.

"Don't call me that!" she hissed.

Oh she was mad mad. Mm. I wished I felt bad.

"So are you upset that we met, or are you mad that Fab told me about your lil plot to dump both of us?" Cash asked.

Gloria's top lip twitched violently while her hands wrang together.

"What do y'all want?" she asked.

Tact was wasted on her.

"Well, I for one, would like some clarification on whatever is happening between us," I answered.

"I'm dating you both," she said plainly.

"No, we got that from earlier," Cash intervened. "We wanna know why you weren't honest with me, and why you're avoiding us."

Glory's shoulders slumped in defeat. Her lip stopped twitching and instead started puckering. Then she started to cry.

"I want both of y'all, ok!? I fucking like y'all both. I don't do relationships. I don't want to need people, but then you two fucking idiots blew up my life at the exact same time, and I accidentally started needing you both in different ways," she sighed.

"I need you, Cash because I never had someone see me and meet me wherever I am and I need Frankie because he's the only other person who's ever made me feel like I might deserve love. But I can't choose, or I don't want to, so I figured the easiest thing would be dumping both of y'all!" she screamed.

With the confession out of the way, we both rushed to comfort our sobbing ball of frustration. Glory was a difficult headache incapable of being upfront about how she felt, but I think we both knew that, and so did she.

She clung to Cash while I rested my chin on the top of her head and we all cuddled in close. Her sniffling eventually slowed, she took a deep breath before squeezing both of our hands, then her lip puckered some more.

"I'm sorry. I still don't know what to do," she whimpered.

Me and Cash chuckled, likely because we were both on the same page.

"You don't have to choose, Glory," he said.

"Really?" she mumbled.

"Really," I nodded. "We can share."

"You wanna share?" she asked skeptically.

"I mean, all three of us can share if y'all with it. You got good taste, shawty," Cash laughed, eyeing me.

Oh, we really were on the same page. Cause I had been thinking that since we drummed up our little ambush.

"I'm down with that," I shrugged. "You thick and rich? Who am I to deny myself a good time?" I chuckled.

"What is happening!?" Glory shrieked.

"Everybody's gonna practice sharing, Essie," I clarified. "Sharing is caring."

Glory's lips parted slightly to reveal her little bright pink tongue. It darted out to lick her bottom lip while she stared between us, practically undressing us where we sat.

"Ok, this was a good prank," she sighed. "Where are the cameras?"

Cash turned to me with a charming smile.

"She doesn't believe us," he laughed.

"I guess not," I smiled.

"Maybe we should kiss on it. Don't you think?"

I nodded and leaned forward to meet Cash's soft lips before parting mine in an excited frenzy. Cash was a good kisser. Not too much tongue, just the right amount of pressure, slow and deliberate. I could kiss him all night and it pained me to pull away, but I noticed Glory squirming in her seat.

"What's wrong, Essie?" I asked. "Did that make your lil pussy hot?"

She was quietly looking between us, maybe shocked, maybe jealous, maybe hoping that we did it again.

"Maybe I should check," Cash suggested.

He pulled Glory's chair closer to us before slipping his hand underneath her dress and inside her panties.

"Can I check, baby girl?" he asked sweetly.

Glory didn't respond, but she did spread those long legs of hers, allowing Cash to slip inside her deliciously fat sex. He smiled contently before adding another finger and making a come hither motion to tease her. Then she moaned, making him withdraw his sticky digits.

"It's definitely hot," he said, sucking his pointer finger clean. "Want a taste, Fab?"

I nodded and took his coated middle finger in my mouth, sucking off the taste of Glory hungrily.

"That was good. I think I want some more," I sighed.

"Me too," Cash said, licking his lips. "Let's eat while it's hot."

Chapter Thirteen

⁂

G lory

Fuck.

I was living out my fantasy. Two fine ass men were servicing me at the same time. Licking me, caressing me, filling me. I was so excited I could scream.

Except I couldn't.

I moaned too much, causing Cash to withdraw his tongue and Frankie to exit my throat. They both watched me come down from the brink of an orgasm for the fourth time with big bright smiles. Did I say fantasy? I meant nightmare.

They wouldn't let me cum.

Yes, I had been a selfish, neglectful, mean brat, but that didn't mean I deserved to be edged. Especially not at a time like this.

Cash signaled Frankie and they resumed their torture. I opened my mouth for Frankie and spread my legs for Cash. Frankie rolled his thumbs over my rigid nipples while Cash licked my swollen clit. It was heaven. How could it be anything other than heaven?

"Mmmm," I groaned.

They stopped immediately.

I take it back, it was hell.

"Please, please, please. I'm sorry," I cried.

The boys ignored my cries and went back to what they were doing. Except this time Cash fucked my pussy while Frankie fucked my throat. Their strokes synced while they kissed above me, making me moan once again.

They pulled out of me at the same time, leaving me to switch places. I watched them conspire against me before Frankie dropped to his knees and sucked Cash's dick clean of my wetness. Cash pulled Frankie's hair and shot me a knowing smile before he came up, then Frankie licked my pussy while Cash fucked my face. I held out longer this time, about five minutes, but I couldn't make it any further when Frankie stretched me open. God, it felt so good to be used that way.

"Fuck, Frankie!" I cried.

They stopped again.

"I'm sorry! I'm sorry, I won't do it again!" I sobbed.

"We know," they answered simultaneously.

I thought that might grant me amnesty, but they switched positions again. This time Cash pressed against me in missionary, and Frankie stood behind him.

Wait.

Were they about to human centipede it? I wanted to ask but I got my answer when Cash stretched me open after Frankie stretched him open.

"Fuck," they groaned.

There was so much happening. Two different sets of hands were caressing my love handles. Balls were slapping against several asses while I got double pounded into the mattress. The boys were moaning and moving in perfect harmony, and I was about to pass out. Especially when Cash swelled against me from an impending orgasm. His mushroom head kissed my walls just right, and I couldn't make a sound even if I wanted to.

"Wait, stop," Cash warned Frankie. "I'm about to cum and she can feel it."

Fuck!

They say it's better to have sex with people who know you, but I beg to differ. Cause they were using their knowledge for evil.

"Maybe we should let her?" Cash teased. "She looks so frustrated," he said, slipping a finger in my mouth.

I sucked eagerly, hoping to override Cash and sneak my way into an orgasm. Unfortunately it wasn't that simple.

"No," Frankie barked. "I don't think she's learned her lesson yet."

The boys laughed at my dumb face before pulling out and rolling on new condoms. Then they stood before me, hard, hot, and ready.

"Pick," they demanded.

I'm pretty sure it was a test. Actually, I'm completely sure it was a test. They wanted to see if I really learned my lesson, and I had. So I cocked my head to the side, glancing between them. Cash with his stocky frame, sultry earthen skin, meticulous fade, and strong jaw. Then Frankie, tall and lean, with skin like ancient clay, and his fairytale hair tickling the top of his ass.

They were beautiful, and they were mine.

Both of them were.

"Both," I purred.

The boys exchanged sweet smiles before confirming my choice.

"Both?" they asked.

"Both," I nodded.

I answered correctly, so there I was with my head resting against Frankie's chest while Cash pressed against my back.

"Are you sure, Essie?" Frankie asked.

The easiest way to take them both was double penetration. That way they could both get a hole and my nethers could be completely filled. I had never done double penetration despite it being on my bucket list for years, and I was still new to anal, but I trusted them to be gentle. I trusted both of them.

"Yes, I'm sure. I trust y'all," I nodded.

Frankie carefully eased into my pussy while Cash lubed my ass. I was used to having objects inserted a few inches, but having Cash's entire middle finger probing me felt ridiculously foreign. So my entire body tensed instinctively before Frankie and Cash massaged my back and neck.

"Relax, Glory," they both purred.

I started to melt into their gentle caresses and my muscles eased automatically until I completely liquefied.

"We're gonna go slow," Cash cooed. "And you're new to this, so you'll have to work your way up to Frankie."

He rubbed his cheeks afterwards and Frankie grimaced. "Sorry," he whispered.

Cash shrugged it off before taking position behind me.

"It wasn't bad, Fab. It's just… nigga yo shit hanging. I thought I was working with something," he laughed.

"You got a good dick," Frankie countered. "It's the perfect size."

"That's exactly what I said," I offered.

The laughing continued until the boys passed each other a quick glance, then Cash stretched my virgin ass open. It hurt. Well, it burned at first, but the pain was non-existent after my body adjusted to being completely full. Then the fun started.

"We're all in agreement then, Glory," he moaned. "We're the perfect fit."

Cash was in a position to control our speed, so everything moved slowly, pulling me between torture and ecstasy as the boys overwhelmed me. I was sandwiched between heaven and hell. One gentle and one rough, working in tandem. Frankie's hand wrapped around my throat while Cash's hand threaded through my curls. Cash fucked my ass with gentle measured strokes while Frankie fucked my pussy deep and hard. Somehow they kept the same tempo which was a problem because I couldn't hold out any longer.

"Can I please cum?" I begged.

The boys laughed in my ears before Frankie found my clit.

"You been a brat, Essie. You hurt our feelings. Especially Cash," he purred.

His thumb stroked my pearl gently while they continued to pound their frustrations into me. I blinked too long and I saw another plane of existence. If I didn't cum soon I was going to pass out.

"I know, I'm sorry. I won't do it again," I panted.

"I don't know," Cash teased. "That didn't sound real convincing, Glory. You didn't even say what you were sorry for."

I whimpered. I whimpered like a punk bitch. I whimpered so loud that I could feel my throat rattle. I whimpered in frustration. I never had anyone deny me for so long at their own expense. I never had someone deny me at all. I had met my fucking matches.

"I'm sorry for ghosting y'all, being weird, and trying to break up with you both. I'm sorry for hurting your feelings, and I'm sorry that I wasn't honest. I was scared, ok!?" I shouted.

The boys surprised me by kissing all over my forehead and jaw, easing my emotional frustration. Then Frankie tightened his grip on my throat, and Cash tightened his on my ass.

"You good with that, Fab?" Cash asked.

"Yeah," Frankie nodded. "She sounded sincere."

"I'm right here," I hissed.

"We know," they replied.

Cash pulled me up slightly, aligning my nipple with Frankie's mouth so he could suck while stroking my clit. His tongue glided over my skin in slow circles that matched the rhythm of their eager strokes.

Bliss.

At least I think it was. I blacked out while they split me in two. Every one of my holes was preoccupied, they were so hard, and they fucked me so good. I had never been so full and wet. My pussy throbbed while my ass tightened around Cash, making me tighten around Frankie and cum on both of them.

Both of them.

"Boys," I cried.

Their strokes were getting more and more impatient and they were so stiff that I could feel them rubbing against each other through my walls. I was trying to hold some composure, but Frankie pulled Cash closer so they were both completely inside me.

It was so damn good, but finally too much, and it overwhelmed me in a way I never thought possible.

My heart skipped while my mind completely detached from reality. I saw auras, spirits, and prophecies before I squirted all over them both in a spectacular release. My entire pelvis tensed so hard that the boys had to fight to stay inside me, but I milked them in the process, earning myself a double fill, a sore pussy, and a hot ass.

"Good job, Glory," Cash cooed.

"You did so well for us, Essie," Frankie purred.

I smiled while their affirmations blanketed my brain, but then I blinked too long, passing out in between them.

Cash

My body woke me at eight on the dot like usual, ready to start our weekend routine. So I stretched onto my toes before rolling the blanket off my eyes, completely forgetting about last night.

"So it wasn't a dream?" My panicked brain asked.

Nope, it wasn't. That was clear from the woman pressed against my chest and the man who was also waking up behind her. I thought my hoe days were behind me, but here I was having threesomes with fine ass artists and shit.

"Cash," Fab yawned. "You good?"

I ain't even realize I was staring at him. I had never been shocked to wake up after the deed, but here I was, completely appalled by my own behavior. I'd do it again though.

"Uh, we fucked," I squeaked.

Frankie's lips parted slightly to let the laughter escape, revealing a set of gold plated canines I hadn't noticed in the frenzy of last night.

"Yeah, Cash. We fucked," he chuckled. "You regretting it?"

I stared at my hands considering the question before looking back into dark piercing eyes.

"Not really," I confessed.

"Good. You hungry?" Fab asked.

"Yeah, but what about Glory?"

We both looked down at a blanket wrapped Glory, who was completely dead to the world.

"We'll let her sleep while I raid your fridge. I think we wore her out."

I'd never thought I'd see the day when someone tuckered Glory out.

"I thought that was impossible," I laughed.

"Shit, me too," Frankie shrugged, getting out of bed. "Turns out the no-limits soldier has a ceiling."

"You mind if I cook this?" Fab asked, holding out a filet of smoked salmon. "I wanna make frittatas."

Frittatas? Threesomes? Fine ass Glory? Fine ass Fab? What was happening?

"Cash, you good?" he asked again, shaking me from my thoughts. I thought I initially replied, but it turns out I was just staring at him. I think I was still in shock about last night.

"Uh, yeah," I grumbled. "Sorry, I just, was last night real?"

Frankie grinned like a Cheshire cat before looking down at our feet.

"Is yo ass still sore?" he asked slyly.

Wowwww. I wanted to scoff, but fine cocky niggas are my kryptonite, and this one in particular was about to make what was now brunch.

"You think you funny?" I teased.

"Hilarious," he replied. "But, forreal. What's on your mind, Cash?" he asked softly.

He used the same tone he used for Glory on me. It was empathetic and kind without being condescending, and his concern was palpable. Then he was rubbing my sore shoulders, easing a confession out of me.

"I'm not gone lie, I had a ball last night, and it would be nice to do it again. But I'm worried it's gonna be a one time thing."

Glory could wake up, freak out, block us both, or her religious trauma could pop back up and vomit on everything. Or she could just decide she didn't want us. Nothing was really stopping her.

"It doesn't have to be a one time thing," Fab shrugged. "You worried about Essie, but here's the thing. Glory's pride is a mother fucker, but not unmanageable. She does well with honest conversations and planning. Her lil ass been sleeping ten hours and she never sleeps this long. I don't have the urge to drink, you seem relaxed. I think we could be good for each other. What do you think?" he asked tenderly.

I think I had just woken up from the best sleep of my life, happy and renewed. I think that I loved Glory's smile, and I loved Fab's laugh, and I think experiencing them both at the same time was sending me straight to heaven. I think I wanted us to get matching Christmas PJs and do a group Halloween costume. Hopefully I wasn't getting ahead of myself.

"I think you're right," I admitted. "Hopefully Glory feels the same way."

Frankie kissed his teeth and waved me off.

"Glory couldn't even pick between us. She don't run nothing."

We both exchanged eye contact before bussing into laughter.

"Oh shit, that was good," I chuckled.

"I know, it sounded so convincing," Fab snickered. "Whew, ok. Point being, Glory ain't the issue. We just all need to sit down and have an honest conversation."

Frankie eased my worry with a gentle temple peck. He was beautiful, smart, funny, and wise beyond his years. I'd be so lucky to share a sandwich with him. Hell, even a conversation with him. So yeah, I could share a boyfriend with my girlfriend.

I was busy picking potatoes out of Fab's pan after he told me to sit down somewhere when Glory finally rejoined the land of the living. She trudged in the kitchen wrapped in a throw with her wild curls blown in every direction and her lips still swollen from last night.

"What time is it?" she squeaked, voice dry from disuse.

"Twelve twenty," Fab answered while brushing honey over biscuits.

I handed her an ibuprofen with a cold Body armor and urged her to drink before guiding her over to the set table.

"Can I start making plates?" I asked Fab.

He nodded before throwing a bit of basil onto our frittatas. He hitched his elbow up to his neck to hit the salt bae, making Glory snicker.

"Yep, everything's ready," he called.

Damn, I wouldn't have picked either if I was Glory. I cut into the last third of my frittata with glee. I was eating the fluffiest eggs I could ever dream of. Then the sun dried tomato with the smoked salmon? Heaven. WITH THE CHEESE!? Lawd. Good dick and good cooking, he could've bought me for a nickel.

"How is everything?" Fab asked anxiously.

I smiled while chewing my last few bites. I needed seconds, thirds, and maybe even fourths.

"Really really good," I chuckled, pecking him. "Thanks for brunch."

Glory once again glanced between us. Her rapt eyes darted back and forth in somber analysis. Last night I thought it was jealousy, but I now realized she enjoyed watching us kiss. I wasn't sure if that's adorable or depraved, but I was fine with it either way.

"Am I high?" she asked, finally breaking her hour long silence.

"What?" Fab chuckled.

Glory sucked the food out of her teeth before leaning forward. Fab had lit a candle for ambiance that sat between us all as a centerpiece, and we both watched in horror as she tried to burn her hand with it.

"Gloria, what the fuck?" I screeched, snatching her lil ass up.

"THIS IS NOT REAL!" she hollered. "I want to wake up or be kicked out, or end whatever this is!"

She tried to swing free of my hold before Fab pushed back from the table with a gaze so sharp it could cut diamonds.

"ESSIE!" he boomed. "Stop swinging on Cash and sit yo lil ass down somewhere."

Glory's motion paused abruptly and she wilted in my arms before I dragged her over to the couch.

Fab sat on the side of her, sandwiching the panicked lady between us before letting out a deep groan.

"Essie, you are twenty-seven," he started.

Glory rolled her eyes dismissively while folding her arms over that imposing chest of hers.

"Duh, Frankie. I know how old I am. That's not news."

Man, I thought I was a brat. *Sometimes.*

"Essie," Fab snarled. "You gone sit still and stay quiet while I speak."

What's that they be saying? I'm sat? Yeah, I was. There was a whole lot of universal big dick energy floating around, and we knew what Frankie was capable of, so that shut both of us down.

"Gloria, you are grown. Grown people can make their own decisions. Grown people don't have to listen to other people's opinions about what makes them happy if it don't hurt nobody," he said.

"But..."

"But nothing," Fab chided. "Do we make you happy?"

I patiently waited for the answer with Fab while Glory's lip quivered. Our poor baby was stressed.

"Yes," she admitted.

"Does having to choose make you happy?" he asked.

She shook her head and the relief I felt was exponential. Thank God she still wanted us.

"Did both of us fucking that fat pussy and tight ass make you happy?"

Fab asked, biting his lip.

My heart started beating in my dick when I noticed Glory's hardening nipples and quickening breath. She was turned on by mere memory. I liked the way this was leaning.

"Yes," she whimpered.

Fab smiled at both of us before raising Glory's chin to meet his gaze.

"Yes what, Essie?" he teased.

Ok, I needed her to hurry up and answer, because I was seconds away from bussing it open with the way he was speaking. Glory could feel it too though. So she parted those pretty lips to tell the man what he wanted to hear.

"Yes, y'all fucking my pussy and ass together makes me happy," she answered.

"Good," he said, snatching away. "We gone set some rules then take a shower, and if you're good for us, sweetheart, we can make you happy all weekend long.

Father God in heaven, I was about to pass out. An entire weekend being fucked and sucked by two of the prettiest people I've ever seen in my life? Absolutely.

"Please be good," I whispered to Glory.

She inhaled sharply as my breath tickled her nape, making control harder for all three of us. Her voice was the equivalent of Viagra, all light, pretty, and high.

"Ok," she nodded quietly.

We sat in front of a giant calendar an hour later, rules set and plans made. Fab would see Glory for lunch Monday and Tuesday. I would have her evenings. Wednesday and Thursday were Fab's days, Friday was for me and him alone. Then Saturday and Sunday were group days or toss ups. It was flexible, but fair, and seeing everything on paper made managing expectations a lot easier. I thought I'd feel jealous or irritated trying to divide Glory's time, but I was excited. I could watch anime with Fab, see art exhibits with Glory, cuddle on the couch with both of them. It was truly amazing, and I'm not sure why I never tried it before.

"Mkay," Fab clapped. "That covers the next month and a half and holidays. The only thing we have to worry about is my birthday and our families, but we'll cross that bridge when we get to it," he shrugged.

"Wait, when's your birthday?" I asked.

Gloria erupted into ear splitting laughter, prompting us to both raise our brows.

"November fifteenth," he answered, watching Glory.

FUCK! That fine-ass nigga was a Scorpio. She knew it too. The way he was fucking us, I should've known. He was trouble all the way around. I started to groan, but Fab seemingly read my mind.

"We get a bad rap. It's all unfounded rumors," he sighed.

Nah. I ain't believe him. The nigga was fucking us, making breakfast, and being a fine-ass menacing dom.

"Yeah, ok. Says the nigga who asked me if my ass was sore."

"Is it?" Fab asked.

"Nah," I lied with a smile.

"What about you, Essie?" he chuckled.

Glory's breath hitched while I slid my hands down her silky robe, kneading her warm breast and flicking her rigid nipples. Fab moved his chair in front of her before spreading her legs onto mine and strumming her already slick pearl.

"What do you say, Glory?" I asked. "Are you too sore to play with us, baby girl?"

I made myself busy by kissing her neck while we waited on an answer. Fab was still circling her clit, I was still rubbing her titties. Then Glory panted while orgasm took her, making her shake and writhe against both of us.

"No, I'm not too sore," she whimpered.

Fab smiled before extending his wet fingers to me, and I happily tasted her clean pussy while she groaned.

"That's what I like to hear," Fab chuckled. "Come on, Cash. Let's reward our good girl."

Glory was feeling confident, so I watched with curiosity as she backed her tight ass down Fab's monstrous member. Her hole stretched around him, tightening every time he exhaled.

"Jesus, Cash. How'd you make it?" he moaned.

I could ask him the same thing while I eased in her pussy. Glory's shit was the equivalent of a hot spring. Wet, torrid, and inviting. So inviting I could die there. I didn't think anything could feel this good. Nor should it. Plus it didn't help that I could feel Fab's hard dick between her walls, throbbing and twitching with every stroke.

"Glory," I moaned. "You thought we could only do this once, baby?"

Glory couldn't respond since her orgasm was knocking the wind out of her, but she did whimper, making me and Fab bite our lips.

"Nah," I panted, allowing her surge to consume me. "You ours."

Fab drove those canines of his into his upper lip while Glory's cum trailed down both of our sacks.

"Damn right. Me and Cash gone take good care of you, Essie baby," he groaned.

Glory's muscles jerked while her scream ripped through the humid air between us. Her pussy and ass tightened and squeezed around us so hard that I almost passed out. Reminding me that there was a thin line between pleasure and pain.

"Keep taking care of me, then," she panted. "Take care of me, boys. I'll be good for y'all."

She ain't even have to ask because the look Fab shot me told me that was the only option. We were gone take real good care of our baby.

Chapter Fourteen

Glory

I never liked Sundays after age thirteen. Mostly because I used have to see Frankie for three hours every Sunday and resist the overwhelming urge to talk to him. Then eventually I had to go through the heartbreak of instinctively searching for his face when I knew he was away at school. But now as an adult, Sunday is just pre-Monday. Sure you get to sleep in late, but Monday's responsibilities are looming in the background. So it's no Saturday. Speaking of Saturdays, I spent this Saturday in a daze made up of out of body experiences and dream-like memories.

I remembered waking up in Cash's velvet-covered bed. It was sinfully soft like it contained the feathers of an entire flock of Canadian geese, but it also smelled just like him. Rich, earthy, and intoxicating. Teakwood, lavender, and something slightly spicy. Maybe cardamon? I'm not too sure, but it's a heavenly combo. So I remembered that. Then I vaguely remembered Frankie making me brunch, lunch, and two separate dinners. Can't recall what we had each time. All I can say for sure is that it was refreshing and hearty, and it kept my energy up in between our sessions. Which I was immensely grateful for because they had wore me the fuck out. So much so that I became angry knowing that I had settled for anything less than total satisfaction all these years.

Somewhere down the line people stopped trying when it came to me. I guess they figured any sex was good sex for a hypersexual. But honestly, it had been like that my entire life. I had to settle for any amount of effort whether it was genuine or not. My dad using my birthday to recruit new members to the church? At least it was acknowledged. I finally get a break from cooking, only to be served something I didn't eat? At least I had food on my plate. Some people were starving. Catering to someone else's pleasure during sex only for it to go unreciprocated? At least someone was interested in my black ass. It was a story as old as time. So this situation, being the center of attention with the boys, was a cold-water-shock to my system.

It was also a powerful and addictive feeling that I wanted to drown in. I hoped the boys would let me spend my entire weekend doing just that, but they clearly had other plans. I woke up alone in bed once again, but this time there was no set table greeting me in the company of half-naked moisturized black men. It was a regular-ass Sunday that was way too hot, and also too loud since Cash lived up the street from yet another church. Or so I thought. I begrudgingly started my morning routine only to find a brand new dress greeting me in the downstairs bathroom. It was a silk, not satin, midi-length wrap dress in a lovely shade of sage green. Which just so happened to be my favorite color. It was accompanied by chunky gold earrings, a coordinating head scarf, a bottle of Creed Spring Beauty, and a neatly wrapped bar of cold-pressed cherry blossom milk soap. Presumably courtesy of Frankie. There was also a note covered in two different distinctive handwritings.

"Good morning, beautiful. We went to grab a quick breakfast. Get dressed and put on comfortable shoes. We'll be back before ten."

Just like that, I was excited for Sundays again.

"Where are we going?" I asked for the third time.

I got two separate responses at once.

"Somewhere special," as well as, *"Hush, you'll find out soon."*

We left after a breakfast of croissants, fruit, and iberico ham that only Cash would be brazen enough to buy, but they wouldn't tell me where we were headed. I guess it was a surprise. So I crossed my arms playfully in defeat before my reflection caught my eye. I had a supercharged glow, almost like someone was beaming a ring light directly onto my skin. My hair, which was usually kept in wigs, was coily and free, with little ringlets cascading over the edges of my hair wrap. I looked and felt more like myself than I had in years. No small part thanks to the boys and their *concentrated* efforts.

I was given a sketch pad and some colored pencils to pass the time while I enjoyed my brief stint as a passenger princess. We were heading into the countryside, passing a plethora of breathtaking naturescapes including rushing streams and ethereal orchards, yet I chose to once again draw dicks. Some things truly never changed, but luckily my subjects had. Instead of drawing deacons with inflated egos and little pistols, I was drawing from memory. Cash's thick and heavy member, hooked, smooth, and picturesque. Frankie's monstrous third leg, veiny and long, with a bulbous head to match. Frankie in Cash, Cash in Frankie. Both of them in me. It didn't take long for the pages to devolve into total chaos and debauchery. I was certain that anyone who saw it would conclude it was porn, or perhaps Boy Love manga given my current art style. Anyone including the boys.

"Essie, is that my dick?" Frankie asked, catching a glimpse of my turning page.

I always wondered if men could recognize their own dick out of context, and I was tickled by the recent revelation that most could.

"And Cash's. Oh, wow. This is why niggas don't need art supplies," he sighed.

"You'd take this joy from me?" I pouted, knowing the answer.

"Not at all, my glittering little pervert," Frankie confirmed. "But you can't blame a man for being shocked at the way he's depicted on paper."

"Cash isn't shocked," I countered.

We stopped at a red light just as I said that, allowing Cassius's eyes to meet mine in the rearview.

"I'm sure I would be, Princessa. You never fail to amaze me."

And just like that, I was blushing, and perfectly content riding into the unknown with my book full of big black dicks.

We entered Canton, Texas about forty minutes later. City Lake greeted me from my immediate left, sparkling like a blue pool of natural glitter in the morning sun. Soon, I was too consumed by the natural beauty of the city to care where we were headed. Canton was only an hour away, but it felt like an entirely different state than Dallas. There were trees, lakes, horses, little local shops, and crisp fresh air. It felt like somewhere I wanted to be instead of somewhere I was dragged to, and I loved it.

We soon parked at Trade Days, a giant outdoor flea market lined with hundreds of booths offering everything from jewelry, to books, to livestock, to food, and I squealed with excitement. I loved flea markets and the boys had brought me to the flea market mecca. It was a good thing I chose to listen about the shoes, because I was in heaven, and not even bad footwear could stop me from walking around that entire post.

"Do we have room for this?" I asked, pointing to a hand-carved cherry wood media shelf.

Frankie passed Cash his share of my bagged goodies with a laugh and took out a tape measure from his back pocket. One that he knew to bring as soon as Cash mentioned the idea of Trade Days. I watched him meticulously notate the dimensions and cross-reference them with Cash's available cargo space, which he'd gotten before we entered the market.

"Yes, but you won't be able to take anything else big," he warned.

That was fine because I was $500 in and the boys were running out of arm space. The money thing didn't matter so much since they were bankrolling me, but still, greed is a sin and all that.

We stopped at one more booth before leaving. It caught my eye when we first walked in, but I wanted to save the best for last. It was a husband and wife team, one was a leather worker, and the other a tailor. Originally, it was a dress that had caught my eye, but two shelves in and I had found the buy to top all buys. A pair of my-favorite-green leather knee-high cowgirl boots. The color was gorgeous, of course, but it was all the detail work that caught my eye. A familiar constellation was etched then bejeweled into the thick material with gold and black beads, the bootstraps were encrusted with a thousand tiny black stones, then the inside had a butter-soft ebony lining to match.

They were perfect.

If they weren't $350. I rarely balked at a price, but there was no way I was spending nearly a thousand dollars in just four short hours. That was too much, even for me, with my two boyfriends and all.

But maybe, just maybe, they wouldn't fit. I wore a size ten, and there weren't a whole lot of custom boots for big-foot baddies. The possibility of them running too small was high. Or so I convinced myself. Believing that an ill fit would break the spell the boots had on me, I carefully plucked the left boot from the stand and tried it on, hoping to be met with resistance of any kind, only for it to fit like a fucking glove.

And it wasn't even broken in!

"Ah, you got your eye on Poison Ivy. She's a beauty," the owner said. "Customs, but the lady changed her mind about the color last minute. Said she didn't know about going to the rodeo in sage green boots."

A bad decision on her part, really, and also mine.

"Sage green is my favorite color," I sighed.

"Oh really?" the owner said excitedly. "Maybe it was meant to be. They look like they fit perfectly."

She was making this way harder than it had to be. Elsie, as she introduced herself, not only gave me the entire backstory of the boots, but also the shop and how she and her husband donated profits made in the summer to back-to-school fairs for kids in the fall. She was kind, personable, and way too charming. If only she treated me with the same disinterest as some of the other vendors. I'd be on my way out, holding a giant chicharron and probably putting those boots in the back of my mind.

Probably.

Yet, somehow, I still found the power to take them off and put them back where I found them.

"Is it the price?" Elsie asked. "I know they're a little more expensive than most, but that's just because of the beadwork. Still, we'd be willing to work with you. You belong in those boots," she affirmed.

I would negotiate the scales off of a snake given the chance, but I believed in paying for the handiwork of small business owners after witnessing Frankie pour hours of effort into candle and soap making.

"No, no. It's no…"

My explanation was interrupted by Frankie, who took the boots from my hand and gave them to Elsie's husband Hank at the register.

"No need for a discount, we'll take them at the full price," he said, waving off my indecisiveness and producing his card.

"Frankie, no! You cannot buy me a pair of $350 boots while you're on leave!" I hissed quietly.

Franklin's entire face balled up as if I called him and everything he stood for bitch made.

"I have savings, Essie. I'm not that irresponsible," he replied.

"Savings are for emergencies!" I countered.

"Savings are for lots of things, Essie. Emergencies, vacations, once-in-a-lifetime boots that make your little heart happy. What's the point of saving if I only spend money on bills and antidepressants?" he laughed.

I had no counter, and it was evident. I stood in the center of the booth with my mouth gaping like an out-of-water catfish while Hank proceeded to wrap my order.

"Looks like you bought her silence. Money well spent," Hank chuckled.

A smiling Elsie popped him on his shoulder.

"Hush!" she chided. "We want them to come back!"

Sympathetic Frankie was quick to come to his defense.

"Don't worry, Hank. It was a good joke. And we'll probably be back. She loves spending money."

Libel, slander, and half-truths! I loved spending *my* money, but this just made me feel bad and he knew it. So Frankie joined him in the popped shoulder club as we headed back to the car.

"Stop looking so sour, Princessa," Cash said while helping Frankie pack the wagon. "It's just money."

"Yeah, but it's Frankie's money, and he's poor," I countered.

Frankie sprang up like a dick in the 70's hard off Pamela Grier.

"First off, rude. Rude as a muhfucka. Second off, I'm not poor. I've been saving money since my very first check. I have $35k in savings, which is why I went ahead and paid that rent on the hoe apartment this month. Then third and final, you do not get to decide how I spend my money, little girl. If I say I got it, then I got it. It's not your job to decide whether or not I'm bluffing. I'm grown. Do you understand me, Gloria?"

The attitude evaporated from my body as my name left his lips, and I managed a nod.

"Yes or no, Essie," he replied tersely.

"Yes," I susurrated.

"And with that," Cash interrupted, checking his watch. "Let's grab lunch."

We stopped at a totilleria closer to the city limits since I was craving tacos, and my purchases were once again covered. The boys would go back and forth about who would pay for what, but I was strictly forbidden from producing any money of my own. I have to admit it was nice to be treated to an entire day, even if it was an unusual feeling. I kinda just got to exist.

I didn't have to worry about clothes, schedules, meals, or money. I could just float around, be pretty, point out stuff I wanted, and be fed a platter of lingua and al pastor tacos. You know how people say, *"Living the life?"*

Yeah.

This was that life, and I was living it. I'm sure my ancestors were somewhere jigging.

And so was I two bites into my tacos, right along with the boys. The food more than made up for the fat unfriendly chairs in the dining room. It was so good that Frankie's smile was no longer agitated once he got three tacos and a few stolen sips of my jamaica in him, and he spared me an apologetic glance.

"Sorry for snapping at you earlier, Essie," he cooed.

Frankie was a secret softie, and as cranky as he was, I know he didn't enjoy raising his voice at me. He'd rather annoy me to no end or hide my wigs. I knew that because recently he'd been doing both.

"It's okie. I know I work your nerves. Sometimes I do it on purpose," I admitted.

The boys spent all day telling me that I was actually an unmanaged brat, and the more I thought about it, the more sense it made. Getting on my dom's nerves for the hell of it? Check. Refusing to do tasks just to see what I could win? Check. Complaining about my inevitable punishment, only to enjoy it? Big ole check.

"You need a whooping," Cash added.

I smiled, showing off all my white teeth. Perhaps they were right. Maybe I was a brat, because being bent over a big man's knee and having my ass palmed sounded like the perfect way to end an already perfect day.

"Maybe you can give me one when we get home. Before we get comfy for the day," I purred.

"Whoa, whoa, whoa. Who said anything about getting comfy?" Frankie asked.

"I'm confused," I said, fixing my posture where I sat. "Do we have something else to do?"

"As a matter of fact," Cash smiled, while passing me an invitation. "We do."

I looked down at the gold embossed card stock invite. It was beautiful and well-made, and it kinda looked like a wedding invitation so I knew I would keep it just based on that. But the description on it really sealed the deal. I was warmly invited to dinner and entertainment at a location to be revealed at a later time. Their handwritings once again combined to provide instructions and set expectations ahead of time. Then an adorable P.S marked the bottom, a reminder not to stress because I deserved everything. Which definitely screamed Cash.

"So dinner?" I asked.

"Dinner," the boys confirmed excitedly.

The green dress was beautiful, but my dinner dress was divine. My body had been poured into a slinky burgundy glitter mini dress with a draped cowl hem. The dress was all Cash, but the coordinating onyx jewelry and satin heels were the works of Frankie. My hair was in a rounded afro adorned with new diamond pins that I got from Trade Days, I was doused in yet another new perfume from Cash, and my limbs had been rubbed with bronze body shimmer which was also courtesy of Frankie. The boys were black girl glam dream team. Cause thanks to both of them, I looked like sin and smelled like seduction.

We arrived at an intimate Italian restaurant that was strangely empty for a weekend. That'd be a red flag in another scenario. An unsuspecting woman, all dolled up and wearing shoes only useful for sex and sitting, lured to an untimely end at an abandoned restaurant sounded like a very plausible First 48 wet dream, and the nightmare of overly-concerned anti-internet dating grandmas nationwide. Fortunately, I trusted my guys and I knew the only screaming I'd be doing that night would be done face-down ass-up in the comfort of one of our homes.

We parked, and I waited patiently as the boys got out to tend to me. Everyone thinks the best thing about two guys is the sex. And while that is a very good thing, the best thing is having two thoughtful gentlemen who make your comfort their respective priorities. Case and point, Frankie opening my door and Cash helping me out. Frankie pushing in my chair at the table, and Cash pouring my wine. Frankie telling me how breathtaking I looked and Cash asking me if the ambiance was pleasing enough for me since I looked the way I did.

Priorities.

Speaking of priorities, I usually make it my business to scope out the crowd in any public setting. Only this time, there was no crowd. It was just the three of us and the very attentive staff who were distinguishable by their impeccably kept uniforms.

"Where is everyone?" I asked, while looking over the candlelit tables surrounding us.

Cash offered me either his heart or a lopsided grin as he explained how he had reserved the entire restaurant for us so we could have a peaceful official first date. Either way, I was more than happy to accept. Even if this was absolutely over the top.

"Cassius, are you rich?" I asked skeptically.

That lopsided smile returned and it was accompanied by a mischievous twinkle in his eyes. Frankie's smile also seemed suspicious.

"No, of course not. Why do you ask, Princessa?" he cooed.

I narrowed my gaze at him while he poured me yet another generous glass of $200 a bottle wine.

"Just curious," I mumbled.

"So, Essie dear. The specialty here is squid ink tortellini alongside Parmesan veal. Do either of those interest you or would you like to see a menu?" Frankie asked.

I swirled the sweet red wine in my glass with a slow and fluid roll of my wrist. It was full-bodied and a beautiful complex color that matched

Frankie's shirt and Cash's slacks. I noted how well everything the boys wore coordinated. Their pants, shoes, accessories and smiles. Everything was in sync, and I got the feeling that they'd be in sync all night.

"You two can pick," I purred seductively.

I think that was the moment I forgave most, if not all, my feminine suffering. Because I had never felt more powerful in that moment while making two intelligent grown ass men blush in warm candlelight.

"You're not being fair," Cash hissed.

I trailed my pointed toe down his leg before resting my folded hands in my lap. So I used a little voice on them. A voice I usually reserved for the bedroom. They were big boys, they could handle a soft tone. So no harm done, right?

"I'm innocent," I pleaded.

"Impossible," Frankie protested.

"Prove it," I challenged.

Frankie placed his hands on the table, ready to answer my call before Cash rudely brought him back to reality.

"She's fucking with us," he said while holding Frankie's hand to calm him. "It's what all pussycats do with their prey. But that's ok, because we're going to sit here and get through dinner without issue. Then handle it at home. Isn't that right, Princessa?"

A thousand defiant replies filled my mind. I could go with *maybe* or *never*. Or possibly even *make me*. But when I saw Cash run his thumb over Frankie's tight clenched knuckles I decided to take the scenic route.

"That depends on what you pick," I giggled.

That made them both sit up and adjust their volatile reactions, just like I planned, so I added,

"For dinner."

They ordered the veal and ravioli, but we all knew I was the only thing they actually had a taste for.

"Everything was so good," I yawned.

And it was. We had pink beet heart-shaped ravioli with spicy marinara, crunchy and tender garlic-marinated veal, as well as an addictively bright asparagus and mint salad. It was probably one of the best meals of my life, and that said a lot considering I had Frankie.

"It was delicious," Cash said. "But do you still have room for something sweet?"

I couldn't believe he had to ask. Everyone knows the dessert stomach is separate from the actual food stomach. There was always room for something sweet.

"Of course. What'd you have in mind?" I asked.

Cash's top lip curled excitedly as he gave a subtle nod to the waitress behind him. I'm guessing yet another surprise.

"When did you two find the time to plan all of this?" I asked in astonishment.

They had somehow crammed a week's worth of planning into twenty-four hours which was both impressive and scary. They could probably take over the world with enough motivation. Sometimes it was difficult to believe they had just met. It it wasn't for me, I'd say Cash and Frankie were perfect for each other.

"Yesterday when we went to get groceries. You didn't notice we were gone for like three hours?" Frankie replied.

"Oh, really?" I grimaced, trying to recall the fragmented memory of them leaving.

Sad to say my attempt at remembering was unsuccessful. Likely because my brain had been cooked.

"To be honest, I don't remember a whole lot about yesterday. Except the kitchen, and the living room, and the stairs, also…"

The pastry chef and his team interrupted before I could finish relaying my tale. I'd been had the pleasure of experiencing fine dining a few times in my life, but it had never been like this. The very personal service and exceptionally crafted meal were already next level, but then I noticed the staff were holding sparklers as the chef sat down a cake too gorgeous to eat. Luckily, I got a glimpse of what was written on it before I started bawling.

"Be our girlfriend?" it said.

"Seriously, y'all?" I gurgled.

I hoped they didn't plan on taking pictures because I was not a photogenic crier at all. The mask was off and they were about to find out I was an emotional, crybaby mess.

"Yes, seriously, Princessa," Cash started. "You don't date, and I thought you were joking at first, but Frankie was quick to inform me that it's absolutely true. You don't do relationships. So according to the history of Glory, we're your first actual boyfriends."

"And we figured we should ask you to be ours properly," Frankie asked.

I needed to see a dentist immediately, because my teeth were going to rot right out of my head from how sweet they were. And Lazarus said sinners and saints never intermingled.

"But you asked yesterday," I laughed.

"And we're asking *properly* today, Essie," Frankie chided, emphasizing the properly.

"So," Cash interjected by nudging Frankie. "Will you have us?"

Did I want to be Cassius Monroe's and Franklin Myer-Smythe's girlfriend? Was fire hot? Did mustard start from the same seed as broccoli? Did horses sleep standing up?

Yes. The answer was yes.

"I'll take whatever you want to give me," I laughed. "Especially if it's from behind."

The chef and some of his staff snorted behind us.

Oops.

I forgot we weren't completely alone, but I still meant it. We could even start right now since Cash's wagon had tints. Perfect for a sex addict with two boyfriends.

Fifteen

Chapter Fifteen

Frankie

I had a blast fucking my whole weekend away until I woke up on Monday with a painful realization. I was still temporarily unemployed. See, I've been working since I was fourteen. It started as a way to make sure I had money for extracurriculars during the summer, but I eventually started helping my mama with the bills since my daddy was fucking up money. Unfortunately it never stopped. I've always had a job, even in college when I was double majoring. It was just kind of baked into me at this point. Glory knows that though, and that's why she "forgot" to return my keys and left me in the hoe apartment with a stocked fridge, a new kindle, and candle making supplies. Her and Cash had been checking on me since they dipped out to go to work, but that didn't make the time pass any faster.

"I wanna leave," I pouted.

Glory sucked her teeth and then her nails resumed clattering against her keyboard, typing away. She clearly wasn't interested in telling me what I wanted to hear.

"Essie!" I fussed.

"Frankie, you can't leave. You can't go back to work, and you have no other business. So download a few books, eat a snack, and get comfortable. I'll be home for lunch," she sighed.

"I'm not a concubine," I seethed. "You think you just finna have me chained up, giving you dick, and waiting on you to come home like some sad-ass trophy wife."

I heard her huff before the line clicked. She hung up on me. I then got a text, telling me to go find some other business.

Fine.

I guess I could read Made To Love. I could also go for a walk. Or, or, or, I could bother Cash instead.

Having a boyfriend was a weird in a good way. I got excited about Cash, and that was new when it came to men. Maybe it's because I never really liked my boyfriends before, maybe it's because we had so much in common. Maybe it's because he understood what a headache Glory was. He usually had my back. Except for this time.

"Nah, I ain't helping," he said smoothly.

"What?" I tutted.

"I'm not helping you escape. Glory told me about the hospital. I'm super good on helping you rush the healing process. Make a candle or something," he suggested.

"Cash!" I shouted.

I expected to hear the line click once again, but Cash was employing a different tactic to keep me in line.

"I'm gonna tell Glory you're trying to coerce me," he laughed.

Not he was snitching! Who did he think he was, threatening me like that?

"Real niggas don't snitch!" I scoffed.

His butter smooth chuckle rang in my ear before he caught his breath.

"Real niggas don't try to escape. Bye, Fab. I'll see you Wednesday for lunch," he cooed.

"Whatever," I grumbled. "I hope she annihilates you in court today."

Cash snickered before blowing me a kiss.

"Mhm. Keep talking and the lemonade train stops."

Damn, he had my ass good.

They left me with no choice, so there I was pouring my fifth candle. I didn't like the way the first two smelled, and the third and fourth weren't shaped right. I hadn't made candles in years due to low funds and zero time, but I quickly remembered why I loved the craft. It was relaxing. Stress melted from my back while I tipped the beaker towards the silicone mold. It was relaxing even when I was formulating scent combinations or trying to free a stubborn candle from a mold. It was also fulfilling. I could design something hypothetical and make it come to life. I could turn Glory's favorite flower into a soothing scent. I could draw inspiration from Cash's velvety smooth voice and intoxicating teakwood cologne, and I could pour my anxiety about sobriety into something new and beautiful. I found satisfaction in that, and simple contentment was something I thought would be lost forever.

"Honey, I'm home!" Essie called in her best Nanny impersonation. I hate to admit she'd gotten much better at duplicating that woman's voice. I would have thrown something at her, but I was busy freeing my latest candle. A butterscotch oatmeal cookie one, shaped like a heart.

"Oh Frankie, these are so pretty," Glory cooed.

They weren't, but I guess girlfriends are supposed to make you feel better about your failures. Or maybe that's just a Glory thing.

"Eh, they aight. They kinda fucked up like how them first couple pancakes be," I replied, attempting to swipe them in the trash.

However Glory popped my outstretched hand before gathering the disfigured wax statues.

"Aht, aht! Take yo perfectionist ass on somewhere," she chided.

I sighed, dropping my shoulders in defeat before following her into the dining room. She brought back fancy ass sandwiches and a pitcher of lemonade, presumably from Cash.

"I got you a steak and pepper with a smoked tomato bisque," she explained, freeing the food. She plated it with such concern. Then her eyes searched mine for satisfaction, hoping that she picked well.

I wasn't too terribly picky after living off rice and old chicken thighs for years. Even still, Gloria knew my heart. It's exactly what I would've gotten for myself.

"Thank you, Essie," I replied, pecking her.

Her shoulders relaxed before she settled into the chair next to me. She started eating immediately, but I was too busy watching her to eat my own food. I could see the stress of her day digging into her under eye and it made me feel worse for relaxing on her dime like a bum. *Just like your daddy.* An intrusive voice called.

"Frankie," she snapped. "Stop it. Take your time to recover. I'm just fatigued because of PMS."

"I didn't even do anything!" I argued.

Glory narrowed her eyes at me, analyzing my expression before tutting.

"You sighed weird," she replied.

"I sighed weird?"

"Yeah," she shrugged.

"Huh?" I asked again, in disbelief that my sigh had so many layers.

"Yeah, it was all depressing and dejected. Like you failed or something," she whispered.

Honestly I felt like a failure. I was thirty one with nothing to my name outside my savings except a 2008 Honda Civic, 6 pairs of drawls, and a substance abuse diagnosis. Plus I didn't even have a job. I was not winning life.

"I feel unproductive," I admitted. I know it had barely been a month, but it was a month longer than I was used to. I had been waking up at seven for no reason at all. Just to shower, change clothes, and twiddle my thumbs.

How she expected me to do this for three months, I don't know. I was going stir crazy, plus I knew I needed to be able to help her with bills long term.

Glory's lips pulled into a gentle smile before she raised a spoonful of soup to my lips, urging me to sip. So I did, melting into the buttery bliss of the bisque.

"Do you remember when you got your first job and you took me to the art supply store with your free check?" she asked.

I remember it like it just happened yesterday. Mr. King let me and Glory skip church to hang out because she had been in a mood. She had filled her shitty notebooks to the brim, so we caught the bus downtown to get her some more supplies from Pete's Paints. We spent four hours there, and I happily scooped up everything she had touched and rang it out despite her protest. It was one hundred and thirty-three dollars, the most I had ever spent as a teenager, and yet I didn't wince. That's when I started to realize I was a goner.

"Yeah, but that's not the same, Essie," I chided.

"That's not my point, Frankie. Hush and let me finish," she fussed.

She brought more soup to my lips, once again raising her shoulders so I would sip.

"You did that for me because I was having a hard time with anxiety. You could have done much less and I would've been happy, or nothing at all. But you chose to take care of me then, so I'm choosing to take care of you now," she whispered, drying my fresh tears.

"Essie…" I started.

"No, sir. You are more than your ability to provide a check, Frankie. Resting is productive. Creating art is productive. Healing is productive, and you need to heal so you can be the best Frankie possible. The Frankie who watches shitty scary movies, pours candles, and tries to coerce me into using homemade lotion because of the fillers in store-bought shit. My Frankie."

Glory's Frankie.

I had to admit I missed him. I was honestly scared he died after I fucked up the first candle. I was honestly scared he died at sixteen. But he was starting to show back up now, while Glory fed me soup that was so good it made me scared to ask how much it cost. Glory's Frankie was peeking out from behind the wall, blushing at the force of a woman sitting in front of me. The one I adored and would do anything for. Even rest.

"Ok, Essie. I'll slow down," I murmured.

I took over feeding myself when Glory started on her spinach artichoke Panini, but I couldn't help but notice her staring at me.

"What's up, Essie?" I asked.

Glory's lip quivered slightly before she abandoned her lunch, and that's when I knew it would be a doozy.

"I think you should see a therapist. I found a counselor who's nearby," she stated.

Did I need therapy? Absolutely. I previously could not handle the public without liquor. That in itself is warranting. However, did I want my girlfriend who was effectively doing everything else for me picking out my therapist? No.

"Thank you for that, but I think I'll take some time and do my own research," I replied.

"But, Frankie I…"

"No, Glory," I gritted. It came out harsher than intended, but I had to make her drop it. See, Glory was a fixer. That was one of the few things she had in common with my mama. She fixed all the time for everybody. She fixed everything from her parents, to her siblings, to her friends and coworkers. But I was not going to let her fix me. It wasn't her job. Hell, the others also weren't her job, but I couldn't control everyone else. I could put my foot down here though.

"I will find a therapist when I'm ready. I will quit my job when I'm ready. I know I put you through a lot, and I know it wasn't fair. I know you're trying to help me work through this, but I'm uncomfortable with you managing my life. I am an adult capable of making my own decisions, Gloria."

It was a hard stop when I called her Gloria. Essie was Gloria to everyone else, but never me. Her lip twisted while she worked to swallow her brewing tears. Shit, I had hurt her feelings. I didn't mean to, but I had to stand firm in this. I couldn't let her fix me. Then I'd really be no better than Greg. My baby deserved better than a stainless steel version of Greg. I pulled her close to me with an exhausted sigh,

"Essie, my love. I'm sorry. I'm sorry for being harsh. But you can't do this for me, no matter how efficient you are, ok? This is a solo journey, and I will take it when I'm ready."

Glory buried her head in my chest to hide her hot tears. I guess some discretion was better than none, even though I could see evidence of her waterworks staining my canary yellow tee. But I made myself busy rubbing her back before a pitchy, strained voice conceded to my earlier request.

"Ok," she mumbled.

"I gotta go back to work, Frankie. I'll see you tomorrow," Glory yawned.

We were waking up from a short nap after accidentally incurring the itis. Plus I just needed to hold her. I massaged her shoulders which were tense from the weight of her breast. So I stroked her spine with soft circles as I dozed. Then her grating lunch alarm woke us up. An hour and a half flies by when you spend it with someone you love, and it hurts doubly as bad when it's over.

"Alright, Essie. Text me when you make it to Cash's," I pouted.

Glory covered me in soft, placating kisses before rubbing my nape.

"I will, Suge. Be good in your tower, Rapunzel," she laughed.

I rolled my eyes before kissing her back. There was always a joke. Her Frankie enjoyed corny jokes.

"Yeah, yeah. I'll figure out how to escape by this time tomorrow. Just you wait, Essie."

Glory

"How was your lunch?" Caris purred.

I clutched my chest to keep my heart from leaping on to my fucking desk. Caris was just as black as me and they were sitting in the dark on my office couch like a fucking creep.

"Caris! What the fuck are you doing?" I exclaimed. "I told you I do not consent to you practicing how you surprise Adam on me!"

"Girl, hush! I wanna hear the tea about your two boyfriends," they chirped. "But I didn't know you'd be out for lunch."

"How do you know I got two boyfriends?" I replied.

I hadn't had the chance to update anyone involved in my Friday abduction because of my, ahem, *long* weekend. So there's no way they should've known. Then in walked Tilly.

"Hey, boss. So…"

I interrupted her by kissing my teeth.

"Maybelline, why is this person in here asking me about having two boyfriends?"

Tilly furrowed her sparse brows, and tilted her pretty little head in confusion. Sending her bone-straight hair cascading over her narrow shoulders.

"Do you not have two boyfriends?" she replied.

"Tilly! That's not the point!" I fussed.

Then something else clicked.

"How do you even know I have two boyfriends?"

"Oh that's easy," Tilly shrugged. "Mister Monroe sent his usual weekly bouquet of flowers, but I overheard you talking to Frankie about coming home from lunch. Seeing as you were escorted out of Adam's by both of them Friday night, I figured you came to some sort of agreement. Besides, ain't they both bi?"

"Mhm. I told her to introduce them a month ago," Caris chimed in.

"Damn, bitch. You could have been living the dream a whole month ago?"

Tilly asked.

I pinched my bridge to keep my demons at bay, but it was too late. My head was already throbbing.

"I ain't want two boyfriends to begin with!" I scoffed.

"Why, cause of Lazarus?" Caris asked.

Yes.

"No, cause two men is greedy!" I replied.

"Three mens is greedy. Two is reasonable. No one looks at you wild if you order a double cheeseburger, but a triple is just egregious," Tilly countered.

"Men and cheeseburgers are not the same," I sighed.

"I disagree," Caris shrugged. "Both things contain meat that ends up in your mouth."

This is was Presley Law paid me and Tilly for. Dick and burger comparisons. If I was a partner overhearing this, I would fire me. National accreditation be damned.

"Ok. I have two boyfriends. Is that what y'all want to hear?" I asked, hoping to bring the topic of conversation to a close.

"Yes, girl. Duh," Caris scoffed. "How…"

"How are you gonna tell your parents if y'all get serious?" Tilly asked.

Shit.

I honestly hadn't thought about that. Mostly because I never dated before. I'd forgotten that was a normal part of courtship. Introducing your partner to your family when you saw it going somewhere. Or in my case, partners.

"Oof. Uhm. I'm not," I answered.

"Wait, why not?" Caris asked.

Caris and I met when we were eighteen so they missed some of the previous season's plotlines. One being my parent's preference for hetero-monogamy, and elective ignorance regarding everything else.

"Cause her daddy homophobic as hell and still tries to control her life," Tilly sighed.

Eh. I wouldn't exactly call Lazarus homophobic. He's more like a diet bigot. Michael finally came out of that glass closet he was living in five years ago, and he's made changes and gained understanding. However reluctant he originally was.

"Wayment, ain't yo daddy gay?" Caris asked.

"What? Lazarus is not gay!" I laughed.

Tilly gave me a skeptical sideye. One I knew all too well. She was finna start.

"Mmmm, IDK friend. You ever peep how he be watching the congregation flag football team in the summer? He be looking harder than I do."

"That's because he's their coach," I sighed.

"What about how close he is with Fab's daddy?" Caris added. "It's weird that two grown married men have sleepovers."

"They've been friends since the boys were babies. And Frankie's homophobic ass daddy is not gay," I explained.

"Them be the ones you gotta watch for high-key," Tilly said with a pointed finger.

Caris nodded fiercely in agreement. Much to my chagrin.

"Y'all, Lazarus is not gay. Just fucking weird."

I wasn't one to defend my father and his bullshit, but him being gay was far-fetched in any world of possibility. The man didn't even let us watch Batman because of, and I quote, *"homoerotic wetsuit themes."* Tilly raised her hands in defeat, but Caris wasn't convinced.

"Glory, I think you might be floating on the river denial, bitch. Papa G said that when you got in trouble for spying on the men's locker room, it was because Lazarus knew about the hole and you blew up his spot. I think he might be right. Ain't no way that man spent all that time in that study and ain't notice that fucking hole."

Of course Mister Gemison said that.

"Papa G is a gossip monger just like your nosey-ass husband. Lazarus is not gay y'all. I got my ass whooped because I was a pervert, and that's the end of it!"

My argument came out in a yell on accident, prompting grimaces and surrenders all around.

"Sorry, y'all," I sighed. "I just get kinda stressed about the whole two boyfriend thing the more I think about what it means for my future," I confessed.

My girls surrounded me with warm hugs and friendly giggles.

"I know this is a lot," Tilly sighed. "Plus I'll be out next week and I'm sticking you with a temp. So all is forgiven, babe."

I hated working with temps, but Tilly was my girl so I'd allow it. Besides, she had forgiven me for blowing up a second ago.

"Yep, all is forgiven," Caris nodded. "Just as soon as you tell as about that nasty ass sex you spent the whole weekend ignoring us for."

I erupted into a fit of laughter. If Caris was gonna do one thing, it was get their cup of tea.

Chapter Sixteen

I was finally off work, and thank God because leaving Frankie's put me in a mood. Not necessarily a bad one, but a mood nonetheless. I think I finally started realizing just how much damage Frankie had been dealt. That terrified me to be completely honest. He was incapable of being still and enjoying free time. His measure of manhood was dependent on whatever money he could generate, and he was obsessed with a standard of perfection that was unreal. He needed therapy like yesterday.

Do you know why he seemed those first few candles defective? One had a small chip on the bottom, and the other had a slight color variation. I couldn't even save the first two, so who knows what was happening there. Point being, Frankie was exceptionally hard on himself, which meant his healing would be messier than usual. That also scared me because I didn't know where that would leave us when he got out from the other side, especially if he didn't get help, and I selfishly worried that he wouldn't want me anymore.

It wasn't fair to think like that, and I know it wasn't. People grow and change and healing encourages growth, but part of me always worried that Frankie would outgrow us. Or worse, that I would start reminding him of his shitty childhood, and he'd be repulsed by our probably trauma-bonded relationship. Unfortunately I had already discovered just how dull my life was without him, and I wasn't really looking to rediscover that sensation any time soon. So yes, I was in a mood. Because I, Gloria Esther King, am I selfish asshole, who overthinks at every given opportunity.

"Glory, relax your brows," Cash cooed as soon as I stepped through the door.

I guess my mood was visual too. Cassius took off my heels before forcing my brow bone to ease.

"What's wrong, baby?" he asked gently.

Hm. I know my boyfriends know about each other and were also involved, but something about expressing my concerns about Frankie to Cash seemed wrong.

"Nothing," I lied.

Cassius carefully pecked my temple. It was a tender gesture that reminded me of that time a butterfly landed on my head. Graceful, delicate, and full of magic.

"You're worried about Fab, aren't you?" he asked.

Damn his perceptive ass! How was I supposed to maintain my air of indifference with Cash noticing every damn thing? He even noticed when my wigs were too tight. Always in women's business and shit.

"Can't you let me worry in peace?" I groaned.

"Nope," Cash exclaimed cheerfully.

I watched him plate our dinner and pour me a glass of white wine with a sadistic smile on his face. He was going to probe.

"Cassius," I sighed.

Cash sat beside me at the bar to feed me a bite of truffle mash and asparagus. It instantly soothed the hangry monster I was becoming despite my best effort to remain tense. Damn, Lena's had good food.

"Tell me about lunch, baby," he whispered.

Cassius listened patiently while I walked him through my minefield of a thought process, carefully nodding as I did so. I thought he might interrupt me with his own perspective, but he never did, even when I was finished.

"So, what do you think?" I asked, rolling my hand.

Cash finished his last few bites of food slowly before ultimately shrugging.

"It doesn't matter what I think," he replied.

What a diplomatic answer. I don't know what I expected, but it wasn't litigious Cash.

"Cassius!" I yelled, pushing his shoulder.

"Glory," he said smoothly, collecting the plates.

Was he really going to be difficult about this after forcing me to open up?

"I don't need lawyer Cash, I need boyfriend Cash!"

"I am being boyfriend Cash," he replied.

He was being careful boyfriend Cash, and I didn't need him either. I needed the Cash that ambushed me at the club last weekend. Cash who didn't give a fuck about hurting my feelings to correct me.

"I want to hear your opinion!" I tutted. "Not this considerate ass, *"You're entitled to your feelings, Glory,"* bullshit!"

Cassius met my gaze before leaning against the sink with folded arms. Then he watched me. His eyes tracked every huff, shuffle, and quiver my body produced for at least a minute before he shrugged.

"I think that you're overthinking, Glory."

"What!?" I shrieked.

Cash huffed before pinching the bridge of his wide nose, seemingly disciplining himself for falling for my bullshit.

Fair.

"Glory," he sighed. "I highly doubt a man who has been in love with you for fifteen years would just discard you because he healed on his own. I've been dealing with you for a little over a month and I'm already in too deep!"

he roared.

Did Cash have a point? Yes, of course he did. Did that stop my anxiety from doing doubles? No, unfortunately not.

"But wh…"

Cash threw the sponge in the sink with an irritated groan before grabbing my shoulders. Then he tilted my chin upward just slightly.

"Gloria, look at me," he demanded with a flickering gaze.

Ok, Papi Cash. Don't hurt yourself now. My instinct was to show my ass, but I could tell Cash didn't come to play so I followed directions.

This time.

He exhaled sharply after searching my eyes for an indeterminate amount of time. Indeterminate because it was so easy to get lost in Cassius Monroe's eyes, especially if you were a sucker like me.

"Frankie is not going to cut you off. He literally cannot. He has tried, and yes, he told me he tried. You're worse than cocaine. Now Fab has a lot of shit to sift through, but it's not impossible. Franklin is more than capable of recovering without you hovering. Give him time and room, Gloria. It's not your job to fix him, and it's good that Fab doesn't want you to."

There it was. The quiet part I didn't want to say out loud. I wanted to fix Frankie. I wanted to use all my love to glue him back together good as new. I wanted to protect him and make up for everything I missed. But he didn't want that. He wanted to set his own pace. That made me feel like I wasn't a part of his healing process. I know that isn't true, but him refusing my help felt like rejection, and I couldn't deal with him rejecting me again.

"Some days will feel like he's sliding backwards, but you have to let him work through it in his own way. That includes trusting him with a key and freewill, baby girl. I know the hospital was scary, but Fab is incredibly smart. He'll figure it out," Cash explained.

Cassius was right. I know he was. Unfortunately I couldn't help how I felt. I guess that's why Cash leaned towards validating me first before I went and blew it up.

"Alright," I sighed. "I'll ease up."

I meant it. If Frankie was going to get therapy, it needed to be on his terms. Not mine or anyone else's. I loved him so I accepted it, no matter how much it hurt to watch him struggle for now.

"Good. You know what this calls for?" Cash asked excitedly.

"Dick?" I questioned.

"**Dessert**, Glory. Jesus," he scoffed.

Dessert sounded good, but dick sounded better. I hadn't had sex with either of the boys in twenty-four hours, and I was fighting a losing battle after being pressed against Frankie's generous erection for the better part of an hour.

Cash handed me a good spoon and a fancy pint of my favorite key lime pie gelato with a snide smile.

"Come on, we're eating upstairs," he said, pulling me along.

"Oh, are we sharing?" I asked, eyeing the lil ass serving.

"Nah, my dessert is warming up now," he chuckled.

"Oh," I moaned.

"Eat," Cash boomed.

I guess he decided his dessert was warm enough. So there I was, spread over his shoulders with my gelato in hand. The tip of his tongue expertly traced my clit while I sucked the gold off the spoon. God, Cash could eat pussy like nobody's business. I tried to scoop up another bite but I accidentally dropped the spoon when Cash tugged at my piercing. How he expected me to divide my focus was a mystery for another time.

"Cassius," I moaned, feeling the push of a cresting wave.

I abandoned the ice cream on the nightstand and laid against the headboard, eager to avoid crashing to the floor instead. Every carefully calculated swirl, eager lick, and gentle suck compiled into mind numbing pleasure that soothed my anxious day.

"Fuck, Cassius," I whimpered, falling closer to ecstasy. "Please, baby."

Cash laughed while he continued to eat me like a peach parfait. His full lips and butter-smooth chuckle only aided in my torture, and my hips bucked uncontrollably while I rode his face through my release.

"Shit, shit, shit. Cash!" I screamed.

I came three times in the span of a minute, forcing my belly to contract so much that I squirted right onto his grinning smug face.

"Thanks for dessert, Glory, baby," he purred.

He rolled from under me, leaving me a wet shaking mess. Then he pushed me forward, letting my head rest in the pillows while my ass remained in the air.

Two of his digits stretched my pussy open with diligence, with his pointer finger hooking to press that spot behind my clit. I'm sure he learned that from Frankie, but I definitely wasn't mad. It was a tried and true method of making me whimper. Case and point, now. Where I was melting into the bed with my knees wobbling like those of a drunk choir member. All because of that little spot Fab saw me touching one morning.

"Why?" I cried, seeking amnesty from the overwhelming pleasure.

"Because," Cash whispered. "You're less of a headache when you're taken care of. So we're gonna get it all out so we can have peace until you see Fab tomorrow."

Shit, had they been coordinating to keep me from being an irritating brat? This had Frankie written all over it. His meticulous ass would plan an entire town if we let him.

"Casshhh," I hissed.

He was still stretching me with his fingers, but now his thumb had found my clit and my heart was racing to the finish line with my pussy. My eyes started watering and my pussy clenched around the three fingers coaxing such a reaction.

"Cassius," I panted with my voice higher than God's nut sack.

No response.

Baby boy didn't ease up, so I tried to suck in enough air to keep from tumbling into unconsciousness. It felt so good, too good. I'm not sure how the boys expected me to clown less with this type of treatment on the regular, cause this was how crazos were made.

Especially when Cash slammed into me, giving me all he had to offer. "Fuck," I cussed. I hitched my right leg just slightly so I could deepen my arch which aided in my destruction. Cash pressed a new wand to my now exposed clit while his hips carried a wicked rhythm. He stroked me so deep that his balls tickled my slit with every measured thrust. I think he was serious about fucking the brat out of me.

"Cassius, please baby," I cried.

My legs shook while violent pleasure consumed all my senses. I came so hard that I saw the shadow from the veins in my eyelids. All while Cash enjoyed a laugh at my expense.

"That's right, Glory, Princessa. Get it all out, baby," he purred.

It was already out, and it was leaking on a set of luxury 3,000 thread count sheets. It was trailing Cash's heavy sack, and literally dripping from my pussy.

"Cash," I whined.

Another orgasm rushed me when Cassius gripped the space between my hips and fupa. His hand was so soft, so strong, so overwhelming. His fingertips dug into my pliant flesh, making me melt into him. THWACK. THWACK. THWACK. I tried to zone out to the symphony of our sex, but it wasn't much better. His mattress didn't have springs, but he was still making the bed creak, and my pussy sounded like somebody was stirring a pot of brown sugar oatmeal. I looked back to watch him pound into me for a second, and that also proved to be a mistake. That telling tingle started to spread from my clit downward while every expertly carved groove and ridge of Cassius Monroe filled me.

"Cassius, baby. Pl-please," I stammered.

The hand that I tried to slow him with was quickly pinned to the middle of my back, and I was forced to submit to his weight.

"Nah, gone head and take it. Ain't no point in holding back, baby. I'mma get what I want one way or another. Me gusta verte derretir."

Oh shit, was Cash a switch? What happened to the sweet man who let me choke him in his office? Cause there was no way him and disrespectful, push my head in the pillows, Cash were the same person. The realization that I bit off more than I could chew hit me at the same time as my orgasm. My shoulders relaxed completely, nearly allowing my titties to smother me. Then my core trembled while the tangible proof dribbled down my thighs.

"There you go, Glory. That's such a good job, mi Princessa," Cash cooed. "Tu sientes bien? You feel better?"

Honestly, I did. The anxiety that had taken up residence in my belly had disappeared, and I was worn out like I took a good run. But I was too sensitive to let Cash continue wrecking my shit.

"Yes, Cash. Please cum," I whimpered.

Cash laughed before flipping me over and bringing his warm mouth to my nipples.

"That's all you had to say, baby," he purred, flicking his tongue over my areola.

I dissolved into the mattress while I savored his release. Everything about that tender moment was magical. Especially his moan, his eager strokes, his sated smile, and the twinkle in his captivating brown eyes. Letting Cassius be one of my exceptions was the best decision I ever made. Even if that meant him plotting to knock the attitude out of me.

"Gloria," my father's voice called. "Are you ok?"

I snapped out of my daze and looked around the table. I was at our monthly catch-up lunch, courtesy of Kimberly King, completely out of my person. All three of my siblings were staring at me like I'd grown a second head, but my mother just gave me a sly smile.

"I'm sorry, did I miss something?" I asked.

"Just Michael saying he was moving in with you. He asked if that was cool and you just nodded *"mhm"* and continued to float off in space.

Shit! My attitude was my first line of defense. My newfound lack of an attitude was about to land me with an unwanted house pest. Damn the boys and that fantastic, wonderful, dastardly dick schedule.

"Hard pass," I cringed. "I don't like roommates. Especially not broke ones."

Halle seemed suddenly interested in the conversation, clearing her throat before throwing me a shit-eating grin plus a curve ball.

"What about the person you're seeing? Are you not living together?" she asked.

It took everything in me not to immediately respond with, *what the fuck?* Not to say I didn't love my sister, but we were not close by any stretch of the definition. She judged me for living how I wanted, and I though she was goody-two shoes, holier-than-thou, wet carpet. So I was at a complete lost trying to figure out how she knew I was even seeing someone.

"Um…. I don't really," I started.

"Oh, I was just asking because Chris and I were in your neighborhood and we saw you walking in the house with a real tall man," she explained, spearing a bite of salad.

She was talking about Frankie. Ok, this was salvageable. Everyone knew Frankie and he was mostly harmless. I mean, my daddy clocked that he was in love with me over fifteen years ago when we were children, but he was still harmless. Mostly.

"Oh yeah, Frankie. He's just crashing in my spare for a few days," I said.

I started drafting up possible responses from my parents and siblings and believable responses I could provide them. Everyone knew Frankie was my soft spot. So me letting him stay at my place for a bit during his recovery was basically a no-brainer.

"Remind me again why you have an entire spare apartment," Michael chimed.

He cast me an impish smile laced with knowing and malice. Knowing because he also frequented Adam's and I tended to have a bit of a love em and leave em reputation amongst other regular patrons. This nigga

Michael was bound and determined to heel-toe on my last nerve.

"Because I do," I said curtly.

More like hissed, but still. I couldn't have my spot blowing up any more than it currently was.

"Well, I think it's nice you found your way back to each other after all these years," Mama interjected, smile also laced with knowing.

"It's not like that," I argued, piercing a potato.

"It sure feels like it might be like that the way you spoke to us at that hospital a few weeks back," My father replied.

Ah, yes. When I put them all out for attempting to make light about Frankie almost dying. It was indeed due to the fact that it was like that. Still, this was the fifth time he brought that up since I walked onto the porch. Not gone lie, on the off chance that Tilly and Caris weren't wrong about his interest in men, he was giving messy gay.

"Dad, please," I gritted, gripping my fork tighter.

Responding to my Bat-signal like the deranged vigilante he was, Marcus jumped to my rescue.

"Why does it matter if Glory is seeing Franklin? He's probably the best thing for her," he started.

I had to admit, he was definitely one of the best.

"Franklin's respectful, kind, and most importantly, he's down bad like a clown without face paint for Glory. Let her have this. Just like y'all let Halle have that fucking weirdo she married," he scoffed.

The floodgates opened and the table descended into spite-fueled chaos. Halle was cursing out Marcus while Michael fueled their flames. Mama was likely praying for peace and common sense to come down and punch us in our chests, and my father was staring me down like that one time I tried to renounce the Bible at Thanksgiving.

"Fix the mess you made," he hissed, leaving the table.

I suddenly felt thirteen years old again, when I would hear my daddy's car turn onto the gravel driveway and scramble to hide any evidence of enjoyment. All this time and nothing had changed on the inside.

"Guys!" I called to my siblings, channeling my irritation into my tone.

No one stopped running their mouths long enough for me to get a word in so I had to take the head of the table my father abandoned to project my voice.

"QUIET!" I yelled.

I could barely hear myself over the thump of my pounding heart. My brow began to cover itself in a cold sweat and my fingertips swelled with evidence of my newly elevated blood pressure. I hated this.

"Marcus, apologize to Halle. Halle, stay out of my business and stop cursing in front of Mama. Michael, stop being an instigating di… dookie head," I instructed each of them.

They looked at me briefly, casting their own respective looks of guilt before apologizing to each other and then my mom.

"Ok. Now that that's settled, I'm out. I'll catch y'all later," I said after they finished.

I was itching to leave. The last thing I needed was more follow-ups about Frankie or a *conversation* with my father. Still I took my time gathering my things, careful to maintain my air of indifference and calm. Even if it wasn't true. Even though I was screaming on the inside. No one needed to know that. It certainly wouldn't make my life any easier. I could cry in the car.

"Glory!" A familiar deep voice called.

Fuck, I kinda wish I had ran like I wanted to. But it was too late for that, so I turned around, hoping he'd make it quick. Except it wasn't who I was expecting.

"Marc?" I answered.

My brother jogged towards me with an apologetic smirk. We'd be twins if he was prettier, but God, he sounded so much like my daddy in his older age.

"Hey, I'm sorry. I didn't mean for shit to get out of hand. I just wanted to help," he explained.

His voice was thick with sincerity. His eyes were apologetic. He *looked* sorry. Sure, he fucked up by bringing up Halle's husband, but I knew my brother really did have my best interests in mind.

"It's ok. Thanks for looking out for me," I mumbled.

Marcus nodded before squeezing around my shoulders.

"Always, kid. But real quick, do you have two boyfriends?" he asked.

You could hear the sound my heart made as it clattered against my other organs and fell into my ass.

"Hehe, whaaaaaa…" I mumbled while violently ransacking my tote for my car keys.

My brother had my back, but I did not want to have that conversation with him. Unfortunately I couldn't find my keys underneath all my junk. So Marcus pinned my arm to my side with his hand then spun me around to face him.

"I always kinda figured you and Frankie would be a thing, even with your no dating rule and shit. But when I called your office last week to check on you, Tilly's temp told me you were having a "very important meeting" with Cassius Monroe. Who just so happens to go by @Cash4the2000s on Instagram. You know, the guy who comments something cute in Spanish every time you post. Coincidentally, the same guy who also pops up in Frankie's comments," he explained.

The funny thing is, no one truly knew what Marcus did for work. Except for maybe Alayssa, but his wife was ten toes down loyal to him and his secrets. That left us to our own separate theories. My father and mother said he was a handyman when asked, Halle thought him a government worker/agent, Michael said he was living pretty off his wife's money, (Which was definitely not true.) and me? I could never pitch a theory in the hat. All I knew was that his investigative skills were second only to the CIA.

"Hey, what do you do for work again?" I asked.

Marcus gave me a friendly push in the shoulder before redirecting the conversation.

"A little of this, a little of that. Don't try to change the subject. Do you have two men?"

Damn it. I could lie. Lying would make this whole day a lot less fucking awkward. But I knew if Marcus was asking he likely already knew the truth.

"Honestly? Yes. However, I would not like to discuss my relationships with you because that's too weird for even me."

So my brother knew I had two boyfriends. Fine, I guess. But there was no reason for him to know that most of my sexual encounters consisted of threesomes and Lucky Pierres nowadays.

"Totally fine with that," Marc conceded with raised hands. "Hearing about that stuff with Frankie a couple months ago nearly gave me a stroke. I don't wanna hear about my little sister being spit roasted."

"Marc! What the fuck!" I shouted, punching his arm.

"Hey, don't assault me! I was just checking in with you so I can help with damage control if need be! Also, as your family publicist, I need a raise for this shit," he said.

"I'm not paying you!" I scoffed.

"Yeah, but you should! Tell Mister Monroe to put me on payroll. I know that rich nigga got it. Hell, Frankie might have it soon too. At least yo niggas got money," he laughed.

That was another dig at Halle's abysmal excuse for a husband. Between Chris' cheating, manipulation, and constant disrespect, Marcus' disdain was completely warranted. Yet, I knew we would be entering dangerous waters if I let him continue airing his grievances. Soon enough he'd piss himself off enough to air out Halle's house. Like he'd done before...

"Mkay, this has been fun, but I really gotta go. I know you wanna talk about Alyassa's baby shower tomorrow, but I have a standing brunch date. So it'll have to be next week," I said, finally locating my keys.

Marcus gave me a lazily shrug before pushing me towards my car. He always watched me get in no matter what.

"I'll talk to you Friday if no one's died," he replied.

That felt like a loaded statement. Perhaps I needed to warn Alyassa that her husband was back on his bullshit. But that could wait until I got home and took off the bra that was digging into my sides.

"Friday it is!" I agreed.

Chapter Seventeen

Cash

I'm starting to love Fridays just as much as Mondays now. I wake up, try not to bust my ass in crane pose, take a long shower, then head to work. My cases are usually easy wins on Fridays because the judges be ready for the weekend, and I'm rarely tied up in consultations. Sometimes I eat lunch with Glory, sometimes I do my own thing. But easiness and guaranteed wins aside, that's not why I was falling in love with Fridays. I think I was actually falling in love with Frankie.

Now Glory had pretty much been a done deal as soon as I kissed her, but Fab was a different story. I never really dated a boy. Yeah I fucked them, but most niggas were too down low or immature for me to deal with long term. Then Fab was just… truly and remarkably an experience. This was my first experience with polyamory, and I didn't really have many expectations. At first I thought me and Fab would be friends that occasionally fucked. Attraction and chemistry aside, we were still getting to know each other when that shit with Glory happened. I liked him, but I had no intention of being for anybody except Glory. That was until our first date.

Our first solo date was about six weeks ago, and he asked Glory what my favorite appetizers were so that we could have an appy hour since neither one of us drank. So we spent a Friday night in sharing homemade mozzarella sticks, smoked wings, and a guacamole so fire I was starting to question if I was really Latino. If I was, I would have never let Frankie out guac me.

Bomb ass food aside though, our first date was magical. Like white girl in a rom-com level magical. Frankie made a pillow fort before I got there, and we enjoyed anime on the wall projector in soft candlelit comfort. I never knew niggas could be so sweet and thoughtful. Especially since I was usually the one being sweet and thoughtful. I liked being on the receiving end for once. In more ways then one.

It was no secret that I liked giving head. I was so good at it that I high-key wished I could put it as a skill on my resume. A munch? Yeah, I was that. I could eat pussy for hours, especially Glory's, and I had never heard of lock jaw. Receiving, however, was a different story. I hate to say it, but a lot of women were fucking awful at sucking dick. Niggas were slightly better, but by and large, not by much. I'd gotten nipped, scraped and cotton-mouthed more times than I could count, and I never ever came from head. So imagine my surprise when I watched Fab swallow two consecutive loads with a smile. The only other person who made me cum from head was Glory, and she was a known throat G.O.A.T.

So I got sucked, fucked, fed, and bed. Bed because I had no intentions of spending the night on our first date, but I woke up at 9 A.M on Saturday morning wrapped in Frankie's arms anyway. He was just absentmindedly rubbing the knots from my shoulders while he shook his own haze, and the auric sunlight that managed to creep through the blinds was dancing across his smooth terracotta skin. He was warm and those big ass hands made me feel safe. Then he smelled like a Lush bodywork shop that discovered brown people perfume oils. So there I was laid up, completely entranced with my pretty girlfriend's pretty boyfriend. So much for just being friendly.

"Hey, babe. How was your day?" Frankie asked excitedly.

I blinked back to the present at Frankie's command. I used to think my voice was deep, but Fab's shit? His shit was eight feet under. His shit was deeper than The Titanic. His shit was was deeper than a 5G conspiracy theory.

"It was cool. Glory played me for lunch though," I shrugged.

I was really hurt by it even though I was trying to play it off. I guess I wasn't doing too good of a job though because Frankie threw his head back and sighed.

"I told her ass to text you. She all the way in Houston and ain't say shit to nobody," Fab scoffed.

Pause. I asked her what her day looked like and she said nothing major. In fact, I distinctly remember her saying she wasn't planning on doing much. How the fuck a day trip to Houston classified as nothing major, I'm not sure.

"What the fuck you mean she in Houston?"

"I mean she got her ass on a plane and flew to Houston," Fab shrugged. "Marcus told me something might be going on with Miss Lailah though."

Ah, that explains it. Miss Lailah was Glory's maternal grandmother. Glory was her spitting image in both looks and personality, and she loved that potty-mouthed old woman down to the sockets. That was easy to do cause Miss Lailah was Glory's cheerleader no matter what. She supported her decision to go to law school instead of teaching, her historical choice to *enjoy* the single life, and most recently, her choice to deal with us. Her love for her granddaughter really was unconditional, so it didn't surprise me that she'd dip in an instant. I just wish she told me that.

"Don't feel bad, babe. The only reason I found out was because she added a new delivery address to the GroceryGo account," Fab grumbled.

So we were both blindsided? That honestly tracks. If a person could be a phrase, Glory's would be Fuck Around And Find Out. That applied to almost everything she did. I groaned and stretched to release the stress accumulating in my shoulders. There was no point in calling to bitch at her now. Besides, it wouldn't make me feel better.

"She say when she was coming back?" I asked.

"She said she'll be back before our date night tomorrow," Fab chuckled.

At least I'd get to see mí Princessa tomorrow, and we'd still have brunch. That was fine, because Fab had made comfort pasta.

"Black truffle angel hair linguine with scallops, lemon seared mussels, and pesto shrimp," he exclaimed, setting the plate down. I could smell every single ingredient, including the garlic and fresh roasted pine nuts. A generous pile of pasta adorned with an equally generous pile of mixed shellfish greeted me next to balsamic asparagus and fresh bread. God, Frankie was good.

I pushed my offering forward. A sangria inspired orange-ade with fresh thyme and blackberries. It was a new recipe and decidedly not a lemonade, but I hoped he'd enjoy it anyway. So I watched with bated breath while he poured a fat ass glass.

"Gah damn, this shit fire," he exclaimed, puckering his lips.

He pecked me on the temple as a thanks and I damn near melted into the chair. Yeah, the man upstairs was working overtime when he made Frankie's ass.

"Hey, are you busy on the morning of the 28th?" Fab asked.

That was Halloween weekend, and I only planned on doing three things. Movie bingeing, eating, and fucking.

"Not particularly. You know we're going to that lil costume party on Tuesday, then our after party. So I'm prepping for that, but that's it. What's up?" I asked.

Frankie anxiously nibbled at his bottom lip, drawing all my attention to his pinched mouth and perfect, rapt, eyes that were racing with proof of a thousand thoughts.

"What's up Frijoles?" I pressed, rolling my hand to coax him.

"Um… Would you mind taking a few things to the Community Market for me? My car isn't big enough for everything," he whispered.

I froze, trying to stifle a scream. Frankie had about three weeks of his leave left and Glory was concerned that he hadn't made much progress outside of maintaining sobriety. He hadn't found a therapist, or given more thought to quitting his uncle's, but that doesn't mean he wasn't healing. He was grocery shopping on his own, taking evening walks, and journaling. He was buying clothes that actually fit his slender frame, and most importantly, he was trying.

"Of course, babe. You just wanna take the wagon?" I offered.

"Absolutely not," Fab replied instantly.

Frankie had a weird beef with SUV's. Weird because he was well over six feet tall, yet he was determined to stick to his low-ride civic with barely enough space for him to stretch his long-ass spider legs in. Partly because he was really, really big on statistical analysis. Much to my dismay.

"Fab," I sighed.

"Nope, I'm not rolling over in that muhfucka," he insisted.

According to Frankie, SUV's have four times a greater rollover risk than sedans. He also didn't like how much gas they consumed, how much insurance cost, and finally, he didn't like that the standard paint colors were boring.

"Lawd babe. Fine, you ain't gotta drive it. I'll drop everything off for you, Statistic Sadist," I sighed.

"Thank you," he sassed. "And statistics save lives."

Ah, Fab, always putting that mathematics master's to use. Getting to know Frankie this last few months has been so fucking refreshing. I loved that he didn't fit into anyone's boxes, especially given who I thought he was when we met at Adam's.

"Everyone thinks you're some big, scary player, but you're just a cute ass nerd with a big dick," I laughed.

Frankie stabbed at the last of his asparagus with a slick little grin before wiping the pesto off my top lip. Then I watched him lick it off his pointer finger.

"Correction, I'm a cute ass nerd with a big dick who can cook," he chuckled.

Frankie flashed me the golds lining his pretty white teeth, and that told me that the bulge between his legs wasn't just for show.

"Right. You're so good at that. Just like statistics," I purred. "So can you predict the probability of us fucking around tonight?" I asked.

Frankie inched closer until the tip of his nose rested against mine.

"I would say 100%," he purred.

I took back what I said earlier, I actually loved how much he considered statistics.

"What the fuck?" Fab exclaimed.

It was still dark out when I lazily cracked my lids to see what had him in a tizzy so early, only to make creepily clear eye contact with Glory.

"Jesus, Gloria! What the hell? When did you get here?" I grumbled.

"Three," she whispered.

"In the morning?" Fab asked.

She nodded before shimmying back under the covers, clearly done with our conversation.

"Glory," I clicked. "We need to talk about yesterday."

I understood it was an emergency, but communication was essential. Anything could have happened and we wouldn't have known. Fab reminded me of that last night.

"Yeah, Essie. You can't just dip out without saying anything," he admonished.

"I'm cold, hold me," she demanded, dismissing our concerns.

Wow. The little brat was unremorseful. She was just making demands. Demands that we'd likely meet, but still.

"Essie," Fab gritted.

I didn't have that much willpower at 6 am on a Saturday, so I did what the little gremlin asked while Fab scoffed at me. I knew I shouldn't have given in, but I what can I say? She was convincing. Soft, warm, and squeezeable. He should know.

"Y'all can yell at me at like 12 or something. I had a rough night," she murmured, pulling Frankie into our huddle.

"Fine," Fab grumbled, wrapping around us.

I could tell he wanted to be a crab apple about this, but Glory nuzzled in between us, strumming our sides with her tender palms. Frankie's eyes fluttered while he fought to keep his attitude, but his lour relaxed while her soft petting lulled us all back to sleep.

"Shit!" I gasped, registering Glory's absence.

I woke up in complete panic because it was just me and Frankie in bed again. I was wrapped in his arms like I was before Glory squeezed between us. Did she leave? Was she ever here? I started to wonder if I was having trippy dreams again before I noticed the easel in the corner.

"Princessa!" I called loudly.

That made Frankie join me in wakefulness, however reluctant he was.

"Cash, she's probably in the bathroom," he yawned.

Glory strolled back in from the bathroom with perfect timing, but she scowled seeing us now awake.

"Fuck, I knew I should've took a picture," she sighed. "Hopefully I can pull this off from memory."

She repositioned herself on a bar stool in front of the large canvas, completely oblivious to our growing concern.

"Essie, what are you doing?" Frankie sighed, trying to blink awake.

Glory pressed her arches to the support bar on the stool to get comfortable before grabbing a smaller brush.

"Painting, duh," she replied.

She returned to silence while we stared her down, mentally demanding that she provide more context. Only she didn't care. She was happy to mind her own business and ignore us.

"Whatcha painting?" I asked.

"Y'all," she said flatly, allowing no indication of excitement or pleasure into her tone.

That concerned me. Glory loved to paint, and while I've never witnessed her in the zone, it was weird that she wasn't excited. Maybe it was bad?

Curiosity overwhelmed me so I left bed to find out. Maybe she was just rusty. Maybe her references moving did fuck up her process. Maybe… she was full of shit. I joined her side to be greeted by an absolute masterpiece. I lay in Fab's arms, wrapped in his thick burgundy quilt, while his head tucked mine in the crook of his neck for safekeeping. She had gotten every single detail. My two-toned stretch marks, Fab's frizzy edges peeking from underneath his velvet durag, the contrasting textures of the hair trimming our forearms, even the peace and security etched into our expressions.

"Oh, Princessa. This is remarkable," I mumbled, noticing the small specks of drool on the pillow that she took the time to illustrate.

"You're my boyfriend. You have to say that," she waved dismissively.

I have never been one to lie. In fact, I was often branded as too honest if you ask my mama. It wasn't my fault I told that lady she was stinking. She should've washed her ass. You don't go out in public with a hot ass.

"Gloria, baby. This looks like something in a snobby ass gallery. You could be a professional with this much skill."

Glory snorted while replacing her detailing brush with a larger angled one.

"Please, like Lazarus would've allowed that. It's bad enough I defied him and went to law school. He would've disowned me," she laughed.

She said that shit like it was the most normal thing in the world. Meanwhile my chest was burning. The more I learned about her father, the less I was looking forward to meeting him. A few months ago I thought Glory was swimming in confidence, but I quickly learned it was a coping mechanism. Because her first bully raised her. I ground my jaw before turning to Fab, curious if he was feeling it too. The hurt, anger, and guilt rimming his sleep-deprived eyes told me he was feeling it tenfold. But all we could do right then was hug Glory tight and remind her how amazing she was.

Chapter Eighteen

Cash

Glory showered when she finished painting since we were migrating to my house for the weekend. We alternated between Glory's apartment and mine for our group days since Fab's place only had one bathroom, and no one was willing to piss down the sink when Glory was busy taking marathon showers with the door locked.

"Ready?" I asked.

"Yeah, I just need to grab a few herbs," Fab replied.

That man and his seasonings. I would be offended if anyone else brought their own seasoning to my crib, but Frankie was a man with a vision. Every flavor had to layer exactly as he imagined it, or there would be hell to pay.

"Babe, we'll just stop at the store on the way. I need to grab a light bulb and shit too."

"What are we doing?" Glory inquired, fresh from her shower.

I got too distracted looking at her to reply. Glory's rich skin was slick with a generous layer of Shea butter. Her face was glowing from her expensive ass moisturizer. Then her kinky curls were piled into a soft, damp pineapple bun that made her look like a magical little Tinkerbell, instead of the complete menace she actually was.

"Headed to Cash's," Fab replied. "Put on clothes."

"But I wanted to have sex first," she pouted.

If Gloria Esther King ain't have shit else, she had the audacity. She left the city, said nothing, popped back home at 3am, scared the shit outta us, then demanded sex with no explanation or follow up. Like I said, a menace.

"Sex?" I asked, slightly in disbelief.

"Yes, Cash. Sex. Yo quiero chingao. It's been a minute," she said, letting her attitude coat my brain.

I was about to tell her some things, but Fab beat me to it.

"You think you deserve some ass after you left outta here and ain't say shit to nobody?" he asked.

The little brat stuck out that kissable bottom lip while glancing between us, likely hoping to find a friend in me, but I shot that down quick by crossing my arms over my chest in defiance to her usually-captivating feminine wiles.

"That's not fair!" she pouted.

"Essie, it ain't fair to leave us in the dark either! Anything could've happened to yo ass and we wouldn't have known! You think that's fair for us to find out you in a whole nother city through a grocery delivery app?" he asked.

Glory knew she was wrong. She searched the hurt on our faces for no longer than ten seconds before her shoulders slumped in defeat.

"You're right, and I'm sorry, but it was an emergency," she mumbled.

Her lip quivered just enough to make me abandon my grievances and I rushed to her side to provide us both with some comfort.

"Communication is important, Princessa. Especially given what we got going on. It's not just you, or you and me, or you and Frankie. It's all three of us. It's irresponsible to have us worry like that. You know we would've had your back and adjusted our plans to make sure you were good," I explained.

She nodded while tucking her head onto my shoulder, then she broke down into tears. Probably because she was stressed beyond what she was letting on.

"Shit, Essie," Fab sighed, joining the huddle. "I ain't mean to make you cry, baby."

"It's not y'all. I'm just… Granny's been having strokes," she sobbed.

Been having? That's not something you want to be recurring. Did her parents know? Her siblings? Was it even safe for her to be in Houston by herself at eighty-seven?

"What? She done had multiple?" Fab asked. "Wait, start from the beginning."

We sat down on the couch while Glory told us about Miss Lailah's growing health concerns. Apparently she had fallen in her garden a couple months back and that's what caused the first stroke. Then yesterday's was brought on by her refusal to sit still. Man, if Glory wasn't that lady's reincarnate.

"So what does that mean? Is Ms. Kim really gone let her live there by herself with all this going on?" Fab asked.

Glory dropped her head onto her chest while releasing the most stressed sigh I've ever heard in my life.

"She tried to pay me a thousand dollars not to tell mama," she whispered.

Honestly, I wasn't mad at it. From what I had heard, Miss Lailah was the OG definition of miss independent. She had bought her first house at eighteen after impersonating her father, she taught herself to code, and also to swap engines. So I could see why she might have been unwilling to relinquish that title after all that. Besides, she was funny as hell. I was trying not to laugh because Glory was clearly bothered, but Fab beat me to it.

"Heh, I'm sorry," he snickered. "Not she tried to bribe yo ass like Boosie. Put ya mama on ice I'll give you a thousand dollars."

Glory sucked her teeth irritably while we tried our best to table our laughter.

"Y'all finished?" she asked.

I slowed my chuckling to nudge Fab who was still at it, and only then did his laughter fade.

"My bad, Essie," he chortled. "So you gone tell her?"

Glory shrugged before locating her phone and checking her email.

"The moving crew packing Granny's house as we speak. She's *"visiting"* Marcus for now," she said.

The Devil worked hard, but Glory worked harder. It hadn't been a full twenty four hours and she had already relocated Miss Lailah. Oh shit, that's exactly what she did to Fab. Yeah, I was starting to see the problem.

Fab pinched the bridge of his nose to steady his exhale before reigning us in.

"Cash, go start the car. Glory, go put some clothes on your ass. Come on so I can make breakfast, and yes, you can diddle us or me once we get some food in our systems," he said, offering our sex-starved gremlin appeasement.

Oh my fucking God. That shit was too good. By that shit I meant Fab's cooking. We had blackberry and orange cream stuffed French toast with sweet potato hash and cracked pepper bacon for breakfast. I was never a fan of sweet potatoes like that before Frankie, but now I understand that they were made for breakfast. That or Fab was on some Harry Potter shit. Honestly, magic seemed likely in this case. How else could I explain my continued urge to lick the lingering grease off my fork?

"Ok, I ate. Can somebody please play with my pussy now?" Glory asked.

Fab peeked over the top of his newspaper with curiosity, then he furrowed his brows, seeing Glory's plate.

"Eat the fruit, Essie. And finish that glass of water," he grumbled.

"Ugh! I don't wanna eat the fruit! I wanna do butt stuff!" she hollered.

I'm not gonna lie, I wasn't a fan of her tone. Glory was being such a brat that I was switching, something I rarely did around Fab.

"Essie," Frankie boomed. "Eat. Your. Fruit. Or you can enjoy a timeout instead."

Never mind, he had it covered. Because Glory picked up her fork immediately after and shoveled the apple slices into her mouth. Her compliance wasn't free though, and she began to antagonize Fab as soon as she finished.

"There, I ate the bitch ass apples," she whined, ejecting her tongue as proof.

"Now fuck me or I'll find someone else."

That did it. Me and Fab were on her like white on rice as soon as she finished her sentence.

"You gone do what?" I asked, grabbing her throat.

"I'm gonna find somebody else to fuck me," she hissed, eyes sparkling with chaotic amusement.

"Oh, Essie. It seems like you didn't learn your lesson. Maybe we need a chapter review on what happens when you're a disrespectful, belligerent, brat. What do you think, Cash?"

I looked down at the beautiful woman with a wicked smile and an excessive amount of misplaced confidence.

"I think you're right, Frankie. Let's play red light, green light this time," I suggested.

Glory's pupils dilated when she realized the hole she talked herself into, but it was too late, we were already carrying her upstairs.

Frankie made quick work of Glory's flimsy ass lace panties while I got rid of her bra. Then we switched places for me to eat her and Fab to fuck her throat. God, Glory had such a pretty pussy. Pink, fat, waxed, and sticky. It was basically a honey trap. Because once you went in, it was impossible to come out. I made myself busy kissing her, and I was beginning to find out how many licks it took to reach the center of a Tootsie pop right when the doorbell rang.

"Expecting something?" Fab asked.

Glory gurgled his nuts in an attempt to join in our conversation.

"Nah, it's probably just the mail or something. Don't worry about it," I shrugged. "Hush, Princessa."

With that, we went back to torturing Glory, and it was the easily the most peaceful sixty seconds of my day.

"I feel like you should get that," Fab grumbled, withdrawing from Glory.

The bell had been ringing nonstop for two minutes. I wasn't sure who it was that couldn't take the fucking hint, but I wasn't interested in stopping what I was doing.

"Frankie," Glory wined. "Come back."

Frankie refused because the bell didn't stop. He looked at me with hitched brows while the unexpected visitor rang the buzzer along to the symphony of Pop, Lock, And Drop It. Then the unexpected happened.

"Ok seriously, Cash. Go get the door," Glory instructed, pulling away.

Ugh. I was actually just as frustrated as Glory, and I just wanted to eat my brat and get fucked on. I was about to fight them on it but then my phone rang. Great. More unnecessary noise. I grabbed my phone off the nightstand, fully intending to switch it to DND, but then I noticed the caller ID.

"Mama?" I answered.

"Hola, Mijo. Why aren't you answering the door?"

I swallowed a futbol-sized lump in my throat. Had I forgotten my mama was visiting?

"Is that you down there?" I asked.

My mama laughed loudly like I was missing a joke.

"No, you know I don't just drop by," she answered.

Oh, thank God. I was about to cry if this happened to be the time when I explained our relationship to my family.

"Cookie is there," she laughed. "She called me to get you to let her in."

FUCK! That was exponentially worse. I would rather explain everything to my mama than Constance. Constance asked too many questions, had too many comments, and expressed too many concerns.

"Cookie?" I repeated anxiously.

"Yes, Mijo. Tu Hermana. Go let her in, Cassius."

Mama said that with enough irritation to will my legs to move towards my dresser and find pants.

"Ok, ok. I'm headed down now. Tell her here I come."

She hung up on me before I turned back to Fab and Glory who were seemingly unbothered.

"Hey…" I groaned, unable to verbalize the fact that I needed them to stay hidden.

"Cash, it's cool. Me and Glory come from church folks. We get it," he shrugged.

"Ok, but this isn't a long-term thing. I just would rather have a formal…"

"Cash, baby. Stop talking and go let your sister in," Glory said. "We're about to catch up on Project Runway since I know you two been watching without me."

Her sharp gaze completely erased the nervousness I felt about my sister's impromptu visit, and replaced it with dread. Especially given how close she was to a very nervous and newly avoidant Fab. Yeah, he was about to suffer for both of us.

"Sorry, Princessa. I'll make it up to you," I said racing to leave.

"Coward!" Frankie hissed, hearing my departing footsteps.

I was so nervous that I couldn't even reply. Yes, I was a coward for dipping. I was also a coward for being afraid that my sister would find out about my partners. And I was a super coward for how I answered the door.

"Cookie, hi. Do you plan on staying long?" I asked, leaning against the door frame.

Constance's top lip quickly met her nose while she made her way inside my living room. I watched as she removed her jacket, shoes, and even her hoops, which answered my question. She was getting comfortable to stay a *while*.

"It's nice to see you too, little brother. After all, it's only been what? A whole year?"

Shit, I ain't mean it like that. See, me and Cookie were close growing up. So much so that I cried for a whole week after she left to LA for college. She really was my best friend, my hype man, and my confidant. I guess that's why I felt so weird about hiding my relationship from her. I rarely kept secrets from my sister.

"Sorry, I just wasn't expecting company," I explained.

Cookie offered me a sympathetic sigh and a quick hug before settling into the recliner.

"I didn't mean to drop by, but I was here on a work trip and I had an entire day of meetings rescheduled, so I figured I'd come check on you."

That made me feel even worse. Cookie had a whole day, suddenly free, and the first thing she thought about was me. Damn, I was a shitty brother.

"Don't look like that, Cash. You didn't know I was stopping by," she chided, seemingly reading my thoughts.

She held my gaze to make sure I was processing her lecture before hopping up and strolling into the kitchen. Likely entranced by the smell of Frankie's leftovers.

"I'm hungry, it smells good in here," she announced, confirming my theory.

She made herself busy making a plate while I texted Glory and Fab to make sure they were good. Only for Fab to text back,

"I'm being abused."

Honestly, I wasn't surprised, and it took everything in me not to chuckle at that update.

"Oh shit, this is hella good," Cookie exclaimed. "You made this?" she asked, eyebrows raised in disbelief.

"Aye, I'm not a bad cook!" I responding, knowing damn well I ain't have shit to do with that magic.

Cookie raised her hands in surrender before stabbing at a potato and checking the crisp.

"I didn't say you were. I just asked because your specialty starts at steak, and ends at mashed potatoes. I ain't never seen you even glance at sweet potatoes."

All I could do was sigh, because she had me there. It had only been two months since I started seeing Fab and I had tried more new shit in that month than I had in four years. He was good for me.

"Are you blushing?" Cookie asked.

Damn it! I was blushing. What the fuck had Fab done to me?

"No! I'm cold!" I said, trying to convince myself.

"Mm, I don't see how with this heat on hell," Cookie remarked. "Anyway."

She started looking through the fridge for a drink, uninterested in my reasoning. Which was honestly good since the house was hot because of Glory's ass. I see why Fab made her start taking iron. She was about to put Sonic out of business for their ice.

"Damn, you ain't got no more Olipops in here?" she asked.

I did, but they were upstairs in my mini fridge.

"Wait. They're probably upstairs, I'll be back."

I started to nod before I realized what was happening. Glory and Fab were upstairs, Cookie was heading upstairs. I was still firmly downstairs. SHIT!

"Wait! Wait! Wait! I'll get it for you!" I shouted, chasing after her.

Unfortunately, she was already at the top. Damn her and those spider legs. Who the fuck skips two steps at a time as an adult? She had a whole child and a mortgage. That tactic was childish as fuck.

"Cash, stop being weird. No one cares about your dildos," she admonished.

Heh. If only she fucking knew. But that discovery was for a later time. Not right now, while I was still heaving my big ass up the stairs, and my sister was about to literally open a can of worms. I shouted after her as her meaty hand turned the Victorian-style knob,

"Cookie, please respect my personal space as an ad..."

Unfortunately, my speech fell onto deaf ears, and she rolled her eyes before swinging open my door, and accidentally soliciting Glory's high-pitched screech.

"Finally! We were about to start w… Eep!" she shouted.

It was too late, and I was too terrified to use my brain. So I froze while my sister came face to face with my half-naked partners.

Frankie

"And she looked at me. And I looked at her. And she looked at me, while I looked at her."

That was the only thing bouncing around in my mind while I made increasingly awkward eye contact with Cash's sister. I knew it was her because they had the same face. The only difference was her slightly darker complexion and hip-length box braids. Her eyes were roving over the room a thousand times a minute while she put all the pieces in place. Glory was hiding in the covers, Cash was obviously mortified, and I was just twiddling my thumbs. Thank God I made Glory put on a nightie earlier, cause this could've been a whole lot worse.

"Can… Can you hand me an Olipop?" she asked, breaking the minute-long silence.

I reached over and opened the fridge, my eyes never leaving hers as I did.

"There's lime, peach, and watermelon. Which one would you like?" I replied.

"Peach please," she mumbled.

I had spent some time organizing the shelves, so I immediately produced her requested selection and passed her the refreshment. Which she cracked open and knocked back like an ice-cold White Claw.

"Cookie, I can explain," Cash mumbled.

To be honest, I'm sure she could've done fine without his explanation. There were two half-naked people on her brother's bed with a bowl of condoms between them. I'm sure whatever conclusion she came to on her own was valid. The math was most definitely mathing.

"Fuck," she hissed.

Cash's entire expression dropped into a deeply depressing frown as soon as she said that, and I had to stop myself from matching energy or rushing to hug him. Until she continued.

"I owe Mama $300. Thanks a lot, Poquito."

I wasn't expecting that. I mean, I wasn't expecting for her to be up here either. But life is funny that way.

"Excuse me?" Cash asked, snapping his head back.

"I owe Mama M-O-N-E-Y," she responded. "Dinero, la mosca, cheddar."

"You've been betting on my life?" he asked in disbelief.

"First off, yo mama been betting on your life. You knew that old woman had a gambling problem with all them damn scratchers," she tutted. "Ain't my fault it's genetic…"

Glory finally peeked from under the covers with a bright laugh to join us.

"Well I guess we might as well have a proper introduction," she whispered. "Let us put some clothes on."

Glory was a true Southern Hostess, setting out drinks, cookies, and fruit for Constance. Despite the awkward first look, the two were becoming fast friends. It made perfect sense. Constance was a lot like Cash. She was funny, sweet, but also mildly inappropriate. She had so many dick jokes. *So many.* The only other woman I've met as equally unhinged was sitting across from her. So it seemed Glory and Cookie were meant to be sisters.

"So she just casually called and told you, *I bet your brother's gonna be in a triad,*?" Glory asked.

Constance nodded while noshing on another shortbread cookie. Making me glad I ignored them when they said shortbread was boring.

"Yeah, basically. Although she did think the group would be bigger. Like a harem situation," she laughed.

"Oh no," Glory exclaimed. "These two stress me out enough."

"Says the woman who left town yesterday without saying nothing," Cash barked.

Oop. He was gonna be mad about that for a minute. His anger was warranted though. Anything could have happened. Plans change all the time. Like how we had plans to get nasty, but instead we spent the afternoon meeting Cash's fam.

"So you're the one who's been fattening Cash up?" she asked, pointing to me.

Glory had spent the last six minutes ranting about everything we'd eaten over the week. From the hash, to the smoked snapper, and the oxtail ramen.

"Yeah," I mumbled. "I really like cooking. My parent's weren't really big into that so I became the family cook."

Shit. There I went oversharing again. Why did I say that? No one asked me the reason. Th…

"Same! But with barbecue. Cash and Mama were hopeless, so I became the family grill master," she beamed. "This is so exciting! I'll finally have some help for the holidays."

If my skin wasn't so red, I'd be blushing. I hadn't made it awkward, and Cookie actually seemed happy to have us around. Being wanted. What a novel feeling. I liked it.

"I'd love to help!" I replied with way too much excitement for a woman I'd literally just met.

"Whoa, whoa, whoa. Who said we were spending the holidays with y'all?" Cash asked.

Cookie stirred her lemonade while sucking her teeth.

"Tu madre, y tu sobrino," she replied. "I already texted her and said you were coming."

Jesus. Cash had been raised with one menace only to end up with another. Glory and Cookie were two sides of the same slightly controlling coin. You really do learn how to love from your family. Oop, let me tuck that knowledge back into my denial sock.

"No," he waved.

"We'd love to!" Glory chimed.

Cash narrowed his neat brows at her while his mouth hung open like a catfish, probably holding back some choice words. Or a promising threat.

"Fine," he grumbled. "But don't think you're off the hook. Especially for that bet."

"Mhm, I'm listening. Anyway, I gotta get going, Poquito. I might as well find me a Dallas dingaling while Rory has Rio."

I promise you that's something Glory would say. Holy shit, Cash was a psychologist's wet dream.

"Ew, te veo nunca," Cash replied with a furrowed lip.

"Don't ew me, you greedy pansexual. Te veo las Navidad, Poquito," she said firmly.

She kissed Cash on top of his meticulous head and I watched a sly smirk appear then quickly fade. He was terrible at hiding his hand, and it was adorable.

"Let me walk you out so Mama can't blame me if you get snatched," Cash quipped.

I scurried off the couch to join him while Glory waved goodbye from the window.

"Get back to LA safe!" we called.

"I will!" Cookie shouted. "We'll work on that Christmas menu in a couple of weeks, Frankie!"

My face warmed while we watched Cookie depart in her little rental hatchback. I was actually excited for the holidays. I was looking forward to spending Christmas with her. With them. Yeah, Cash was good for me.

Chapter Nineteen

Frankie

You know what's not good for me, though? Public settings. Public settings make me anxious. Anxiety makes me overshare. Oversharing makes me want to jump. So yeah, me and the public do not get along. Then to make matters worse, I had to sell them shit. Shit that I made. Ugh, fuck capitalism. Capitalism felt like a neuro-divergent hate crime.

"Nope, I can't do it."

I tried to spin away on my heels after that announcement, but Cash quickly caught me and put another crate in my hand.

"Frankie, I done gassed up the car, loaded six crates of candles, scrubs, and lotion, and lied to Glory for you. Get yo ass in the car. You said we were selling candles today so we're selling candles. **Today.**"

Dammit! Dom Cash was a fucking buzzkill. Anyone with eyes could see that I was not cut out to do business of any kind. I just wanted to be the creative goblin who made shit, and had interaction-free earnings deposited into my account. This is why middle-men were so damn popular.

"I hope this crashes and burns so I can go back to my shitty desk job in peace," I mumbled.

Cash laughed in my face before pulling his phone out his back pocket.

"Take it back, or I'm calling Glory," he sneered.

"You wouldn't dare," I hissed.

Cash's head snapped back before immediately pulling her up on speed dial. He put it on speaker and the phone rang once before she answered.

"Hi, Cassius. Good morning," she cooed.

"Morning, Princessa. You have plans today?"

"Fine!" I whisper-yelled. "I take it back."

I couldn't believe he had the audacity to call my bluff. Fortunately Glory's busy body-ass already made plans.

"I'm hanging out with Granny today. Running her around a few places. Why, what's going on?" she asked.

Cash looked at me, hazel eyes brimming with chaos. Daring me to try it again. All I could do was suck my teeth and accept defeat.

"Nothing, Princessa. Just called to check on you. Call me if you get some free time before our date tonight."

"Mmhkay, will do," she yawned.

And with that, I knew backing out was no longer an option for me.

"You're maniacal," I mumbled, loading the last few crates.

I somehow survived three hours of peddling my wares by nothing less than a divine miracle. I hadn't done as well as I hoped, but I wasn't completely failing either. Most customers were buying multiple items at once, so that was a win. The main downside was that I only had about six people stop by my table.

"I think I should call it," I sighed.

Cash didn't immediately respond. He instead unwrapped two egg and ham bagels before sitting in the chair to my right.

"I think you should take a breakfast break and stretch yo spider legs," he mumbled with a mouthful of bread. "Then I think we should stay just a little longer before calling it. Only old ladies and statistics nerds wake up before six for community markets."

He passed me my sandwich with a delightful smile that prevented my expression from further curdling. But I still wasn't convinced.

"For me?" he begged.

Damn Cash and his buttery ass voice and fire ass smile! I was gonna do it, but I wasn't gone be happy about it.

"Ugh! Fine. We'll give it until like eleven," I offered.

"Noon," he countered.

"An hour isn't that much of a difference, Cash," I argued.

Cash flashed me a shit eating grin before sipping an herbal tea he got from one of the other stands.

"I'm glad you agree! Noon it is," he laughed.

And with that I was sent on my way to stretch my legs or whatever.

Honestly, it was nice to walk around. There were so many vendors that I hadn't seen from my little reclusive corner. A tea lady, a couple selling various oils and seasonings, an auntie selling hand fans, and a barrage of farmers. The older farmers were the best at crowd work. They drew people in with steady voices, relatable jokes, and friendly smiles. So I wasn't ashamed to admit I walked away with two pounds of turkey breast to smoke at Cash's later. That shit was gone hit with some elotes, rice, and cranberry-orange chutney.

I wandered around as a patron for twenty minutes before I decided to head back and serve out my sentence. Maybe noon wouldn't be so bad. When I was shopping, I noticed that most of the vendors had repeat customers. I listened closely to the friendly exchanges as I picked out fruit, meat, and tea, and one thing was commonly present. Genuine interest in each other's lives and well being. It had me rethinking my own strategy. Maybe I needed to share a little more for once in my life.

I practiced in my head as I walked, *"Hi, I'm Franklin and I make candles and body scrubs because the woman I'm in love with has serious allergies when it comes to cheap chemical-ladden fragrance."*

I grimaced, maybe that was too honest. Maybe I needed to treat this whole thing like a bushel of greens. Cut the stems, rinse the leaves, and put some meat in it. I make high quality candles because people have allergies to artificial fragrance. Simple enough right?

"Ion know." Inner Frankie shrugged lazily.

Ugh. Unhelpful, anxious, bastard.

I was relieved to see Glory and Cash chatting at the stand when I rounded the corner because that meant I could get both opinions on my new elevator pitch.

Wait.

Glory was now at the market. I thought she had shit to do with Mama Lailah? Fuck, I hadn't expected to see her then. Especially not with how shitty the stand was doing. It was bad enough I hadn't committed to a therapist, attended an AA meeting, or quit my job. It was bad enough I was living in her shit. It was bad enough I was bringing all my problems to her doorstep when she had plenty going on with Miss Lailah and them.

I tried to reason with myself. This was probably just my long-term boo, anxiety talking. Glory never said she was mad at me for staying at Curtis's. She never said I had to commit to a therapist immediately, she just wanted me to give it a try. She also never told me I was a burden, despite how I felt in my head and heart. She had never verbalized anything other than support. Yet I felt like a fucking failure while staring at her magnificent, deserving, face, and I couldn't handle another disappointed lip twitch from her when I told her that again.

"Essie?" I called.

"Frankie," she responded.

Shit, she was real. She was real and in a pretty maroon sweater dress with her nipples poking through the knit.

"Dammit!" I scolded internally. *"Now is not the time for that!"*

"What are you doing here?" I asked, trying not to sound as panicked as I actually was.

What was she talking about with Cash? Did she know how low sales were? Is that why she popped by? Was she disappointed?

"Granny wanted to grab some herbs and stuff because she said the only spice Lazarus likes is salt, but I've just been watching her flirt with the florist for the last twenty minutes," she sighed, pointing her head towards the specialty flower booth.

I followed her sight line, and sure enough, Miss Lailah was busy giving Old Man Gonzalez the *business*. He had to be at least twenty years her junior, but she still had it by the way he was leaning towards her, smile all wide and goofy. I swear Glory was that woman's reincarnate.

"Ah," I laughed, watching the seniors whisper undoubtedly sinful things to one another. "Spice has multiple meanings."

She sucked her teeth before eventually breaking into laughter that rang through my anxiety-prone mind and soothed it like fresh aloe on a blistered sunburn. God, Glory was so beautiful. So sweet. So observant. Shit, too observant.

"So, I noticed you were having some trouble with sales," she started.

I turned to Cash with a tense jaw. There was only one way she could've known sales were rough, and while it was true, I did not want her fixing this. I didn't want her fixing me.

I shook my head, rejecting whatever plan she was about to pitch, but she doubled down.

"Frankie, jus…"

"No, Essie. I will figure it out," I gritted.

"Please, Frankie! I know what I'm doing! I have a whole bachelors in business and economics," she argued.

I knew that to be true, but Essie ain't just have any old business degree, she had a Spellman business degree. I knew for a fact that muhfucka was solid, but even still I was uninterested in once again dumping my problems on my girlfriend's lap.

"Mhm. That's nice. You should probably grab Miss Lailah before she gets arrested for indecent exposure."

Glory tilted her head in an effort to locate her grandmother, only to find her under a nearby tree, showing Ernesto the flower peddler all her goods and services.

"Ugh! I'll be right back, and we'll talk some more!" she shouted, stomping off to bust up an elderly striptease.

With Glory off being Miss Lailah's fun police, I was left to perfect my pitch. I had since discovered that my biggest competitor when it came to candles was Yodels, and after reading hundreds of reviews, I knew most consumer's biggest complaints when it came to their product.

"Hi!" I called to a lingering couple. "Do you like Yodels candles?" I asked.

The Pink Berry of a woman immediately nodded yes while her storm cloud partner grimaced.

"They make my nose itch," he replied.

Bingo. This was as good as done.

"Me too," I laughed. "That's why I started making my own. I wanted to burn a candle without my sinuses getting inflamed, but I didn't wanna smell just plain wax. So I came up with these."

I offered them both a small tea light to smell. One honeysuckle and cream, and one tangerine. The woman immediately sniffed hers and her partners before eagerly pulling him closer to the stand. She then spent ten minutes going through the modest collection and asking questions before picking up the last unsniffed scent, Campfire S'mores.

"Oh my goodness. This smells so dang good! Babe, it's just like s'mores!" she squealed.

She offered it to her grumpy companion and while his mouth did curl into a slight smirk, he ultimately shrugged it off.

"It's not bad," he sighed. "It's up to you, Cherub."

They stepped away to talk amongst themselves before the guy came back with a wad of cash extended.

"We'll take two of each, and two hibiscus brown sugar body scrubs," he stated.

His partner joined his side with a new tote and extra newspaper, flashing a sly grin that seemed to calm his agitation.

"Thank you, Anais," she cooed, before turning back towards me. "Do you have a website? We're not in the city often," she explained.

Shit, a website. That would be helpful when it came to long-distance customers. Especially ones who were just visiting Dallas. How did I miss that? Oh yeah, anxiety.

"It's currently under construction, but if you'd like to give me your email I can add you to the newsletter and also give you 25% off your next order," I offered.

The woman reached into her purse for a pen before her storm cloud stopped her and extended me an engraved matte black business card. Whatever money this nigga had was ludicrous, because I'm sure the card itself was printed on aluminum. He also bought out half my remaining candle inventory just to make his partner smile. Yet, somehow, according to the card, he was just a chicken farmer.

"Thanks, we hope to hear from you soon," he said curtly, scooching the little woman along.

I did a little fist pump once they left. Yes! I had made my first major sale without help. It was mere pennies in the bucket compared to my biggest competitor, but I didn't care, because it was the start of something great. Something that was mine. Then along came Glory.

"These are the best candles you'll ever buy. Plus a portion of every sale benefits therapy for local black men!" she exclaimed.

She had a crowd in tow. A crowd I likely didn't even have enough product for consider Mr. Aluminum Business Card just bought two of nearly everything. After I explicitly expressed to her that did not want help and would figure it out. Plus she had lied to these damn folks.

But I didn't have time to address that right then, because we were getting swarmed. I rang out the first few orders before getting overwhelmed and Cash was nice enough to takeover for me. Then I stepped away to talk to Glory.

"Glory," I chided. "I asked you not to meddle, and you did it anyway! Then you lied to these folks about it benefiting charity!"

"First off, I did not lie, I stretched the truth a tiny bit," she explained, measuring the amount between her thumb and pointer finger. "Second, I didn't meddle. I simply gave an honest product review seeing as I own a few."

Her shrill voice carried not an ounce of regret even as I pinched the bridge of my nose to ward off a headache from all the sudden stimulation. She continued reciting her business plan for my business as I tried to ground myself, talking about business cards, merch, and an eventual brick and mortar location. Her checklist was unrelenting and overwhelming, causing my already-present anxiety to roil in the pit of my stomach. Then, as suddenly as the headache I found myself nursing formed, I snapped.

"GLORIA!" I seethed. "For the thousandth time, I do not want your help! This is not your business, it's mine. These are not your candles, they're mine. And this is not how I want to gain customers! You are hard headed, impatient, and inconsiderate!"

I'm sure Glory heard the latter of my argument countless times before, but that didn't stop warm tears from making their way down her cheeks and neck. It also didn't stop her from backing away from me after I reached for, realizing I had yelled at her. And it definitely didn't stop me from feeling like an absolute pile of shit when Cash ran after her, trying to console her very public emotional breakdown. So there I stood in the center of the market, with a sold-out stand, a tearful girlfriend, and a back pocket full of self-righteous validation that I never really wanted.

Fuck.

Twenty

Chapter Twenty

Frankie

"She's doing ok. Still mopey. Idk about the Halloween party tomorrow."

I was on hour 36 of a Glory iceout so Cash and Caris were doing God's work by checking on her. Truthfully, I originally planned to spend today in the crack of her ass, but instead, I found myself wandering around the grocery store. I planned to grab a pack of chicken thighs and go, but then I started searching for something I knew could emulate her warmth. I stopped in the center of the whiskey aisle and stared. I stared for a really long time. Long enough to notice the slight color variations between the top shelf whiskey and the cheap shit. I thought I would immediately grab a pint and head for self-checkout but the urge to do that never came. It instead felt wrong to be there. Like I was a kid with a fake ID trying to get a bottle to impress his friends.

That feeling worsened when I remembered how uneasy Glory was being in my apartment after I came home from the hospital. The anxiety radiating off of her was palpable. Hell, it was radiating off me too. Seeing thousands of dollars and hundreds of wasted days stacked against the wall was jarring.

Especially because it almost spelled the end for me. And now the liquor aisle felt like dejavu of that revelation. The habit no longer served me. I turned on my heels to find something safe to do only to feel a familiar small hand to tug on the hem of my shirt. Shit, Glory was gonna lose her fucking mind seeing me here.

"This isn't what it looks like!" I exclaimed, knowing exactly what it looked like.

"Franklin," my name came not from Glory, but from her grandmother.

She didn't have to say anything else to drive her disappointment home. Her graying brow was knit against her midnight skin and her mouth tight.

"Hi, Mama Lailah," I mumbled.

She looked me over slowly before tapping her foot. I expected to get the lecture of a life time but she simply sighed and motioned for me to follow.

"Come put these two cases of water in my cart, baby," she called.

An hour passed before I realized I was acting as her grocery assistant. I'd gotten all her out of reach can goods, loaded water, juice, and a body bag worth of rice into the cart, then helped bag everything after checkout.

"Just follow me over so you ain't gotta leave your car," Mama Lailah said.

That finally snapped me out of autopilot and I realized I had put all of the groceries in her car, even my own. This was who Glory got her Southern Belle charm from.

"Follow you where?" I asked skeptically.

Mama Lailah sucked her teeth just like Glory did before motioning me back to my vehicle.

"To Kimberly's," she answered. "Come on, boy. It's getting late nie. I gotta start on my turkey tails and collards."

"To the King's?" I stammered.

"To Kimberly's," Mama Lailah clarified. "Put some mustard on it."

I stumbled into the kitchen after Mama Lailah, arms wracked with grocery bags and rice slung over my shoulders like a fresh hunt. I hadn't been back to the King's since everything happened with Glory, but everything still felt the same. Well oiled-range, hand carved tables, yellowing overhead light. Crippling religious judgment. Everything.

"Mama! No you didn't make Frankie do your bidding!" Miss Kimberly chided.

Everything including Miss Kim.

"Girl, hush up with all that hollering and carrying on. He was already there, I just gave him somethin' to do," she replied.

Miss Kim took a few bags from me and started putting things away for her mom while they fussed at each other.

"I'm sure Frankie had his own plans," she replied.

"He ain't," Mama Lailah replied.

And I didn't. My plans for the day included consuming more sugar than a person should reasonably eat in a week while binging questionable Netflix shows.

"Besides, he need his braids done. Glory ain't doing them cause they had a falling out."

The lump of guilt swelling in my throat made it difficult to reply when Miss Kim asked what happened.

"Glory was being Glory," Mama Lailah replied. "Hardheaded and bossy. She get that from you," she said, waving towards Miss Kim.

This was after she hijacked my day with an unexpected grocery run and dinner. Lawd, denial was a river in Egypt. Me and Miss Kim exchanged a look that said exactly what I was thinking.

"Miss Kim had to get it from somebody, Mama Lailah," I mumbled.

Mama Lailah simply laughed in response before handing me an apron and three bushels of greens.

"Now you on picking duty," she smiled haughtily.

"Franklin?" Mr. King asked. "What are you doing here?"

I scraped the greens into Mama Lailah's pot so she wouldn't pop me before I turned to answer him.

"Helping Mama Lailah. We ran into each other at the grocery store."

Mr. King's face scrunched into a tight ball while he stared at the lil old woman, only she didn't care.

"I see you looking at me. I just don't give a damn. You pick out mushy ass greens, and Kim got enough going on between helping you with your sermons and grading her own student's work."

"Lailah…" he grumbled.

"Lazarus," she replied. "Don't you got something better to do? You ain't got no friends or nothing? A grown ass man with no friends… I always knew you were a lil off," she shrugged.

The tension in that room was thicker than Glory. I always knew they had their differences, but I ain't think it was that bad.

"I think I should head out," I announced.

"Good i… The food will be ready by time I finish your hair," Mama Lailah interjected, silencing Lazarus.

I watched in awe while she used one weathered hand to cut a sweet onion into the boiling pot and the other to wave Lazarus away.

"Get out or get busy, little boy," she hissed. "You see Frankie working and he ain't no less man than you."

My jaw became one with the floor, watching a lil old woman body a grown ass man in his own house. It took less than fifteen seconds for Lazarus to whisk out of that kitchen with a new attitude while Mama Lailah remained unbothered. As if this was their normal. I wondered if they had always been that way and if I had just been too young and absorbed in Glory to notice it.

"Come on. Take them braids down," Lailah directed, breaking me from my thoughts.

She offered to re-braid my hair for the help with dinner, but I would've helped either way. She was the closest thing I had to a grandmother. Her greens were also the best in all of Texas. Which is probably why Glory's were so damn fire.

"Are you sure, Mama? I don't want you over-extending yourself."

"Boy! I'm old, not vegetative. Everybody just think I'm supposed to quit my life and sit still. That's how you end up dying. I ain't gonna die of boredom. Come on nie."

I chuckled and obliged her by sitting at the table. But my mind kept wondering to her spat with Lazarus while I worked through my platted ends.

"Mama, what's you and Lazarus's beef?" I asked, unable to quiet my growing curiosity.

"We ain't got no beef. That boy a punk," she muttered. "Always hollering at my granddaughters and talking to them fucked up. Treating them like maids and treating the boys like gold. That's why they got the jitters now."

"The jitters?" I asked.

"Yeah ahn-ziety," she said, showing off that Southern Mississippi accent. "You thought it was just you who had it?"

Selfishly, yes. Glory was everything I wasn't. Outspoken, ambitious, and constantly productive. In my mind that made her normal, unaffected by internal hardship. I had taken my required psychology courses and I knew that anxiety presented differently in black women, yet I continued to let ingrained societal bias affect my perspective of my own girlfriend.

"Is it weird that she never cries?" I asked, testing a theory.

Mama Lailah hitched one perfectly arched brow in my direction, prompting me to reexamine my question.

"You don't think Gloria cries?" she replied before motioning for me to sit at the kitchen table.

I could tell by her slightly concerned tone that it wasn't so much a question, but rather a, *"You can't be that damn slow,"* statement.

"I mean, I'm sure she does. It's just really rare," I explained.

Mama Lailah snorted before wetting my hair and combing through the ends.

"Franklin, Gloria cries every single day. She'll never show it, but that girl is a bleeding heart."

"Huh?" I asked, dumbfounded.

"Mhm. Cries in the shower. That's why it takes her so long in the bathroom," she explained.

Well I now knew why she took an hour or better under running water. It made sense if she didn't want anyone to know. But why didn't she want me to know?

"Did she ever tell you why?" I asked.

Mama Lailah huffed, seemingly pained by the explanation.

"There's a price for being a strong woman. No one ever thinks you need a soft place to land."

"I don't feel like that's not true," I argued.

"Your perception and reality are two different things, Franklin," Mama Lailah sighed. "You wanted to know why, and that's why. She's been everybody's everything since the moment she started forming coherent thoughts. She's had twenty-something years for that mask of indifference to harden."

That was the nail that drove Mama Lailah's point home. Glory was masking. A skill I had perfected over the years. For as different as we were, we were also very much the same. Knowing that meant knowing I had made a monumental mistake. This was on me to fix. *Really fix.*

"Thank you," I whispered.

"Mhm," Mama Lailah hummed knowingly. "Take her a plate when you stop by."

Glory

I was done crying. Mostly. Sometimes it started up again when I let my mind idle. Embarrassment would creep across my skin while doubt settled into my stomach. Then the wretched pair would spend an hour wringing me for more tears. I would cry out of frustration, out of stubbornness, and especially because of our newfound distance. We even missed brunch for the first time ever since we started dating. It was the first in a month of

Sunday's that I'd gone without seeing his face, and it felt just like old times. I loathed those times.

Caris and Cash were working in tandem to keep my mind busy though. I had plans to eat a pound of mozzarella sticks and sob on the couch, but Caris's ass popped up with very little warning and made me get dressed. We got brunch and pedis, then I sobbed into their shirt. I was a fucked up, anxious mess. So they let me blubber for an hour before kindly suggesting I get my meds adjusted. Because they said the whole situation with Frankie and Granny reeked of unmanaged anxiety, and honestly, they were right.

I felt things getting out of hand months ago, but I wasn't ready to go on the hunt for another psychiatrist then. Or endure the grueling trial and error process of finding a new med combo. All the tapering and increases, withdrawals, or flat out medication rejections were exhausting, and I just wanted to save my energy to enjoy where I was with the boys. Although that reasoning was ultimately proved unproductive. Because I had meddled and messed everything up. *"Just like always."*

And with that pleasant thought, I was back to doom watching British baking competitions. I always found them soothing, because not gonna lie, Europeans could fuck up some pies and custards.

I was vegging out to the chaos of making four tarts in 90 minutes when there was a knock at the door. The rapping was urgent and loud, eliminating all possibility for it to be Cash Or Caris. They had no inclination to fuck up a manicure by banging on my door when they could call. Knowing that, I tried to refocus on my show and ignore it. Unfortunately, my visitor wouldn't take the fucking hint. So I threw on a robe and my stiff-ass Wanda from Holiday's Heart wig before making my way to the door. Where somebody was still banging like Twelve. I had an attitude before I could even turn the lock all the way.

"Can I…"

"Glory, hi."

Frankie. His eyes were wide and brimming with tears while his outstretched arms offered me a triple-wrapped plate with a torn cardboard note attached.

"Work that shit out, baby." -Granny.

Ah. So that's why his forehead was tucked into his braids. I knew that facelift looked familiar. I could feel his throbbing temples from here. I could feel a lot of things from here.

"Hi, Frankie," I mumbled, taking the plate.

"Hi, Essie. Can I come in?" he asked.

I didn't hesitate to nod yes. Although I made him grovel at my feet in my OG mental rehearsals of this scenario. I also had a better wig and a glass of expensive champagne in those rehearsals. I wish delusion was a resume skill sometimes.

Frankie politely removed his shoes before exhaling a lengthy, tired, sigh. It kinda triggered me because that's what Dad did every time he came home and saw us laughing, but then Frankie held my hands to ease that fear of familiarity. Now all I had to do was open my mouth and organize my hundreds of racing thoughts into a coherent sentence. Damn it. That was the hardest part. Shit like this had me wondering how I survived law school. I'm sure it was just the anxiety, but I still had to try and prove I had a working brain.

"I, um," I started.

"Essie, I'm sorry," Frankie finished.

Tears stung the corners of my eyes instantly. I was not successful in my attempt to cry it all out, and that was unreasonably embarrassing. So I tried to snatch away and run to the bathroom, but Frankie refused that me that luxury and held me firm.

"No, Essie. You can't just hide in the bathroom right now and tape everything back together until later," he admonished.

My lips curled like an old-school press and bump. He was looking at me with those rum-colored eyes, full of adoration and concern just like when we were little. It was unfair and even a little cruel.

"Let me go," I gurgled while trying to swallow emerging tears. "Let me go! Let me go!"

Frankie didn't budge so I desperately pounded against his chest in hopes that it'd mean something. Only it didn't. His big tree branch arms wrapped around me to squeeze me tight, causing me to completely unravel. Dignity was only a theory in that moment. Because I was a snotty, sobbing, slobbery mess, *and* my wig was stiff as fuck.

"I'm sorry, Essie," Frankie repeated. "I'm sorry I yelled. I'm sorry I made you feel unwanted. I'm sorry I haven't been your soft place to land. There are no excuses, I'm just sorry," he cooed.

I wanted to tell him it was ok and all was forgiven, but the only thing I could do was sniffle in response.

"Oh, Essie," Frankie sighed, before reaching to stroke my hair and then instantly retracting when he saw what I was working with.

"You took hard wig-soft life, serious huh?" he asked.

"Shut up," I scoffed, popping his arm.

"No, but seriously, Essie. You deserve better than what I've been giving you. I've been so stuck on proving myself that I failed to see you were drowning. I haven't been as patient or as understanding as I should've been. Because I wrongly assumed you had all your stuff under control and didn't need help," Frankie explained.

"I don't," I mumbled.

"Eep!" I yelped, feeling my ass cheek sting from contact with his open palm.

"Hush, woman. You do too and that's ok. Cause I wanna be your soft spot to land," Frankie replied.

Suddenly, it hit me. I was being provided a space to be vulnerable for the first time in a really long time. I was being seen, and I was being acknowledged. Two things that didn't always happen in tandem. Especially not to me. Just like that, I was crying again. Boo-hoo bawling.

"Oh, baby. C'mere," Frankie whispered, pulling me closer. "You don't have to do anything but be you to deserve love, respect, and attention, Glory. You don't have to prove you have value in abilities. You don't have to prove you're strong. You can just exist. You can just be and we'll take care of the rest."

My shoulders relaxed and I felt physically lighter. Maybe I wasn't all I had in this world. Maybe I could depend on a few people to take care of my heart. Especially Frankie and Cash. Especially right now.

"I haven't slept more than six hours in months, and I'm anxious all the time, and I hate driving, and I don't like sleeping alone, and I really really..."

"Take a breath, Essie," Frankie interjected.

I sucked in a sharp one then let my heart steady before pulling away and looking in Frankie's eyes.

"I really missed you. I know it's only been two days but it sucked," I admitted tearfully.

Frankie leaned forward slightly and pressed his tender lips to my throbbing temple. It was so reassuring I almost didn't need words, but he provided them anyway.

"I missed you too, Essie. A lot," he whispered before holding me closer.

"I'm sorry for meddling," I sniffled. "I'm just worried about you going back to work. I keep thinking that you're going to fall back into that mental space and I'll lose you. "

"I know," Frankie nodded. "Me too. But at least I only have two days this week. Then it's our weekend together. And Essie?"

"Hm?" I asked.

"You don't have anything to worry about. No part of almost losing you is an experience I care to relive. I finally got you and I'm not giving you up," he whispered.

His smooth voice coated my brain, soothing my anxiousness. But my tears fell faster instead of slowing, because he said what I needed to hear. I clung to Frankie's chest, desperate to hold him and be held.

"Stay," I pleaded.

He chuckled, then his big hands circled my waist and head to support me.

"Of course, Essie. But we need to call Cash and let him know we're ok."

"Yeah, he'll be happy to know we're going to the Halloween thing tomorrow," I sighed.

Frankie's spine became ramrod straight as soon as I said that.

"We are?" he gulped.

I could tell that he intended to escape his fate, but alas, he was granted no such luck.

"Of course," I nodded. "You're going to love our costumes."

"Shit," he grumbled.

Chapter Twenty-one

Glory

I finished curling the layers in my 613 wig just in time to watch Frankie slip his yellow and green, felt mask over his head.

"I hate you both," he grumbled while me and Cash cackled at the majesty of the full ensemble.

Just like that, he had the costume to match his grumpy personality. It was honestly the perfect choice. Frankie was definitely the Bowser of our group despite his lean muscles. A tall, cranky, dom with a kidnapping problem.

"Put me down!" I shrieked.

The hem of my frilly gown lifted with my person to expose my nearly bare thong-clad ass, which Frankie popped before taking off with me slung over his shoulder.

"Peaches, peaches, peaches, peaches, peaches. I love you, oh," he sang.

Cassius ran behind us expectantly in his own costume, very much giving Mario's fine-ass second cousin with his glowing chestnut skin, glossy fake mustache, and glove clad hands that were still adorned by his favorite Tissot watch.

"Frijoles!" Cash shouted. "You said you'd give me a head start!"

"I lied!" Frankie shouted before placing me into the Muver.

The car sped off as soon as Frankie climbed in, leaving Cassius on the curb with a furrowed brow and a lour. Just like actual Mario.

I now understood why Cash was so excited we were going. It turns out they had planned this for weeks. I wasn't privy to all the details, but I knew this night was basically role play on steroids for us.

"This is… different," Adam mumbled, looking us up and down. "Mario? Seriously?" he asked over the blaring melodies of Big Titties by Rico Nasty.

He had been at the door to observe the costumed patrons for the contest. While we were good, we definitely weren't the best. This was a gay club, and there was a group who had The Sanderson Sisters down pat. Don't even get me started on all the Chers.

"If I explain it, I might ruin your childhood," Cash warned.

Adam shrugged, thinking he was too buzzed to be affected by whatever Cash had to say.

"Go for it, Monroe," he laughed.

"There's a theory that explains Peaches' kidnapping is nothing more than a roleplaying kink for the triad Bowser, Peach, and Mario is in. That the thrill of the chase makes it more exciting to them."

"Really?" Adam laughed looking between us. "Well, that is something. I guess we'll never know."

"No, we will," Frankie cackled, as he picked me up once more to sprint away.

Even though we were moving fast, I could still hear Adam sighing loudly behind us.

"Y'all freaky as fuck," he snickered.

"What's going on?" Caris asked as Cash placed me on near them on a couch, partially occluded from the general view of the club.

It was the fourth time I'd been relocated that night, but no one was too concerned because Halloween at Adam's was always wild.

"Princess Peach kidnapping," I answered nonchalantly. "I thought Adam would've told you."

I probably would have answered someone else a little more vaguely, but Caris was not only unbothered by my odd little relationship dynamics, they also demanded to know the details.

"Is that a sex thing?" they replied.

"Probably," I shrugged. "Yes," I added, remembering Cash's kink comment to Adam.

Our loud laughter gave way to the melodic hymns of Destiny's child as an on-stage dance troupe acted out a murder scene where the black girl lived. I cheered for her as she twerked away victoriously. Then my expression settled into subtle euphoria when I saw Frankie smile at me through the crowd.

"You look really happy, Glo," Caris said, squeezing my hand.

They weren't the first one to tell me that. My mama also mentioned how happy I looked when I stopped by to have lunch with her and granny. My mama was prone to using flattery as a tactic to get you to open up, but I knew she wasn't lying to make me feel better as mothers do because I felt happy. I still had a thousand and one things to do one a daily basis, but when it came to the boys, life had been easy besides that little tiff with Frankie.

"Thanks, babe," I blushed. "I think I am."

Caris was a softie just like Frankie. They placed their hands over their tender heart with a big grin and released a satisfied, "Aww," right before Frankie plucked me from the couch and put me over his shoulder. And yes, that also made my black ass blush.

"Ok, Fab!" they cheered. "If this what y'all doing in y'all free time, we gone need to do a weekly catch up. How about brunch?"

"Brunch is kinda tradition for us," Frankie answered. "Her Saturday's are pretty free though."

The plain audacity of that nosey, lumbering, fastidious man. I was perfectly capable of telling Caris brunch was something me and the boys did together before he interrupted. Who did he think he was? You call a man daddy during sex one time…

"Stay out of Fem's business!" I chided.

"Y'all have a standing weekly brunch?" Caris laughed. "That's so gay."

"You didn't get your copy of the gay agenda?" Frankie replied. "Standing weekly brunches are the first item listed. God, Car it's 2019. Get with the times," he laughed.

Caris stood to place a kiss on my forehead before Frankie could dash off with me.

"Call me when you have some time and we'll do lunch. I'm off to see if I can get Adam to give me some head. Y'all got me riled up," they laughed.

I gasped in disbelief. I was usually the nasty one, but the tables had turned. Caris's announcement came as a surprise considering how much of the prude they used to be. But it was Halloween, the perfect time to let your demons out. So who knew what else the night had in store?

The night was fun. We had scheduled breaks in between my kidnappings so we could dance and talk. The boys were nearly neck-and-neck with Frankie slightly in the lead with four kidnaps to Cash's three. But I had a feeling that was about to change when the sweet scent of teakwood and lavender invaded my nose. *Not again.* Unfortunately I never knew when their truces were until we were in the middle of one. This game was fun and all, but a bitch needed a minute. Mostly to eat.

"Wait! Tim…"

I was snatched before I could even wrap my lips around the square of spanakopita I had just recently procured.

"Cash!" I hissed. "I was eating that!"

"Lo siento, mi Princessa. We only have five minutes left."

I sighed as Cash spun us around, searching for a hiding spot among the crowded bar patrons. The club was dimmed with blue light, but I could still see the horns of Frankie's mask wading through the crowd. He was moving in strides but staying in Cash's blind spots. I thought about warning him, but I was still mad about my snack so I stayed quiet and swung my feet instead.

"Gotcha!" Frankie cackled, attempting to slip me off Cash's shoulders.

Cassius fought a good fight with his little foam mallet, but Frankie was determined and full of brute strength, so I knew he'd probably win. Unfortunately for Frankie, the timer buzzed right before he could steal me back, ending the night in a tie.

"It's midnight already?" Frankie huffed.

"Yep. We're tied, Frijoles. Unless…"

The boys looked to me with cute-ass pouts that might have worked if I wasn't so fucking hungry.

"No, absolutely not. I'm going to stuff my face. You two rock-paper-scissor it out!" I shouted.

Finally. I ditched the boys and headed straight for the appetizer table, but it was looking a little sparser than it did ten minutes previous. The shrimp cocktails were gone, but here were still mini lobster grilled cheeses and spanakopita left. That was all I really needed. Seafood, dairy, carbs, and spinach. A love affair for the ages. Neu Roses by Daniel Caesar blasted through the speakers just as I took my first bite, and my voice synced to the hook right before one of my own transgressions entered my peripheral. Elias Oscar, weirdo fucking extraordinaire.

I ain't have inherent beef with weirdos. A lot of them were cool. Then, depending on who you asked, Frankie was a big weirdo. This nigga Elias, however, was slimey weird. Even his appearance was a red flag, specifically his eyes. Elias' eyes were dull and lifeless. It looked like the original host of his body died a decade earlier, and whatever took over the skin had begun to rot from the inside out.

"Gloria," Elias almost snarled, walking past me.

I flashed him a tepid wave, unwilling to engage in him more than I absolutely had to. I hadn't seen him since I found out what actually happened between him and Frankie. But we weren't friendly before that either. Looking back on our childhood interactions made me realize he was creepy, and that hadn't changed. So I avoided him. It was easy because no one liked him, Adam included. Which made me wonder how the fuck he got in here.

Fortunately I ain't have to wonder too long, because I heard Adam radio security to remove Elias before joining my side.

"You gotta go, miss mamas," he sighed, finger-combing my wig.

"What, why?" I asked, curious as to what he knew.

"Well."

He motioned to Frankie who was leaning against a cocktail table. Any enjoyment he might have been experiencing earlier had been washed from his expression. Then poor Cash was being completely ignored while Frankie busied himself tracking Elias in relation to me.

"I just bought these tables, babe. I love you and Fab, but that nigga can't keep busting shit up in here. The toilet paper dispenser y'all humped on was $200," Adam chided.

Heat crept onto my cheeks, nearly darkening the blush I packed on in the beginning of the night. I heard something break that night, but I figured it was just a weak hinge.

"My bad, hun. You need me to write a check?" I asked.

Adam scoffed before turning me back towards the boys.

"Girl, boo. You can pay me back by letting me be y'all brand manager when y'all start an OnlyFans. Caris wants to be the content editor," he chuckled.

The way my head snapped back in surprise should've given me whiplash. Meanwhile Adam was completely unphased, eyes sparkling and smile gleaming. He was serious as hell.

"Goodbye with your nasty ass!" I scoffed.

"Says the lady role-playing a beloved children's character for her nastiness!" he shouted as I pranced back to safety.

Not true. I was role-playing a beloved children's character for *the boy's* nastiness.

Cash knew about Elias, but hadn't been able to put a face to the name. I remember watching his skin crawl when Frankie told him what happened, yet he was the epitome of calm when I told him why we needed to leave. It was probably a facade to avoid riling Frankie's unhinged ass, but it was appreciated regardless.

"Hey, babe," he cooed while rubbing Frankie's back. "It's time to go. Muver's pulling up outside."

Frankie was still watching Elias intently, completely oblivious to both me and Cash.

"I'll meet y'all outside, I need to p…"

"You don't even use public bathrooms. Bring ya ass, nigga," Cash scolded.

Frankie was the type to hold it for ten hours straight instead of using a public toilet. He had all sorts of statistics on the families of bacteria in them, and the general public bathroom smell also didn't help. Frankie knew he'd been clocked, so he turned towards the exit with a reluctant huff.

"Fine. Let's go," he grumbled before guiding me to the doors.

I noticed the boys acting weird the closer we got to Cash's. *Real weird.* Hiding phones, exchanging looks, speaking in codes, weird. And I, super-nosey-extraordinaire, was not a fan.

"Um, what's going on?" I asked after intercepting a second nudge between Cash and Frankie.

"Nothing, we're just trying to settle the tie," Frankie responded quickly.

Too quickly in my opinion.

I stared him down like we were in a Wild West shootout only for him to laugh in my face.

"That don't work on me, Essie. Gone somewhere with all that," he chuckled.

Well damn.

Maybe I could get Cash?

"No ma'am," he said, before I could even turn his way.

"Ugh, whatever!" I grumbled. "Keep your secrets then!"

"We will," they said in unison.

Men were already frustrating and my goofy ass decided to go out and get two. What was I thinking when I agreed to this?

Oh yeah, I was thinking about dick. Don't get me wrong, the boys mean the world to me, but when I decided two boyfriends was a good idea, I was buzzed and mostly thinking about dick. Kinda like now.

"Essie, stop trying to take off my pants," Frankie admonished.

He drew me a bath while I removed my makeup, then warmed my robe and towel before carefully undressing me. I assumed he was also going to get naked, but alas, it seems I had no such luck.

"You're not getting in?" I pouted.

"No, Essie. As much as I like being pressed against your very alluring body, I am not getting in," he sighed.

I couldn't help the ugly way my face twisted. I was in a serious mood after spending my night getting lifted and carried and neither one of the boys seemed interested in relieving me. Seriously, what was I thinking?

"Don't look so sour, baby. We're just doing stuff a little different tonight," Frankie said, before once again lifting me and placing me in the tub.

I noticed I was in a bubble bath when I finally relaxed. I never got to take bubble baths growing up because my skin was so sensitive, and that was something Frankie knew.

"Different how?" I asked softly.

"Good different," Frankie replied while washing the highlight off my right arm.

"Like the bubble bath?" I asked.

He flashed me a gentle smirk and I lost my breath. I guess I'd let them have their little secrets. I had no choice but to surrender my apprehension after that. Still, Frankie amused me.

"Yes, Glory. Like the bubble bath. Do you like it?" he cooed.

I took the time to consider my answer. The water was steaming, tinted pink, and scented with alluring scents of chamomile and blackberry. Then the bubbles were abundant and so soft against my skin. I was wrapped in liquefied winter Cashmere.

"I love it," I nodded drowsily.

"Good," Frankie replied. "I made it with you in mind."

God, Franklin. My teeth were going to rot right out of my head if he got any sweeter. This man made me my own bubble bath. I can't believe I once considered avoiding him forever. Jesus, I can hold a grudge well. Maybe a bit too well.

"We're working on it." My brain reminded me.

I was released from myself criticisms by the feel of gentle fingers lacing underneath the strands of curls at my nape. Something so familiar yet so foreign.

"What are you doing?" I asked, sitting up.

"Taking down your hair," Frankie answered.

"Why?"

"To wash it," he laughed.

I had to remind myself to relax. I hadn't had my hair washed by anyone other than myself or Caris since I was seven. Then I hardly let anyone see my wig braids, let alone take them down. Still, this was Frankie. A man who'd been taking care of me in different ways my whole life. Even when I didn't want to let him.

"Thank you," I whispered as he scrubbed between my parts.

"It's my pleasure, Essie," he purred while pecking me.

Frankie slipped out the bathroom once my hair was washed, conditioned, detangled, *and* plaited. All the products he used were from a new mint and Shea butter hair care line he was developing. A line inspired by my persistent complaints about fighting with my consistently knotted hair. He seemed nervous to try them on me at first, and hell, I was too. But I have to admit he was onto something because my 4c curlies were singing. I was stressed out my mind a week ago, but tonight had made up for it tenfold.

Life couldn't get any better. Or so I thought.

"How was your bath?" Cash inquired.

He was a vision darkening my doorway wearing nothing but a pair of blue silk pajama pants and a wicked smile.

"It was nice," I replied, eyes still on the door.

"Good," he chuckled.

Cash stepped forward, falling just underneath the still of the moon-illuminated window. Strands of silver light danced across the slight sheen of oil covering his broad chest, rendering my heart all but useless.

"I think I need another one," I whispered, eyes wide and head tilted.

I watched him not-so-subtly adjust himself before padding over to the tub. He dropped his arm toward me, dragged his thick pointer finger over a few remaining bubbles that were guarding my thighs, then pulled the drain plug at my feet.

"I think you're good, Princessa. Let's restore you to your Glory," he smiled.

"Fuck," I moaned.

Every busty best friend knows about the inherent back pain that comes with having a rack. It even rhymes. If you got a rack, it comes with a bad back. I had been a victim of the chesty curse since these things grew in, but tonight the tension was eased by two strong hands and some wonderful jasmine-scented body oil.

"How's the pressure?" Cash asked.

"R-real… Really good," I blubbered in response.

He gave my shoulders one last tentative squeeze before moving down to the back of my ribs and I shuddered. I never thought a massage could feel better than sex.

"What's this about?" I asked.

Call it curiosity or maybe even cynicism, but a night full of freely given service had me wondering. I thought I'd be getting dug out right now but I was instead getting treated to an at-home spa night. It wasn't necessarily suspicious, just unexpected.

"Making you feel good," Cassius answered.

"You always make me feel good," I chuckled.

"Making you feel good in other ways, Princessa. Making you feel cared for and cherished," he replied.

Oh. That's why it felt so foreign. My relationships were strictly sexual before the boys. Like I said, it was easier that way. Even after they broke me down the first weekend, I tried to tell myself that it was just a crush and unhinged libido making me so attached to them. Until I didn't talk to Frankie for a few days. I cried the entire time and it made me realize I was previously affection starved. Most people were happy to give what I took and never reciprocate. I kept telling myself that distance and separation from love and sex was what I wanted, hell *needed*. But clearly, that wasn't the case, and I didn't know how damaging those habits were until these two knuckleheads popped into my life. I needed meaning. I needed connection. I needed them.

However, I also needed dinner. The echo of my growling stomach filled the room just as Cassius finished oiling my soles. My body was just trying to embarrass me at this point. It was bad enough I got so relaxed that I farted when Frankie scrubbed my scalp. Then now this? Luckily he only chuckled at the Whitney Houston-level performance my belly was putting on and slid my feet into new houseshoes.

Oh, my Jesus.

They were the softest things I ever stepped in. It felt like the adult version of that time when young Glory tried to make moon shoes by tapping pillows to the bottom of tissue boxes. In other words, heavenly.

What was happening? What had I done to deserve this? Was this just a really long version of foreplay?

"You're thinking about it too much, Princessa," Cash said while wrapping me in a robe.

"I am not!" I argued.

He gave me a side eye before mimicking my bottom lip, calling my attention to my quivering mouth in the mirror.

"Shut up!" I scoffed while snatching my robe closed.

Unfortunately, I couldn't quite get my bust covered, and Cassius made it known that he was looking disrespectfully. My eyes quickly darted down to the generous bulge straining against the seam of his pants. Lord, Cash had a glorious dick. Perfect for sucking. I could probably swallow the whole thing if I really tried. I'd have to belly breathe the entire time, but I could do it.

"You need to eat food, Glory," Cash clicked while guiding me to the door.

"Dick can be food," I quipped.

"Ok, cannibal concubine. Take yo fast ass in the room," he chided.

My breath hitched and my heart stopped when I stepped out of the bathroom. Frankie was also clad in silk pajama pants, his the color of smoke. The room had been decorated with a mini-hanging solar system, and a swirling Pisces constellation was projected onto the ceiling, making my eyes sparkle full of resplendent silver stars and midnight skies. I knew this vision anywhere. It was my favorite painting brought to life.

"How," I gasped, eyes brimming with tears.

I looked between the boys who briefly shared a sweet smile. I knew they were up to something, but I never imagined this. I never expected this. I never knew that people could be so considerate and thoughtful. And again, I never knew how much I wanted it.

"So," Cassius started. "We were looking through some of your work, and I noticed this one painting with a woman who looked a lot like you, sitting on Neptune."

"Then he asked me about it, and I completely nerded out while explaining your love of The Big Blue Planet and how you painted Stargazer shortly after I sent you Black Sun Signs. It was one of the only paintings you ever posted and I remembered you mentioned how healing it was for you,"

Frankie added.

For one, I never knew he sent me that book. It just appeared in my mailbox one day in a big yellow envelope with no return address. I should've been concerned, but I was instead curious and I opened it to find what would eventually become one of my favorite books. From who I now know as one of my favorite people.

I was bawling. Snotty nose, hot tears, swollen lips, blubbering. Completely and utterly wrecked. Stargazer was so long ago and my skills had grown leaps since then, but it always held a special place in my heart. I didn't think anyone noticed or cared and it didn't matter to me that much anyway, but hearing Frankie say he noticed and he cared was something magical.

"Aw, baby. Don't cry," Frankie cooed.

Him and Cash pulled me into a tight hug that stabilized my ragged breathing. Which helped me speak in a kinda-sorta coherent sentence. I again found myself asking,

"Why?"

"Well," Cash started. "You've been running around helping Mama Lailah, helping with Alayssa's baby shower, and coordinating all your donation drives without missing a beat. So we figured we'd take over for you tonight and be your Glories. Like how you are for everybody else."

That was it. I was certain life could get no better. I was blessed, lucky, fulfilled, anointed, wholly and unashamedly lost, and irretrievable in the warmth of my men's embraces. Feeling a kind of freedom I previously thought unattainable for an unrepentant sinner such as myself.

Emotions made me horny, but I still hadn't eaten and Frankie had gone all out on dinner. Smoked turkey, elotes, and maybe some kind of fruit jam? I'm not sure, but it was all delicious and itis-inducing. So we laid in a cuddle puddle afterward instead of launching into R-rated activity. Honestly, I wasn't mad. I mean, I was still horny, but being held is a form of intimacy I never tire of. Cash was wrapped around my back while I laid on Frankie's chest and we had formed a love ring with our hands resting against each other's thighs. The boys were warm, strong, and they both smelled like their own respective version of bliss. If my father's prophetic inclinations were correct, then I knew this sensation was the closest a human being could get to heaven without dying.

"Princessa, are you crying again?" Cash asked.

I touched my fingertips to my warmed cheek, pulling back to examine the warm thick tears that they were coated with.

"Happy tears," I murmured.

The boys suppressed their own versions of "aw" before they peppered my face and ears in kisses. Soft, sweet, luxuriated kisses that made me giggle. Kisses that quickly morphed into something else when my shoulder slipped out of my robe.

Cash trailed my shoulder towards my collar while Frankie concentrated on teasing the opposite direction towards my breasts. I'd never loved being me more than in that moment. Cause my entire areola was in Frankie's mouth while Cash was trying his best to leave a hickey between my shoulder blades despite my complexion. That sensation alone nearly made up for all my feminine suffering.

"Let's take this off," Cash mumbled, tugging at my robe tie.

I nodded and I was undressed that instant without having to lift a finger. Then the boys took their time undressing each other, making sure to put on a show for my eager ass. Silk was a great choice. Because the way it slid down moisturized brown skin was unfairly mesmerizing.

"We have a dilemma, Essie," Frankie cooed.

It took me a while to fully process what he said. Mostly because they were fully naked and erect and I was busy wondering if it was the day I fit two dicks in my mouth simultaneously. I was sure I could swallow them both if I *really* tried.

"Hm?" I hummed, still dazed.

The boys surrounded me on either side of the bed while looking at me with hungry eyes. They were looking at me like starving jaguars eyeing a fattened hog.

"See, whoever won tonight was supposed to take the lead, but we tied," Cash explained.

"Oh yeah," I nodded.

"Yeah," Frankie purred, tipping my chin. "It's too late for a tiebreaker, so now you're stuck with two doms and we've decided we're just gonna fuck your tight little holes until you pass out."

"Again," Cash added.

"Right. Again," Frankie agreed.

That's right. I passed out the first time we all fucked. Not sure how I forgot, but I'd bet I had a mini-stroke from cumming so hard. They inched closer and my bedroom suddenly felt like a Casting Couch video gone off script. I trusted the boys, but being that out of control made me nervous as hell.

"W-wait, come again?" I stuttered.

"Cum as much as you want, Princessa," Cash cooed. "Can I?" he asked while separating my thighs.

Cassius's warm skin on mind was addicting, and although I was still nervous to get fucked into literal oblivion, I managed a nod.

"Don't you wanna cum all over us, Essie?" Frankie asked, sensing my hesitation.

Of course, I did, but I wanted to remember it this time. Then again, leaking all over the boys was my favorite pastime. Especially when their bodies dominated mine and left me breathless and sore.

I quickly nodded again only to be met with a reprimanding scoff.

"Aht, aht. Words, baby," Frankie purred.

Damn it! This is the problem with doms! They want absolute consent all the damn time. I just wanted to be filled with no questions asked. This was too much. The entire night had been one giant panty-drenching tease. Then the glide of their hands against my thighs and curves was driving me mad.

"Yes," I whined.

"Yes, what?" Cash chuckled while nipping my ear.

Frankie took my distraction as an opportunity to tease me further by gently sweeping his thumb over the hood of my clit. My nerves ignited, sending a surge of electricity straight to my sex-starved brain. I tilted my hips, chasing more of the promising pleasure to no avail. Frankie rescinded his touch with a hitched brow that urged me to answer.

"Please," I begged softly.

"Please what, Essie?" he grinned.

"Please touch me. Please fuck me. Please let me cum all over y'all," I whimpered.

Pride? Out of stock. Dignity? In shambles. Pussy? Soaked.

"Say no more," Cash chuckled.

I found myself in a fold I previously thought impossible. I was spatchcocked like a roast chicken with Cash licking my pussy underneath me, and Frankie behind me licking my ass. I think I was supposed to be sucking Cash, but I was too overwhelmed to do anything besides pump his length and give him the occasional lick. Frankie's tongue expertly traced the sensitive ridges of my ass while Cash sucked my clit like a watermelon Dum Dum pop. Then two different pointer fingers eased into my tight pussy, both eager to stroke my slick walls, and I was eager to accommodate them.

"Yesss," I purred.

There was soft romantic jazz blaring over the speakers, yet I only heard my soul being sucked out of my body. I was literally being swallowed alive and tortured, yet I hoped it never stopped. The boys clearly shared my sentiments since they pulled release after release from my shuddering, limp body. Still, I wanted more. I needed someone inside me.

"Fuck me," I begged. "Please."

Frankie stood with a demented chuckle before pressing his tip to my sticky-wet entrance while Cash remained otherwise occupied.

"Aw Essie, you want me inside you?" he teased while rubbing his rigid head over my slit.

I was in no mood for games, so I tried to take matters into my own hands by backing my ass down Frankie's length. However, my hips were locked in place by Cash who was still underneath me.

"Not so fast, sweetheart," Frankie chided. "If you wanna get fucked, tonight's on our terms."

I loved Frankie but I really fucking hated doms. Be good, this. Eat your fruit, that. I fuck you when I feel like it. Blah blah blah.

Yet I was still willing to comply. God, they had ruined me.

"What do you want?" I whined.

"First off, fix your tone," Frankie barked before popping my ass.

The sting of his palm brought me closer to a new edge and my pussy clenched tight, immediately aching from the emptiness. I got my act together quickly after that.

"I'm sorry," I pouted sweetly. "I need it."

"Aw, baby. I know. I know you need that hot lil pussy filled. So here's what's gonna happen," Frankie purred while bending over my back.

"You gone open that pretty little mouth of yours and let Cash inside first. And if I like the way your cheeks look while full of my boyfriend's dick, then I'll fuck you."

I just know somebody at Merriam-Webster was scrambling to put Franklin Myer-Smythe's picture underneath the definition of nasty, because that made me blush. *Me.* An OG who fucked in offices and at glory holes. I can't believe he had me squirming. Or maybe that's just because Cash was still sucking my clit. The heat from his tongue was mesmerizing. So I accepted that as the reason when my mouth dropped to release a breathless scream. How was I supposed to suck dick with such a distraction?

"Frankie. I can't," I whined.

"Yes you can, baby. If you wanna get fucked, then two of your holes need to be filled with us at all times tonight. We wanna see you full and wide open. Are you gonna let us have that, sweetheart?" he asked.

I nodded weakly while my body was wrecked with another belligerent orgasm. Then Cash lifted his mouth from me and granted me temporary reprieve with a gentle command.

"Let me inside, Princessa," he cooed.

My eyes were trained on Cash's polished member while I caught my breath. The veins straining against his skin were glistening with precum that was oozing down his length. He looked delicious, like a phallic maple-glazed longjohn. I parted my lips, eager to prove he tasted as good as he looked, and sunk down his shaft.

"Mmm," I moaned, nuzzling his base.

Franklin's idyllic moan harmonized with mine when he eased inside of me. Cussing inch by inch until he was fully buried. Sex had always been my vice, but Hoe my God, I was officially ruined. The slight sting of his dick stretching me open while Cash fucked my throat and laved my clit was bliss.

"Look at you, Essie," Frankie purred. "So tight and full. You look so pretty with your mouth wrapped around Cash, baby."

I whimpered. Ok, more like gurgled. The caption would have read, "unintelligible sound," but still. Who could blame me? I was getting fucked and eaten at the same damn time. I was more sensitive than I ever thought possible, and every push, pull, and stroke made me melt into a hormone-driven high. My eyes fluttered uncontrollably while Cash used Frankie's momentum to thrust in and out of my mouth. I was too overwhelmed to focus on one thing, yet I was too mesmerized to look away. I had to bear witness to the madness of it all.

Then Frankie got stiffer. He hadn't stopped cussing since he started stroking, but his string of expletives were suddenly replaced by exhausted grunts. His strokes got faster and one of Cash's hands left my hip to cradle Frankie's sack. I was convinced that was the only thing stopping him from trying to fill me literally balls deep when his hand replaced the spot on my hip Cash has abandoned. Everything was tightening. Hands, pussies, sacks. I noticed Cash swelling with an impending release when I gave his nuts the same treatment, and I knew we wouldn't be long. Which was good because I was one breath closer to passing out.

I looked up, noticing the glint of Frankie's slugs in a mirror placed in front of me. Sweat sheened our skin and moonlight reflected off our jewelry, making the vision of our love-making akin to an impressionist painting of marbled browns and hazy golds. It was intoxicating to watch us move in complete harmony and indulge our most hedonistic desires. It was almost peaceful to see the dopey look in my eyes as I watched myself be dominated and used. Suddenly the warmth in my core intensified. It crept down my belly and thighs like a vining ivy, wrapping around my sex with concerning consumption. My orgasm started and the cursing was back. This time coming from both Cash and Frankie.

"Fuck, Glory," they snapped and growled.

I relished the feel of their rough grips tightening around my hips and hair, forcing me to take everything they had with no chance of reprieve. It was euphoric the way they commanded me. So I finally let go of everything. Fear and anxiety alike. My orgasm came first, soaking both of them like I wanted, then Cash came down my throat in hot bursts, then finally Frankie. Who narrowly succeeded in pulling out to cum on my ass and into Cash's open mouth. I came again while watching it all, and that's when I knew I was definitely a succubus.

"That was..."

"Everything," Cash sighed.

Frankie nodded and I released a satisfied breath before attempting to pull myself upright. Only to be stopped.

"Where do you think you're going?" Cash asked.

His voice was raspy from his constant moaning, yet still creamy and undulating. But his eyes? They were charged with undeniable lust and want, despite the taste of his release still lingering on my tongue.

"To freshen up?" I half-asked.

"No ma'am," Frankie chuckled before rearranging my body.

"No?" I asked, genuinely confused.

"That's right, Princessa. No," Cash purred.

"Why not?" I inquired.

"We said until you pass out, baby. You're still very much alert," he growled.

His hand cupped my now exposed breast, massaging it until my nipple pebbled against his palm.

"You were serious?" I moaned as Cash's hardening dick rubbed against my sensitive folds.

"Very," Frankie answered while stroking his member. "Open wide for me, Essie. You got a busy night ahead of you, sweetheart."

I opened my mouth eagerly to taste my essence on Frankie's skin. Then I shuddered when both boys sank into me. It was a busy night indeed. I just wished it was a Friday.

Chapter Twenty-two

Cash

Ugh. Fucking Friday. Fridays are back to being my least favorite day, and let me tell you why. First thing, no matter what occupation and/or title you hold, Friday is the least productive day of the week. Everyone exerted most of their energy making it until Wednesday or Thursday, and therefore the focus has shifted to the weekend by Friday. Then for me and Glory, Friday is basically a half day for judges and bailiffs. If it's not said and done by noon, it's waiting until Monday. Don't even get me started on meetings. Friday meetings are the epitome of, "This could have been an email." Friday is basically added on to the work week for production value, and I'd rather be treating it like the weekend day it is rather than listening to Vick Spencer drone on about average appeal rates.

"And lastly, due to company budgetary constraints, associates and junior partners making $150,000 or greater will not be eligible for a salary increase this quarter."

Err. The record playing in my head scratched before coming to a stop.

What the fuck did this cheap bastard mean, *"Will not be eligible for a salary increase?"*

"Excuse me," I said, throwing my hand in the air. "Are you able to elaborate on the reasoning for such a decision?"

It was clear by the increasingly confused looks circulating in the room that hardly anyone was listening. S&D's announcement would have slid right on by, buried by the monotonous recitation of projections and table data if I hadn't been paying attention. Friday's Absentminded Fuckery struck again. I knew I had asked the right question when Vick gave me a sly "fuck you" smile before once again finding his seat at the end of the table.

"We're in the business of staying in business, and in order to do that, we will have to make adjustments," he explained rather calmly.

"Right, I understand," I nodded. "It's just, it targets a very specific group of us. Excuse me if this sounds ostentatious, but $150,000 is not a lot of money in this economy when you have loans to repay and a family to support. Additionally, many of us work here for decades before ever seeing that kind of money. So it almost feels like we're being punished for being loyal and working hard."

Strained murmurs and glances joined the conversation as my coworkers realized the validity of my argument. I don't consider myself a glutton, however this decision had very real effects on the very real human beings under this dirt bag's employ. Then again, maybe my concern was a little selfish. It wasn't just mine and my mother's occasional needs I had to meet. I had Glory and Cash to worry about now too. Especially if we decided to have kids someday soon. As soon as Vick made his little announcement I realized **I** was becoming one of those people with a family to provide for.

Vick's usually lax jaw tightened while he glared at me. Eyes icy blue and unremorseful. The disdain was intense and evident, and I might have even backed down if I was the pussy nigga he took me for.

"I can certainly understand the concern surrounding such a sensitive topic, but I can assure you this decision was not made lightly. We have the best interest of all of our employees and have approached this solution after careful deliberation. "

Yeah, deliberation of the profits and the interest of his wallet. His traitorous ass fucked his brother's wife. I highly doubted he gave a fuck about the people he considered below him. Luckily, so did my coworkers. Hands shot in the air with the urgency of a Tuesday conference while their accompanying questions filled the room, but Vick was still slick.

"I appreciate all these thoughtful questions, but we've actually gone a bit over on time. So please feel free to drop them in the town hall slack channel and we'll do our best to address them," he said curtly.

Ha. I'd been working in corporations since I was seventeen years old and I knew that dismissal anywhere. That's professionalese for, *"Fuck y'all, you can't change my mind."*

Vick then turned back to me with a set jaw and a lackluster smirk after addressing the chaos I created.

"And Cassius, I'll be meeting with you directly before the end of the day," he nearly growled.

Fuck, that one needed no translation. Everyone could see I had put a target on my back.

I left the office early after an uncharacteristically lengthy private conversation with Victor Spencer. Simply put, I had blown up his spot. It was clear that S&D was banking on the announcement going unnoticed and they were unprepared for the push back it was now receiving due to my decision to speak out. So for that, I was reminded to ensure I aligned myself with company interests and remain competent in the responsibilities of my current role if I didn't want to face the possibility of demotion. In other words, sit down and shut up or hit the door. Yeah, fuck Fridays.

I was a chin hair's width away from just saying fuck S&D, poaching my clients, and quitting in a belligerent haze, but Friday reminded me of what was waiting for me at home. Friday was the start of our group hang. This week had been deemed Frijoles Friday in honor of the vegetarian dinner Glory had prepared for us. Three-bean chili with cornbread. She said we were getting older and we needed to focus more on macro nutrients like fiber. She almost sounded like Fab when he gripped about the importance of eating colors. I guess his lectures had been working on both of us. God, I loved that man.

Shit.

I realized I was in love. I was in love with a boy at that. I mean, he was a gentle and kind boy who rubbed my back while he cooked, sang along to Sade, and did everything in his anxious, number-crunching power to ensure my happiness. But a boy nonetheless. A boy who I honestly couldn't picture living without. A boy whose gold-adorned smile lit up my entire soul. *My boy.* I was so concerned about Glory swallowing my goofy ass whole, that I completely forgot to watch for Fab. And now my heart was hammering in my chest, seemingly unable to contain my recent revelation.

Yet I had to. Partly because I didn't know how to express it, and partly because I didn't know if the feeling was mutual. Plus I wasn't there with Glory either. Which made me feel a way. Now I know relationships move at different paces, but sometimes I felt like a third wheel. I know for a fact that they loved each other cause they said it all the time. The twinkle in their eyes told me they meant it too. So I was starting to feel like I was interrupting something real between Glory and Fab. I was out of my element in more ways than one lately.

"Cassius!"

I was bombarded with lip gloss kisses and sultry scents as soon as I stepped off my porch. The house smelled like slow-simmered cumin, tomatoes, and freshly baked bread. It also smelled like Glory, who was too busy peppering my face to notice my previously sour mood.

"Hi, Princessa," I sighed.

I thought I was doing a decent job at compartmentalizing and neutralizing my issues, but then Glory pulled away like I had the cooties.

"What's wrong?" she asked, soft voice inundated with genuine concern.

Is there a good way to tell someone, *"I'm in love with you and every day we spend apart feels like I'm being torn to shreds and rebuilt, but I fear you may not feel the same way because our boyfriend who I also love is probably your actual soulmate and I'm just something fun for now?"* Probably not. So I just went with,

"Shitty day at work."

I was guided into the kitchen where a huge pan of honey glazed cornbread sat. Glory made quick work of cutting it into perfect squares before hand-feeding me a piece.

"Tell me about it," she requested.

Damn. Her cornbread damn near tasted like cake. It was fluffy, butter-rich, and sugary. Kind of like her. I was almost sad when I finished my piece. Luckily Glory gave me another after I told her about the meeting.

"So what, it's just basically fuck y'all?" she asked in disbelief.

"Basically," I nodded.

"Wow. I'm sorry, my love."

My love? Was I tripping? Did she love me? Did she slip up? I wanted to process that but she continued the conversation so quickly that I thought I was hearing things.

"Have you considered maybe opening your o…"

She was interrupted by the chime of the front door. In walked Frankie with disheveled, unbraided hair and glassy eyes. Fab was usually pressed and dressed when he went to work, and he tried to remain that way.

"Hey, are you ok, babe?" I asked, sensing his apparent anguish.

He didn't answer. Glory tried to follow up and he ignored her too. He simply washed his hands, knocked back a bottle of water, then picked up two pieces of cornbread. One for each hand.

Then it got weirdly quiet for the three of us. Freakishly quiet.

"Fab," I urged again, seeing discomfort etching itself into Glory's features.

"What's up?"

He took a break from dual-wielding his cornbread to finally look up at us. The confusion scrunched into his eyebrows told me he wasn't even aware we had been talking to him.

"Oh, sorry. I had a long day," he said, swallowingly thickly. "My bad y'all."

So we were all having rough days. Ok. Understandable. Shit always got weird towards the end of the year. Especially with corporations. Especially with black people.

"Wanna talk about it?" I asked.

Frankie shrugged before sweeping his crumb fallout into his hand.

"Nah. It ain't nothing important. I just quit my job is all," he said calmly. A little too calmly if I'm being honest. Luckily I wasn't alone in the feeling.

"Huh!?" Me and Glory exclaimed in tandem.

Frankie

I'm what I like to call an optimistic grouch. I'm always secretly hopeful that things will work out, but I know better than to let it show. No one needs to see the physical proof of my sanguineness, but it's nice knowing I'm not completely dead inside. I'm like if Oscar lived in a recycling bin instead of a garbage can. Trash, but make it renewable.

So when I popped into work on Thursday, I naively hoped everything would be how I left it. Instead, I walked into a garbage fire that somehow developed an infestation of flying cockroaches covered in shit. The entire department had disintegrated without my presence. No budgets had been revised. No expenses were cataloged. No bills paid. The only thing Curtis ensured got done was the deposits. Then, to make matters worse, someone had "accidentally" leaked the reason for my leave. I had everything from alcohol-free beer suggestions to full-blown AA meeting invites. To say I was irritated and overwhelmed was an understatement.

But again, optimism. So I went in Friday with a new attitude and Thursday's scowl, only to find both ineffective for the new pile of shit thrown on my lap.

"Good to see you back in action Fab," Curtis said, plopping a stack of files on the corner of my already overcrowded desk. It wasn't even 10am and I was already burnt out.

I gave him a grunt, hoping he'd go away and let me run my budget projections in peace, but my dear uncle instead pulled up a chair.

"So we need to talk about your leave," he continued.

"What's there to talk about? All my paperwork was sent and signed," I replied.

Curtis scoffed as if I said something to make his unwashed ass itch. Then he gave me the "you really don't know?" look before I became frustrated and raised my brow to coax his point so I could get back to losing my fucking mind in the mess of accounts.

"Yeah, I know. I know about your paperwork. I made sure Mindy got it back to you in a timely manner cause we kin. That's what kin do. They look out for each other. I thought you'd return the favor and end your lil vacation early, but you just said fuck us," he exclaimed.

My lil vacation? This nigga said it like I was backpacking through Europe for three months. Floating on canoes, fucking in Amsterdam, and eating lemon prawns.

I wasn't.

I was trying to recover after having a tube shoved down my throat to save my body from shock. I was trying to remember what happiness felt like. I was trying to live because I almost squandered my chance to.

"I almost died," I whispered.

"Yeah, I hear you Fab. But..."

I tuned Curtis out as my mind finally came to grips with what really could have been my unfortunate reality. Franklin Jameson Myer-Smythe, 31 years old, husband to nobody, father to no one, tolerated only for his usefulness. Survived by Glory, the only person to ever hold his hand. The only person to ever love him. That was almost how my story ended. No

Cash. No inside jokes. No nothing.

"I almost died," I repeat again, this time almost laughing.

"I almost died, and you got the audacity to feel some kind of way cause I ain't ignore my needs and put your shit first!?" I shouted.

The cubicles rattled from the bass in my voice, and normally that'd be enough to shock me back in submission, but a decade of silent enduring had broken my reserves.

"Aye, calm all that loud shit down," Curtis gritted, sensing my coworkers' interest.

I looked around the room at what would have been my legacy if not for Glory. Gray low pile carpet swimming in mysterious brown stains, a windowless cubicle, and a never-ending pile of someone else's problems.

"I'm done," I chuckled.

"W-what?" Curtis stammered.

I watched his internal panic appear on his face briefly before he shook his head, attempting to dismiss my statement.

"You can be done for to..."

"Naw. You ain't hearing me. I quit. Fuck this."

"You can't just quit, Fab. You know we got an agreement in place."

The agreement? Right, my indentured servitude. Yeah, no.

"We ain't got shit in place but a whole lotta bad blood, nigga. I quit. Fuck you and your brother. Fuck this office. Fuck that investment. You can't hold nothing over me. I'll be a legal snitch and whistle blow for I come back in this hoe."

"Oh, I can't hold nothing over you? What about that Cuck situation you got going on with Glo..."

I was on his ass before he could utter the second syllable of her name. All my life I've been non-confrontational. I practically coined the term Gentle Giant. Letting shit slide was a pillar of my personality. Except for any-and-everything concerning Glory. I'd become Heath Ledger's Joker for her. Leading me to then. Standing in a mildewed office building with my hands wrapped around my uncle's thick neck, fingers itching to end it all. Luckily, logic found me. I couldn't choke Curtis' pitiful ass, let alone kill him. Doing so would make my life a thousand times more complicated, and I was finally ready for peace. I was ready to heal.

"Mention Glory again and I'll set your life on fire. Stay out my way and I'll stay out yours. You understand?" I snarled.

I had years of information and evidence documenting everything from property and wire fraud, to tax evasion, to money laundering. Enough to put him in jail for two lifetimes. So Curtis would be a fool not to take me for my word. He nodded his head quickly, and I threw him back on the ground just in case his bitch ass pissed himself as he had done during fights previous.

Then I left.

I tried to will myself to go back to the apartment and start on a plan, but I instead found myself in Leigh-Hold Park, walking through the gardens. Parks always brought me peace. Probably because Glory is a big outdoor person and she used to force me on hikes with her despite my insistence that the statistical probability of us getting bitten by ticks was abnormally high in our state. I started taking evening walks at fourteen and everyone found it odd that a teenager would spend precious free time that way, but it made me feel close to her. It was a way to stay sane when I had to go home and be without her. A personal Glory pick-me-up.

Fuck.

I could have used one of those in that moment, cause my lungs seized up the moment I realized I was unemployed. I had been working more than half of my life, and then suddenly, I wasn't? My mind immediately itemized an invoice for everything I needed to pay for. Rent, clothes, food, business supplies, gifts for my partners, trips I wanted us to take, shit to torture them with. I still had a few thousand to make it through the winter and perhaps get the ball rolling with the apothecary line. But for all intents and purposes, I was broke with no job. I was a bum.

Again.

I briefly considered walking into the street and seeing which way oncoming traffic carried me until I remembered the concern on both their faces when I insisted on going back to work. They were nervous, scared even. I knew I couldn't validate that fear. I couldn't do that to my loved ones. Still, I wasn't ok, but this time I knew I needed help. So a quick Google search landed me in Fort Worth at a black-owned therapy practice.

"Hi, can I help you?" the receptionist asked.

It took me a minute to process her question since I was zoning out. It seemed like every square inch of available space in this office was covered in plants. The greenery calmed me instantly, and my thoughts slowed.

"Si…"

"Sorry. Do you all take walk-ins?" I inquired, cutting her off.

She started to sigh before a flip switched, and then a light of an idea flickered almost visibly above her head.

"Not typically, but we do have a new associate with an open schedule if you're comfortable with a male therapist?"

"Yeah, absolutely," I nodded. "But um…"

I trailed off, considering the best way to pose my question. Unfortunately, the socially appropriate way never came.

"I'm broke. So what can I get for $50?" I asked sheepishly.

The receptionist, who I named Tina in my mind once again started to sigh. Except she didn't stop herself this time.

"Sir, I'm not trying to be funny, but I'm not the Flo with the name your price tool."

Ah, so her name was Flo. She definitely didn't look like a Flo.

"You may need to find a practice that does sl…"

She paused with a new idea illuminating her eyes, then held out a single finger before picking up the office phone.

"Hey, Jer. You wanna try that sliding scale experiment right now?" she asked.

Something was said before she gave me a one-over, then she asked another question.

"Sir, how much do you make a year?"

For the first time, the answer was,

"Zero. I don't have a job at the moment," I answered.

The first human reaction I got to that statement was probably the oddest.

"Perfect," she squealed.

An hour later I was down $50, up a therapist, and equipped with enough de-escalation skills to avoid an all-inclusive grippy sock vacation. That made me wish I'd gotten therapy sooner. Plus Jeremiah was cool as fuck, and very professional and respectful when I told him I was in a poly-pocket. To be completely honest, I've only told one other person, and that was my lawyer friend. He ain't say anything outright, but his usually aloof demeanor oozed judgment. It was an interaction that exposed an uncomfortable truth. Polyamory still wasn't normalized and accepted. So it was safe to say I was a little apprehensive to tell a man who was a $50 stranger that I had two partners. However, he just said,

"That's awesome! More people to love and support you," and kept it pushing.

The only downside to seeing Jeremiah was the whole cost thing. I didn't have insurance, nor a job, so maintaining regular appointments would be difficult. But I after a panic attack in the middle of his office, I knew it was something I needed, and had to plan for. I was done putting me on the back burner.

Yet I put a pin in my life planning and drove to Cash's. It was our weekend together and Glory had cooked. Glory had always been an amazing cook, she just rarely chose to use those skills. I'm not completely sure why, but I kinda think it's kind of in protest to how Lazarus raised her and Halle. While I think it's sad, I also understand. If Lazarus had it his way, she'd be a barefoot housewife with a horde of crumb-snatchers and I just couldn't see that for her. Glory wouldn't be Glory if she'd let herself fall into a routine of domestication. And I love that woman.

I sat in the car for a bit, wondering how to tell the loves of my life that I was once again without anything useful to do. But then I saw Cash pull up. He waited in his car for a while too. I could see angst twisting his handsome face into a heartbreaking lour, then he tapped his head to the steering wheel a few times before getting out. I kinda felt like a sleazebag for watching my boyfriend struggle, but I also didn't want to interrupt whatever he was processing. Cause when Glory greeted him at the click of his keys, I watched him put on a mask so thick it was scary. He instantly discarded his issues for her, and there I was, likely about to contribute to it.

"That'll do it." I thought, as I slipped into another heart gripping anxiety attack.

That little episode led me to now. Where I was truly not in reality, but still acutely aware that my announcement worried my partners. Then I said the most unhelpful thing you can say in a high-stress situation.

"Don't freak out," I replied.

Cash left the room in a huff after shooting me a bombastic side-eye. That truly was the worst thing to say.

"Frankie, baby, what happened?" Glory asked.

I needed to ground myself, so I did that ghetto power ranger pose Jeremiah taught me. New coping skills activate! I had recently run into some hard truths. I got on Glory for being Saint-Save-A-Sucker when I did the same thing. Saving other motherfuckers absorbed that last decade of my life. Why did I even decide that was my responsibility?

"I realized my family uses me and I didn't want to waste my life there, with Curtis, so I quit."

"I'm sorry," I whispered, realizing how impulsive that was.

I quit a guaranteed job with no backup plan or readily available alternative. I was just doing shit. Stressing my partners out. Putting Glory back in fix-it mode. God, I felt like shit. I wanted to express that, but then Essie shook her head and distracted me.

"No," she mumbled tearfully.

"N-no?" I stammered.

She nodded in agreement,

"No apologies. You did the right thing."

It definitely ain't feel like it. It felt like yet another mark in my Big Book Of Fuck Ups. I was about to run out of room at this point.

"But, I'm broke," I mumbled. "Like, dog food for dinner, broke."

Suddenly Cash was back and actively pulling me into a hug huddle. I expected him to fuss me out but he instead seemed relieved. *Really* relieved.

"Shut up, Frankie. We'll figure it out. You're worth more than a check to us," he cooed.

I had just acquired a fancy new set of de-escalation skills, but I couldn't help but revisit ole' reliable. Joking to escape tense situations.

"Right. How could I forget I'm also dick?" I laughed.

That got me popped and pinched before soothing kisses were placed in the same spots. Then we squeezed tight, coiling around each other like a pile of warm cats.

"We got this," Cash affirmed, with Glory nodding in agreement.

I was still anxious as hell. Still unsure. Still cynical. But the light shining in my love's eyes told me we really did have this, and that was enough for me.

Chapter Twenty-three

⧫

Frankie

One thing I could never get enough of? Holding Glory. I'm generally not great at cuddling because I'm incapable of sitting still for periods longer than five minutes, but I could have her in my arms for a lifetime. Don't get me wrong, I like holding my boyfriend too, but he liked to get up at the ass crack of dawn to do yoga and read the news. Whereas I adopted a semi-night owl routine since quitting Curtis'. That left us with a very limited window in between my lying down and his getting up. But my little snuggle bug Glory? She'd remain asleep for as long as someone was holding her.

Unless her phone was ringing.

"Fuck."

I thought about silencing it and blaming it on Cash and his hatred for sudden loud noise, but he was already gone to work. Glory was off so she could drop off a few things to the women's shelter, and I hoped we'd get to sleep in since the last few weeks had been so busy, but no such luck awaited me. Besides, it was Marcus calling and he hardly ever called Glory to bother her.

"Hello?" she squeaked after I reluctantly passed her the phone.

Her voice was dry and her eyelids still fluttered with drowsiness, threatening to snap shut at any given moment, until he said the thing she'd been waiting to hear all month.

"SHE'S HERE!?" she screeched.

Glory leaped out of bed with the energy of a coked-up Energizer bunny because her niece was here. Her usually well-organized room became a tornado of outfits, wigs, and accessories as Marcus relayed the story of Penny's birth. Then, upon hearing that they were at home, accepting visitors, she settled on a pair of my jogging pants and one of Cash's sweatshirts.

"Frankie! Come on, get dressed!" she exclaimed.

I laughed because she didn't even ask, not that I minded. It only took once for Glory to tell me she hated driving and I was happy to be her chauffeur. The first few times she seemed embarrassed to ask, so I started doing it automatically only for her to try and fight me on it. But today was different. There was no embarrassment, excessive apologies, or petty fights. It was just me, my passenger princess, and sweet nibbles of our shared raspberry bear claw as we made our way over to Fort Worth.

While Glory left home at the first opportunity presented, Marcus and his wife Alayssa stayed in the neighborhood we grew up in. That meant he was 10 minutes away from the King's and just up the street from my parents. Personally, that sounded like my worst nightmare, but I guess he had his reasons. Reasons he wasn't keen on disclosing.

"Fab! I see Glory put you to work," Marcus said, greeting both us and the mountain of gifts I was lugging. I had four boxes of organic diapers, lovies galore, and a truly innumerable amount of pink and frilly clothes piled onto my arms while she held a basket for Alayssa.

"Always," I laughed.

Fed up with our apparently lengthy pleasantries, Glory pushed Marcus out of the way like he weighed nothing and headed inside.

"Rude!" he shouted.

"Ain't nobody here to see you, Otis!" she yelled back.

And with that, we were banished to unpacking all of the baby shit.

"How's fatherhood?" I asked, passing Marcus a pack of diapers.

We hadn't hung out in a year or better. Partially because he and Alayssa were growing their family, partially because I was busy drowning my sorrows in liquor, and also partially because I was now knocking the Sonic Rings out of his sister in a way that made me ashamed to look him in the eye.

"Honestly? Kind of otherworldly," he sighed.

That wasn't really what I expected. Out of all the times I asked a new dad how it was, they never answered otherworldly.

"How so?" I replied.

Marcus placed his work on the ground and sat down beside me. The action was so familiar, reminding me of all the time we used to spend together.

"It's different during pregnancy, you know? You got all these unrealistic expectations of the type of parent you'll be. I'll never let my kids… blah, blah, blah. But when they come out, and you see all the love your wife poured into making this tiny person who has your same face. It's…."

"Humbling," I finished.

"Yeah, exactly. Humbling. How'd you know?"

It was funny. I actually didn't want children for a really long time. My parents weren't parents and I never wanted my children to suffer that same brand of emotional immaturity. Then I turned twenty-five. I was seeing this alt boy who was really into shrooms. He told me that shroom sex was unbelievable, and me being curious, I tried them. He was right, the sex was unbelievable, but so were my dreams. I saw Glory, pretty, pregnant, and round. Then I blinked and she was lying in a hospital bed, wrapped in white, handing me a baby. My little chocolate drop had wild-spiraled hair, bottom-heavy lips, and wide, curious eyes. Just like their mama. I cooed, causing them to look me right in the face, and in the moment, I felt exactly what Marcus was describing.

Humility of the utmost degree. Peace, and a kind of happiness I've yet to replicate. All thanks to the efforts of the woman I loved.

"Just a hunch," I shrugged haphazardly.

Me and Marcus fell back into an easy rhythm as we unboxed everything. We talked about everything from the trash TV the girls made us watch, to the vacations we planned on taking, to how business was going. Funny enough, none of the Kings knew what Marcus did for a living. Now I had heard the theories. He got everything from CIA officer, to construction worker, to dope dealer, and even sugar baby. And knowing what he actually did made that last one particularly hilarious.

"So, I see you out here trying to be Bed Bath And Beyond and shit," he started.

"Wrong store," I laughed. "Niggas is selling candles, not overpriced towels."

"You know what I mean," he said with a wave.

"Do I?" I smiled.

I got chin checked.

"Point is, I'm proud of you. I always knew you were gonna be my sister's rich husband," he chuckled.

"Cash is her rich husband," I corrected. "I'm her well-off husband. I can afford a 3 bedroom 3 bath in a decent school district. Cash can afford Beverly Hills and pre-Harvard."

We both laughed, but it was true. Sometimes it felt like Cash was Target and I was Walmart. Albeit, the good Walmart on Lyndon B Johnson, but a Walmart nonetheless.

"Speaking of, how's it going with Cash?" Marcus asked while mating the tiniest pairs of socks I've ever seen.

I was so shocked that I almost dropped the lamp I was freeing.

"What?" I replied, my flabber clearly gasted.

"How's it going with your boyfriend?" Marcus clarified.

Ok, so he did ask what I thought he asked. Not sure why it threw me off guard so bad, but I think I just expected general disinterest from others when it came to my relationship with Cash. Don't get me wrong, no one was busting out my windows or throwing rocks at me for liking boys, but homophobia was still around, often in the form of disassociation.

"You wanna hear about my gay shit?" I asked.

"Yeah, bruh. I mean, Ion need to hear about you bending nobody over. But, yeah. Tell me how it's going. We're friends and I wanna be a part of your life," he shrugged.

Glory and Marcus had a lot in common. I mean, duh, they were siblings, but even the subtle way they showed genuine interest and love was familiar. Because not only was he the first person I talked to in a long time to ask about how things were going with Cash, but he also sat and listened to me tell him about every date, smile, and cheesy joke between me and my boyfriend. And if that's not love between friends, then I don't know what is.

Glory was too busy doting on Alayssa and Penny to pay us any mind so we'd been taking the time to catch up. Outside of entering his fatherhood era, he'd also been doing some programming work on the side and working to get rid of Halle's husband. Honestly, I understood. Chris was bottom barrel and I don't think anyone pictured someone like him for the King's youngest daughter, but that's what happens when you let your parents run your life. Speaking of...

"Aye, your phone's ringing again," Marcus pointed out.

It nearly killed me to stifle that sigh. My phone rang six times in the last hour. I had missed calls from three different numbers, but it was the same person each time.

"Oh, is it?" I asked, pretending to be dumbfounded. "I guess let me answer."

"Hi, Mom. What's up?" I sighed.

I hadn't talked to either of my parents since quitting Curtis's. Mostly because I didn't have the bandwidth for their interrogation or gas lighting.

The thing is, Glory never liked my parents. Not even as a little girl, and especially not as an adult. Don't get me wrong, Essie was never disrespectful, because she is the queen of cordiality, of course. But every once in a while I'd notice her eyes gloss over with a distinct brand of hatred when she intercepted a conversation between myself and my parents. My mom especially. I asked her why recently, and she gave me a very straightforward answer.

"Regina is manipulative and selfish, and I don't appreciate how she uses you."

Two years ago those might have been fighting words, but I had started to see it more and more the longer I was outside of her immediate orbit. Especially since starting therapy. Thanks to Jeremiah, I'd come to realize how much of my childhood was outside of the norm. It wasn't normal for my mom to use me as an emotional sounding board from ten to twenty and tell me how much she regretted marrying my father, and how she wished she could get a do-over. It wasn't normal for my parents to use me as a conflict mediator after days of screaming matches. It wasn't normal for them to pass the blame back and forth and try to make me pick sides. And working to pay off *their* bad decisions, definitely was not fucking normal.

"Yeah, I'm visiting with Glory. Her niece was born," I explained.

"Oh, Gloria's there?" she all but grumbled.

"Yes, I just said that," I replied.

Silence briefly filled the line before her tone changed in a way that unsettled me.

"Can you walk over? I'd like to talk to you about something."

"What do we need to talk about?" I asked.

More silence before her tone changed again, and this time the manipulation was right in my face.

"Just come over," she cried. "We'll talk about it when you get here."

She hung up and I stared at the phone, wondering how to avoid speaking to her in person altogether. Glory wasn't ready to go. That much was clear from all the laughter and awwing coming from Penny's nursery, and I wasn't selfish enough to rush her anyway. Then if I didn't go, she'd just call back until she annoyed me enough to produce a response. I didn't want that. The holidays were nipping at our heels and the last thing I wanted was to be in a stank-ass mood on vacation with my partners because of my mommy issues. So that left me with one real choice. Face my mother head-on and get it over with, because I was done letting her control my life.

She stood on the porch, picking at the peeling paint with a gray expression and defeated body language. When I got within ten feet of her, she sighed like her lungs were about to collapse. It was funny, because before I would've rushed to try to fix everything for her, but now I could see clear as day that this was a performance, just like everyone else.

"Hey, Mom. What's going on?" I asked.

I watched her kick at a loose brick before meeting my eyes.

"Frankie, look at this porch. I can't believe your daddy lets us live like this," she lamented.

That porch had been raggedy for the last ten years. And I'd given her money towards getting it fixed every two years during that stretch.

"Yeah, it has gotten bad. But the house is paid off, you could just set aside some money and hire someone to fix it," I suggested.

"Nah," she waved. "You know how your daddy is about other men fixing his house. He says that's the next step to someone fixing his wife."

Weird thing to tell your son, but aight.

"I'm just saying, Ma. It's your house too. What's he really gone be able to do besides complain?" I asked.

"Oh, Franklin. Last time I outright defied your father we argued for three days and nine months later, you were the result."

My face scrunched up something nasty. Like mayonnaise spread on gym panties left out on a July summer day nasty.

"There's so much to unpack with what you just said to me, that it'd take a hoarder's crew," I said shaking my head. "Anyway, what'd you wanna talk about?"

More silence. Then,

"Why'd you quit your job?"

Nope.

"I still sell my stuff downtown on the weekends. I'm actually looking at a d…"

"No! Not that Bath And Body Works shit!" she shouted. "Why'd you quit your actual job?"

My heart was pounding, my ears were ringing, and I was a good minute away from crouching on the ground to keep from completely passing out. Even therapy couldn't change how I felt about being hollered at.

"Ah, you mean Curtis'?" I huffed.

She nodded, eyes fierce and expression annoyed.

"Because driving to that building five days a week made me want to commit suicide," I answered bluntly.

That was the truth. I felt suffocated every time I got near the parking lot on Jackson and S Pearl. I wanted to crawl out of my skin and leave it there as evidence that I had finally died. That I was finally no longer of use to them. To anyone.

"Ok," she said. "What about part-time?"

It was like I was speaking Klingon. I told her I wanted to end my life, and she asked me if I could do it slower instead. I shifted my weight back, ready to flee. I was in a great mood this morning. Hell, I was in a great mood half an hour ago. But now? Now I was seeing red, and this was supposed to be my mama. *My* protector.

"No," I gritted.

Shock settled onto her familiar brown face, then our expressions began to mirror. We were at an intersection, both standing firm on our side of the road.

"Franklin, it's not that long left. Only three years," she urged.

"That's three years too long on an already ten-year sentence," I shrugged.

"Franklin, that's not right. I raised you better…"

"You do it then," I hissed. "You have a degree. You can take my spot since you're so embarrassed I upped and quit."

My mother looked at me like she was seeing a random grown man on the street she had never seen before. Then she asked,

"Is Glory pregnant or something?"

"No, she's not. And don't involve her either."

"I don't understand then," she said, shaking her head. "What about me and Daddy?"

I didn't understand what she wasn't understanding. I didn't care. My answer was unchanging. They were on their own.

"You and him can fix y'all own damn mess!" I shouted, finally feeling everything from the last three decades.

"What kind of so…"

I cut her off, because one thing I couldn't do was listen to one more iteration of the, *What Kind Of Son Would Leave His Parents To Perish?* speech. It was always, *"What kind of son would leave his parents without a car?"* or *"What kind of son would let his mother sit in the dark?"* and finally, *"What kind of son would refuse a job just to see his parents suffer?"* I had heard them all, and now I had an answer.

"Me! I'm the kind of son who's saying fuck y'all, that's not my damn problem. You ask me that every single time I don't want to give you my fucking soul! Let me ask you something, Regina. What kind of mother knows her son is an alcoholic, and never encourages him to get help? What kind of mother screams and cries in her son's face to the point that he has PTSD? What kind of mother sees her son struggling, and still finds a way to pivot back to herself and her bullshit?"

I finally had silence, but it was a little too late if you ask me.

"Oh, you can't answer that huh? Well, since you think the question is rhetorical, let me answer it for you! The kind of mother who would rather spend her Tuesday morning, begging her son to go back into a toxic workplace, than to stand on her own two fucking feet and get her shit together! I do not owe you my life because you and that man had unprotected sex! I do not exist to ensure your comfort! I am not your fucking husband!" I seethed.

I left before she could respond. Hot, salty tears were streaming down my face. My hands were shaking, and my ears were ringing. All the grounding techniques in the world wouldn't be able to stop the hurt I was feeling, and luckily, they didn't have to. Glory was sitting in the living room with Marcus when I got back.

"Hey, whe…"

She stopped herself, rose from the couch, and grabbed a wad of Marcus's bougie-ass facial tissues to blot my face. And while I was appreciative that I was no longer a snotty, sobbing, mess, there was only one thing I needed Glory to do for me in the moment.

"Can I please have a hug?" I asked.

Glory, ever the empath, kissed my reddened cheek with a tenderness only described in romance novels before wrapping herself around me tight.

"Oh, Frankie," she cooed. "It's alright, I got you. Always."

I never had to question Glory because I felt the confidence in her voice. I always had her.

I composed myself enough to drive even though Glory insisted she wouldn't mind taking over. I would've let her, but some things are tradition.

"You were right. I feel so much better."

We were sitting on the stairs at Dagget Park with a bucket of truffle fries from Roger's Smokehouse between us. The sun was setting with the urgency of an office worker after five, and the winter dusk highlighted Glory's nitid midnight complexion in a way that was nothing short of seraphic. Just like old times.

"I told you," she laughed. "Greasy fries heal all."

And so did she. I mean, I still had a long way to go. That much I knew. But there wasn't much I couldn't conquer with her and Cash by my side. Wait a minute, I was forgetting something.

Dammit! Cash!

"Shit! I need to get our tickets today. Cash is going to kill me," I said, rushing to pull out my phone.

I had completely forgotten we were leaving for the mountains in less than a month with all the commotion and celebration of today. And apparently, so did Glory.

"Dammit! I have to book the rental!" she gasped.

"I'll just grab it with the flights and you can take over entertainment," I offered.

Glory nodded in agreement before exhaling in relief.

"Thank you, Frankie. You know how OD he is about Christmas," she mumbled.

We had a month to go and our bags and PJ's were already packed and sitting in the coat closet. Cash was managing Christmas like we were the Jackson Five and he was Big Joe.

"Very," I agreed.

Chapter Twenty-four

C ash

Ah, Christmas. Sweet, joyful, unreasonably fucking stressful Christmas. See, the month preceding Christmas was super busy for all three of us even though we didn't do anything big for Frankie's birthday, much to my chagrin. Frankie was busy with his business, specifically getting his website optimized. Glory was busy with her multitude of donation drives, and I was busy assisting with drop offs for her as well as coordinating our holiday with my family. Despite the crunch and as much as I hated my presence being volunteered, I was excited to spend Christmas in Colorado. Especially since we were spending New Year's in Heaven's Peak, a small mountain town about 3 hours away from my mama in Colorado Springs.

That guaranteed alone time meant we had a chance to slow down and enjoy each other before the new year started, which I desperately needed. I'd become accustomed to weekly if not damn near daily dates in the four months since we all started dating, but we were so damn busy we hadn't been on one in the last three weeks. Let alone had sex. Not to cheapen my longing for my partners, but I really missed sex. Especially Glory's pussy. Burning on both ends yet being deprived of intimacy is a special kind of hell.

Which is why I screamed in relief when my checklist was finished. I didn't even care that the Target aunties were looking at me like I'd lost my God-given sense. Gifts, check. Accommodations, check. Flights, luggage, and snacks. Check, check, check. All three houses were clean, Glory was finished with all her philanthropic efforts, now free to focus on phallic efforts, and I was officially on vacation. Then there was Fab...

"Frijoles, put the laptop away! We have four hours until our flight leaves. We are on vacation!" I chided.

"Sorry! I just got one little email to send and then I'm done," he replied.

Frankie, who once tried to leave the community market only three hours in had become quite the workaholic since leaving his family's multi-level marketing scheme. He started as a GroceryGo driver shortly after quitting, using his free time to work on his website, and then he had the brilliant idea to start attaching new user coupons for his products to delivery orders. Needless to say, it'd been a great success because he was responding to the fifth retail expansion offer he'd gotten that month. After watching him spend countless hours in his makeshift lab, contacting vendors, sourcing supplies, manufacturers, and even renting a warehouse to catalog and ship from. I was beyond happy for him.

"I need one of y'all to look over this contract for me when we ge..."

Glory shut his laptop, pulled him from the desk, and placed a suitcase in his open palm.

"Set your inbox to away, create an auto-reply, and leave the laptop. We. Are. Leaving. Cash did a lot of work planning this getaway and you are not going to capitalism it up!" she admonished.

Glory couldn't pass up the opportunity to boss somebody around despite us insisting that she could be hands-off. That created a strange conflict in my mind. I couldn't decide if she was adorable or hard-headed. Fortunately, I knew it was both.

"You lucky I love you," Frankie grumbled while doing exactly as she asked.

My stomach was suddenly rumbling and twisting. It had been hurting a lot lately, but I think it was just IBS. Cause what else was it? Definitely not jealousy or anything. Heheh no. Definitely not.

"I love you too, nerve-wracking," she cooed sweetly.

I had the immediate urge to purge my early breakfast.

Weird.

That fruit and toast must've been too heavy for me.

"Be right back, I need to hit the bathroom before we leave," I hollered, trekking to the bathroom.

I was slow enough to catch a glimpse of Glory's face. Cute, shiny, and twisted with worry. My poor baby was back stressed, and it was all my fault.

Fuck.

"What the fuck!?" Glory exclaimed while exiting the car.

I knew she wouldn't try to conceal her honest reaction. Her analytical ass kept herself busy pummeling me with a thousand questions on the hour drive from the airport. Questions about the area, questions about my mama, questions about our traditions. So many questions, which I had artfully and diplomatically answered for the time being. Because I knew everything would be clear when we made it to the house.

"You are rich!" she shouted. "Like, Bezos rich!"

I knew she was dramatic, but that was crazy. No one was Bezos rich. Yet, the Gilrados came close…

"No, my mama is rich. I am firmly middle class," I corrected.

"That's literally what every silver spoon baby says!" she scoffed.

"And you are **not** middle class," Frankie added.

I disagreed. $380,000 a year was definitely middle class for a family of three.

Fab helped me with the plethora of bags while Glory took to examining the holly wood topiary art trimming the house. Elephants, giraffes, and zebras brought The Sahara to the Midwest in a tasteful light-trimmed hedge display. Mama had outdone herself this year.

"I am never paying for anything ever again!" she whisper-hissed.

I encouraged her not to all the time, and she hardly listened. Either way I didn't mind being her azucar papi.

"Fine by me," I smiled.

The door swung open to a grinning, graying, beauty who scooped an unexpecting Glory into a tight hug.

"Hola, Mija. You're so pretty. Your Instagram pictures don't do you justice," she fawned.

Glory stood with her mouth wide open, wordless. I think Mama caught her off guard. I'm not sure how when she had Mama Lailah, but I get it. Finding out you'd been researched by your significant other's parents isn't the best holiday greeting.

"Mama!" I chided. "Stop internet stalking people!"

"Hush, Poquito! What else am I supposed to do? Ay! I'm so bored, you never come and visit anymore. I almost miss the cancer," she said with a shrug.

"Mama!" Cookie admonished.

Glory then stepped inside the house to scream-greet Cookie and Rio, allowing me to pull my mother into a long-overdue hug.

"I'm sorry, Mama. I'll visit more often next year. I promise," I sighed.

My mama pulled back to take a good look at me, pinching my face and patting my arm. I had a good look at her too. Her signature plump cheeks had returned, her hair had grown to her ears, and her eyelashes had come back to frame her shimmering hazel eyes. I realized how lucky I truly was. Not many people got to see their loved ones on the other side of chemo.

"Or you could just give me a granddaughter and we'll call it even. You don't have to do anything besides make her. I got the rest covered," she said, breaking me from my thoughts.

"Mama!" I hissed.

"What? What's the big deal? Glory, Franklin, do you not want children?" she asked.

Sweet Jesus of Nazareth, she wasted no time.

"Uhm," Frankie started.

"Yes!" Glory finished.

We had the kid conversation after The Great Halloween Cest Fest. No one bothered with a condom so we had to go through the hell of getting a morning after pill for Glory. We all wanted kids, and Glory offered to give us one biological child each then a toss up on the third and final. I was kinda ready, Glory seemed really ready, but Fab was still trying to get his footing with entrepreneurship so we agreed to revisit the logistics of kids in two years or so.

"We're taking it slow, Mama," I sighed. "Not everyone has kids three months after getting together."

"People do that?" Fab asked.

"Our whole family does, actually. We get married and have babies pretty immediately," Cookie answered. "Speaking of Mama, isn't cousin Nat getting married soon? I'm sure he'll have nothing but girls with the way he acts."

My Mama's mouth drew in tight to conceal what was likely a grimace. She was grimacing because she knew something, and the only way she could possibly know something was if she had been gossiping with our Tia Cecilia. My cousin was too private otherwise.

"Spill it," I sighed.

"Well Mijo, we always said that girl was no good for him. She liked the life, not the man."

"She dumped him?" Cookie gasped.

"He dumped her. You know how he feels about infidelity," Mama said, wagging a finger.

"She cheated!?" Glory exclaimed, fully invested in a story she knew hardly anything about.

"Mhm, with her bodyguard that he pays at that. In his house. Maldita Muchacha. He was so pissed, he burned the whole thing to the ground with all her worldly possessions inside," Mama nodded.

I palmed my forehead as my mother continued telling my partners about my unhinged cousin's bout of rage-induced arson. Yeah, Christmas was off to a great start.

"You're wondering what kind of rich we are?" Mama asked Glory.

After getting us all caught up on the family tea, we retired to the kitchen to sip virgin coquito and eat bimuelos. Fab had settled in quickly, alternating between chatting with Mama and discussing dinner ideas with Cookie. Meanwhile Glory sat perfectly still and looked as if she was too scared to touch anything. It was as if she was seeing the world in Technicolor for the first time ever.

"Kinda," she whispered sheepishly.

Mama smiled and gave her a gentle pat.

"Let's see, now their late father was an oil tycoon. That really should've been the first red flag, but arranged marriages and all," she shrugged. "I got a little under half in the divorce, but I also had money from my family. I spent the early years investing in safe stocks, but once the kids were old enough to mind themselves I opened a few little casinos. You've heard of Casa La Negra?"

"NO FUCKING WAY!" Glory screeched.

A few little casinos was a major understatement. If there was a desert, there was a Casa La Negra. She also had her own margarita mix, jarred salsa, and frozen arepas in the local grocery stores. My mother was Caesar's Entertainment with Sazon and Cumbia.

"Yes fucking way," she nodded.

"Shit, sorry!" Glory exclaimed, covering her mouth.

I burst into laughter, noticing that she couldn't stop cussing if she wanted to. And she really wanted to.

"I am so sorry for being disrespectful. I'm gonna get some air. I heard the adult puppet theater is walking distance from here. I might go by there," she rambled awkwardly.

Ugh. Her and those creepy ass puppets. I also learned she was a fan of claymation in recent months. Figures.

"Don't apologize, Mija. I love a good cuss word. Cassius won't even sit next to me at funerals cause every other word out my mouth is an expletive," Mama laughed.

That was absolutely true. My grandfather died four years ago, and while the service was probably beautiful, all I could hear was Cookie and Mama saying "desabrido" in response to every third dress they saw. To be fair, a lot of them were inappropriate. But hey, I guess there's no handbook to being a dead billionaires side-piece.

"Oh, but this is the last night they're open, Glory," Cookie chimed in. "So do you wanna pop by? I could go for the puppet, *Why Did I Get Married?*"

"Let me change into actual clothes and we can catch one of the late shows," Glory responded. "Boys, you down? I can buy the tickets online."

"I'm down, my love," Fab laughed.

Weird. My stomach was hurting again. Maybe it was from the turbulence.

"You guys go ahead. I think I had too many sweets. I need water and a nap," I waved.

Glory's gorgeous eyes narrowed in disappointment and confusion. Then Frankie joined her. Damn it, I should have thrown in a yawn for good measure.

"Cassius, are you sure? We can go to the last show if you need time to rest," she offered.

I put my college theater years to the test of time, patting my belly and smacking my lips exhaustively.

"Nah, it's ok. You know puppets creep me out. Besides, if you go now we can wake up early for a hike," I suggested.

Princessa reluctantly accepted my excuse, but her little lip quiver wasn't at all lost on me. It was burned into my brain, actually.

"Ok, I guess," she sighed. "Come on y'all."

After everyone left, I put on pajamas and snuggled into one of the recliners to hate-watch BET. There were only ever three things playing and I hoped it was something I could use for background noise while I tried to read. You know how you keep stuff playing so you don't have to be alone with your thoughts? Yeah, I was in that stage of delusion. Ironically, *Why Did I Get Married?* was playing. This was probably the first time they took Baby Boy out of the VCR in eight years, and I caught it just in time to get gut-punched with a reminder of my avoidant misery

Fuck.

At least I was alone.

"What are you hiding from?" A distant voice asked.

I leaped out of that chair so quickly you would've thought my ass crack was on fire. But it might as well have been because I, Cassius Julian Monroe, do not like surprises. My heart races every time I hear the syllable Sur.

"Jesus fuck!" I hollered as my Mama stepped from the shadows.

"Who are you tryna be? The hat man!?" I panted.

"Cassius, what's going on?" Mama asked as if she didn't just make me stress fart.

"Nothing, I'm just watching TV," I answered while getting her a blanket.

She, like Cookie, also took her hoops off to stay a while.

"I've never known you to watch this bullshit channel," she said, letting that Colombiana accent shine.

It was something I envied at times, despite being perfectly fluent in Spanish. The way she rolled her R's, automatically turned her Y's into J's, or how perfectly she could cuss someone out in her mother tongue, speaking no less than 150 words per minute.

"I..."

"No mientas," she scolded.

Right, don't lie. That thing I generally have no problem with not doing. Yet, in the moment, that's all I was compelled to do.

Cause truthfully, I was jealous. Envy snuck into my blood every time I even heard the word, "love." Every time I caught them looking at each other with that fantastic twinkle that could light up a midnight sky. It didn't make sense because I knew Fab and Glory had known each other since forever, but I still couldn't help the way I felt. It was like watching my friends be let into the club to party behind the glass without me. Even though I was on the same list.

"I love them," I mumbled.

"Yes, I can see that," Mama nodded while flicking channels. "So answer my question. What's the problem, Mijo?"

Ah, a snare of my own creation. I should've just gone to bed. I knew she would pry. But I stayed up because I wanted to hear Glory tell me all about the creepy puppet show. I hated puppets, but I would listen to her rant and rave about anything.

Ugh.

Love is poison.

"Mijo," Mama warned.

She looked at me with a look I'm convinced mothers start developing as soon as they find out they're pregnant. It's too precise to be anything otherwise, cause I immediately spilled my guts.

"I love them, but I don't know if they love me and sometimes I feel like a weird third-wheel-ass nigga who can't take a hint," I sighed.

We sat in silence for far longer than I was comfortable with until my Mama turned to me with a lour.

"Cassius, you are so smart," she said, sounding pained.

"Thank you?" I half-asked.

"Yet, you are also a bruto," she continued

"A mother's love…" I mumbled.

She waved me off with a swish of her manicured hand before resuming.

"Did you tell them how you felt or did you just hide it and make yourself sick?" she asked.

I stayed silent because we both knew the answer. My toxic trait was letting issues fester after overthinking and underestimating my value in relationships.

"This is something that can be resolved with a simple conversation. Figure out what you need to say. I want my granddaughter before I die," she advised.

Ah, Mothers.

Glory

I loved theater. I wish I could go more often, but between work, the shelter, granny, and the boys I never really find the time. I'm sure either one of them would love to accompany me, but I've just never had the courage to ask. Especially since Cash started acting weird. I don't know why, but I get the feeling he's keeping a secret from me. Technically I have no right to be upset about something like that since I neglected to inform him about Frankie initially, but my racing heart didn't know that. He told me no thanks to hanging out and I wanted to vomit. This is the first night we all had free in a month and he didn't want to spend it with us. Didn't want to spend it with **me.**

"What are you freaking out about, Essie?" Frankie asked as we walked to get intermission snacks.

I knew I couldn't lie. My lip quiver was a dead giveaway.

"Cash has been acting weird," I admitted. "Do you think he wants to break up with us?"

Frankie burst into laughter. I'm talking gut-clenching, knee-slapping, cough-inducing laughter. Nigga was acting like Hannibal Buress told a joke.

"Frankie!" I scoffed.

"Oh shit. I'm sorry," he chuckled. "It's just… You think Cash wants to break up with us? Really, that's what you think?"

What else was I supposed to think with how weird and distant he was being?

"Yeah, kinda! I don't know how this shit works. I thought those were signs of eminent demise or whatever!" I shouted.

Frankie pulled me close and hugged me tight. Forcing me to calm myself with an obnoxiously deep breath. I really really liked Cassius. I liked waking up to his perfect smile. I liked having his butter-smooth radio personality voice interrupt my panicked thoughts. I liked how excited he got when we visited bookstores, or when he got a new journal. I liked him so much I think I actually loved him. Then the crazy part? I realized I'd loved him for a while. Typical Glory to be so emotionally lacking that I don't even notice when I've fallen in love.

Again.

"Baby, Cash is not trying to break up with us," Frankie said sweetly.

He was also drying my tears. Tears I hadn't even felt until then. Ugh. I was turning into a crybaby.

"How do you know that?" I murmured.

"Because I'm a boy," he laughed. "I know when other boys are on B.S. Case and point, Elias Oscar."

"That can't be your only reference," I argued.

"Ok, fine," Frankie shrugged. "Then you'll just have to trust me on this. You trust me, Essie?"

I loosened my hold on his shirt so I could peer into his rum-colored eyes, deep and sincere.

"More than I probably should," I admitted.

"Mkay. Then let's get you some caramel and cheese corn, watch the rest of the show, then talk to Cash when we get home. Aight?"

Meet Frankie Jameson Myer-Smythe, everyone. Brat soother and tamer extraordinaire.

"Alright," I nodded.

Unfortunately for the boys, taming only did so much without action, and they hadn't had the time to check me recently. Cookie had wandered off with one of the string pullers for the night after getting the ok from Dalia, so all I had to worry about was ditching Frankie.

"Essie, wait!" Frankie shouted as I kicked off my shoes and raced off in search of Cassius.

Nothing could sway me from my objective, and I soon found him in the second sitting room of that big ass house watching BET of all things.

Ew.

"Princessa, what's wrong?" Cassius asked.

Why did he automatically assume something was wrong? Maybe it was because I looked unhinged. I caught a glimpse of myself in the mirror. Smeared lipstick, unbuttoned top, skin glistening with sweat. The only time I ever let myself sweat was during sex. What had love done to me?

"Nothing, why would something be wrong?" I asked, somewhat smoothing my wild hair back into place before fixing my disheveled clothing.

"You're running," he pointed out.

"People run, Cassius," I replied.

"Yeah, but you don't. You might briskly glide, but running isn't really your thing. Also y…"

"Are we breaking up!?" I shouted tearfully.

Frankie had caught up too little too late, and all he could do was bow his head and pray. He was logical, and ain't believe in confrontation, but I did.

"Gloria, what?" Cash asked, sounding horrifically amazed.

He asked as if I was imagining things. Had I been? Cause the way his brows remained knit made me feel out of my mind.

"You've been weird! You don't want to hang out, you keep disappearing, what's going on with you! Do you w…"

"Glory, I love you," he sighed.

"W-what?" I stammered.

I was confused. Duh. Cause what the fuck did love have to do with this?

"Can we go talk in private?" he asked.

I finally noticed we had an audience. Mama Dalia, Frankie, and even Rio, who had questions.

"Abuela, I thought you said Uncle Cash was a ba…"

"Shush," Dalia grumbled before turning to Frankie.

"This is a very dramatic confession. Is this all the time?" she whispered motioning at me and Cash.

"For the last four months," Frankie nodded.

"I don't know how you do it," she replied.

"I'm a saint," he shrugged.

Wow, ok. Homie was lying, but Cash did have a point. I gave him a nod in an attempt not to be included in Dalia and Cecilia's weekly gossip, even though I was sure we were well past that.

"You too, Frijoles," Cash sighed to a still gossiping Frankie while guiding me to our room.

By the time we hit the door, I was fully sobbing. It felt like the boys couldn't collect Kleenex fast enough to dry my tears. I was so confused, scared, and frustrated. Then it didn't help that I had weakened my ability to mask by listening to Frankie.

Damn, these men.

"Glory, Princessa. Please calm down. I didn't mean to make you cry," Cassius cooed.

His voice was so sweet but that was unhelpful as hell. He wanted me to stop crying and I wanted him to stop avoiding me. Seems we were at an impasse.

"Why are you being so fucking w-weird," I blubbered.

"Cause…"

"Cause what!?" I hollered.

"Because I'm jealous!" Cash replied, voice raised.

"What? Jealous of what?"

I never took Cassius as the jealous type. Hell, he told me he was ok with me sexing other people in the beginning of our relationship. So him being jealous of his own boyfriend was not on my bingo card.

"I'm jealous because I love you and Frankie, and you love each other, but I don't know if you feel the same about me and I always feel like a third wheel. Like I'm j..."

"You don't think I love you?" I asked, interrupting his rant.

Silence gave way to a disheartened shrug. My poor sweet Cash. He really didn't. I can't say I blame him though. I never felt like I was good enough for love, and I was, therefore, quite terrible at expressing positive emotions. I still told Frankie his food was just alright even though the first bite almost always made me cry. Being happy out loud felt too foreign. But that was on me, not Cash. So I had to fix this. I had to try.

"Well, I love how excited you get for Mondays. It makes me more optimistic than I would be otherwise. I also love how many lemonades you keep on hand. You spend so much time perfecting flavors and combinations. Every time I think you've bested yourself you prove me wrong. I love that you smile every time I just barely brush your arm. It's so fucking cute, and it makes me feel like we're teenagers who've never held hands before. I love how you cherish your poetry journals, and I love how loyal you are to paperback books, even if e-readers are better, and I love your hatred of animated clay and puppets and how you try to accept them because I love those things. I love every single thing about you, Cassius. I have for a while now."

"Y-you love me?" Cash stammered.

"I do," I nodded. "So much. Which is why I need you to stop being all distant and closed off. It's hurting my lil feelings," I admitted.

"I love you too," Cash said, pulling me close.

We were ok, we were just in love and equally bad at it. I snuggled into his chest, drying the last of my tears on his flannel and finding peace before we were interrupted.

"Fucking finally!" Frankie groaned, interrupting the sentimental soundtrack playing in my head."God, y'all took a long-ass time."

"Seriously, Fab?" Cash chuckled.

"Yes, seriously!" Frankie scoffed while changing into pajamas. "Had me holding in my shit cause y'all emotionally constipated. Glory loves Cash. Cash loves Glory. I love both of you, but I'm going to gossip with Mama Dalia. Enjoy y'all alone time."

Frankie skirted away before we could protest, leaving us wrapped in each other's arms. I loved it here, but not gone lie, it had been a while.

"So hey…" I started.

"You wanna have sex?" Cash asked.

I, Gloria Esther King, was the luckiest girl in the world. Not only did my boyfriend love me, he also knew me like the back of his hand, and he knew I needed my back blown to smithereens after all this.

"Absolutely," I nodded.

I didn't waste time pulling off my shirt but I had to take a pause when I noticed the luminous twinkle in his hazel eyes. Maybe love wasn't too good for me.

Chapter Twenty-five

G
lory

"I'm too good for this," Cassius grumbled.

He was upset because it was *"the devil's pacing hours"* as he had put it, and we were awake and dressed.

"You made me cry and you promised me a hike," I reminded him. "You're too good for nothing."

"Fine. But why the fuck is Frijoles so chipper?" he asked, pointing to a jigging Frankie.

Frankie had been oddly sunshiney since we landed yesterday. Why? I'm not entirely sure. I knew he was really excited to spend the holidays outside of Dallas and to cook with Constance, but even then, his newfound cheeriness was overwhelming and also slightly unsettling.

"I'm not sure. He either has plans to off us and collect the insurance money, or he's hiding something," I replied.

"Well, which one is it?" Cash asked Frankie with crossed arms.

"I'm hiding something," Frankie shrugged lazily.

"You wanna share with the class?" I asked.

"Nope!" he exclaimed. "I want to leave and start this hike so I can stuff myself with that breakfast burrito Mama Dalia suggested after."

I won't lie, breakfast burritos after did sound fantastic. Especially since I'd fallen asleep without eating last night. Cash was a show instead of a tell kind of lover. The best kind.

"Fine," I pouted. "Keep your little secret. Just carry my pack."

"Done and done," Frankie replied. "Let's head out."

We packed into the rental and drove six miles to Palmer Park. I had researched a few spots when Cash told me what area we'd been staying in, but I decided to forgo my research last minute and let the boys take me wherever they thought would be good. Which happened to be a place at the top of my discarded list.

"Yucca Flat Trailheads?" I confirmed as Frankie opened my door.

"Yep," Cash nodded. "It's rocky and might be a little icy, but there's a great view at the end. Hopefully, we make it in time."

"Make it in time for what?" I asked.

"You'll see," Cash replied, taking my hand. "Get to stepping, Princessa."

I was so anxious to see what Cash was talking about that I had outpaced the boys about a mile into the trail. They were about a good ten feet behind me, swinging hands and giggling the whole time. Being ridiculously adorable. That gave me time to enjoy the mountain air. The air was noticeably thinner and Colorado and that contributed to my overall feeling of ditzy care-free joy. Skeletal winter trees, winter-hardy bushes, and rocks looked like they'd been perfectly placed as if Palmer Park were a real-live mini model built by some ethereal artistic visionary, and the dark morning sky reminded me that life and the unknown could be as beautifully complex as it could be scary. Suddenly, it all clicked, and I think that was the moment I fully understood the importance of balance.

"Glory, what's wrong? Are you hurt?" Cash asked.

Shit I was crying again, but I didn't get the chance to explain why before the boys caught up to me and started examining me.

"Did you step on something sharp? Was it rusted? Cause if so you need a tetanus shot ASAP," Frankie explained while pulling off my boot.

"Frankie, Cassius. I'm fine. I'm not injured. Nothing poked me. I'm just having a little Aha moment," I sighed.

"Whew, little crybaby," Cash chuckled. "You water signs are so emotional and stressful."

"And wet, don't forget wet," I shot back.

Both the boys blushed before their faces settled into relief and chaotic amusement. One dismissive and one grieved. Both sweet and handsome. Further making my heart trip into something inescapable.

"What's with the waterworks, Essie?" Frankie asked, interrupting my daydream.

I considered my words carefully. We'd had a hectic year end between Frankie and Cash's jobs, not to mention everything going on with my family and Cash's, and the last thing I wanted to do was add to the uncertainty. Still, their gentle smiles told me it was ok. That we'd figure it out. Just like always.

"I'm really happy right now, and I think my life back home makes me not so happy," I admitted.

Frankie made a face but Cash was quick to take his hand to comfort him before following up with me.

"How so, Princessa?" he asked.

I told the boys everything I'd been considering for the last half mile. I told them how I loved Colorado, how I loved theater, how much I missed painting, and how I realized I wasn't able to indulge in those things because of the position I'd taken in adulthood. I told them how I felt out of balance, how I hated that our relationship was basically a dirty secret back in Dallas, and how I didn't want it to be. Then I cried some more before telling them I loved them, and they just listened patiently the whole time. Only occasionally breaking eye contact to dry my tears. It was one of the simplest acts of love I've ever experienced, yet one of the best.

"So, in short, I'd just like to be pretty and useless for a while," I explained.

"Ok," they said in unison.

I started chuckling because they said it so earnestly. Like it was just that easy. But then my laughter slowed when they didn't join me. Their faces remained straight beside a raised brow or two. They really were serious.

"What really? Just like that? No questions asked?"

"No preguntas necesitas," Cash replied.

Frankie nodded in agreement.

"We told you we wanted to be your soft spots, and if you're tired, we're happy to pick up the slack. Really," he explained.

What did that even look like? Would I just dawdle around, paint, and take walks all day? What about working? What about the boys?

"I was just kidding, y'all," I said, shaking my head. "I can't just mooch off of y'all even if Cash is kind of rich. And Frankie, you're still working on your business and g…"

My mouth was covered by Cash, effectively stopping my snowballing rant.

"I think we should talk about this more after Christmas," Frankie sighed. "Ok?"

He sounded so sure. Like everything was just going to magically fall into place. Yet, something about the look on his face told me there was a chance it could. So I said,

"Ok."

"Ok," the boys chimed simultaneously.

We finished the rest of the hike, and we made it just in time for me to witness the most magically aureate sunrise I'd ever seen float over the jagged mountain tops. Which the sight of made me teary for a different reason than the first cry thirty minutes earlier.

Life really was so perplexingly winsome.

Chapter Twenty-six

G lory

"Where's Frankie?" I groaned.

It was Christmas morning and I was hungover. We got to Colorado Springs three days ahead of everyone else in Cash's family and we spent the cozy days beforehand with Mama Dalia, Cookie, and Rio alone, giving me a false sense of tranquility. I thought the holidays in Colorado would be chill and intimate, but I was wrong. Mama Dalia and her sister Cecilia could party and out-drink an Irish King. Or in my case, a lightweight Black one.

"Cooking with Cookie," Cash replied, pulling me back into the downy blankets.

The velvet duvets were tempting but I noticed that the morning was still dark, not even blue yet.

"Did he ever come to bed?" I asked, voice craggly and dry.

"Nah. He fell asleep on the couch while waiting on the roast," Cash yawned.

Right the roast. Yesterday he was asking me which flavor combos I liked the most based on what he'd gotten at the market. I picked rosemary plum. Maybe I could watch him work his seasoning magic.

"Should I help?" I asked.

"No, he specifically requested that I do not encourage or allow any such interference," Cassius grumbled.

Excuse me? Who did these two think they were? I don't recall getting *"Glory is a punk bitch"* tattooed on my forehead. All that love shit had bit me in the ass. They had no business conspiring on telling me what I could and couldn't do.

"What? Are you gonna keep me locked in here all morning?" I scoffed.

"If I must," Cassius shrugged lazily.

He didn't seem confident in that answer. Honestly, I didn't even think he was awake. His almond eyes were still half-lidded and his usually smooth voice was dripping with exhaustion. Besides there was the fact that Cash wouldn't hurt a fly. So I was plenty doubtful that he was going to keep me captive.

"Glory, be still or I'm gonna make you be still," he sighed.

"You won't make me do shit!" I argued.

Cassius jerked back, looking at me as if I'd grown a second head. I expected a lecture, a fuss, or even a scoff but I got nothing except silence. Then he slowly rose from the bed, stretched on his tip-toes, and walked over to the door to twist the lock. That little *snick* should have caused concern, but I was too high on my horse to notice the shark-infested waters I was wading in.

Suddenly, I was pinned to the bed. Cassius and I are roughly the same width and height, but I'm soft allover whereas Cash, like Frankie, is mostly solid, heavy muscle underneath his fluff. Body composition makes all the difference in a fight, and I was already set up for failure.

"I won't make you do shit?" Cash teased.

The fire in me was still burning despite the fact that I couldn't move anything besides my fingers and toes.

"Nope," I sneered.

Cassius's lips curled into a devious smile. One I could never see myself losing fondness for.

"Ok," he chuckled. "I won't make you do shit."

"Exactly," I said, attempting to sit up fully.

Only I couldn't because more of Cash's weighted body was pressed against mine. Completely overpowering the strength my muscles had. A weird little intrusive thought reminded me it would be easy for him to hurt me if he really wanted to and I had to quickly push it away. Cash was safe, he was just trying to be a big man. And he was succeeding judging by the bulge pressing against my stomach.

"Let me up," I demanded.

"Make me," Cash purred before pressing his mouth against my neck.

I immediately went for ole reliable. The hip tickle. Cash was deadly ticklish in his hips and it was usually a free square on my escape bingo card. Except for this time. This time he didn't laugh or squirm. He instead pinned my right arm above my head and guided my left inside his boxers.

"If you're going to touch me, do it right, Princessa," he snarled.

Jesus, Mary, and Joseph, he was hard as iron. His dick felt like warm stainless steel in my hand. Rise and shine was about to have a new meaning because I was so tempted to pump his length. But I also wasn't willing to let a nice dick distract me from my goal of leaving that room.

"Pervert," I tsked.

"Your pervert," he replied, making his member twitch in my palm.

This battle was going downhill fast. My chained horn dog was biting at it's own leash, growling to be freed and chase the rabbit that was teasing it. Any other concerns had quickly become irrelevant.

"Princessa," Cassius cooed so sweetly. "You still wanna get up?"

Yes. Kinda. Not really.

"I wish you could be pressed against me like this forever." I thought.

It was true. I felt so safe and relaxed, and I never wanted that feeling to end, but something defiant in me was still telling me to fight. So I answered,

"Duh," in the snarkiest tone possible.

I waited and waited for him to move, but the only movement between us was the slight involuntary grind my hips did against his. He was fucking with me.

"If you wanna get up so bad, then push me off of you," Cash laughed.

Yep, fucking with me. I tried again and of course failed. Cassius grew harder against me and his smile grew wider, making me realize this was a very sick game for him.

"I can't," I said, finally falling limp underneath him.

"Aw, Glory. Are you really gonna let me make you lay here? I thought you said I couldn't make you do shit," Cash teased.

Arrogant.

I tried to ignore him so he cupped my chin and forced me to meet his heated gaze. His eyes flickered over my body like an uncontrolled flame, determined to burn a path into my skin.

"Gloria," he snarled. "You're just giving up?"

"Yes," I nodded while attempting to snatch away. "You won. Happy?"

"No," he answered. "I'd be happier if you laid back down the first time I asked. But now I'm awake, and unfortunately for you, alert."

"Unfortunately for me?" I asked, with confusion lacing my tone.

"Sí, Princessa. Porque ahora te joda hasta que no puedas camina," he replied sweetly.

My Spanish was still iffy and I didn't understand much besides because and can but I didn't care because it sounded so poetic coming from his mouth. So I shrugged and foolishly said,

"Fine."

I understood why Satan was rumored to be one of God's most handsome creations. Because the smile Cash gave me was sinfully wicked, and yet I couldn't be bothered to look away. He was as beautiful as he was depraved. Cassius finally let me up, taking my previous position by lying flat on his back and making me straddle him. Then he very rudely ripped my nightgown down the center of its neckline to expose my breasts.

"Cash!" I scolded.

"It's fine, Princessa. Your rich boyfriend will buy you a new one," he chuckled.

At least he could admit it. Still, it was my favorite, and it had been reduced to a dishrag in an instant.

I playfully squeezed his throat to express my irritation with his dismissive comment, and Cash wrapped his hand around mine. Encouraging it instead of pulling away.

"If you're going to choke me, I need you to use both hands, baby," he purred.

It was too early for me to realize I was making a mistake. So fuck around was about to meet find out.

"What?" I gasped.

Cassius smiled again before slipping his dick out the seam of his boxers. He was now harder than diamond. His pulsing tip was already slick and shiny, dribbling with precum, but I guess he wanted more. So he slowly eased inside of me to take advantage of my dripping sex.

Fuck it was perfect.

"Use both hands, mi vida," he said, making my right hand join my left over his throat.

Yet, it somehow got better. Then when he moved? God. He fucked exactly how he danced. Hips rhythmic and coordinated. Touches tender and consuming. With his whole body leading mine. I think I collapsed against his chest on my own before he could reposition me but his hands still snaked around my thick waist, seeking control while he rocked against me. Then he rocked me right onto the edge of a cliff.

"Cash," I groaned. "You're gonna make me c..."

He stopped before I could complete the sentence. Instantly pulling me back from the brink of bliss and pissing me off with that priggish-ass grin.

"What the fuck!?" I hissed.

"Oh, I'm sorry," Cash chuckled. "I just remember you said I won't make you do shit. And I'd hate to keep you in a warm bed and make you cum when you *actually* wanna go sweat over a stove at four in the morning."

Check-fucking-mate. This irritatingly smug handsome asshole had my number. He had even developed immunity to my pout and lour combo. He just shrugged and smiled at me as if we were exchanging a hilarious inside joke.

"Unless you want to use my lap as your cum catcher?" he asked.

Of course I did! What kind of question was that? Who in their right mind wouldn't want to use Cash's lap as their cum catcher?

"Words, Princessa," he laughed in response to my modest nod.

Something about our little game of cat and mouse made me fall deeper in love with him. Maybe it was the way his nose crinkled when he smiled that mischievous smile. Maybe it was the sure yet playful glint in his eyes. Or maybe it was because he was willing to give me exactly what I wanted as soon as I said,

"Yes."

Whatever the reason, I was perfectly content being told what to do that morning.

Frankie

It was really magical seeing my partners snuggling underneath a tomb of blankets on Christmas morning. The morning outside was frosty and gleaming white, casting a natural spotlight on Glory's little upturned button nose and Cash's hand, which were the only two distinguishable body parts in the sea of fluff. With the exception of my side of the bed. I guess they had been waiting for me to come back, so there was a perfect-sized spot for me to crawl into and curl up with them. While everything else remained securely tucked under the quilt covering.

Cookie and I had finished all the mains at 7 that morning, and Mama Dalia and her sister had taken over breakfast, telling us to go rest for a bit.

It was a rest well earned because we were exhausted, still, it was one of the best exhaustions I've ever experienced. Aside from that time me and Cash collapsed inside of Glory after fucking her into oblivion. That was fun. I wondered if they'd want to recreate that sometime soon. But the gratification of cooking a big meal for my loved ones during the holidays was something I'd always cherish. Especially when Mama Dalia pinched my cheek and told me my tortillas reminded her of her Abuela's. That alone would probably get me through next year.

I started to stretch in hopes of releasing some of the pressure on my throbbing feet. Instead, I released a long-winded yawn in the middle of it. My eyelids heavied when they blinked from the force of my yawn, and my body suddenly felt slow. I had plans to do one thing and one thing only, but then my phone rang.

"Yo, These. Merry Christmas!" I greeted.

"Oh, yeah. Shit, it's Christmas," he grumbled.

I met Thebes Dacres at Stanford in 2008 when he was there for an engineering seminar. He was fresh-faced, tall, quiet, and also an asshole. We got along based off that alone, but he turned out to be pretty cool once I got to know him. Also really into Manga, food, and numbers. Then imagine my surprise when this kid, who I definitely thought was a student like me, actually turned out to be a visiting instructor. That humbled me quickly. I was smart, but not Thebes Dacres smart.

"Yeah, aren't you home for the holidays?" I asked.

"No," he responded quickly. "I got cheated on last year and they want me to *"get back out there"* I can't physically stomach another match-making attempt from my aunties and nem. I wish I just married her anyway so they'd leave me the fuck alone, but I'm hiding out in Arizona for now," he explained.

I also wasn't Thebes Dacres blunt. Whoever he did end up with was going to have their hands full.

"Okie dokie, Grinch. What's the occasion?" I asked.

"What?" Thebes asked.

Oh right. I forgot he was kinda iffy with certain figures of speech.

"You know, why are you calling?" I clarified.

"Right. So I finished reviewing the contract, and everything looks solid. I've emailed you a copy with suggested revisions, but they're just suggestions with no lasting effects on your product or ownership. So other than that you're good to go."

My body was suddenly vibrating. My prior dreariness had been replaced by pulsing energy that felt oddly similar to that time I drank two Bang energies back-to-back. I swear those drinks had amphetamines in them.

"Are you serious?" I asked in sweet disbelief.

"What's that shit y'all be saying? As a heart attack?" Thebes countered. "Yeah, I'm serious. Like I said, I've already emailed everything over."

I checked my inbox, and sure enough, it was sitting right on top marked urgent. Everything suddenly felt really real. I had to suppress my urge to shout for joy in consideration of my sleeping beauties.

"Thanks so much, man. Oh my, God. What do I owe you?" I asked.

Thebes chuckled as he rarely did, making me feel slightly unsettled.

"No money necessary. Instead, I'll take a favor to be discussed at a later date," he responded.

I don't know what was with him and favors, but I knew it was his preferred form of currency. At least three people owed him favors at any given time. I guess you could afford to do that when you're rich. It was weird. Still, I didn't mind.

"Say no more. Thanks, and Merry Christmas again, bruh," I said before hanging up.

I put on a clean T-shirt and slid into bed with my partners. I was too wired from my good news to do anything but stare at the ceiling and fantasize about how different life was about to be for us. Yet, soft warm hands sought mine and pulled me into their cocoon anyway. A luring warmth then enveloped my body along with every racing thought. The heaviness in my eyelids soon returned and my breathing once again slowed. It was a fight I couldn't win. So I decided to clear my mind and let sleep take me. Because nothing would be the same when we woke up.

"Fab," Cash groaned.

I lazily cracked my eyes open to find my boyfriend lying on my bare chest. Funny, I didn't remember taking my shirt off, but regardless, it was lying next to me where I expected Glory to be.

"What's up?" I yawned, seeking a few more minutes of sleep.

"You're laying on my arm and I need to pee," he grumbled.

"Oh shit, sorry."

I rolled to my left to free him and accidentally caught the time on the bedside clock. It was 11am.

Damn.

I was sure we missed presents and also breakfast. I honestly expected the noise to wake us up, but I guess everyone was playing the quiet game.

"Can we share the toilet?" I asked, scrambling out of bed.

I had this theory that two penis people could use a standard-sized toilet at the same time, and therefore conserve water. I was so sure of it, that I almost submitted it as a final project for my environmental chemistry class. Until Marcus told me that it was, and I quote, *"Some weird ass shit I didn't need to say out loud ever again."*

"Frijoles, I'm not crossing streams with you. Wait two minutes like a normal person," Cash grumbled.

Ouch, ok. Perhaps Marcus was right.

We both freshened up and put on matching pajamas before slowly cracking the door open.

Weird.

The house was mostly silent except for some light chatter traveling down the main hall. We expected the house to be abuzz with mealtime conversation, Rio's chaos, and laughter, but only Mama Dalia and Glory sat in the living room. They were eating Marrinitos and sipping coffee while discussing baby names. Something that previously would have made my heart fall into my ass, but all that changed after that morning's phone call.

"Where is everyone?" I asked.

"Hangovers," Dalia answered, pinching the bridge of her nose.

Yikes. I had my fair share of hangovers, and they were not missed. If I was groggy in the morning nowadays, it was usually because a certain somebody hogged the covers or got in too late.

That certain somebody was also hungover based on how she winced when I moved from in front of the window and light poured in. My poor baby. She's always been a lightweight, and I've never been prouder.

"So we didn't miss breakfast?" Cash asked in conjunction with his stomach.

"No, Poquito. Everything is in the oven. Make your plates, wake everyone else, and bring us two bottles of water please," she instructed.

With that, we were off on our tasks. I distributed water and Tylenol to the ladies while Cash went down the halls, broadcasting a rather cheerful good morning in Spanish. Everyone else didn't take that well. Especially Tia Cecilia. She cracked her door just to launch a house shoe at him.

Soon the house returned to chaos. With toddlers running around talking a mile a minute, hungover, pajama-clad adults scowling at the plate of eggs, and Cash who was busy irritating Glory and Mama with Christmas songs.

"Alright," Mama Dalia called, voice gruff. "Let's start opening gifts so I can take a nap. Niños first. Todos aqui."

Oh to be a kid from a good family on Christmas. The massive tree in the main sitting room was flooded with gifts, and more than half belonged to the children. I watched with awe and slight jealousy while the little ones unwrapped toy after toy, smiles beaming bright the entire time.

Rio unwrapped a set of tools and was overcome with absolute joy. The kind of joy only present in childhood. In contrast, his cousin Mimi, unwrapped a simple art set and bounced around the room like the embodiment of a kangaroo. It was the cutest thing I ever witnessed, and it made me excited to think about a future where we had our own kids participating in Christmas presents. With the adults pitching in to clear the mountains of wrapping paper out of the way, the giggly, energetic kids dispatched to their own separate corners to enjoy their new gifts.

"Alright, all you grown motherfuckers can open your stuff now," Mama Dalia said, handing Cash, Cookie, me, and Glory our own small boxes.

"You still have to hold it up and show it off though," she laughed.

Each of us were gifted a set of jewelry. Cookie and Glory got glittering gold birthstone earrings and matching pendants. While Cash and I were gifted chains and corresponding bracelets. The gesture was insanely thoughtful. I had just met Mama Dalia less than a week ago, but she welcomed me into her and her family's life. She radiated kindness and warmth the entire time and treated us like we were participating in a standard monogamous partnership. My heart twinged as tears threatened to escape my lower lash line. Picking your family really was the best gift.

I was content watching the scene before me, in a room full of people who were strangers less than a week ago. The glittering room was filled with light-hearted conversation about gag gifts and sentimental tokens alike. I was delighted to find I had received a hand-stitched extra-long quilt from Glory, and 7 physical volumes of One Punch Man from Cash. Then an extra long *something* else for my gag gift. They thought they were funny. But despite that, this was the best Christmas yet, until Cash opened his gift from me.

"Uh, Frijoles. Did you get me two gag gifts?" he asked, holding up a $10.57 gift card from Market West.

Market West or Markie's as it was dubbed by its Millennial customer base, was a department store chain that was making its way through the

South and Midwest. They were a relatively new company, but they were able to expand quickly with help from wholesale partnerships with local farmers and artisans in their service areas, as well as the quirky ads that usually went viral. They were also black-owned. Like I was.

"Nope, you said you wanted something to match with Glory," I chuckled.

Glory abandoned her gift swap with Cookie upon hearing that, and tore into a similarly wrapped gift with her name on it. Producing the exact same card, and scowling intently.

"That gift is lame," Rio announced, breaking the loaded silence. "You can't even get a clearance toy with that! Not even good snacks!"

Little man was right. Ten dollars and fifty-seven cents wouldn't get you far. Especially not in this economy. It wasn't enough to buy Cash's office snacks or Glory's favorite OPI nail polish. It wasn't even enough for a pack of decent toilet paper. However, it was the exact amount needed to buy one Smythe's Fine Apothecary two-wick candle after tax. Plus their actual gifts were waiting in our room. Matching embroidered sweatsuits, an original cover of Indigo for Cash, and a custom wood and resin paint palette for Glory.

"Read the card in the envelope," I instructed.

The duo hastily pulled out their coordinating cards, Cash finishing before Glory.

"Franklin, is this for real?" he asked.

I nodded earnestly.

"What? What's happening?" Tia Cecilia asked.

Cash ignored her and pounced on me, pulling me to the ground by my shoulders and peppering my jaw with kisses. I expected Glory to join us soon after, but a quick peek-up told me she was still sitting exactly how we left her. Except for the addition of fresh tears.

"Everything ok, Mija?" Mama Dalia asked.

It was silent until Glory pulled a Kleenex out of the box on the console and nodded. Then she set her sniffling sights on me.

Cash once left his poetry journal on the coffee table, and I helped myself to a sample of his written work detailing the majesty of Gloria's eyes. He described them as divine anodyne pools of onyx, coaxing their viewer into a vortex of mind-numbing pleasure, and separating them from their sensibilities. Oh, how right he was in that assessment. Just a few seconds in, and I was completely numb to the world outside of our shared gaze.

"Frankie," she choked, drawing me back to reality. "I could never be prouder."

My heart squeezed me breathless. What she said was so simple, and yet it meant the heavens above to me. Gloria was proud of me. My sweet baby who listened to my lofty dreams wrapped in rambling thoughts all those years ago. I had made her proud. Finally. It felt better than crack I think.

"Can somebody please tell us what's going on!?" Mama Dalia exclaimed impatiently.

Cash brought Glory in for a hug while I explained.

"Part of my product line, candles specifically, is going to be sold in Market West starting in February," I chuckled nervously.

I didn't expect fanfare from anyone except Cash and Glory. Honestly not even from my own parents. I knew I might get a warm or courtly congratulations from a few people in the house, but I ain't mind either way. But then Mama Dalia got up and squeezed me so tight that the air in my lungs pushed downward against my diaphragm and made me burp.

"Excuse me," I said hurriedly.

She waved me off and instead took my cheek in her small palm, giving me another loving pinch, which I'd come to appreciate.

"Ay, Mijo. Congratulations. You've worked so hard and now you're going to be everywhere. Cassius, get the good champagne. We're celebrating!" she exclaimed.

Her heart was in the right place despite the fact that she was definitely hung over. Plus she was forgetting one small detail…

"Sober, Mama," I gently reminded her.

"Oh, shit. Right, lo siento. Cassius, scratch that. Get the good leche helada! And bring fresas con crema!"

Getting an ice cream party as an adult hit different, and so did the conversations. We gossiped, rattled off jokes, and spoke about all the monotonous things most adults do to maintain life. But people also liked to ask difficult questions instead of asking about your favorite comic or your new shoes. Carlos, one of Cash's second cousins, seemed particularly determined to stick to the hard questions.

Hard. Questions.

"So like, I kinda get the poly thing. But I thought it was usually one man and two women," he started.

"That's polygyny. We're polygamists," Cash replied calmly.

Carlos nodded before ultimately waving his hand and dismissing Cash's answer, much to my chagrin.

"Yeah, Ok. But how does that work when you decide to get married? Who gets the girl?"

If Carlos wasn't Cash's cousin, I would've cursed him smooth out. All the questions were invasive and unnecessary, but that one, in particular, rubbed me like a cat who decided to scratch their ass on a cactus. In other words, the wrong way.

"Glory will decide who she wants to legally marry. We're a team, not opponents, and Glory isn't some shining, brainless, trophy who has no say," I spat.

With that, Mama Dalia stepped in to diffuse the brewing tension.

"Carlos, why are you so bothered? Are you mad that your primo has two lovers while you can't pay someone to kiss those ashy-ass lips?" she asked.

Carlos was light enough to visibly blush which only further confirmed his well-deserved embarrassment.

"No, Tia. I was just curious," he mumbled quietly.

Mama didn't buy his answer for a second. She shot him a look that quietly said, *"get uncurious"*, before addressing everyone else.

"Anyone else curious?" she asked.

Leave it to the kids to boldly go where no one else dared. While everyone shuffled about awkwardly and avoided Mama's gaze, seven-year-old Rio's hand shot up like a violently popped champagne cork.

"Uncle Cash," he started. "How'd you get a boyfriend and a girlfriend?" he asked.

Fucking yikes. I'm so glad he ain't ask me because there were so many parts of our story that were inappropriate for young ears. The short answer was sex. However, Cash handled it with absolute grace.

"I was nice and respectful to both of them and they were nice and respectful to me. So we decided that we liked each other and wanted to be boyfriends and girlfriends," he explained calmly.

Rio seemed content with that answer. Then he said,

"I'm gonna get a boyfriend and a girlfriend too since it's that easy."

I froze, momentarily concerned that I witnessed a kid come out to his family, but Mama Dalia and Cookie didn't bat an eye.

"You're seven. You will not be dating anyone. But when you're old enough, make sure you got money to spoil them both," Cookie said lazily while chewing a chunk of sugarcane.

Rio shrugged and said, OK. Then just like that, we were back to regular conversation as he skittered off to find a new piece of wood to tinker with. I almost wanted to cry. That was how uneventful coming out should be. I was so happy Rio wasn't traumatized. The Gilrados were alright.

Dinner went well. Really well. Maybe too well? Mama Dalia praised the roast and ginger duck I made and saved herself a few tortillas, but she was also trying to keep me.

"Franklin, how about you stay here after the New Year and let them go back to Dallas? That way they have a reason to visit, I can spoil you until I get my granddaughter and eat like a king every night," Mama Dalia pitched.

Tia Cecilia seemed to nod in agreement even though she lived in Alabama.

"Mama, you can't keep my boyfriend," Cash replied hurriedly.

His arm hooked around mine protectively like he was defending me from a surging crowd instead of his family. It was dramatic and cute, making his mother roll her eyes.

"Greedy," she sighed.

Her attention was then claimed by Carlos attempting to scoop the last of Glory's greens onto his plate. Effectively marking it his *fifth* serving.

"Aht! Drop the spoon!" Mama Dalia chided. "No one wants to smell what happens once you digest all of that. Plus, hardly anyone else got seconds."

Carlos tried to state his case,

"Tia, I just didn't want them to go to waste. No one else seemed interested when I asked," he explained.

His explanation immediately produced several narrowed gazes and scoffs.

"Oh, I must ain't hear you ask," Cookie said, taking the spoon. "Me, Rio, and Tia Cecilia want the rest. Don't worry, they won't go to waste."

Chaos ensued. Cousins, elders, and children alike were arguing over how the remaining two cups of greens should be divided. Carlos was being heckled and harassed for eating more than his fair share while Mama Dalia sat bemused, sipping a cup of hot jamaica. Glory's greens induced madness among the Gilrados.

"I'm so glad we leave tomorrow," Cash sighed.

That's right. We were leaving for Heaven's Peak the next day. It would just be me, Cash, and Essie for a whole week. Living in the mountains and enjoying each other's company. Peacefully and quietly.

"Maybe we can visit again for the summer," I suggested, watching his lively family continue to bicker.

Cash seemed like he wanted to protest, but then he caught my gaze and gave me a gentle smile. Snuggling against my shoulder, he conceded,

"Yeah, maybe."

Chapter Twenty-Seven

Heaven's Peak, Colorado, was absolutely breathtaking. The welcome sign was situated at the beginning of a low valley, which gave way to an awe-inducing view of the picturesque cabin town situated in the center of it. Population 3,700. Full of snow-kissed slopes, natural hot springs, and lakes. It was a tiny jewel nestled in a rocky foothold of majestic Colorado. Very different from desert-like, fast-paced and huge, Dallas.

"So what do you think?" Cash asked, as we drove through downtown.

My response was interrupted by the sight of a bubbling creek that split the median of the road. It was contained by a high fence bordering the entrance until you reached the larger, rushing river it was connected to. Several shops and businesses composed the town's skyline welcoming us in, and locals selling hometown delicacies such as kabobs of grilled elk and cellophane packages of candied crickets greeted us with a friendly wave.

"I think I won't want to leave," Glory answered, reading my mind.

"Frijoles?" Cash asked.

"I think I could die here," I answered. "It's beautiful."

Cash gave us both a light snicker.

"Just wait until you see the cabin," he replied.

We arrived to our rental ten minutes later, and it was clear Cassius was his mother's son. A huge wood and brick home greeted us as we parked in the icy shadow of it's balcony. It was surrounded on all sides by flowering ivory Daphne coupled with vividly green Wintergreen Boxwood, and the pathway to the ornate hand-carved wood door was paved with bricks of varying colors, reminding me of autumn.

Glory noticed the eight-foot fireplace through the front window and squealed.

"Cassius, how much did you pay for this?" she asked.

We tried to keep things split pretty even lately. I did fairly well last quarter so I got our flights and rental. Glory got food and entertainment, and Cash took care of lodging. Really he knocked that shit out of the park. The cabin was insane with two decks, a hot tub, five bedrooms, and a central location. So I was curious too. And also slightly concerned.

"Just enough but not too much," he replied, keeping his answer vague. "If you're worried, you can just make me a pan of cornbread and all will be well again."

I snorted.

Everyone loved Glory's greens, but Cash was flat-out addicted to her cornbread. He also refused to share with anyone. Me included.

"I'll think about making some for dinner. Right now I'm going to change boots and look around," she said as he turned the lock.

Leave it to Glory to be that curious black person. Her curiosity concerned me at times as her paranoid, high-strung, partner, but I'd never tried to deter her from exploring it. Curiosity made her brave. That bravery made her Glory.

"Do you want some company?" I offered.

Glory quickly shook her curly lil head, slipped on her hiking boots, and gave me and Cash a few sweet pecks.

"Nah, enjoy some alone time guys. My location's on, I have a backup battery pack, snacks, and a paper map. Love y'all."

She dragged the door shut before we could form a protest and skipped down the stone path towards the small woods east of the cabin. Leaving us standing in the center of the living room staring at the door like bored ducks.

"So," Cash started. "What do you wanna do now?"

Our girlfriend was gone and we were alone for the first time in a week. There was only one thing we could do. I pulled Cash close to me and gave him my most dazzling smile to get him on board.

"I have a few ideas," I purred seductively.

"You cheated!" I yelled.

"No, you just suck," Cash laughed while shuffling the deck. "In more ways than one."

He gave me a little wink and I was almost inclined to explore it, but he was definitely cheating.

"Roll up your sleeve," I demanded.

"What? No, Frijoles. It's just Uno. It's not that serious."

Yes, we were two grown men playing Uno while our girlfriend dallied around in the woods. No shame about it. See, Essie hated Uno after Marcus lifted a year's worth of allowance off her at age ten and refused to allow it in her presence. Because of that, I knew a cheating hand when I saw one. I had twenty cards in my hand from an assault of draw twos when Cash called his Uno.

"You fibber!" I laughed, tackling Cash to the ground. "Let me see them arms!"

Cash put up a good fight, rolling and swinging in an effort to avoid my invasive search. But he eventually bumped into the couch, and I had him with nowhere to run. I lifted his tight-fitting sleeves and a slew of draw twos and wild cards slid to the Sedona Red hardwood.

"I knew it!" I screeched victoriously. "You little pretty-eyed grifter!"

Cash smiled beneath me, and his usually smooth voice morphed into lighthearted laughter that tickled my eardrums melodically.

"You're lucky you're so cute," I scoffed, rolling my eyes.

"I'm cute?" Cash chuckled.

His smile gave way to deep-set dimples that were competing with his glowing hazel eyes for my heart. His chestnut skin contrasted beautifully against the red of mine, and his soft yet strong body cradled mine perfectly.

"Kinda. The whole sun kissed thing is working for you," I responded.

He placed a kiss on my throat with a snort.

"I wonder what else I could get to work for me?" he laughed.

I had to make a joke.

"The TV remote is right there, baby. No need to wonder," I replied.

Cash sucked his teeth while I cackled at my own joke.

"Akiki. Pull out your dick, nigga," he scoffed.

Cash

Shit.

The French and their colorful language have a word for this. They call it frottage and it feels so fucking good. Not as good as fucking, but still.

"Sword fighting is so fun," Frankie mumbled.

I reeled my head back in slight disbelief, reluctantly parting my sight from Franklin's unethically large dick.

"What? You call it sword fighting?" I asked.

"Well, yeah. It's literally meat fencing," he replied.

I lost myself in a fit of laughter. Tears were streaming down my cheeks and I was hunched over on my knees. The moment was definitely ruined.

"Are you finished?" an unamused Frankie asked while crossing his arms.

"Aye, don't get sassy with me! You called it meat fencing! How is that not funny?"

I started laughing again as soon as the words left my mouth. I can't tell you why I found that phrase so damn funny, but the image of two people vigorously dueling with salami that populated my mind definitely didn't help.

"Whatever," Fab pouted. "I'm putting my dick away."

"Wait babe, no. I can get it together," I countered.

I could not get it together. I once again found myself crying laughing, this time sliding down the wall.

"Whew, shit. Ok, ok," I chuckled. "Come on, nigga. Let's do a pickle tickle."

Fab pushed me on the bed with a defeated sigh while I was in the middle of howling then I watched him and his fairy-tale hair float downstairs to the living room. I was on my way after him when I saw him scrambling out the door with a blanket, moving with an unexpected amount of urgency.

"GLORIA! WHY ARE YOU NAKED IN 32 DEGREE WEATHER!" he hollered.

I put on slides to run after him, and sure as shit, our girlfriend was walking across the property's bridge in a pair of undies, boots, and a soaked sports bra.

"Princessa, what the fuck?" I exclaimed, running after her. "Where are the rest of your clothes? Esta helado! Tienes de ganas enferma!"

"My clothes are in my hands, Cash. Duh!" she spat back.

My pulse raced. What an irritating, bratty, little woman. She tossed me a mischievous smirk that said she knew exactly what she was doing. Yet I still fell for it.

"I should whoop you," I gritted.

"Now who has a sick desire?" she chuckled.

"Glory," Fab snarled while wrapping her in a blanket. "Why are you running round out here half-naked?"

"I could ask you two the same thing. Cash is also in undies."

I looked down to spot my exposed black boxer briefs along with my half-chub. I forgot to put on pants the moment I saw her.

"Were y'all meat mincing?" she asked.

That was worse than meat fencing and a few wanton chuckles escaped before Fab glared at me.

"Don't start," he commanded.

Glory waved off our concern while trotting back inside, distracting us both from our grievances with the bounce of her breasts and the sway of her hips.

"I took an accidental dip in a shallow hot spring that wasn't marked on the map. I'm fine y'all," she insisted.

Fuck.

I don't usually condone lying, but there were some instances where it was absolutely necessary. Take for example, this one. To know Fab was to know he didn't like to fuck around and find out, wait and see, or take action after the fact. Which led us to…

"YOU FELL IN MYSTERIOUS WATER!? No, no, no!" Fab screamed. "We're going to Urgent Care for cultures now!"

Glory couldn't even protest because he pulled a clean gown over her head, handed her a pair of pants, and *carried* her out to the car. Hell, I didn't even have time to react before he threatened to leave me. Which was unexpected because we had rented an SUV and that nigga lived by his car safety statistics.

"Cash! Let's go!" he called from the driver's seat.

"I'm coming!" I shouted while pulling a pair of Glory's velvet pajama pants over my legs.

Damn, it all! That little exploration discovery girlfriend of mine had our retreat off to a rough start.

It took twenty-six hours for Glory's cultures to come back negative. Fab forbade us to have sex until we knew she was for sure not carrying some rare parasite that could ruin our immune systems and kill us all, but by the time we confirmed she wasn't, she was pissed. She took the largest room since it had a soaking tub and an accompanying balcony, and she'd been in it ignoring us since we'd gotten home from urgent care nearly two days previous. I was heartbroken.

"Princessa, please. I'm sorry," I sighed.

My forehead was pressed against her locked door and I was listening for any sound or vibration to indicate she might open up and let me inside.

But instead, I got a firm,

"Go away, Cassius."

"Glorrryyy," I whined. "It wasn't even me! It was Fab's fault!"

Suddenly my boyfriend materialized out of thin air and lingering spite to scare the shit out of me.

"And I don't regret it. But thanks for throwing me under the bus, babe," he scoffed.

"Babe, wait," I tried.

Frijoles ignored me and continued on his journey downstairs, casting me a stank-ass grimace the entire time.

Great.

Now both their dramatic asses were upset with me. Everyone loves water signs until they remember that passion swings both ways. Spiteful, grudging, unfairly beautiful water signs. I never considered drowning an ideal way to die, yet here I was.

I found Frijoles outside, gaze set on the small frozen lake located in the back of the cabin. His large hand clutched a few winter blooms tight. He seemed to be deep in thought, notating the flowers for future scent ideas, but my presence wasn't lost on him. His eyes cut over to where I stood for a split second before he went back to ignoring me, and in that moment I decided enough was enough.

"Cassius! What the fuck!?" he hollered.

Wet clumps of snow dripped from his hair and he scowled at me while I packed my hands tight with more ammunition.

"We are not spending all week in a literal winter wonderland ignoring each other," I shrugged, tossing my next snowball.

He tried to turn and duck but it was too little too late and I pegged him square in his big-ass forehead.

"Stop that!" he spat.

"No thank you," I replied curtly.

I quickly shaped my third and fourth snowball, hoping to get back at him for his equally crotchety and cantankerous behavior, but he had all but vanished by the time I looked up.

The air outside whipped past me and whistled in my ear. It was way too quiet for me to be comfortable. No crunch of frozen snow, no doors opening or closing, and no belligerent cursing followed. It was just me and the song of the winter wind. Until I turned around. One. Two. Three. I was pelted with solid, powdery snowballs coming from multiple directions. I randomly fired at what I could, but it hit nothing. Frankie wouldn't let up, and I couldn't even get a chance to defend myself.

"Show yourself, coward!" I yelled.

"Surrender and I will!" Fab replied.

I was outfoxed, but not for long. While the area was wooded, the trees surrounding us were skeletal and too barren for someone as large as Fab to hide behind. That left either the bushes, the car, or the shed. But my clothes would be frosted long before I could locate him by process of elimination.

"Why should I surrender!?" I shouted back. "You scared that I'll win again and get to be the dom for a week?"

I was taunting him but I was already in too deep to care. Fab was a dominant. Glory was a brat even though she didn't know it. Then I was somewhere in the middle. Able to assert authority and protect, but also able to ride a dom's last nerve.

"Pfft. You don't even know where I'm at. How can I lose?" Frankie replied.

He was playing right into my hand, little did he know.

"I'm just saying. I'm sure Glory would appreciate the change in scenery. And don't even get me started on the aftercare," I laughed.

"What's wrong with my aftercare?" Frankie scoffed.

I followed that irritated sound over over to the hedges trimming the porch but that seemed too obvious. So I continued with my search.

"Nothing if you like being put to sleep with fan theories," I replied. "You basically turn into a white noise machine."

"Oh really? You don't seem to mind when I be putting you to sleep," he spat.

"Mmhm," I replied. "Ok."

Something about the phrase "Ok" as a response in an argument always set Frankie off, no matter how minor or friendly the disagreement had been. If I had to guess based on our time together, I'd say it's because of his parents. His dad was the personification of a dry text.

So I tried to avoid using it as much as possible, but he was getting OK'd today. We had wasted a whole day of beautiful mountain sunshine being distant and griping at each other. That had to end immediately. I ain't plan this trip for my health.

"And another thing!" Fab barked.

He was still going. Just fussing and cussing. It's no wonder he fits right in with my Mama and sister. The three of them could pass for sisters if you got them in the same room with the right prompt. Again, normally I'd try to soothe him, but his argumentative nature was working to my advantage. He was too busy repining to notice I was approaching his location among the boxwoods.

"If you had something you needed me to change, you could've just told me! But naw, you out here att…"

I finally silenced him by dumping him in a bucket of snow I dug out during his rant. Was it childish? Yes. Was it effective? Also yes. Effective as hell. Right up until he stood and chased after me.

I was hauling ass then suddenly, we were on ice. I had forgotten about the lake and apparently so had Frankie, because his long legs were wobbling like an unsteady calf standing for the first time. Luckily I knew how not to bust my ass after growing up here, but I knew Fab held no such skills.

"Hold on, I'm coming," I laughed, watching him grab at the air for support. "I won't let yo cranky ass fall."

I penguin hobbled over to him and pulled him upright. But his expression reminded me of Goofy's for a second as he threw himself forward then back to stay straight, and we both fell over when I started laughing.

"Ugh! You did that on purpose!" he groaned.

I definitely didn't. Mostly because I did not possess the knees of someone who could afford a fall on hard ice.

"I did," I lied.

Fab let his limbs fall limp and turned to me with a pout. His deep brown eyes shined like unclaimed riches against the bright white mid-day sun and those full lips slowly pulled into a forgiving sugar-sweet smile. There was a reason he was saved as Azucar Morena in my phone.

"Let me be mad at you," he sighed.

"Nope," I shrugged. "Not allowed."

I kissed Fab eagerly and he reciprocated. I thought we might be making up for lost time, but he suddenly broke us off and placed a kosher kiss on the tip of my nose. A nose that was probably going to freeze off if we didn't get the fuck off the ice.

"Fine I guess," he conceded. "Let's go inside though. Making out on the ice is white people shit."

"Definitely is," I agreed while helping him up.

Glory's door was open when we came back upstairs. She was listening to Neo-soul on the balcony, accompanied by her easel and a fresh canvas stained with wet paint. She looked just as stunning as you expected a divinity to look. Me and Fab exchanged a skeptical look before easing closer. While walking through her room, I noticed she had several canvases filled with work in various stages of creation. Some were still sketches, some had been outlined, and some were nearly complete, just missing her meticulous shading work. But I noticed that they all lent their viewer a sense of freedom and curiosity. Glory was thriving in the Colorado mountains.

"What are you painting?" Fab asked as we reached the balcony.

Glory didn't respond audibly. She instead tilted her body left, allowing us a view. It was us. Us throwing snowballs, slipping on ice, and sharing a kiss in the winter sun. It was a living document of the last hour we'd spent together. Something she believed was worthy of taking the time to create a physical memory of. She believed we were worthy.

"Amour, this is breathtaking," I whispered, sounding more like my mama than ever before.

"It really is," Frankie agreed.

Glory gave us a proud smile and a gentle nod but still remained silent. That was fine though, because I was prepared to grovel. On bended knee while singing a 90's love song. Man, they need to bring back hairy coochie music.

"You still mad at us?" I asked.

Another non-verbal response. This time a head shake indicated she wasn't.

"What's going on then?" Fab asked.

Glory's round mouth pulled into a slight grimace. I saw the thoughts racing past in her big brown eyes, and then she sighed, almost in defeat, and parted her lips to finally speak.

"I got a sore throat," she said hoarsely.

I thought she was mad when she told me to beat it earlier, but no, her usually delicate voice was shot and strangled. She sounded dry and gravely like Wilhelmina Packard from Atlantis: The Lost Empire.

Shit. Damn it!

I hated that Fab was right about the mystery water. So much so that I sighed in defeat. RIP to my unhinged plans of sucking Glory's soul out of her pussy.

Chapter Twenty-Eight

Cash

There are perks to having a chemist boyfriend. Fab swabbed Glory himself and sent it off to a local lab. I was surprised when the results came back just two short hours later, confirming that she wasn't contagious, but did have a sinus infection. Much to her upset. Frankie took care of everything from there, getting her results over to the NP who had seen her earlier, and procuring a prescription to treat her inflamed throat. My job was getting her to take it, which really wasn't any less work. She was a fighter, and that worried me for an inevitable future filled with mini Glories. I prepared her a hot ginger and turmeric tea to go along with a sweet potato tart Fab made and placed it on a serving tray along with the antibiotics she originally tried to refuse and went to work. She could tell me no to a lot of things, but she was taking this pill.

I found her on the deck, soaking in the hot tub wearing just what she was born in, with her eyes towards the sky. The clouds above us were gray and ominous, but she was focused on the glittering snow beginning to flurry around us.

"I can't believe you grew up here," she sighed.

She sounded so very content, and I developed a great sense of pride knowing I had a part in that.

"Well, a few towns away. But yeah, Colorado is serene," I agreed.

"Very," she nodded. "If I could ever get out of Dallas I would come here."

A strange heat crept up my spine. I think it was the desire to do whatever I could to make Glory happy. Even if she didn't formally ask.

"You could… I mean, we could live here," I offered.

Her eyes dropped to the mountain peaks and she began to search for something intangible. Maybe a sign. Maybe a solution. Our silence then became loaded instead of peaceful, like we were on the precipice of something undiscovered.

"No, I… the timing isn't right," she sighed.

Glory then rattled off all the reasons why she had to deny herself the luxury of peace. Everything from family and community obligations to housing prices, and work. It was weird. Mostly because she still didn't know that she could just say the word and me and Frankie would take care of everything. Suddenly it was silent again, and I witnessed a singular fresh snowflake melt into the stream of an escaped tear. She was conflicted, but I knew better than to push the issue. So I just said,

"If you ever change your mind, Princessa. Just know I'll make it happen."

And I meant it.

God, life was so hard. Or was that just me? See, I finally got Glory to take her meds after an hour of dancing around, only for her to end both my night and Frankie's by nap-trapping us. Soft women were dangerous, and so were hard men, and I had the most unfortunate pleasure of being trapped between both. Every time I tried to move it got worse. Frankie's unholy dick was resting against my backside and Glory's tear-drop ass was pressed against my front. It was too much, and I'd either pass out or nut attempting to get out of bed without waking either of them.

Still, I managed. It cost me my sanity and I was sweating buckets, but

I finally got out of bed. Only for Glory to immediately wake up. She stretched her arms over her head with a melodic yawn and I watched eagerly as the sheet slid down her shoulders, past her marvelous, jiggling breasts, to gather at her hips, just underneath her soft belly. Gloria Esther King was perfection personified.

"Good morning," she cooed sweetly.

Her eyes briefly darted below my waist and I noticed that I was back on brick, then my dick had somehow made its way into my hand and coaxed me to stroke it. Weird.

"Is that what you're giving me for breakfast?" she giggled.

"Ye…"

"NO!" Frankie groaned. "No one's getting dick for breakfast. I spent all day yesterday making cinnamon rolls and we have somewhere to be in two hours."

"Buzzkill," I hissed in reply.

I didn't know Frankie was awake, yet alone alert enough to tell time and cockblock. Still, I knew he was right, so I took my hand out of my pants and focused.

On Glory's titties.

Man, them muhfuckas were huge.

"Go take a cold shower," Frankie tutted while hitting me with a pillow.

"There's more wood than a 70's sitting room in there," he said, pointing to my bulge.

I looked down and noticed The Sears Building was protruding from my boxers.

Touché, boyfriend. Touché.

One thing I learned pretty early into dating Glory was her love for the outdoors. She liked walking wooded trails, visiting local parks, tending gardens, and even swimming in lakes. I personally thought swimming in lakes was fucking trifling, but she did a lot of research and testing before dipping in so I let her have it. Besides that one lil thing, her outdoorsy nature was admirable, and since we lived in a big concrete metropolis, I took every opportunity I could to indulge her.

"Are we at a ranch?" she asked excitedly.

"Yes, a horse and goat ranch specifically. It's called Hoof And Bleat," I replied.

Frankie had packed her boots in his luggage to keep some parts of our itinerary a surprise but Glory hadn't taken them off since she found them lying in his carry-on. She did all that fussing and fighting about Frankie buying them only for those boots to become her favorite thing.

Typical brat.

We were on vacation, but Frankie had noticed that the owners of Hoof And Bleat were selling goat milk for cheaper than his current wholesaler. They didn't ship, or really even work with companies outside of Colorado, but they gave Frankie an in since he seemed so determined. If he could milk their most belligerent goat within one hour, they'd be open to a partnership with the tall, fast-talking soap maker from Texas. So that left me and Glory to manage the tour alone.

"Come on, Cassius!" she screeched. "Let's go see the chickens."

I wasn't sure how to tell my excited baby that I absolutely hated birds, so I didn't. I just let her pull me along through freshly tilled mud and what was probably goat shit in a new pair of leather dockers.

"God, you're cooked." My subconscious reminded me.

"Yeah, I know." I sighed.

Honestly, it was a great time. Even though a broody hen tried to claim me as her perch. The ranch really was something out of a postcard, with green fields stretching far beyond the horizon and orchards and fruit patches bordering it. They also had complimentary apple cider that tasted like a liquid baked good and leather riding crops, (Which I definitely didn't buy for sex.) Plus Glory loved the animals and they loved her. A pair of cows had followed her through the fields for a mile before they were shooed off, only for an intrigued goat and that same mischievous hen to replace them. She was like a country, dark-skin, Snow White, attracting farm animals with her melodic harmonies and bright smile. Until we got to the horses.

"Cass baby, look," she whispered, tapping the back of my hand.

She was ten feet in front of a beautiful red mare, frozen in awe.

"Do you think she notices me?" she asked.

The horse was staring directly at her as if it was trying to communicate telepathically. Like they knew each other. As if she was saying, *"How you been living, girl?"*

"I think she does," I chuckled.

Glory took two small steps towards the mare, and it was if she was rediscovering her ability to walk. I guess she didn't want to spook her, but the horse didn't seem bothered. If anything she was just as curious, because as soon as Glory raised her palm to greet her, she nuzzled her hand.

"Oh my goodness, you are so pretty, with a personality to match," Glory giggled while stroking her back.

"Look at that! Red's taken a liking to ya," one of the handlers named Bale said.

That had me concerned because Glory was well within kicking distance.

"Is she usually unfriendly?" I asked.

Bale was an all-American white boy with a charming white smile to match. I could see him disarming some poor, unsuspecting woman to the point of getting her right out of her panties.

"Nah, don't worry. She's not aggressive, just kind of aloof. She prefers the company of crickets to most other animals and people."

Ok, so she was the equestrian version of Frankie. That tracked.

"She's for sale too," Bale mentioned.

I was suddenly sure that they were speaking telepathically because Red's ears twitched as if she were asking Glory if she heard the good news.

"Why would anyone wanna get rid of such a beauty?" Gloria cooed to the horse more than anyone else.

Red whinnied and continued nuzzling Glory as if agreeing.

"Cause she's dramatic, likes to be the center of attention, and this is a working farm, but she's not a working horse. She'd be much happier being with a one animal owner," Bale confessed.

"She just like me for real," Glory laughed.

"The one owner thing!?" I panicked.

Glory cut her gaze over to me, damn near slicing my lips off.

"No, Cassius. The dramatics and desire not to work," she sighed.

I couldn't help but pitch my offer again.

"You don't have to work, Princessa. You can just spend your time painting and riding d…"

"HORSES!" Glory shouted, noticing Bale's confused expression.

Out of all the times she cracked an inappropriate joke, now she was embarrassed. Glory was so unserious.

"Can I ride her?" she asked.

"Of course," Bale laughed. "Let me get you a loaner saddle."

I was watching Glory and Red gallop through the fields when Frankie joined my side. He had acquired a cowboy hat which was very on-brand for him, and a large glass carafe of fresh goat milk was tucked into his side.

"I see you got your contract?" I laughed.

"I did. Got bit too," he confirmed. "I see Glory is riding a horse."

"Mhm, they like each other. Her name is Red. She's for sale," I shrugged nonchalantly.

I enjoyed the quiet breeze for a moment before Frankie reclaimed my attention with a loud sigh.

"Cash, you cannot buy Glory a horse," he chided.

"Pfttt. I wasn't gonna buy her a horse," I waved.

I was.

"But just out of curiosity, why not?"

"For one," Frankie said, resting the reason on his pointer finger. "We live in Dallas apartments. For two, this horse is all the way in Colorado, and for three, taking a horse from a farm just to keep it in boarding stables is wrong."

All valid points if I'm being honest. But something about not buying Red for Glory still felt wrong. Maybe it was the knowledge that nothing back home could duplicate the joy she was likely feeling now. Trotting through the fields, with mountain air wrapped around her curls.

"She looks so happy out there," I mumbled.

Frankie rested his head on top of mine with a loud sigh that represented how both of us felt watching our joyful little cowgirl.

"She does, she really does," he replied.

Chapter Twenty-Nine

G lory

The time we spent in the mountains wasn't enough. Even with the seemingly endless starry nights we spent laying on our backs, gazing at the midnight sky, with tenebrosity rivaling my own skin. 16 days felt like 16 hours, and even the best-planned itinerary didn't help the sense of FOMO I got when I found yet another shop or sight we didn't have time to explore. Heaven's Peak was aptly named, and I developed a strange sense of homesickness leaving it behind as we boarded the plane to go back home to Dallas. But then again, it could've just been the antibiotics. Still, I'll admit that touching down on the tarmac of DFW quelled my stomach with anxious nausea. But I'm sure everyone felt like that returning home after a dream vacation, right?

"Hey, we need to stop by Fed-Ex and grab your paintings before we head home," Cash explained.

Oh right. My art. I felt inspiration strike while we were away. Knowing Cash was properly filthy fucking rich did wonders to assuage my Amazon shopping guilt, so I ordered supplies off his card in exchange for the head I was going to give him anyway. It was a win-win situation. We wound up shipping ten paintings of various sizes from Heaven's Peak to Dallas. My favorite, being a piece that I tilted Monday Morning. Forever memorializing the ethereal beauty of a new Colorado sunrise. I already had the perfect place in mind to hang it at home. Which for some new and unexplained reason, felt a lot like Cash's bougie-ass condo. That meant it was probably time to have the, "let's move in" convo. Shit, I was unprepared for that. I can confidently say I didn't expect to be ever having that conversation with anyone, let alone two people, but here we are.

Thoughts and prayers to my dearly departed pimp card.

Out of the few things I missed about Dallas, the traffic wasn't one of them. It was hell wading through weekday traffic at 4 P.M, and if I wasn't so damn excited to get my paintings back in my possession, I would've said fuck it and made the boys take the street way home. That squeamish feeling in my stomach was intensifying and slowly spreading to my still-sensitive throat. It was weird cause I've never been a gagger, but the way the car was stopping and going? One more hard brake and today would be the day a legend fell from grace.

"Shit like this makes me wonder why we even came back," Frankie grumbled.

A sentiment I wholeheartedly agreed with even if I wasn't brave enough to say it out loud.

"All of our shit's here and this is also where me and Glory's jobs live," Cash reminded us.

Right. My lawyering job. The one that I fought tooth and nail to succeed at every day. The one that wasn't at all exhausting and sometimes suffocating. Not at all.

The car lurched forward again, and so did my stomach. I soon broke out in a chilling sweat. Then my brain suddenly started screaming at me to open the door lest I wanted to be covered in regurgitated chicken pesto, and I was quick to listen.

"Cash, pull over! I'm about to…"

I gagged first, but that turned into full-on heaving as soon as Cash pulled onto a shoulder. Frankie ran out, narrowly avoiding being bumped by an angry soccer mom, to help me. It was dangerous and impulsive, but I can't say I wasn't grateful. I wanted someone by my side. Throwing up is just one of those human experiences that humbles you. Plus it fucking hurts.

"Wait, wait. Essie, let's wait for a minute," Frankie instructed.

I thought I was done blowing my guts out and I was eager to leave the scene of the crime, but Frankie kept me still for a few seconds longer. It was a good thing too because the rest of my lunch came up shortly after that, forcing me into my hands and knees. My throat burned like I took a shot of microwaved paint thinner.

"Oh, Essie baby," Frankie sighed, pulling me off the ground.

Mister Meticulous then retrieved a pack of wipes out of his well-organized bag to freshen up my vomit-covered face before arranging the seats in the car quite particularly.

"Change of plans, love. You're going to ride up front, but you're going home," Frankie said firmly.

"What about the art?" I grumbled weakly.

"I'll grab it," he replied. "You need to rest, and Cash is a better cuddler. We all know I can't sit still for long."

Even after spending more than a decade apart, I knew Frankie's rules. No cheap socks, no skipping wash day, no pickles, and absolutely no SUV's. I respected his rules, but there was no way he could cram 10 big-ass wood-framed canvases into his little civic.

"Baby, you won't be able to take your car. It's too much stuff," I sighed.

I was ushered into the car, the seat was reclined, and a cold compress was placed on the sweltering expanse of my forehead.

"I'll take Cash's wagon, Essie," he almost laughed.

He said it was a routine action for him. Like he didn't have a panic attack every time we merged into a different lane on the highway in that same wagon.

"But, your rules," I started.

"You're well worth rule-breaking for, Essie love," he said sweetly.

Well fuck. Suddenly I was hot again, and nothing would stop me from melting into the leather of the seats this time.

"How are you feeling?" Cash asked.

We had been home for thirty minutes. Just long enough for me to suck down a can of cold ginger ale and put on Maury reruns. The ancient healing ritual.

"Better," I whispered.

I tightened the blanket around my shoulders while snuggling into Cash's chest. He wasn't lean and cut like Frankie so he often joked he had a dad-bod in training, much to my chagrin. I felt like he was being unfair to himself even if he didn't mean the remark to be as self-deprecating as it sounded. Cassius was soft, his big thighs had stretch marks, and his tummy shook when he laughed, yet I wouldn't change a single thing about him for everything in the world or the sky above it. Cause all of that made him Cash, the world's most perfect cuddler.

"Much better actually," I added.

"Good," Cassius replied while pecking me.

He wrapped his arms around me tight, inviting me to doze off before his phone vibrated back-to-back. He rolled away from me to answer it, and I almost asked who the fuck was texting him at two in the afternoon like he was single when he reached to check. But he told me before I could open my big mouth.

"Frankie said he's stopping to get you some probiotic smoothies in case it's the antibiotics messing with your stomach. He asked if you needed anything else."

Well, I felt two inches tall. That prompted me to examine my actions. I was cranky all day today, even before I threw up, then I was jealous.

Granted I was jealous over nothing, but the emotion itself was not only unprompted, it was unlike me.

"Can you ask him to grab a pregnancy test please?" I said softly.

While I'd love to blame my unease on the antibiotics, I knew that likely wasn't the case. I only had two days of them left and I'd been fine leading up to today. So maybe all the motion of the journey home unsettled my stomach, or maybe I was reaping the consequences of our lust-filled New Year. I wanted to know either way. I *needed* to know either way.

Chapter Thirty

Glory

It was negative. Just like the last ten I'd taken over the last two weeks. While anyone else in my position would've felt relief, I only felt confusion. Mostly because I was still sick with no other readily available explanation, but also partly because I don't think I would've actually been devastated to see a little blue plus looking back at me. Sure, my life wasn't the neatest. I had two partners, one was recovering from PTSD, the other was my kinda coworker, and my immediate family didn't know about our relationship. But despite all that, it wasn't the worst either. If I had a baby, they'd have two awesome, capable, supportive dads. Frankie would probably talk me into staying home for my pregnancy so I could be stress free, and Cash would definitely be buying out entire Baby Depots to make sure we were prepared. I'd make sure that they'd have the best childhood. I'd give them everything that wasn't given to me. Carefree summer nights filled with brownie sundaes, a home warmed with kindness, and judgment-free unconditional love just to name a few things. We could catch lightning bugs, eat bimuelos, and build pillow forts inspired by the stars.

"I think I want a baby," I whispered.

Tilly looked at me like I grew a second head. Hell, she might've been right. That would be one explanation for the staggering polarity of my thoughts.

"That's an odd confession to have in the middle of a case briefing," she replied.

Right. The case briefing. I was defending a woman charged with alleged child neglect and abandonment. Her and the child's father had a court agreement that he would get partial custody, and have the child every other weekend. Unfortunately he was never consistent, and since she couldn't get help from family or friends, she dropped their child off on his porch after confirming he was home and went to work. It was a bullshit charge. She, like most moms, deserved better.

"I'm sorry, I've just had a long couple of weeks. Forgive me. What were you saying?" I asked.

Tilly gave me a look letting me know she intended to dig.

"We'll circle back to that, but I was letting you know that the firm won't let you do this one pro-bono."

My daydream crashed down around me in a fiery blaze.

"What?" I stammered.

Tilly tucked her lip and gave me a reluctant nod.

"You know how these people are," she sighed. "If it's not making dollars, it's not making sense. They said the decision won't generate enough press to justify letting one of their best attorneys do it for free."

I volunteered my time and expertise often. Church had traumatized me in more ways than one, but it also made me aware of how many people were living without. Life could be cruel enough to cut with steel when you were already down from a kick in the ribs. Especially to black women. That's why I decided to become a lawyer. To make an actual difference. Not a publicly praised one.

"Who made the final decision?" I asked.

Tilly shuddered.

"Theresa Adams," she replied.

The only black female partner in our entire practice. She was the proverbial nail in Kiara Greenly's coffin. The urge to vomit was back and violent.

"No," I said, shuffling to stand. "No, she can't afford it. She'll be in jail by tomorrow if she has to settle for a public defender."

Tilly caught me by my sleeve.

"Glory, I know. I know, and you're not wrong. But hun, I don't think you can change Theresa's mind. Some people just don't care."

That was evident by the state of the country and who was running it. A lot of people just didn't care. Everyone was too concerned with watering their own gardens to notice that their neighbor's house was on fire. But I cared. I was someone. Someone who could prevent something bad from happening to someone else. Someone like twenty-three year old Kiara Greenly.

"Tilly, I have to try," I said, snatching away and heading towards the door. "Wish me luck."

"Ugh," she sighed. "Good luck, Glory Hun."

Cash was right. I never ran, but I did occasionally whisk. And whisk I did. Right down the hall, towards the east elevators, and right up to the fifth floor. I would have torn the door off the hinges if I was any more amped, but Luckily Theresa's office was already open.

"Ms. King. My second favorite attorney in all of Dallas. How can I help you?"

That second favorite thing didn't go unnoticed, but given how vain Theresa was, I'm sure she was her own first favorite. She was nectar complexioned, and a head shorter than me, but her presence was suffocating like the loud flowery perfume she wore. You could tell by her bright, unlined lipstick that she had earned her place by stroking the flames of ego-maniacal men. And their dicks. Or maybe she said cock? She looked like she said the C word.

"Hi, Misses Adams. I was hoping to borrow your ear for a second," I said in a voice I reserved for coons and white folks.

"I have some time," she said, checking her digital planner. "What about?"

"It's actually regarding a denial I got on a proposed pro-bono case. Kiara Greenly, twenty-three, charged with child neglect."

Theresa's brows pinched together, offering her confusion.

"Left the kid at their dad's house and went to work. At an adult entertainment club," I added.

"Oh right, the stripper," she said.

"Bottle girl," I corrected. "Listen, I know everyone thinks that women in the adult entertainment industry have bankrolls, but that's not the case for everyone. Some people barely get by. Take Kiara for example, she drives a 2003 Chevy Cavalier with peeling paint and lives in Stop Six."

"Stop Six?" Theresa asked.

"Meadowbrook," I clarified.

"Oh, egh," she grimaced.

"Exactly," I nodded.

She dropped her shoulders and sighed, and the optimistic little girl who saw the good in everyone thought Theresa might empathize with another human being for a moment.

"Listen, Gloria," she started.

I was wrong.

"We know that philanthropy is important to you personally, and that is an upstanding value to embody. Unfortunately, we just aren't able to afford the hours this early in the quarter if it's not potentially benefiting the firm or attracting new clients."

Lies. All lies. They had just lent a few attorneys to some "Victims of Me Too cancellation" for the free. Still, Granny taught me you caught more flies with honey than salt.

"I completely understand, Misses Adams, and that's why I'm fully prepared to research and compose my argument on my own time. Without it affecting my billable hours."

Theresa smiled.

"Freelance work is forbidden per your employment contract, Gloria."

"Freelance?" I all but scoffed. "But I'm…"

I was interrupted by Theresa quickly flashing me her raised palm. It reminded me of Lazarus shushing me as a child, and I sought her eyes to prepare my temperament not to react. Unfortunately, all I saw there was cruelty and malice.

"Either she pays or she finds someone else, Miss King. This is a business, not your daddy's church. Which reminds me, I have business to discuss somewhere else. So if there's nothing else…"

Resentment settled into my bones. Tilly was right as usual. She did not care and I couldn't change her mind. The only thing I caught with honey was mold.

"No, there's nothing else," I said firmly. "Thank you for your time."

This time I ran. I ran straight to the bathroom and threw up, and it hurt twice as bad as the tears did when they cut through my foundation.

I had no energy left after voiding my entire breakfast in a public bathroom toilet. So I had plans to head home and do what I could while laying in bed and bingeing 90s romcoms. Tilly was quick to reschedule my meetings since that also meant a half day for her, but our leave was interrupted by none other than Granny.

"Hey, Mama Lailah," Tilly called. "What are you doing here?"

My granny's eyes narrowed skeptically while she eyed Tilly, but that apprehension visibly dissolved when she met her eyes.

"Oh, Maybelline! Hi, baby. I almost didn't recognize you with all them titties. I knew they'd grow in once you got over twenty-five," she said casually.

Tilly looked down at her B-cups turned DD and blushed. The memories of bird-chested Tilly had all but left us, but not Granny. Never Granny.

"Nice to see you haven't changed one bit, Mama," she laughed while hugging her.

"Lawd, lady. What are you doing here?" I asked, trading Tilly for her embrace.

My granny patted a few stray curls from my shoulder-length 217 frontal back in place.

"I ain't put eyes on you in almost a month. I ain't even know you was alive the way you barely called and couldn't pick up the phone for nobody. So I wanted to surprise you and see if you wanted to grab lunch."

Ladies and Gentlemen, Lailah Esther Birch. The definition of drama. I visited her three days ago.

"Actually Mama, Glory been sick so she was on her way out," Tilly remarked.

I elbowed her shamelessly. There was a reason me and Granny hadn't talked much since I'd been home. I did not want to stress her out with what I had going on. What kind of granddaughter would I be if I caused her third stroke?

"Glory, you sick how?" Granny asked.

"I'm fine," I answered quickly.

"She throwing up," Tilly added.

I ain't never wanted to twist someone's lips so fucking bad in my entire life. And I grew up with Michael. My granny's eyes expectantly dropped to my stomach. Men threw up all the time, but the second a woman did it…

"Gloria, are you pregnant?" she asked bluntly.

"I am not," I replied.

"You sure?"

"Yes, Granny. All the tests have been negative," I assured her.

Lailah Birch shuffled through her purse with urgency, retrieved a silver cigarette holder given to her by her father, and extracted one joint, artfully wrapped in pink paper.

"Good, you can smoke this then. Come on, baby. Let's go get crab legs," she said, pulling me along.

I generally hated eating out with my family because no matter the setting or occasion, I'd end up footing the bill. They treated my little coinage like I had Jefe Jeff money and would go out of the way to "treat themselves" on my dime. Then there was my granny. Dining with her was always her treat, and she always picked somewhere bougie enough to make me sweat. Even in my good wig and heels.

"You want some more caviar?" she offered.

I watched with hazy vision as she sat down her gold crab cracker to spread a little caviar onto a piece of truffle Melba toast. I was so full that my eyes were blinking separately.

"Granny, I'm gonna pass out if I eat one more thing," I wheezed.

The table housed a spread large enough to satisfy four grown-ass men with labor-intensive jobs. The fact that it was just for the two of us was insane but even more ludicrous, was the idea that we'd get anywhere close to finishing it all. Two crab boils, two fried lobster tails, crawfish souffle, roasted potatoes, and seafood mac with cornbread. Lazarus would have a field day if he could see us. We'd be every glutton in the book.

"Can we please get about four boxes?" Granny asked a passing waiter.

"Good call," I chirped.

We boxed up everything and sat it in an unoccupied corner while we chatted. Granny was still quite the vixen at her age, and she was now going steady with the retired postman, Mister Fred, in addition to seeing Mister Ernesto the florist. My mama was not happy about that seeing as Mister Fred delivered their mail her entire childhood. At least her packages were always on time.

"When's the last time you been to church?" Granny asked, changing the subject.

"Uh, Granny. You know I'm liable to catch on fire for going within 50ft of a church," I replied.

She rolled her eyes as only grandmothers could.

"Girl, hush. I'm being serious nie."

I sighed, for whatever reason she wanted to know. So I might as well have made it easy on myself.

"Not since I kicked Halle's cheating-ass husband in the balls," I replied.

Granny laughed so hard she had to lean against the table to catch herself. Getting to see her laugh so freely wasn't at all lost on me. It was a gift I'd cherish for the rest of my living days.

"Whew, that dirtball deserved it too," she chuckled. "But you and the boys should join me this upcoming Sunday for the noon service."

See, I knew better because she gave me too many details for it to be a request or suggestion.

"Granny, I don't know if that's a good idea. Especially the bringing the boys part," I grimaced.

"Listen, baby. I know how you feel about the church, and I normally wouldn't ask. But that's why I suggested bringing them boys of yours along. There's something I need you to see, Starchild. Please."

Starchild. If being called Essie was rare, Starchild was even rarer. My grandparents drove ten hours to see me when I was first born. I was the darkest child ever born to my parents, and my late grandfather said my big bright eyes looked like majestic stars against my midnight skin. Thus giving me the name, Starchild. Granny knew her way to my heart, that's for sure.

"You know, you ain't have to drop a small fortune on seafood to get me to agree," I chided.

My grandmother dismissed me with a wave, as only grannies can.

"Girl, hush. You were gonna agree regardless, and I was gonna feed you regardless. Two birds, one stone," she shrugged.

I pinched the bridge of my nose to keep my head steady. So I guess we were going to church.

Chapter Thirty-One

I spent a whole week asking Granny what I was looking for, and she just told me I'll know when I see it. I guess she had lived long enough to enjoy her cryptic yet demanding nature. Because she was also dead serious about me bringing the boys along. The boys were unexpectedly excited to join me for service. Even Frankie, who previously called church, *"An archaic social cesspit good for only performative righteousness."* When I asked them why on two separate occasions, they both told me they were looking forward to spending more time with Mama Lailah. Apparently, she was the most memorable part of any King outing. A sentiment shared among many people. Anyway, Frankie was going as my boyfriend since Halle had already outed him, and Cash had been demoted to my curious "work friend." He didn't seem to mind though, because as he put it, *"There's nothing friendly about what I plan on doing to you after brunch."* Then he told me to, *"Make sure you enjoy the mimosas, Princessa."*

Yeah.

I was going to burst into flames as soon as I sat in a pew.

"So how do I look?"

I spun around to greet Cash, who had never seen me in my church clothes before.

"You look….hmmmmghh," he garbled, taking in the full ensemble.

I did a 360 for him. I had on a King classic. A maxi skirt with a wide, fold-over waistband, opaque tights of course, a turtleneck, and accompanying cardigan to maintain some sense of self-respect since having big titties was a sin, and my black Satan Steppers. Which were a pair of two-inch closed-toe kitten heels with gaudy brass buckles on the sides. Cassius slowly examined the outfit again, looking for something worth complimenting only to land back on my face.

"I love your hair, baby girl," he cooed sweetly.

"Cash you always like my hair! I'm being serious! How do I look?"

He grimaced and started to hold up his hands in defeat before Frankie answered for him.

"You look like a woman who got divorced at her adulterous husband's request because he found "a new model." And now she insists she's a widow instead of telling the shameful truth, and says heaven rest his soul every time his name is brought up in conversation," Frankie answered.

My mouth dropped. How long had he been sitting on that?

"That was oddly specific in a real bad way," I mumbled in reply.

Frankie shrugged playfully before pecking my temple.

"You're beautiful no matter what, Essie. Still very fuckable," he said, squeezing my ass.

"That's what I want to hear," I chuckled before patting his chest. I then onced over their outfits, noting how handsome they looked in their coordinating ties and pressed slacks.

"Let's roll fellas."

I was happy it was raining when we left. It gave us a valid excuse for running behind if we were asked. We actually arrived late so I didn't have to deal with introductions and small talk twice, but unfortunately, we weren't able to go unnoticed. Marcus and Alayssa hadn't been out of the house since my niece Penny was born, but I guess Granny was able to convince them to come too. They sat in the third from the front row right next to her, patting the seats they saved for us and motioning for us to come sit. Then directly across from them sat my mama, Halle, and her pathetic ass husband, Chris, who was about to pass out trying to avoid my gaze.

Ah, praise be.

"I think they want us up there," Cash whispered while waving to Granny.

"Yes, I see that," I replied, eyeing a kinda clear pew near the back.

"So what are we doing?" Frankie asked.

Suddenly, I received divine confirmation that God had a twisted sense of humor. The storm clouds outside shifted, and morning light beamed through the blue-stained windowpane before falling onto my face and highlighting my discomfort. Prompting my father to smile.

"We were trying to avoid him," I mumbled, accepting my fate.

I busied myself by fawning over my niece to avoid thinking about all the eyes on me. Everyone was staring, and it certainly didn't help that I let the boys convince me to wear my hair out. My afro was like a honing beacon for attic moths. I attracted glances from everywhere, even from the careful eyes of the devout clergyman. Good thing Penny was so gorgeous. I could stare at her pretty chocolate eyes and matching chocolate curls for days and be content.

"Cassius, good to see you again, baby," Granny grinned.

I was too nervous to make introductions, or really even breathe. So Granny took it upon herself to make them for me.

"Alayssa, you know Frankie. But this is Cassius, Glory's other partner," she said in a hushed tone.

"I know, Granny. Marcus tells me everything," she whispered back before extending her hand to Cash. "But it's nice to formally meet you."

"Marc!" I hissed.

I expected some expression of regret, and I was sorely disappointed to find he had none.

"I tell my wife everything," he shrugged. "Marriage ain't the place for secrets."

Damn, that was actually fair reasoning.

Touché, brother. Touché.

My original plan to stay out of the way was foiled because it didn't take Lazarus long to turn my guest appearance into a prodigal son moment. He was rejoicing, reciting scripture like it was renaissance poetry, and he even went so far as to invite me to sing with the choir. Something he knew I detested.

"Oh, no I couldn't," I smiled as he asked a second time. "I wouldn't want to wake Penny."

Baby girl slept like a bear. There was no way she'd wake if I moved, but I had to use what I could in the moment.

"I'll hold my great-grandbaby," Granny said sweetly. "Gone on up there, Gloria," she said, taking my tiny human shield.

Damn it Granny! She smiled through the blatant look of betrayal I gave her as I climbed onto the pulpit and took the mic from my father's outstretched hand.

Fuck, so I guess we were doing this.

I hadn't sung in years. At least not out loud. Sometimes I could feel the urge rushing back to me like an old friend offering a warm embrace, but I refused to give in. I would hum along to create a false sense of satisfaction instead, stopping when someone caught me. My mama always called my refusal to sing one of humanity's most devastating losses, but the truth was stopped simply because I no longer had much to sing about. Not until recently at least.

The room went deadly quiet while I tried to steady my hammering heart, but I was startled when the pianist ripped a note to compliment my hardly noticeable inhale. I let the drums join to map the melody, and I recognized the song immediately. It was Lamar Campbell's Closer To You, one of my old favorites. Suddenly my chin tilted heavenward and the instincts came rushing back. It was like riding a bike. Only this time, I could no longer pull from the glory of God, so I was immensely grateful to be gathering strength from the two men in the third row from the front. Who were giving me their silent yet unwavering support with every single note that left my mouth. Shepard's Hand Baptist church was soon overflowing with a riveting emotional chorus, yet, in the midst of everyone's tears and my own cathartic release, I noticed what Granny wanted me to notice. My father, and his heartfelt gaze, which was set not on my mother, but two seats behind her, on none other than infamous con-artist, Curtis Myer-Smythe.

Service couldn't end fast enough. Even with my mind running a thousand miles a minute, trying to process what I had seen. Yes, it was just a passing glance. A brief look. Sure, it could've been an accident, the angle of my vantage point, or even my anxious imagination drawing up images that weren't there. But I had seen that look before. Years ago before I could even comprehend what it really meant. It was the exact same look Frankie gave me. A look of promise, longing, and maybe even heartache. A look cast out to another soul in search of warmth and comfort.

Something was going on.

If my granny knew, had she told my mother? Was she certain, or was she also just noticing the fine print of Lazarus' expression? Was there proof? Did Frankie know? A thousand questions avalanched me in a manner that felt deadly, and soon I was running down the hall to prevent my breakfast from spilling into the collection tray making its way down our aisle. Oh, what a tithe that would be.

I returned just past the concluding prayer after voiding my bagel breakfast, and it was right in time for my daddy to suck me into an unwanted conversation.

"Gloria! There are some people here I want you to meet," he cheered. "They're good company."

A similar-looking man and woman stood before him with Uncanny Valley smiles. I would have rather taken an ass whooping than taken my ass over there to meet anyone Lazarus considered good company. Especially if he was doing what I thought he was doing. Plus the man who was wearing a cheap version of a Mister Rogers sweater had a friendly grin. A little too friendly if you asked me.

"Essie," Frankie purred. "Let's just get this over with so we can head to brunch, and I'll suck the stress out your asshole to make it up to you after that."

Getting my soul removed from my booty hole did sound tempting, but their smiles…

"You promise?" I pouted.

"Yes, baby. I promise. Get to stepping, me and Cash are right behind you," he laughed.

Granny was right about bringing the boys along, cause they lent me strength and calm where I had none.

"Alright, fine," I sighed.

The group was a bunch of wet carpets just as I suspected. I don't expect everyone to match my energy because even I can admit I'm too much at times, but good God, they were boring. I'd never talked about flood insurance and wheat germ for this long in my life.

"Gloria, you have a wonderful voice," a nervous, lean woman, introduced to me as Vanessa lamented.

"Thank you," I nodded.

The more they spoke, the more I honed in on the pair's unsettling body language. Their gazes were shifty as if they were children who had stolen sweets and were paranoid about getting caught. I was giving clipped answers in hopes of icing them out, but it simply did not work. They just switched subjects when I got short instead of releasing me from the conversation like normal people. People capable of reading a room.

"What about your little friend?" Friendly Bob Cheap Sweater asked, pointing behind me. "Does he sing?"

Weird.

Weird because the group hardly acknowledged the guys besides my father greeting Frankie tepidly and asking Cash's name. The boys were well aware of the cold reception and opted to hang a bit farther back than I would've liked.

"What little friend?" Frankie spat.

Venom laced every single word and his expression was deadly if looks *could* kill. However, I got the feeling that his sour face wasn't going to be my biggest concern.

"I… I didn't mean it… I just thought, I assumed you were friends," Cheap Sweater said.

"Well you assumed wrong," Frankie huffed. "I'm her man, and ain't nothing little about me."

My father's eyes bulged out of his head like he was a cartoon cat and the look he gave me made my stomach flip yet again.

"Gloria," he seethed, hands twitching.

Frankie, who had made it clear he didn't care for the dynamics of my father's relationship with me, snatched me out of Lazarus' reach. It was unmistakably protective as if he were silently saying, *"Watch that hollering shit."* But the look my father gave him in return caused my stomach to issue a final warning, and then I felt the last of my breakfast threaten to offer itself as a response to all of this.

"Please excuse me," I rushed. "I need to use the restroom."

"Glory, wait!" My daddy called.

He could call all he wanted, but we were at the mercy of my testy stomach and I was honestly a little grateful.

I guess there's more than one way to effectively end a conversation.

I was in the bathroom longer than normal since this was my second visit. Frankie thinks that my inability to let my body settle after a traumatic physical event such as vomiting is what makes it such a persistent occurrence, and I hate to say it, but I think that nerd was right. I passed the time by picking my pew-flattened fro back out and wiping up water from the counter when suddenly I heard two very familiar voices flowing from the vent of the second to the last stall. One much softer than the other.

"Did you talk to her?" the soft voice asked.

Damn it, I wish I knew who's office was behind the lady's room. It'd make eavesdropping so much easier. I grew up here, but it had been years since I'd been at church, and especially upstairs. While I knew the building layout, the office spaces and who they belonged to were bound to have changed. So I had to concentrate my efforts on recognizing the voice.

"No, she ran off," my father replied.

Were they talking about me? Was that what that weird ass introduction was about?

"Shit, he's going to need a lawyer," the voice replied.

Yep, definitely talking about me. Well, that mission was DED anyway. I never represented men for free, and especially not randos.

"She's not going to take his case for free. You know how Glory feels about men," My father explained.

I had to stop myself from laughing. At least he knew that much.

"Yeah, you really fucked her up. I don't know how my nephew hanging in there," the second voice laughed.

"Nephew?" I said out loud.

Shit.

I hoped I wasn't heard, but the other room went quiet, and then I heard the swing of a door shortly after. Footsteps clomped against the antique hardwood with urgency, and a slew of hushed murmurings followed.

So Lazarus did have *something* going on with Curtis. What he had going on was an entirely different question for another day and another Glory, because I was literally itching to leave. I washed my hands one more time for good measure and flew out the door. I knew for certain that I needed to talk to Marcus. Because if there was anyone who could figure out what

Lazarus King was up to, it was him. I was halfway down the expansive hall, brainstorming the speech I was going to give him when a hand darted out of an open door and caught my wrist, causing me to jump.

"Essie, are you ok?" Frankie cooed. "Did I hurt you?"

I looked down at our connected hands and swallowed the lemon-sized lump in my throat. It hadn't even been an hour and I was paranoid. Bad news bears.

"No, sorry. I just thought I was alone up here. What are y'all doing?" I asked.

"We came up here to check on you, but then Frankie noticed that the door to your old domain was open," Cash laughed.

That's right. We were standing in the OG study. I guess it looked a lot different without the furniture and artwork in it. That's why it was my favorite room growing up. All the paintings taught me there is value in art. Even if wasn't mine.

"Ah, yes. Where I'd lure young boys to their downfall," I chuckled. "Frankie included."

"Mhhm," Frankie smiled. "And look, your old peeping hole is still there."

I looked down and nearly jumped out of my skin. Frankie was right, the hole was back like it never left. But that didn't make sense because I distinctly remembered watching Lazarus nail it shut while preaching to me about the importance of chasteness. I remembered how disgusted he was that I would even think about doing something as vile as peeping on naked men. I remembered how angry he was. I remembered everything.

I couldn't even force myself to laugh before I was cupping my hands together to catch more bile.

Something was most certainly amiss in The Good Christian House Of King.

I had every intention to leave and let the boys baby my sick ass, but there was a lengthy set of handwritten instructions waiting on me when I got downstairs. I pulled the taped note off the wall with a lour.

Unfucking-believable.

I pop in once a year and somehow still get stuck with vacuum duty. Apparently, my parents had "errands" to run and they were confident the boys wouldn't mind helping me. I mean they didn't, but damn! My mimosas were getting warm. I was hungry! I was also fucking horny. Whatever. At least Frankie brought snacks for me.

"Dammmmmnnnnn," the boys exclaimed in unison.

They were done dusting and vacuuming the pews, but I was on all fours, reaching under the podium for a stray gum wrapper so it didn't get sucked into the brush, and they were being men. Mannish, uncouth, perverted men.

"Stop staring at my ass," I chided.

"That muhfucka poking tho," Cash said, sucking his teeth.

"Really, Cassius? In front of our lord and savior?" I asked, pointing to the mounted cross sculpture above the pulpit.

"That's not my lord and savior," Cash replied. "The only thing we worship is that pussy," Frankie added.

I flung my gum wrapper at them, creating more work for myself.

"Y'all are being nasty," I admonished.

Suddenly I was surrounded on both sides with Cash at my back and Frankie at my front. Two sets of hands busied themselves squeezing and caressing my curves while their owners chuckled in my ear.

"We can show you nasty, Glory," Cash growled. "Just say the word, baby girl."

"You can bend back over and we'll even spell it out for you," Frankie laughed.

Nasty indeed. I hid myself in Frankie's hard chest. I knew for a fact that I was blushing because my pupils felt like they had gotten hit with dilation drops on a sunny day. I dressed warm because it was only 50 degrees outside but suddenly it was burning hot and I needed everything to come off. Especially my panties.

Unfortunately, my good ole Christian guilt kicked in.

"We can't have sex in a church," I sighed.

It actually came out more like a moan because Frankie's fingers had already wiggled between my thighs. He brushed my lips and I became acutely aware of how wet I was, feeling my moisture cling to the pads of his fingers when he pulled away.

"Are you sure, Princessa?" Cash asked.

"No," I admitted.

Having sex in a church was wrong. Having sex in my father's church was doubly wrong. Having sex in the pulpit? First class ticket to hell, champagne and breakfast included, no blackout dates. But something about the way they kissed me felt like I might get to witness heaven first, even if it was only for a few seconds.

"Conditions," I gasped while Cash unhooked my bra.

"We're listening," they agreed.

"This is a quickie."

Laughter. If they had any say, this would be no such thing. Still, I deceived myself and moved on to the next item.

"No moaning," I bit.

That was met with flat-out refusal, yet I persisted and kept rambling off requirements that we all knew they wouldn't meet.

"And lastly, we never mention this again, and you will both buy me the greasiest potatoes and the stiffest mimosa money can obtain after this."

"Done," they nodded.

At least we could agree on one thing.

The boys wasted no time getting me indecent. I had on garters so I got to keep my skirt, but my sweater was pulled over my shoulders, exposing my round breast to the entire room. I felt so exposed that I started wondering if my kitty was an outdoor cat. Because crazy enough, I loved the idea of a crowd watching me get ravaged by two strapping young men as my Granny would say.

I didn't have time to get a wax before we left for Christmas, so Henrietta was covered in a light thicket of curls, slicked with wetness. The fuzzy look was starting to grow on me, and it was clear that the boys preferred it. Frankie twirled his fingers in the patch on top of my mound before spreading my lips, and I watched chaos blaze in his eyes before he dipped down to place a soft kiss on my sex. It was so sweet that it was almost innocent, but then his tongue snaked out and wrapped around my throbbing clit. Suddenly, I had a vision. One of Eden, the forbidden fruit, and the serpent that coveted them both. The first sin of the first daughter. Ironic, given my current state.

Of course, I was the one to break my own "no-moaning" rule. To be fair, I wasn't expecting to be spread on the stage stairs getting my titties sucked and my pussy ate when I proposed it, but I still felt like a dirty little hypocrite. But again, it wasn't my fault. It was theirs with their salacious tongues, probing fingers, and perfect rhythm. They were making me leak all over the carpet. They were making me test the acoustics of the sky-high ceilings and antique stones. They were making the stained glass morph into kaleidoscopes. They were my undoing.

"Fuck," I muttered.

The precursor to my orgasm was barely heard over the sounds of their licks. But when I tightened around Frankie's fingers and almost pushed him out, suddenly they were all ears.

Or maybe eyes. Frankie pulled away after I finished cumming and watched the aftermath. His face was dripping with my essence, his eyes still hungry and his jaw set. Cash noticed and freed my nipple from his mouth with a satisfying pop to join his boyfriend. So I did my best to spread my shaking legs further and put on a show. I could see why they were so enamored when I spread my lips. I was sticky beyond reason and almost burning hot. Perfect to sink inside of.

The boys quickly freed their dicks, revealing a similar state of want. They were throbbing and their swollen tips leaked precum like faucets. They pumped each other's lengths while watching me play with my pussy until Frankie couldn't take it anymore. Then they quickly sandwiched me between them with Frankie underneath me and Cash on top.

"Wait, I'm not prepped for anal," I whispered.

I was nasty, but not dookie-on-dick nasty. Plus I still wanted my brunch. Those two things did not mix.

"That's fine," Cash cooed. "You're wet enough for us to try something else."

What hadn't we tried? I was under the impression that they had violated all my holes in every way you could.

"What?" I asked curiously.

I was met with silence and action. First from Frankie easing inside me, then from Cash who joined him. In the same hole. We were all very still following the moment the boys settled inside me, yet I still managed to cum. It was really inevitable. There's only so much fullness one woman can take before madness ensued.

"Oh my God," I panted while feeling their first strokes.

"Naw, baby," Cash chuckled. "God ain't got shit to do with this."

"Fuck, Essie. You feel so damn good," Frankie groaned.

"So soft," Cash added.

Frankie's arms wrapped around my waist to steady my position with one of his hands settling on my clit, and Cash divided his touch between my throat and breasts, then they rocked. It was so coordinated that it felt like a dance. A seductive tango gone wonderfully wrong.

"Fab, damn. You hard as hell," Cash muttered.

Frankie was throbbing and stiffer than a fresh silicone dildo, but then again so was Cash. If I was seeing stars when I blinked I was sure the boys weren't too far behind me. Especially with all the friction. They were basically frotting inside me.

"How does it feel for you two?" I asked.

It was a bit of an awkward question for some, but hell, I was curious. Plus I needed conversation so I could stay tethered to reality. Because I was a few minutes out from passing out or maybe even on to the next realm.

"You're very wet and it's very tight. It feels like we're going to be picking out baby names in a few months," Frankie moaned.

"I always liked the name Sebastian," Cash laughed.

"Selena for a girl," Frankie replied.

"This isn't sounding like a joke," I gasped.

I was briefly treated to strained grunts and heavy breathing while the boys increased their speed. Then my focus shifted to the dramatic squelching sound coming from between my thighs. I couldn't see much past my heaving chest and pert nipples, but I could tell I was soaked by the sheen coating Cash's lower belly. I had never been so full and wet before. My body started to warm and I sought to maximize touch any way I could. My hands caressed Frankie's soft exposed forearms, I brought my lips to Cassius's and kissed him as if he were a cool drink of water on a burning summer day, and I pulled both of them closer to me like my life depended on my ability to cling to their arms and backs. Maybe it did based on the way my clit was throbbing.

"Who said we were joking?" Someone whispered.

"You better be," I hissed.

"Fine," Cash sighed. "This time," Frankie finished.

"Okie," I agreed. "This time."

With that out of the way, I was left to focus on the overwhelming pleasure of it all. Frankie's strong hands were gripping and massaging my bouncing belly and breasts. He always told me he loved how soft I was. I never doubted it because he worshiped every part of me equally. Just like Cash, who had slipped his right thumb in my mouth while his left swept over my clit. The rest of his hand rested comfortably in the valley of my hip, partially covered by my uncoveted belly. I moaned again from the increasingly intense stretch and this time I didn't hold back. I let my voice carry throughout the entire building. I let it wrap around the boys and dissolve their restraint, and I let it free me from the emotional burden of getting busted open like a sack of dried corn in my parent's church by my two big-dick boyfriends. Because at least I was finally singing again.

Chapter Thirty-Two

I always thought I was pretty good at public speaking. I wasn't easily intimidated by shit like silent stares or light spatterings of mumbling voices, I had a clear voice and perfect posture thanks to Mama, and I always practiced before I presented. Except for this time, because all the preparation in the world was useless when it came time for me to tell my brother my suspicions. Nor could it prepare me for his response.

Laughter.

Like gut-clenching, throat-stripping, knee-slapping laughter.

"Marcus!" I hissed.

"Whew, ok. Ok," he said trying to steady himself against the wall. I had hopes that we could get through it this time.

But, nope. He was back at it. Sliding down that muhfucka like he didn't have a whole entire child and wife.

Childish.

"Babe, seriously. Get it together," Alayssa chided.

My girl. I don't know where we'd be if it wasn't for her. Because Unserious should have been Marcus' King's middle name.

"Alright! Alright! I'm sorry! But it's not my fault! Why she call that man a

Propheteering Power Bottom?!" he wheezed.

Ok, admittedly, I could've rephrased that. But it's all I had in the moment. Lazarus definitely wasn't nobody's top with the way Granny bodied him on the regular.

"Marc, I'm serious though. Something is going on."

My brother straightened his back and then shook my shoulder in the endearing way only he could.

"Listen, I believe you, Glory. There's a reason I've always stayed kinda close. Someone has to look out for Mom," he said.

Well fuck, that made me feel an inch tall. Had I been that bad of a daughter?

"Don't look like that. You didn't know because they didn't want you to know. Hell, they didn't want anyone to know. But it's my job to keep a healthy amount of dirt on everyone. Just in case."

"Excuse me?" I squeaked.

What the fuck kinda dirt did he have on me?

"You're excused," My brother laughed. "But no seriously, I'll look into it and keep you updated. In the meantime, try to avoid getting involved in whatever plans you overheard and stay out of the way. Dad knows something too. He didn't even flinch when Elias Oscar mentioned seeing you with two different men on the same night."

Fuck, that wasn't good. If he was unphased by learning something like that and not bringing it to me, it meant he had definitive proof beforehand. Which meant he was saving it for something…

The nausea was back. I reached into my clutch for a Zofran, prompting worry from my brother and his wife.

"It's fine," I assured them. "I have a doctor's appointment for it today."

My OBGYN was on vacation, but the lady at the desk was able to squeeze me in with another doctor at the practice. My pregnancy test were still coming up negative, which in itself wasn't that concerning, but my period was also late. I could count on one hand the amount of times I'd been late. So whatever was going on was starting to throw my body off wack, and

I ain't have time for that right now. Especially since it was worrying the boys.

"Let us know how it goes," Alayssa said, passing me a ginger ale. "Hopefully it's nothing."

Hopefully.

I filled out my usual questionnaire before I was handed the infamous pee cup. They'd asked me no less than three times if there was a possibility I was pregnant since I arrived and that meant absolutely nothing in the grand scheme of things. We all submit to the clean catch eventually. The nurse who escorted me back immediately recognized my name and gave me a warm greeting before pitching me a concerned glance.

"You aren't switching doctors are you?" she asked.

"Um, no," I responded. "I've just been really sick for the last three weeks and I needed to get seen. I know Doctor Pritchette is on sabbatical though."

That did nothing to ease her mind.

"Are you sure you don't just want to reschedule? Doctor Pritchette comes back the first week of March. I can give you her first open appointment," she offered.

Maybe she was just trying to help me stay consistent with one doctor since they'd gotten complaints about that recently, but I was OK. I could handle a little change if it helped me get answers.

"It's fine, but thank you. I'll just be sure to keep my annual with Doctor Pritchette in case I need to follow up," I affirmed.

She sighed so deeply that it felt pained, but then she was quick to fix her face after handing me a gown.

"Alright, Miss King. The doctor will be in shortly."

Roughly half an hour passed before I was greeted by a quick knock. I had to scramble to sit up because the lowered exam table was hell on my lower back, and I wasn't going to spend thirty minutes straining it to keep a paper gown pristine. Pulling upright brought me face-to-face with a thin older black woman with a camel complexion and sock-bunned hair. She looked me head to toe and sighed before introducing herself as Doctor Bradley.

"Hi, Miss King. So I see you're here for vomiting and a delayed period. Any chance you could be pregnant?" she said, ignoring my introduction and zipping through my chart.

"Uh, no," I said. "Nurse Debs let me know my test was negative."

Doctor Bradley quickly flipped back to my vitals and scowled.

"Hm," she said. "I see you only lost four pounds since the last time you were here."

Ok, I get it. I'm fat. I have an apron belly, a round chin, and my hips aren't super curvy like an ideal BBW, but I wasn't morbidly obese. And that wasn't my concern.

"How's your diet?" she asked while listening to my lungs.

She talked with slight dismissiveness in her tone instead of genuine intrigue. Like she already knew the answer but she was just waiting on me to confirm it.

"Fine," I replied. "I eat plant-based meals once a day and avoid surgery drinks."

She harrumphed. I guess I wasn't able to confirm that bias for her today.

"Good, good," she nodded. "Are you currently sexually active?"

"Yes," I confirmed.

"Great. How many partners?"

I winced. The answer was usually unsatisfactory to medical staff no matter how much diversity and inclusion training they went through in an effort to tighten their bedside manners.

"Two," I answered.

"Ok. Any chance you may have been exposed to a sexually transmitted disease?" she asked.

"No," I stated firmly.

"Are you sure? Because you're sleeping with two people, but who knows how many people they're sleeping with?"

I knew how many people they were sleeping with.

"We only sleep with each other. I'm a part of a closed polyamorous triad," I explained.

You know that look older people give you when you say something they feel like you would've gotten stoned when they were coming up? Yeah, that was the look she gave me. The infamous, *"Girl, what the fuck?"* look.

"Let's just order a quick check just to cross it off our list. Ok?"

I agreed just so we can get back on track, only for her to ask me,

"What are you doing for birth control?"

Again, this was a question asked no less than three times on the questionnaire. The answer hadn't changed in the hour I had been there.

"Condoms," I said, motioning to the clipboard.

"Right! Condoms. Condoms are great as a back-up method. But they're only effective 87% of the time you use them," she explained.

"I'm aware," I nodded.

"Good. So how about we look into something a little bit more effective. How about an IUD?"

I jumped. How did we get here? I thought we were talking about my delayed period and extreme bout of nausea.

"I'm actually not comfortable with a long-acting birth control like an IUD. My partners and I are going to start trying for children sometime within the next three years," I explained.

"Oh, ok. That's fine. We have other options like Nexplanon, or the shot. I see you're a lawyer, so I wouldn't recommend something like the pill for a busy girl like you. Plus with your we…"

I interrupted Doctor Bradley with a wave.

"I'm sorry. What does this have to do with my missing period and the nausea?" I asked.

Doctor Bradley sat down her clipboard and gave me a pitying grimace.

"Well, sweetie. Usually bigger girls have problems with hormone balance. Weight gain and upset stomach are often the first symptoms. But if we start you on birth control today, we can help regulate your period and maybe even get you back within normal range. Does that make sense?"

No it didn't. Not really. But I had a migraine from the Zofran and I was tired of gagging and feeling half-dead all the time. Who knows? Maybe Doctor Bradley was right. I'd researched her beforehand and there was a possibility that the fifteen-year difference in experience helped her catch something Doctor Pritchette missed. And putting my faith in another black woman hadn't done me wrong yet.

So I agreed.

Chapter Thirty-Three

F rankie

Something was seriously wrong with Gloria. At first, I thought it was because her client had to settle for a public defender due to the payment conflict with the firm, but Glory remained gray even after receiving the news of her former client's favorable outcome. So I asked Marcus. He was nice enough to let me know that there was something going on with their parents, but when I asked Glory about it she just shook her head and said nothing was wrong.

But she was lying.

Essie didn't want to go on any hikes, hit up any flea markets, go on any dates, or even have sex. That last one hit hard even if everything else wasn't a red flag. Not because of my needs, but because once insatiable Essie was completely uninterested in any kind of pleasure. She just did her job, came home, made herself a peanut butter sandwich *without* jelly, and laid in her room. She wouldn't even talk to me and Cash about anything day-to-day, including moving in together full-time. Which she'd been geeked for previously.

It was scary. I felt like I was watching the beginning of her end, and even Cash who was usually cool, calm, and collected was uneasy about the sudden shift.

"Did you talk to Mama Lailah?" I asked.

We were lying in bed watching Project Runway together since Glory declined our invitation to watch it as a group. She also didn't want to cuddle so the bed felt unusually large.

"Yeah," he whispered. "Did you know her dad was having an affair?"

"LAZARUS!?" I choked.

"The one and only," Cash nodded.

"Does Essie know?"

"Apparently she's known since we went to church a few weeks back. She asked her brother to look into it."

"Is he the reason… Is that why she's so?"

Sad. Dejected. Hopeless.

"I don't think so, babe. I asked her about it and she just said it didn't matter because her mom was choosing to stay."

Fucking yikes. Things were worse than I thought because Glory was never the one to allow her mother to be disrespected by anyone. Especially not him.

"Cassius, something is wrong. She was fine in Colorado. She was smiling, singing, eating shit other than bread and cheap peanut butter. But the second we touched back down in Dallas she got sick. And now she's just… She's not herself," I sobbed.

My shining star was dimming by the second and I couldn't fix it. I felt fucking useless. She had been fixing everything for everybody for years and the one time she needed us, needed me, I was useless.

"Frankie. I know, but she won't talk to us. Depression affects everyone differently," Cash sighed.

"It wasn't like this a month ago," I replied. "She just came home one day and shit started going downhill."

Cash sat up and scrambled out of bed, gears clearly turning.

"Wait!" he exclaimed.

Me and Cash spent an entire weekend gutting one of his guest rooms and turning it into a giant walk-in closet in preparation for us all living together. And Glory's handbag collection was generously allotted a fifth of the total space. So seeing them in a pile on the floor felt criminal.

"Cash! She's going to stab us!" I hissed. "You don't put no black woman's purse on the floor!"

"Hush!" Cash replied, dumping yet another bag. "I'm looking for something."

He was looking for an ass whooping, that's what he was looking for. Cost and ability to replace anything damaged aside, Glory was seriously protective of her leather goods. Something like this was sure to send her swinging.

"Found it!" he screeched.

By "it" he meant a tattered physician summary warped and folded into one of Glory's work totes/recycling centers.

"What is that?" I asked.

"This is what's wrong!" he said, smacking the page. "You said she wasn't like this a month ago, and you're right. A month ago she was sick, but not this moody. Until she went to the doctor."

Cash showed me a page with aftercare directions from one Doctor Veronica Bradley. Aftercare for a birth control implant.

"What? Why would she do this?" I stuttered.

I thought Glory wanted kids. I knew she didn't mean right then, and I mean, we joked about getting her pregnant all the time, but those were just jokes. We'd never, *I'd* never do something like that without her explicit consent. Did she need to protect herself from us?

"I don't think it's anything we did," Cash said, reading my mind.

"It feels like it," I muttered back.

My stomach started to burn from the subtle sting of rejection I felt while reading the summary, and I crushed it in my fist before I could realize it.

"Babe, take a breath. Ground yourself," Cash cooed.

I tried but it was an effort wasted. I was heartbroken because Glory didn't trust us enough to come talk to us before getting a depression rod inserted into her body. I didn't agree with it, but it was ultimately her choice, and we would've still supported her.

"I don't understand," I cried. "Why didn't she just tell us?"

Cash sighed and started moving around the closet, collecting clothes. He eventually threw a pair of pants and a matching shirt my way before dressing himself in a similar outfit.

"Where are we going?" I asked.

"Well, your stomach is growling and emotions are high, so we're going to step out and get some fresh air. And lunch. Cause I need some bacon or something to fix this," Cassius replied.

"But…"

"Get dressed, Frijoles. Let's go and we'll have a town hall meeting after we come back. Glory deserves a calm conversation," he said firmly.

That was all he needed to say. I got off my ass with a grumble and got dressed. My annoyingly logical boyfriend was right. Emotions were high. Because when I saw Glory standing in the kitchen for the first time in five hours, waiting on a piece of wheat toast, all I wanted to do was rip that thing out her arm and get my baby back. So yeah, we needed space.

"Do you feel better?" Cash asked.

I looked down at my half-eaten Santa Fe skillet and nodded. The tension left my shoulders somewhere around the fifth bite and I finally remembered that this wasn't about me. It was about Essie, the changes she was going through, and how we could support her.

"Do you think we should even bring it up?" I asked. "Maybe there's a reason she didn't tell us."

Cash's usually steady features pulled into a grimace. That reminded me I wasn't alone in this, and I reached to hold his hand. He gave my hand a tentative squeeze before pushing his plate away, allowing me to reach across the table and hold both his hands.

"I think we should strive for a really honest conversation. If we did something that influenced her decision, then we need to apologize and correct it. We can't do that if we just pretend we don't know," he explained.

I discovered that Cash had been in therapy for five years right around the time I got consistent with my appointments. He had started going as a way to work through his issues with his dad, and it ended up helping him through Mama Dalia's cancer diagnosis as well. So this pillar of strength that stood before me was the result of years of hard work. And that was something I didn't take for granted.

"Ok. I'm going to grab her a biscuit and some shrimp and grits to go," I said, standing to peck the top of his head.

"Get two orders!" Cash called. "This feels like it's going to be a comfort food kind of situation!"

I ended up ordering a quart. Because this was definitely a comfort food kind of situation.

Glory was on the couch when we got home. It was sunny out and warm enough for us to enjoy lunch on the patio while we were out. Usually, Glory would try to match her wardrobe to reflect the weather. I remember plenty of spring days when I watched her float by as the embodiment of a wildflower garden. Bright, auric, and undeniably beautiful. Glory and her smile made me feel so damn alive. So it was a little soul-crushing seeing her reduced to gray sweats and a pile of blankets on an 80° day.

"Hi, baby," Cash cooed gently. "Can we please interrupt your alone time?"

Glory paused her true crime drama and sat up with a drained nod, and I came over to rest my chin on her head like always.

"How are you feeling today?" I asked.

"Just tired," she replied weakly.

Her eyes had bags deep enough for a girl's trip to Miami and her lips were cracked and peeling. She looked tired. Like she hadn't slept well the entire month.

"Yeah?" Cash chimed. "We noticed you haven't been eating much."

"Yeah," she shrugged. "I don't really have an appetite. But it's fine."

"Baby, it's not fine," I said softly.

Glory's vision shifted to a spot near the downstairs bathroom. Her habit of escaping hard conversations was well known at that point, and honestly expected. But not this time. This time there was no fight or flight and no hiding. This time there were only tears.

"I know," she choked. "I know, but I don't know what's wrong. I'm just fucking sad all the time, and it's so draining. I have no motivation. I don't know what's wrong with me."

"Glory, you're depressed," Cash said quietly.

"Depression isn't real," she laughed awkwardly. "If you ask my daddy, I just need to *"give it to God"* and *"take a walk."*

"Depression is absolutely real, sweetheart," I affirmed. "You're not imagining the way you're feeling. This is real, Glory. Your tears are real."

She cried. Oh, she cried like she did when her Papaw passed. Her heart-wrenching sobs echoed off the walls and cast her song of sorrow onto the ears of anyone unfortunate enough to witness it. She cried so long that I feared she'd make herself sick, but we never left her side. Because we had her. *Always.*

"I don't kn-ow how this happened," she hiccuped. "I was fine a few weeks ago."

"Hey," Cash cooed. "So me and the big guy have to come clean about something. We found the paper about your birth control in your purse."

"Oh," she sniffled.

"Yeah. We didn't mean to violate your privacy if you didn't want to tell us, but we were concerned that the hormones might be messing with you in a bad way," he explained.

"But is there a reason you didn't want to tell us?" I added.

I couldn't help myself. I wasn't strong and calm like Cash. I was emotional and passionate. I would go to the ends of the Earth to keep Glory safe, even if that meant keeping her safe for me.

"No, guys, I…" she sighed. "I didn't want any birth control."

Well, that didn't make sense. Because it was there, chilling in her bicep.

"What do you mean, Princessa?" Cash asked.

Glory raised her sleeve and showed us the jagged horizontal scar on her arm, tracing it with a lour.

"I went to a new doctor about my symptoms. She was kinda in a rush, but she was older, so I assumed she was just used to cases like mine and already had a solution. She suggested birth control because people like me often have problems with hormone levels, and she was talking so fast, and I was so overwhelmed th…"

"What do you mean, people like you?" I asked skeptically.

Glory looked at her soft little tummy with an unexpected amount of shame.

"Bigger girls," she whispered. "It didn't really make sense, but I just agreed so I could leave. I regretted it immediately too. Unfortunately, Doctor Pritchette wasn't available for a removal until March, and the longer it stayed in, the more I convinced myself it was right. What does an anxious sex addict need with a kid? I'd just fuck them up."

Even though she was most certainly a victim of blatant medical bias, I heard Lazarus in every single syllable of that statement. The judgment, the shame, the ignorance. It carried every single reduction Glory had to suffer since she was diagnosed with HD. And she was none of it.

"Glory, that's not true. Please tell me you know that's not true," I chided.

She shrugged, so I tilted her chin to meet my eyes.

"Essie, you would make an amazing Mama. Hell, you're already a great auntie. You make it your business to spend time with Penny once a week.

You read to her, brush her hair, and rock her so Alayssa can get a break. Rio didn't even want you to leave, he spent two days trying to convince you to stay so you could build a birdhouse with him. You are patient, caring, and creative beyond all reason. Any child would be lucky to call you mom. You are not your trauma. You are not Lazarus's perception of you. You deserve to experience life on your terms."

She caught her cry by clamping a shaky hand over her mouth before managing a nod. We could get through this, she just needed to believe that she deserved better than what others were willing to offer her. *Really* believe it.

"Oh, sweet baby," Cash whispered, pulling her into our arms. "It's going to be ok. It is. We got you."

She let us hold her for the first time in weeks, and I made the silent promise that she'd never go this long without being held ever again.

And I meant it.

Glory

Things had gotten better. The day after we all talked, I woke up and ate breakfast with the boys. I still didn't have much of an appetite, but I felt stronger after eating a few bites of chicken sausage, half an apple, and an English muffin. The following week I called and scheduled a removal for my implant. The lady at the desk warned me that my insurance wouldn't cover another long-acting birth control, but I let her know I was completely fine with that because it didn't fit into what I wanted for my life. Not now or ever.

Turns out it would've needed to be removed anyway because it bent during insertion and embedded into some nearby muscle. I took that as a sign that it wasn't meant for me to begin with. I spent a few days healing from the removal before Frankie brought me a bag of new clothes along with some jewelry, and ushered me out of the house. We scooped up Granny and drove an hour to go to a flea market that had a big tiled mirror that I saw on Instagram. Which he happily purchased and loaded for me.

It was a good day made better when I saw Cash was waiting for us at home with takeout and a pillow fort. We snuggled under a pile of clean linens and binged October Faction. It was a great show, plus it made my little fantasy-loving heart happy. It was also a great way to end the night, but then we had sex. We hadn't had sex in almost two months and it was much different from the frantic pace of last time. It was slow, rhythmic, and gentle. The boys spent the whole time telling me how beautiful I was and how much they adored my squishy, soft belly, expansive thighs, and dippy hips. I remembered how much I used to despise slow sex and talking, but it was now a staple in my daily life. Soft and sweet was my new normal. As it always should've been.

Two weeks ago we made the official decision to all live in Cash's condo. It honestly wasn't a whole lot of work since we'd been fluid with belongings and space anyway, but it was nice to really get the chance to make it ours together. We spent an entire week off work consolidating furniture, decorations, and oddly enough, blenders. I guess the gays really do love a festive drink because there was no reason three adults had five blenders. But we figured it out in the end.

I also got my meds adjusted. I had been taking Zoloft since I was thirteen years old, and while it worked then, it didn't work now. Plus my HD diagnosis was no longer a concern for me. I had partners who were supporting me through that, so I switched my focus to my anxiety. It had gone untreated for so long that it became my normal, and I didn't want that anymore. I wanted to laugh without wondering if that ache in my belly was a sign that my heart was exploding. I wanted to sleep for more than five hours straight. I wanted to be better for myself and my partners, and I was getting there. Wanting to be better also made me realize I had some trauma to unpack regarding my childhood, but unfortunately, I had trouble restarting therapy due to the growing concern of COVID-19, but other than that, I was in a good place. A great place even.

Until my dad called. I had been avoiding Lazarus since I went to church. Partially because Marcus confirmed he had been cheating on my mama for decades, and partially because Marcus also found out he wanted me to defend a man accused of sexual assault to help Curtis out. Two things that disgusted my very being. He'd usually take the hint when I ignored his phone calls, but today was different. He had called me seven times since 9am, and twice from a blocked number. I was napping on Frankie when he called for the eighth time, and Frankie answered on my behalf with nothing less than absolute disdain.

"Can I help you?" he growled. No hello, no hi, how are you? Nothing.

I heard my father's voice waver when he asked for me, but I shook my head no.

"She's sleeping," Frankie replied.

They talked a bit longer before Frankie launched into his standard departure, but when my father continued to talk through it he settled for disconnecting the call himself. He was such an asshole at times, but he was my asshole.

"What did he want?" I asked.

Frankie briefly rearranged the pillows before repositioning my head in the crook of his elbow, getting me back comfortable before addressing Lazarus's call.

"Said something about a family reunion happening next month," he grumbled. "He's getting desperate."

"Next month?" I exclaimed. "Aren't COVID cases on the rise? They were talking about a total shutdown?"

"Yes, and yes. It's definitely bad timing, but we don't have to go if you don't want to, Essie. It's your choice. He don't run shit over here."

I noticed he said we. It wasn't the first time and I was sure it wouldn't be the last, but it made me stupidly happy every time one of the boys included themselves in my plans.

"You'd suffer with me?" I asked.

"Yes, sweetheart. And Cash would too. You don't have to face anything alone."

God, sweet Frankie was nothing but panty bait. I snuggled deeper into his frame, subconsciously hoping to climb right into his skin and stay there.

"Thank you, babe," I said, pecking him. "But we're not going."

I wanted no part of whatever Lazarus was up to, and nothing could change my mind.

Chapter Thirty-Four

Glory

Unfortunately, someone could, and it was not who I expected. I told Granny that I had no intention of showing face at whatever little shindig Lazarus was throwing and she said that was a shame, but she understood. When I asked her why she explained that she had a feeling this would be her last chance to be with everyone and she'd miss me. Normally I'd brush it off as a possible guilt trip and hold true to my no, but Lailah didn't guilt trip.

Ever.

Plus I remember when my Grandfather died. It was sudden and unexpected to everyone except him. He'd casually mention how he was running into his last few days, and how he was grateful his life was filled with us in the end. Then he took his last breath three months later. He always did say that babies and old people have more in common than we'd like to believe, one thing being their connection to the next realm. As a preacher, Lazarus didn't like that very much and he forbade me from talking about death with my grandfather. But it was too little too late because that had stuck with me ever since. Elders know when they're running out of time.

So there I was, destroying all of Frankie's hard organizing work by picking through the closet for something modest yet cool to keep me from catching on fire during the day's events.

"Princessa," Cash sighed. "What was wrong with the last dress?"

"Too much leg," I grumbled back.

"Girl, what!? It stopped at your knees!" he exclaimed.

I said what I said. It was too much leg, plus it was the kind of red old women mumbled about. No thank you.

"Too. Much. Leg," I repeated.

Cash, who had been suggesting me outfits since 8 that morning, finally gave up. He rose from the dressing room bench, flung his hands in the air, and hollered for backup.

"FAB!" he yelled. "Come get her!"

In walked Frankie, who was already immaculately dressed. He had on a pair of navy knee-length shorts and a pink polo paired with a Cuban chain and coordinating bracelet. His long hair was unbraided and pulled into a bun piled high on his head, and his mouth was dressed with a scowl.

"Essie, it's o'clock," he said simply.

"Yes, I'm aware, father time," I sneered.

Cash laughed at my remark before leaving with an outfit of his own.

"Good luck," he called to either of us.

He called to either of us, but when Frankie padded over and leaned onto the shelf I was perusing, I felt like it was more for me.

"It's 1'oclock, Essie. And you're still nearly naked," he sighed, flicking my budding nipple. "It's like you're not even trying. Would you rather just spend your day in my lap?"

My heart shot into my throat and I nearly choked on all my pooling spit.

"N-no," I mumbled. "I just don't know what to wear."

"Mm. How about this? How about I pick you something to wear to free you of your decision paralysis now, and you can decide how you want to take it off for me later."

Several breaths passed without my response, so he gently tipped my chin to coax me to meet his luxuriated gaze.

"How does that sound?" he asked.

"That so… Sounds fine," I said, trying to strengthen my shaky voice. "I'm ok with that."

His deep resonance arranged into a sinfully seductive chuckle before he sent me on my merry, dazed, and hypnotized way.

"Alright, Essie. Go sit yo fine ass down and start your makeup. I'll bring your clothes out shortly, sweetheart," he purred before patting my ass.

I shivered as he scooched my lil ass out the closet and into our room with Cash. I had never been more ready for a day to end in my life.

That sentiment increased tenfold as soon as we got out the car. I loved the pink monstera-printed sundress dress Frankie picked out for me at home, but now I wondered if it exposed too much of my bust. Or if my jewelry was too gaudy. Or if my hair was too tangled.

"Relax, Princessa. You look perfectly fine," Cash said sweetly while grabbing his basket.

Mama Dalia had raised Cash right so he brought along a fruit basket offering for my parents that I knew they wouldn't appreciate. Especially considering how they were staring us down when we got to the driveway. My father particularly.

"I'd like to spend no more than an hour here," I whispered before we got too close.

An hour was all I needed. Everyone knew I was only there for Granny and Penny anyway.

"That's not a problem," Frankie replied. "My parents are here."

Frankie hadn't spoken to Gregory or Regina since Penny was born four and a half months ago. He came back to Marcus's in a fit of tears and I knew something had gone wrong, but I never imagined that Regina would insist that he was a bad son for refusing to work off her debt. There was selfish and there was heartless, and that bitch was both bordering on asinine.

"Well, here's to surviving this," I mumbled.

I'll admit it was nice to play catch-up with some of my cousins, but it didn't take long for my initial reservations to become valid concerns. My father kept trying to corner me to talk about Cheap Sweater, and everyone else was louring at the boys. I half-expected that for Frankie given his Fuck You nature, but Cash was sunshine on a cloud personified. Who didn't like sunshine? Apparently the Kings. But that was fine, because as the song went, I wasn't gonna be there for long. I just had one more stop on my list.

"Hi Granny," I called.

I carved out a good chunk of time for her. Because if she was right, if this was her last go round, I wanted to cherish these moments with her. Despite whatever else was going on.

"Starchild, you should take them boys and go home," she said plainly.

"What? Granny, we've only been here twenty minutes," I replied.

"And it's twenty minutes too long. Me and you can catch up over lunch or something as long as they don't do that shutdown stuff they been talking about."

"Granny, what's going on?" I asked.

Lailah never pushed me away. So not only was her insistence that I leave foreign, it was also unnerving.

"They know you dating both of them," she said with a shake of her curly, grey, head. "Save yourself the trouble."

Ah, so my skeletons were falling out of my closet. That was unsurprising considering everything going on with Lazarus and Curtis. I could handle that.

"Granny, it's fine," I waved. "I'm not worried. I need to come clean about it anyway. We might start trying for a baby soon."

"Gloria, no," she said firmly. "Now is not the time for you to be honest with that fucking fool."

I started to argue but my attention was torn from our shared table when I heard the infamous F word sail over the music. A word that I'd previously boxed someone for when they used it to refer to Frankie.

"You got the chance to live right and be with a beautiful black woman, yet you still choose to be a fucking fag," Gregory spat.

"Excuse me!?" I roared, abandoning both my plate and my grandmother.

"Glory, did you know Franklin was fucking around with your work friend?" he announced loudly. "I saw them a few weeks back at Lena's, kissing on the patio. All that talk about not wanting to be like me and he's worse than me. Cheating on a woman with a man."

Frankie didn't waste one breath protesting. He was just taking it. He was probably trying to protect me, but who was going to protect him?

"No, Frankie is not cheating on me," I said, stepping in front of him. "Cash and Frankie are both my partners. We're all dating," I clarified.

Suddenly the nausea was back like it never left.

Everyone within listening distance stopped dancing and started exchanging horrified glances instead. All eyes were on me and my two boyfriends. If the murmuring was any indication, we were now pariahs, and it was simply because I had the audacity to be loved how I wanted. Granny was right, this wasn't the time to be honest.

"Ew what the fuck?" Halle screeched. "You're cool with your boyfriend bending another nigga over?"

"Halle, stop," Marcus warned.

"That is kinda weird," Michael shrugged. "You don't get jealous?"

"Our bedroom isn't your concern," I hissed back. "Respect my privacy like I respect yours."

"I've known for a while," Lazarus added. "It's obvious. They're too touchy feely to be friends."

"You know because of your boyfriend, hypocritical piece of shit."

I narrowed my gaze at him. All those years of preaching about glass houses had done nothing to strengthen his own accountability. He was throwing stones with a house made of crystal. But for the sake of my Mama, I'd try to be the bigger person.

"My relationship with my partners is no one's concern but ours. This is how I'm choosing to live my life, and it doesn't affect you."

"It does too affect us," Halle spat. "You're a reflection of this family. How is the church going to feel when they found out Daddy's oldest daughter is living with and sexing two different men?"

"THAT'S NOT MY FUCKING PROBLEM!" I roared. "I have given this family everything! For years, I've done everything! I've been a second mom, I've been a nurse, a maid, a cook. I've been a protector, I've been a bank, a coordinator, I've been a therapist. I have been everything and no one fucking cares that I'm always one bad day from a full-fledged mental meltdown! I'm one person, but to y'all, I'm this supposed pillar of strength that you all can pile your shit on without any breaks or acknowledgment. Besides Granny, you can't even be bothered to remember to call me on time for my birthday. So why the fuck do you care if two men love me and make me happy!?"

I didn't even notice that I had nearly knocked myself over from screaming until Cash caught me. I was so angry I was hot, but despite all the rage swimming in me from years of neglect, I was mostly sad. Sad because I didn't have unconditional love from the people I should've gotten it from. Sad because I realized I was only tolerated for my usefulness, and sad because my partners didn't deserve any of the heat they were getting just because our happiness looked different from theirs. I was choking too hard to say I was ready to go out loud. So Cash dried my tears with a heartbroken sigh and gave Frankie a look to confirm we were leaving. Still, the little girl in me longed to reconcile with the people I was born loving.

"Why can't you just be happy for me?" I sniffled to my parents. "Am I really such a bad daughter that I don't deserve my own happy ending?"

My mother stepped forward, hand raised in an attempt to soothe me before my dad stepped in front of her.

"You don't get to play the victim like you haven't spent years being a wild whore before this. This was the final straw. You have been given every opportunity to be normal and instead, you do this," he said, motioning to the boys.

You could hear the sound of my heart cracking under the weight of my father's words. It hurt worse than I ever could've imagined. Even with how strained our relationship had become.

"Daddy, pl..."

"Don't daddy me. No daughter of mine would behave like this and embarrass me and her mother!" he spat. "Some days I wished you were swallowed."

Frankie swung left without hesitation, sending Lazarus soaring five feet back. I watched him crash to the ground, spitting blood and hatred onto the fresh spring grass. There was no coming back from this. My father had washed his hands of me, and any hope that our relationship might one day be salvageable truthfully died at the same time the music did.

"Shou... Should I get involved?" Marcus asked, looking between his dad and my boyfriend.

"No," My mama said firmly. "Let them take Glory home."

"Mama," I whispered. "Just let me talk to him."

I knew things were bad, but I could fix it. We just needed to talk and work through it. I knew I could fix it if they let me.

"Gloria, go home!" she shouted.

The finality in her tone was undeniable. I couldn't breathe, think, or move my legs. I felt five years old again, like I was silently screaming for help that would never arrive. So the boys moved for me, and with that, we went home.

Cash

A month of hard work was undone in just twenty minutes. A month of progress. A month of growth. A month of stability.

Gone.

I watched it flush down the drain helplessly, and now we were back at square one. Square one wouldn't have been so bad on its own, but then Mama Lailah passed. Two days before Glory's birthday at that. I didn't think anything extra about it when she asked me to take care of Glory and Fab for her, because that's just what parents and grandparents say. But she knew. Somehow, she knew.

Glory wasn't able to be with her in the hospital due to COVID restrictions, and if that wasn't bad enough, Mama Lailah's service was also done over video chat. That left no space for endearing stories, mournful embraces, or even the expected comfort of something heavy and preferably fried afterward. There was just silence and sobbing. As if the world had been drained of color and painted the darkest shade of gray.

Shit was bad. Me, the king of seeing silver linings, could only find one upside to everything that had happened, and that was Glory's leave of absence from work. So at least her peanut butter toast wasn't tasked with powering a full load. Most days she'd read a little, attempt to paint, and come lay with us if we were home. But the outside world didn't exist to her. There was no Caris, no Miss Kim, no Marcus, no green grass. Some days I wondered how close it was to being no us. It wasn't right to think that way when my partner was going through a literal emotional implosion, but she was a husk of the woman who once told me she'd eat me alive. I didn't know what to do.

But I guess that's why it was a good thing there were two of us.

"Hey, I need you to take two weeks off from the 30th through the 11th," Fab said.

That was the first thing he said to me since Glory came and sat with us four hours ago. He was staring off into space while Princessa slept through most of our best-man re-watch. I assumed he was deep in anxious thought but it turns out he was plotting.

"What's going on, Frijoles?" I asked.

His eyes shined with hope while he told me the plan. Operation Get

Glory Back.

"We're going back to the mountains. I packed her bag already, I booked the same house from New Year's, and I rented one of those death traps you love so much," he explained.

"They're called SUVS, babe," I laughed.

"Same thing," he shrugged.

I had to laugh when he stuck his tongue out at me, and it felt like the first genuine laughter I had experienced in weeks. Ever since…

"Do you think that will actually help? She doesn't seem willing to leave the house much, especially considering the current restrictions," I sighed.

Glory had only left once in three weeks, and it was to lay fresh flowers on her grandmother's grave. I thought I could try and convince her to go to lunch afterward but she burst into tears after running her fingertips across Lailah's engraved headstone. If lunch was hard, a vacation sounded implausible.

Fab wrapped his big hand around mine. I noticed he had a few more calluses than he did nine months ago when we first met. That was because there had been a massive shift in the kind of work he did. He was now spending fourteen hours a day hauling supplies, mixing ingredients, and pouring candles. Some days he'd come home, nursing a blister from an accidental scuffle with hot wax, sometimes he'd smell like a bakery, and some days his hands would be covered in cosmetic glitter. The comfort of his touch remained unchanged, however. It was gentle and sweet, yet so sure and confident. So even if I was still unsure how, I knew we'd get through this.

"I think it's worth a shot," he said firmly.

My mind slipped backward to the morning she sat on the balcony painting. Her wild curls were free, while her lips were wet with local coffee. She radiated pure, unadulterated joy in a way I've never seen anyone attempt. It was infectious and classically Glory. So we went back to the mountains.

The bushes bordering the cabin were now joined by freshly mulched tulips in a spectrum of colors, while the sides of the stone path were lined with marigolds and hyacinths, attracting a myriad of butterflies and bees. A sight that Glory appreciated. She crouched down and took off her mask to smell a nearby patch, causing me and Fab to nearly pass out when we saw her pearly whites peak through her curled lips. It had only been five minutes since we left the car and I was trying not to get my hopes up, but this was good. So good.

An older couple waved to us a good distance away. I couldn't see shit with my dry-ass contacts, but Frankie recognized them as the owners. Glory still wasn't feeling up to socialization, so she headed inside while Fab and I jogged over to meet them. We got within ten feet and Fab stopped me with an outstretched arm, reminding me that my days of friendly greetings were on a hiatus while we were in a new normal.

"Hi," Frankie waved. "Thanks so much for hosting us at the last minute."

A lady I knew as Debbie gave him a friendly wave of dismissal.

"Oh, it's no problem, dear. We were so excited when you reached out, plus you're our last guests."

"What? How come?" I asked.

That was disappointing to hear. I could see us vacationing in the mountains for years and generations to come, and I preferred doing business with the same people every time.

"Well, besides COVID restrictions, we're just too damn old," David said. "The maintenance is a lot of work, and we could hire someone, but we just want to retire somewhere warm without having to worry about the cabin."

"Oh, you're selling?" Fab exclaimed.

I could see the gears turning behind his eyes and I just knew we were on the same page. This house was never going to hit the market.

"Do you take Amex?" I asked, more like blurted, out.

I really didn't identify as rich, but I could *occasionally* see some rich asshole tendencies shining through, and this was definitely one of those times. Offering to buy a whole ass house with a credit card was crazy. So it made sense that the question caught everyone off guard, including me. It also made Frankie shoot me a look that only black people could see. Silently saying, *"Chill tf out."* before re-asking my question in a much more refined manner.

"What my boyfriend meant to say was, when are you looking to sell by, and for how much?"

The last time we visited Heaven's Peak, we spent almost every lunch in an old-school dinner that served 6 different types of loaded potatoes and mile-high burgers. Anyone who knew Glory knew a well-prepared fried potato could cure any mood she was in, and this mood was no different. The magic created by a whole order of Circus Tots with extra jalapenos and green onion was still effective, even though we now had to order carry-out and eat in the car.

"How is it?" I asked.

Glory paused mixing her cheese and leftover bacon jam to answer me with another glowing smile.

"It's really good. I forgot food could taste like this," she laughed.

It was a laugh containing a good amount of shame. Shame I wish I could burden for her.

"Well, thanks to Frijoles, we'll be here for two weeks. So you and good food have plenty of time to rekindle your love story," I said, scratching her curly nape.

Her bottom lip wobbled and I held my breath for fear the tears would start again, but Glory just laid on my chest with a satisfied sigh.

"Thanks, guys. I love you," she mumbled.

"We love you too," We replied simultaneously.

So much.

Two weeks went by so fast. Especially when we spent it laughing together. If you were to tell a random stranger you had two very distinct soulmates, they might be inclined to treat you like you had something in common with old-school plumbers. Crack, and lots of it. But hearing Fab's deep and resonating laugh mixed with Glory's light and rippling giggle confirmed that I was only full by a third before they crashed into my life. And I was so grateful for it.

I was also real grateful that Mama taught me to nurture business relationships because my cousin Nat's nemesis, who also happened to be a fantastic realtor, was able to expedite the purchase of the house for us. There was no official closing date yet, but we spent our last remaining days hiking and exploring the area where we might soon be living, unbeknownst to Glory. We also went back to Hoof And Bleat to see Red. She still wasn't a working horse, but she was still crazy about Glory, and also still for sale. That felt like a sign, and clearly, I wasn't one to ignore signs. So yes, I did use a credit card to purchase a horse for my girlfriend. And no, I didn't care what my boyfriend had to say about it.

Until we were on our flight back to Dallas and he handed me a purchase agreement of his own.

"Fab, what the fuck? You bought a store!?" I whisper-shouted.

A storefront with an attached warehouse to be specific. I couldn't get loud because Glory was stretched out over our laps taking a little snooze. She was so cute when she slept but also real distracting. I didn't even feel Fab slip my phone out of my pocket.

"You bought a horse!" he spat back, showing me the receipt for Red. "That I specifically told you not to buy, on the credit card I told you not to buy it on!"

"It counts as travel! I get points!" I argued. "This is different. You can't run your first brick-and-mortar five states away!"

Fab had both the customer base and the product variety to warrant a brick-and-mortar location, but things were hard enough for small businesses. Without the owner living twelve hours away during a historic pandemic.

"What are you talking about? Who said anything about being five states away?" he grumbled.

"Wait."

I mean, we were buying a house, but that was just for the future. Right? We couldn't possibly pack up, leave Dallas behind, and spend every day literally living in Heaven. Right?

"You wanna move? What about Glory?" I asked.

She was technically still employed, plus her whole family was in Dallas. Her whole family minus one, but still. We couldn't just take off without her.

"We'd just take Essie's little ass with us," he shrugged.

If you searched the internet for what it meant to be an independent woman, you'd likely find a picture of Gloria King. She made her own rules, built her own life, and earned her own money. Plus she did that for everyone else in her circle too. Whether she was sending Halle back to school, setting up Michael with a job interview, or introducing Marcus to his wife. Glory was a force to be reckoned with.

"Fab, I'd love to quit my job and go live in a wonderland with y'all, but shouldn't she get a say?" I asked.

Frankie's hand came up Glory's back to cup her shoulder so he could give her a gentle squeeze. If it were anyone else she would've woken right up with an attitude for being randomly touched, but in our case she just snuggled closer. Still very much dead to the world and its dilemmas.

"Of course, it's her world at the end of the day and what she says goes. But I think Glory could benefit from someone else making the hard decisions for a little while. Someone like her h.. like us," he whispered.

I spent some time thinking about it. Then I asked for a sign. Within seconds Glory's sweet face relaxed. It was because I placed my hand on top of Frankie's, creating a sense of weighted protection for her. We made her feel safe. That was a sign as good as any. So I guess we were making hard decisions.

Chapter Thirty-Five

G lory

Have you ever misplaced something and felt like you were losing your mind? That was me after returning from Colorado. At first it started with something simple, a tea infuser Mama Dalia gifted me over the holidays. It was shaped like a rabbit and it even came with a separate hole for agave. It was my favorite tea accessory so I kept up with it. Which is why I could've sworn I put it back in the drawer with all Cash's juice shit, but it was somehow missing. Just like my red ostrich heels. And my winter pajamas. And all my black purses.

Something was going on, but when I asked the boys about it they just shrugged it off and mentioned something about rotating our clothes. I mean, I guess it tracked. Frankie was good for spring cleaning, so I let it go. Until I woke up two months later and the only thing left in the house was the bed I was sleeping on and an outfit on the corner of it. A floor-length sage green corseted gown with matching underwear and gold jewelry. It was like getting a cool gift from Santa on Christmas, but worse.

"Guys!?" I screeched, flying downstairs. "Where is all our shit?"

They looked up from the dusty milk crates they were sitting on, completely unconcerned with the fact that we didn't even have bulbs in half the lights.

"Ah, we're catching up on maintenance. Some painting, some staging. Don't worry about it, Princessa," Cash said with a wave.

"Wait, some st…"

I was interrupted by Frankie and his offer of a brown sugar blueberry muffin.

"You should eat so we can get going," he said, completely redirecting me. "We wouldn't wanna be late."

I ended up blinking separately trying to focus on two different amused and mischievous grins. Apt representations of the wearers and their coordinated intentions. In other words, they were up to something.

"Late? Late for what?" I asked.

"A surprise," Cash exclaimed.

"A really big one," Frankie cheesed, sounding every bit as vulgar as my thoughts.

We were riding on tarmac ninety minutes later. When the boys said we were getting car service, I thought it was for something fancy like brunch or an art exhibit. Not TSA.

"Guys, this is the airport," I mumbled.

"Good eye, Essie," Frankie said sarcastically. "This is indeed the airport."

Fucker. There were planes taking off above us, everyone knew we were at a damn airport. What I wanted to know was,

"Why?"

"You like that question a lot," Cash sighed.

"We're taking a trip," Frankie replied.

I wasn't packed for a trip. I had on a dress, albeit a beautiful one, a pair of very impractical shoes, and a fun purse. It couldn't even fit my phone.

"What? Where?" I frowned.

I once again got two very different answers. *"It's a surprise,"* and *"You'll see.*"

But I guess I'd let them have it, because at least we were flying private.

After spending the better part of two hours mentally reciting Movin' On Up from The Jeffersons, we landed in Aspen. I was sad to leave the plush butter-leather seats of Mama Dalia's jet, but I was happy to be one step closer to figuring out what was going on. Especially when we piled into a wagon that looked a lot like Cash's. It would've been an exact double if his didn't have that wax stain on the rear of the driver's seat.

"Wait one fucking minute," I exclaimed, noticing that exact stain.

"Cassius, is this your car?"

"Uh, yes," Cash nodded, buckling me in.

He offered no further reason or explanation, nor did Frankie. They just handed me my placation supplies and started up our road trip playlist like a teleporting car was a completely normal occurrence.

"What's your car doing in Colorado, Cassius?" I inquired.

"Well, right now it's driving, Princessa," he laughed.

Sarcastic little shit. Clearly it was driving but I wanted to know how it got there to begin with.

"Frankie's rubbing off on you," I mumbled.

"Well duh, you recorded him doing it last time. Remember?"

Cash was being a perverted bratty asshole, and I should know.

"I want new boyfriends," I hissed.

"Not happening," they said in conjunction.

Wow. One little episode of the sads and my boyfriends thought they were the boss of me. I mean, *sometimes* they were, but that was besides the point. I could replace them if I wanted to!

"*But you don't.*" My subconscious sighed.

Whatever. A threat didn't have to be meaningful to be effective.

The welcome sign for Heaven's Peak came into focus a few hundred miles later and I realized we were back in the mountains.

For the third time that year.

Don't get me wrong, I loved Heaven's Peak but I was growing concerned with the boy's spending habits. Sure Cash's family was rich beyond my povo comprehension and Frankie was doing well, but that Cabin wasn't cheap. I couldn't keep letting them whisk me away simply because I couldn't handle life. That wasn't reality. It wasn't *my* reality. They never said it, but I knew they'd get tired of cleaning up behind me eventually. I needed to stand firm on my own two feet.

"Guys, listen. I think this is a great surprise, but it is also a very expensive surprise. The cabin is $1,200 a week," I said.

"You hear that old money? She said that like she not dating two rich niggas," Frankie laughed.

Leave it to Frankie to crack a joke in the middle of a serious conversation. Everyone constantly harped on how Frankie was so shy and so sweet, but they knew Faux Frankie. Cause this man was an ass.

"First off, you're middle class, Frankie. Second off, I'm serious. These trips cost way too much to be a regular occurrence."

"Don't worry, Princessa," Cash purred. "We got a really good deal. Only $2,050 for the whole month."

Damn. That was a really good deal. An impossibly good deal. A sketchy deal.

"How is that even possible? Do the owners have a panty fetish or something? Is that why I only got two scoops of drawls left at the house?" I asked.

"All your pretty panties are accounted for, Essie," Frankie laughed. "Everything will make sense soon."

Except it didn't. It grew more confusing with every passing moment. Even from what I could see a mile away, the cabin was covered in balloons and party decorations. There was also a myriad of rainbow lawn chairs spaced across the front lawn with people occupying them. *Familiar people.*

"Is that Marcus?" I exclaimed. "And Caris. Halle, Mama, Tia Cecilia. Wait, what is happening?"

Cash passed Frankie a crisp twenty with a sigh.

"You're breaking my heart, princess. I thought you would have figured it out twenty minutes ago," he clicked.

Nothing was making sense. All of our family was in the mountain. We were headed to a party. They were making bets. I couldn't find any of my $60 bras.

"FIGURED OUT WHAT?" I yelled frustratedly.

"I told you we should have fed her more than a muffin," Cash sighed. "Now she's crabby."

"Yeah but then she would've been too full. You know she has a little bird stomach now," Frankie replied.

"Hello? I'm right here!" I hollered.

"We know," they laughed simultaneously.

I was helped out of the car. One man at my door and one at my hand. Then one at my waist and one at my back. We greeted everyone at a respectable distance thanks to Frankie. Which was a little awkward for me considering I hadn't spoken to my family since they found out I had two boyfriends, and had a meltdown, causing Frankie to punch my dad in the face. It came as no surprise that he was absent from the guest count. That was fine, but then everyone started to congratulate me, which was also a little awkward because I didn't know what it was for, which apparently caused Cash great distress.

"Come on, Princessa. Let's go look at our new backyard," he said.

Suddenly everything clicked into place.

"Wait, our new backyard? What? Are we moving?" I asked.

"Technically, we already did," Frankie grimaced. "We'll talk about that more later, but right now we need to head out back."

Fine.

I guess I was so love struck that I was just following whatever they said without a fight.

Yes. I was really that love struck.

Truthfully, I loved the boys enough to follow them to the ends of the Earth. I had felt that way for a while. They were the kerosene to my lamp. The up to my down. The everything to my anything. They were everything right. My namesake. Pure Glory.

And so were the peonies. Hundreds of blooms of varying colors littered the backyard. There were vivid shades of orange, pink, yellow, red, white, and even lavender. I guess they had been out long enough to attract nearby wildlife, so dozens of butterflies floated about spreading a kind of magic I've only ever seen in movies. It was such an incredibly beautiful sight that I was sure I had died. Because nothing could be that perfect in any lifetime.

Except for the boys.

It took me a while, but I finally noticed the flowers were arranged into words. Words I never in my life imagined seeing.

Be our wife?

The events leading up to this moment suddenly made a lot more sense. Especially the gown. I turned to find the boys on their knees, both holding two beautifully coordinated rings. Our family, minus Caris of course, was a respectable distance behind them, sparklers and disposable cameras in hand, cheering us on. And me? I was fucking sobbing. Boo-boo bawling. Because I never set out to be in a relationship, let alone two. Because I never wanted to fall in love. Because I used to think I didn't need anyone until two tenacious knuckleheads proved me wrong. And because my answer was unequivocally,

"Yes. Yes I'll marry you," I choked with a laugh.

"Oh thank God," Cash sighed. "Or else this would've been real fucking awkward."

Cash waved and a man I recognized as Bale from Hoof And Bleat led a beautiful red mare around the corner, her mane decorated with matching florals and bows. Carmine, as I had named her.

"YOU BOUGHT ME A FUCKING HORSE!?" I shouted.

"Yes, baby," Cash purred, taking my hand. "We got you a horse, and a house, but now you have to make a choice."

The choice had been made. I know it took me a little bit to catch on, but I hoped the boys didn't think I was that slow.

"I already said yes," I laughed nervously.

"Yeah, but you didn't hear our conditions," Frankie replied.

"There are conditions?" I asked, chewing my bottom lip.

"We learned from the best," Cash winked.

Funny.

But I distinctly remembered one of my conditions was that we never mentioned that again.

"Seriously, though, baby. We want you here and forever, at your worst and your very best," Frankie explained.

"We want you to sass us around, steal our clothes, spend our money on house decorations, and bully us into watching trash TV with you," Cash laughed.

"But most importantly," Frankie sighed, wiping my tears. "We want you to live freely. Without having to worry and fret over everything and everybody."

"We know you think that love is conditional, but it's not. You deserve happiness Gloria, even if you do nothing to earn it. We don't need you to pay us back for loving you," Cash explained.

"Because we'd do it a thousand times over and still be rewarded with a new way to fall deeper in love with you," Frankie finished. "So only say yes, if you'll let us shoulder your burdens and make the hard decisions necessary to keep your heart safe."

I toiled endlessly for the last decade of my life. I got educated, built my own life, made my own rules, and suddenly they wanted me to give all that up. I think they wanted me to sniff flowers, ride horses, and paint the mountainside. They wanted me to leave my job, leave my state, leave my life, and be theirs. It should've sounded terrifying, but it didn't. It should've sounded unrealistic, but it didn't. I should've said no, but I couldn't. Because love is so stupid like that.

"Yes. Of course I'll let you do all the unfun stuff while I paint you pretty pictures," I laughed. "I'll let you be my decision makers. I'll let you protect me. I'll let you love me unconditionally, and I will never take that for granted," I cried.

"We know," they said in unison. "We know, baby."

Our family interrupted into graduation-volume cheering, and I held my breath while they slipped two rings on my finger. One Aquamarine and one diamond, both perfectly suited for me, both perfect reminders of my men. Both proving once and for all, that sinners did deserve saints.

Thirty-Six

Epilogue

Glory, two years later: Colorado Springs, CO

"Congratulations! You're fourteen weeks and three days," the doctor exclaimed.

My eyes left the wand pressed firmly into my lower belly and focused on the tiny flickering bean on the monitor placed before me, then I broke into a choking sob. I guess there was a different reason for all my nausea and exhaustion this time besides stress from my gallery debut. Alright wax play, I see you.

"Happy birthday, babe," Frankie said, nudging Cash.

We were spending Cash's birthday at Mama Dalia's when I literally passed out in his arms while dancing. I thought it was because I hadn't been eating much, but they boys insisted I go to the ER anyway. The ER gave me a same-day referral for an OBGYN due to some spotting, and that brought me here, where I discovered that two plus one sometimes equaled four. My sweet boys exchanged a kiss, settling into a handhold while that cold-ass gel was wiped from my stomach. Good thing we were getting lunch afterward because all these emotions had me hungry.

"Aw, look at the happy dads," the sonography student cooed. "You're so sweet to bring them along to the first appointment. I always said surrogacy was truly an amazing gift."

The record of sentimental music playing in my head scratched instantly. A hell of a whole lot could change in two years, but some things would always be the same.

"I'd like you to leave," Frankie said to the student plainly.

Some things including cranky Frankie.

But like I said, plenty of things had changed within two years. We had moved, duh. I quit my job to pursue art, Cash opened his own law firm, and Frankie. Well, Frankie was now putting Bath And Body Works to shame. Smythe's Fine Apothecary was not only a staple in Heaven's Peak, it was also nationally loved and gaining international traction with Mama Dalia opening another Casino back home in Bogota. He was her exclusive bath product supplier for all locations and a favorite amenity among guests. Especially the blackberry and gold shimmer bath bomb, aptly named, Glory.

A lot had changed with our families too. My mother and Lazarus were rightfully divorced, Cookie moved closer to us so Rio could spend time with his favorite new aunt and uncle, then Curtis surprised everyone by apologizing to Frankie and working to build a stable relationship with his nephew. I had my reservations, but after Lazarus renounced him and his devilish Myer-Smythe dingaling as unholy temptation, he changed for the better. I guess having the love of your life publicly reject you forces you to acknowledge some hard truths. I was empathetic to being rejected by the pastor, so I played nice. Plus having some immediate family to relate to was so good for Frankie.

The most shocking change happened two years ago though. A week after my engagement, my mother and sister flew back to Colorado courtesy of Cash. We sat down at the dining room table, surrounded by freshly squeezed lemonade and Frankie's orange shortbread cookies, and had a long conversation. At first, I was nervous for fear they'd gaslight me and put me back in fight or flight when I was just starting to unlearn it, but no. It was an apology. A real apology. Mama told me that when I was little, I was determined to do everything. Everybody told her that was an admirable trait to have in a child so she never thought to stop me. Then before she knew it, she looked up and realized I had become someone they relied on to keep the house in order when they couldn't. She didn't know how to undo it so she just accepted it, thinking it couldn't hurt. Unintentionally putting pressure on me that I didn't have the tools to handle in my vulnerable adolescence. I spent a very long time wondering if my parents realized all my sacrifices and it was so healing to learn that they had, and at least one of them regretted putting me in that position.

My sister, on the other hand, was facing a completely different crisis. She felt like she grew up in my shadow being Glory's chaste and quiet sister. Unnoticed and unremarkable. Then as we got older, she struggled seeing who I became, conflicting with how we were raised. She felt cheated. Because I was everything I wasn't supposed to be and I was still thriving, and she had followed the rules only to be discarded and forgotten. Sure, jealousy made her act ugly, but she was still my baby sister. So even though our relationship was frayed, I was willing to do the work to mend it if she was. As long as it didn't disturb my new peace.

Peace was a commodity I never bought into before the boys. Mostly because I didn't understand the long-term implications of it. But two years later, I knew what peace was capable of. Peace could facilitate the deepest of loves. Peace could influence life to influence art. Peace could heal, renew, and clarify. And peace, once elusive, could even create something exciting and new. Full of promise and hope. Like whoever was currently growing in my belly, and whoever might come after them.

"Essie, you can share with us! We share all the time," Frankie pouted as I snatched back my bowl of hash brown casserole.

Cookie made some at my request, but she only made enough for me and the baby before telling the boys to eat fries.

"Don't be a stinge! Sharing is caring, Princessa," Cash cried.

I savored an extra cheesy bite with a smile before addressing the beggars at my side.

"I share my life, my love, my body, and my soul with you both," I said. "And I adore every second of it."

Their beautiful brown eyes both sparkled, full of love and something akin to hope. Which almost made my heart melt. *Almost.*

"But I will not be sharing this," I laughed.

The spell broke and the boys put on a production. Falling to their knees, grabbing at their chests and crying out in pain.

"Glorrryyy!" they whined, forgoing baby, Princessa, and Essie alike.

"That's my name," I laughed, kissing both my guys. "Don't wear it out. Unless it's in bed."

Their melodious laughter mixed to create a sound envied by angels and demons alike. Making my heart feel doubly full. Then I realized there was nothing wrong with gathering my strength from the sins of men. Especially if they were mine.

Burry The Hatchette Sneak Peak (June 2024)

I watched my six bridesmaids float down the aisle while waiting for my father to meet me in the hall. We hadn't spoken since the Governor's Ball, but he was walking me down the aisle no matter how mad I was about this arrangement. Now matter how fucked up it was.

I held my breath while watching Nat watch the door until my Daddy touched the back of my arm.

"You look beautiful, baby," he cooed.

Tears eased down his cheeks and settled into his thick salt and pepper beard while he took me in, and I realized my grudge against him was useless. My daddy had done everything in his power to provide me a good life. I ate like a king, traveled to some of the most beautiful cities, and got the best education money could buy. Meanwhile, my father had toiled tirelessly, only just recently resting after a heart attack and a double bypass. So if I had to marry Nathaniel fucking Burry to ensure my father's hard work wasn't for naught, I would. Because the fact that he was here to see me get married was a gift in itself.

"Thank you, Daddy," I whispered.

He looked surprised to hear my voice, but then his expression settled into a content smile.

"You talking to me again?" he asked. "You not still mad?"

"Oh no, I'm livid," I clarified. "But I also understand why this is a necessary evil, and we're here. So we might as well make cheese out of this spoiled milk."

Daddy gently bent my head forward to kiss my crown, then he straightened me out and looped my arm in his.

"There's my smooth-talking baby girl," he laughed. "Let's get this show on the road, princess."

The doors opened to a florid, gold-trimmed-ballroom, and despite the imposing and demanding crowd, Nat's eyes instantly found mine. One green like jade and one brown like polished oak, both too familiar for my liking. I hoped he would get bored and look away, but his gaze was trained on me the entire half-yard walk to the altar, and it stayed that way until he had to shake hands with my father.

"I trust you'll take care of her," my daddy urged, grasping his palm.

"Of course, Sir," Nat assured, taking my hand. "I have no doubts that she'd poison me in my sleep if I didn't."

And would. At least he knew.

My father found his seat and the pastor began, eliciting silence from everyone besides my soon-to-be husband.

"You nervous or is your skin itching from that white ass dress your whore ass got on?" he whispered.

I was fidgeting because I had on heels. My grandmother's blue satin heels specifically. My something old and something blue that I promised her I would wear at my wedding when I was six. Before Nat fucked up my leg. Fucked up leg aside, I kept my promise to Shirley Hatchette. But now I was paying for it.

"Stop talking to me," I hissed.

I was trying to focus on remaining upright and he was trying to make jokes.

"Aw that's no way to speak to the light of your life, baby doll," he sighed. "You ain't hear Pastor Wilson say honor your husband?"

I ignored him while my legs shook in agony. My calves felt like they were being shredded and set on fire over and over again. It hurt so bad I almost wanted to cry. But Earl and Shirley Hatchette ain't raise no punk bitch, so I suffered through it.

What I didn't count on was Nat noticing my increasing discomfort.

"What's going on, darling? You shaking real bad," he whispered.

"Nothing," I lied.

Nat squeezed my hand while pulling me closer to his center.

"You about to fall over. So I suggest you open your mouth and tell me what's wrong before I call this off," he threatened.

"You wouldn't," I gritted.

"Oh, but I would," he mused. "A couple of million don't make me no difference, but you'd have to start all over. So I'm gone ask one last time and you gone answer me. What's wrong?"

Tears threatened to sabotage my lash line when Pastor Wilson started the second half of his sermon, and I knew I wouldn't benefit from satisfying Nat's ornery ass with a lie.

"I got on heels and they hurt," I confessed.

Nat lifted the hem of my gown with his oxfords to check my legs. Then he sucked his teeth after confirming the ragged state of my person.

"Aye, Pastor. I need you to hurry this along and get to the vowels," he boomed.

Pastor Wilson quieted himself while processing the request and the crowd began murmuring. Both of which pissed Nat off. Dexter wasn't lying when he said Nat let me slide with a lot of shit because Nathaniel Burry was a known menace when it came to everyone else.

"Y'all stop all that whispering," he demanded before turning back to the altar. "Come on Preach, let's skip to the I Do's and shit."

His rolled his shoulders to crack his neck while Pastor Wilson asked me the question of a lifetime.

"Andrea Delphine Hatchette, do you take Nathaniel Beau Burry to be your lawfully wedded husband, for rich or poor, in sickness and in health, as long as you both shall live?"

"I do," I nodded.

He then turned to Nat, voice accidentally wavering when they made eye contact.

"And Nathaniel, do you take Andrea..."

"I do," Nat interjected.

Pastor Wilson was once again flustered and thrown off by Nat's chaos as were the crowd of spectators. If he was my actual man I would've been embarrassed. Hell, I was slightly embarrassed either way to be completely honest.

"Boog, he didn't even finish," I whispered.

Nat rolled his eyes while turning to face me.

"I don't matter, I take you as my lawfully wedded wife regardless. With this ring, I thee wed and all that mess," he said, exchanging our wedding bands. "Wrap this shit up, Preach."

Pastor Wilson quickly reorganized his cards and closed us out.

"Uh, by the power vested in me by that state of Alabama, I now pronounce you man and wife," he blubbered. "You may kiss the bride."

Our immediate family got the crowd clapping while we sealed our disastrous union with a kiss. Despite my mind knowing that the man was a means to an end, my body had gotten crushed under the weight of his kiss. His plush lips parted just slightly to capture my mouth and allow his tongue to curl around mine. A move that suffocated all my apprehension, just like a python did to its prey before they were consumed.

"He could swallow me whole." I thought.

I was unashamed and delirious from the deprivation of oxygen. Unfortunately, I was startled out of my brief moment of marital bliss when everyone, including myself, gasped as Nat swept me off my feet onto his shoulder.

"Please join us for our cocktail hour and reception in the main hall," he announced, striding down the aisle out of earshot.

I waited until he rounded the corner of the expansive hallway to cut up how I wanted to.

"Put me down!" I hissed, swinging my feet.

"Shutcho difficult, bratty ass up," he growled. "Hardheaded ass just had to wear heels. Got me cussing at a Pastor so you don't pass out."

"Like you care!" I spat.

I tried to wiggle down the length of his body before he popped my ass. Which stilled me until we reached our final destination. An office originally belonging to his great-grandfather and rumored to have soundproof walls. He deposited me in a burgundy winged chair in the center of the room before hooking his finger under my chin and forcing me to meet his heated gaze.

"You're right, baby doll. Normally I wouldn't give two fucks if you fainted. Hell, I'd probably even enjoy it. Unfortunately for you, you're my wife now. Which means you're a reflection of me and my choices, and I'll be damned if I let you embarrass me with your spiteful bullshit in front of half the state of Alabama," he barked.

He towered over me with a tight mouth and flared nostrils, clearly pissed beyond what I normally had the privilege of seeing. I was finally starting to realize who I had bound myself to. Or possibly even what. I think my husband, Nathaniel Burry, might be a monster. Whatever he was, put the fear of God in my heart. It was clear our dynamic had changed, and I found myself eager to explain what happened.

"Ain't nobody try to embarrass you. I made a promise to wear heels," I grumbled.

"A promise?" Nat asked. "I'm the only muhfucka you swore your word to today."

Was he jealous? Nah, couldn't be. This was a business arrangement. That was the one thing we could agree on. I might have gotten a Groomzilla though. I heard my Daddy was the same way when he and Mama got married.

But that was different because they were in love. I ain't love this man and he damn sure didn't love me. Still, I found myself considering my mother's advice. If she could soften Daddy's heart, it was a possibility I could soften Nat's.

"I promised my grandmother I'd wear her heels on my wedding day. For my something blue," I explained.

Nat stopped pacing the office and made his way back towards me. Then he squatted on his knees to take off both of my shoes and look at the brand on the sole. I guess he thought I was lying.

However, I was surprised to feel my arches relax from his hand's targeted pressure. Nat had big hands. Strong hands. Hands that were rubbing my entire ten-hour day away. God, it felt good to be rubbed. Especially like this. I was a little ashamed that my disdain for physical touch had deprived me of something this wonderful. Then I remembered why wonderful was bad when it came to Nat.

"From this day forth your promises to everyone else are invalid. I'm the only one you promise anything to until I make you a mother. You understand me, darling?" he asked.

My body immediately tensed. Everything in me wanted to fight, yell, and cuss. But then he stood, directing my attention to those sinister mismatched eyes. Eyes that could light me on fire if I kept staring.

"Open your pretty little mouth and answer me, baby doll," he bellowed, voice now unrecognizable.

I didn't know who this man was or what he had done with the one I spent torturing for the last twenty-something years, but I wasn't a fan. This man was rigid, stern, and demanding. This man was also impatient.

"Andrea," he growled.

"Y-yes. Yes, I understand," I nodded, trying to put my organs back in their rightful spots.

"Good girl," he cooed.

His voice then switched from Nathaniel, the unhinged demon I sold my soul to, back to Nat Burry, the bane of my existence.

"Come on, darling," he called. "Let's go get our pictures taken before yo mama has a conniption."

He reached for my hand and I immediately joined him, slightly afraid to find out if the rumor about the walls was true.

Thank You!

I promised I wouldn't write another bible, and yet here we are a year later. Thank you so much for taking the time to read Glory, and hopefully you've enjoyed the messiness just as much as I have. If you have the time, please consider leaving me a review. Reviews not only help me grow as a writer, but they also help other readers like you find my work and get a shot at seeing themselves represented in romance. Again, thank you for giving me your time and support, and as always, I hope to see you in the next story!

About the Author

Aria is a die-hard romantic whose main goal is to constantly be drying her eyes from something sickly sweet. She has been dreaming up romance stories since she was seven years old, with the first one being a Toy Story fanfic. Her dream is to one day write inclusive stories that center BIPOC full-time, but for now, she labors in fraud as a working stay-at-home mom.

She's also a Neo-soul and R&B enthusiast who's forever got a song stuck in her head. You can find her looking for tasty food, reading, writing, or enjoying time with her family in her free time. She lives happily in Saint Louis, Missouri with her middle-school sweetheart-turned-husband and their adorably chaotic son.

You can connect with me on:

- 🔗 https://www.tiktok.com/@authorariadaze
- 🔗 https://www.instagram.com/ariadazewrites

Candid

Wilhelmina Sturges is not looking for Mr. Right. She has no desire to give up her independence or share her space with someone else. But that starts to change when she meets Thebes.

Thebes Dacres hates socializing, he hates conversation, and he especially hates touching. His disdain for affection knows no bounds, and that's why he's still a virgin at 31 years old. No one ever expected him to get married or fall in love, himself included. But he quickly realizes that life isn't as predictable as he'd like to believe.

Wilhelmina's smart, she's stunning, and she makes his heart beat fast. Attraction is something Thebes never experienced, and their instant chemistry often gets them into trouble. Especially when they realize he's her new boss. But Thebes can't help but risk it all for Wilhelmina, and she must decide if she'll reciprocate.

Bloom

Winifred Walsh is sick of perfect. She's sick of speeches, estate dinners, coordinated undergarments, and dealing with the "perfect" man. Unfortunately, she could never picture anything else for her life, so she was committed to the end. That is until she met Marvin. He's intelligent, handsome, kind, and everything she was raised to avoid. A working-class white man the blue eyes and no money. Her father has made it clear that she is a representative of their family first and foremost, which meant no partying, no boyfriends, and certainly no sex. But the Heiress quickly realizes that making the most out of life means leaving some parts of herself behind, including her not-so-humble beginnings. Set in the early 70s, Bloom details the challenges a young Marvin Rosenbloom and his wife, Winifred face before Rosencorp and strict employee dating policies. Join them on a story filled with scandal, murder, and sex as they start their lives together.

Rudy Jones's New Year's Resolution

Ah, New Year's Eve. The perfect time for the proclamation of better habits and cleaner diets. Unless you're Rudy Jones. His New Year's Resolution is simple; Get back his wife. Who is also technically, and legally, not his. The high school sweethearts have been estranged for six years after a nasty divorce, but Rudy's ready to leave the past behind them. Can he convince Noah to give him one more shot or are some things truly better left unsaid? Join Rudy and Noah on a cozy winter adventure to find out!

Burry The Hatchette

"Andrea Hatchette, a woman after my own soulless void of a heart. Will you do me the honor of being my wife?"

Lots of women dream of moments like this. A calm evening. A party on the lake surrounded by her family and friends. A handsome, rich, educated man asking for their hand in marriage in the middle of a fancy-ass yacht with a big-ass ring. Except for Andrea. Marrying her lifelong enemy, Nathaniel Burry, is her worst nightmare. Still, she knows she has no other choice if she doesn't want to be disowned and thrown from the company she helped build. She supposes there could be worse fates than marrying a billionaire. Right?

Meanwhile, Nat has a plan. Being forced to take a wife isn't the picture of peace he had five years previous, but he's willing to make the best of it with Andrea. After all, even villains deserve happy endings. Can these two find middle ground and make it work, or will they drown in a storm of their own creation?